OTHER BOOKS BY RICH[illegible]NDON

The Final Addiction
Emperor of America
Prizzi's Glory
Prizzi's Family
A Trembling Upon Rome
Prizzi's Honor
The Entwining
Death of a Politician
Bandicoot
The Abandoned Woman
The Whisper of the Axe
Money Is Love
The Star-Spangled Crunch
Winter Kills
Arigato
The Vertical Smile
Mile High
The Ecstasy Business
Any God Will Do
An Infinity of Mirrors
A Talent for Loving
Some Angry Angel
The Manchurian Candidate
The Oldest Confession
And Then We Moved to Rossenarra
The Mexican Stove/Ole Mole (with Wendy Jackson)

RICHARD CONDON

THE VENERABLE BEAD

ST. MARTIN'S PRESS  NEW YORK

DESIGN BY JUDITH A. STAGNITTO

PRODUCTION MANAGER: JIM FORBIN

Library of Congress Cataloging-in-Publication Data

Condon, Richard.
The venerable bead / Richard Condon.
p. cm.
ISBN 0-312-08331-9
I. Title.
PS3553.O487V46 1992
813'.54—dc20 92-24638
CIP

First Edition: November 1992
10 9 8 7 6 5 4 3 2 1

For darling Evelyn
from first to last

A philosopher decided to end his life so that, in his final moments, he could write down what he would be permitted to see as the essence of life itself. With a notebook and pencil beside him, he put his head in the oven and turned on the gas. As consciousness fled, he jotted down the crucial information. Neighbors smelled the escaping gas, broke in, and rescued him. The first thing he did when he regained consciousness was demand the pad on which he had written the secret of the meaning of life. There was only one scrawled sentence. It said, "Think in other categories."

— PHILIP WYLIE

In "Finnley Wren"

PART

1

1

Leila Aluja had never been curious about her own past because the present was always so exciting. Things had happened and she had moved on to the next thing, forgetting where she had come from and wallowing in what was happening now. She had lived in the present with the energy and glee of all the seven dwarfs in their diamond mine.

Tonight things were different. She stared at the stars and remembered what the President's scientific adviser had told her about a galaxy far out beyond the imagination, which was called the Great Wall and which would take five hundred million light-years to cross from edge to edge. Could she suppose it had sparrows throughout all that density? Could He still keep his eye on that many individual sparrows over such enormous distances? Their own solar system was only 5.5 light-years across, from edge to edge, the man had said, so the sparrow-watching responsibility on Earth was considerably reduced. Better His eye should be on the politicians, she thought, which is to say she lacked faith in the group systems. She was her own deity, her sun and moon and stars. This tended to make her somewhat self-centered and more obedient to her own wishes than to those of her neighbors, a common fault but one which tended to make the wearer stand out as being boldly naive.

She was a willowy, andromanic woman, perhaps in her early forties, with a long face that gave nothing away. Her mouth was sensual and as viscous as a bowl of shucked oysters. She had big hair. She was accepted as being a Sicilian aristocrat because she was a billboard Sicilian, in the sense that the complexions and features of Sicilians had been formed forever during the 325-year Arab occupation of their island between A.D. 652 and 977. She could have been bred from the loins of one of the Aghlabid emirs who had ruled Sicily, then swept up through the Alpine passes to mid-Europe.

She had a conspicuous, passionate nose, cinerous eyes, black hair, and white teeth against dark skin like the women of the Abbasid caliphs, like the woman who had told the stories to Hārūn ar-Rashīd under the Green Dome of the palace in Baghdad. She was also a woman who had spent a lot of time and money putting herself together. Expensive clothes from a single (adapted) designer had created great good taste. It is a pleasurable and rewarding thing to look at a beautiful woman, and, throughout her life, Aluja had never let down a beholder.

As if the coastline of Monaco were drifting steadily westward across the night sky, the ocean liner loomed and gleamed with lights, row on terraced row, slithering toward Florida. It was a full ship, bound for Miami on the first leg of a world cruise. Leila Aluja was a short-haul passenger who was crossing from Southampton to Florida.

She had just completed three and a half weeks of intensive, mind-sapping, fourteen-hour days with lawyers, bankers, accountants, and raw-material suppliers acquiring the North American rights to Tofu Pizza, the taste sensation of Europe and Asia that her company expected to ride to enormous profits. The representatives of the Korean conglomerate that owned all the world patents had been hard bargainers. They thought they held all the high cards, but Leila, laid back and seemingly pliable, was the most deceptive negotiator in the international fast food business. She had won over frantic bids from nine other companies.

There was bad feeling throughout the industry about her victory. Her competitors had stated openly that she had won unfairly, which was nonsense, she told the trade press. However, someone had felt badly enough to have slipped a threatening note under her hotel door in London. If she were the sort who lost out on contracts, she told the police, she certainly wouldn't write poison pen letters to even the balance. The prize was hers, and *tant pis* for the losers. It would be a tremendous home delivery winner and quickly become a supermarket item.

Then the unexpected bonanza had fallen upon her and she had had to cancel her holiday: bone fishing at Andros, bullfights in Colombia, and at least two really satisfying meals at La Fonda del Refugio in Mexico City. Instead, she would have to return to her desk and her spotless kitchens in Terre Haute, Indiana, to settle down to make the greatest food discovery in history, the most sought after fast-food item since the tuna burger or the shaved salami mountain on oatmeal bagels.

She had dined in the exclusive ship's grill that evening with Sir Alfred Harrison, the Scottish knight, who, it was rumored, had made the quarter-finals at Wimbledon a few years back and who, someone had said, was heir to an enormous railway fortune accumulated by his grandfather in South America. Shipboard gossip said the handsome baronet was en route to Palm Beach to enjoy a few chukkers of polo leg-to-leg with Prince Charles. He was a tall, blondish man, deeply tanned, who walked with the bent knees of a confirmed horseman or an aristocratic version of Groucho Marx. He had wonderful diction, high-pitched, with each dipthong shaved and apart, as startlingly precise as that of the late actor Terry Thomas. At first meeting, Leila had though he was kidding. He spoke to the maître d' using beautifully gargled French. He had powerful male smells.

The cuisine aboard the *Eros* was far better than adequate, she thought (especially the white truffle sauce over the beef and the heavenly raspberry clafoutis). The service was devout, and the bottle of Bonnes Mares '61, shared with Sir Freddie, had been monumentally memorable. While chewing dreamily, staring into Sir Freddie's blue eyes, she wondered if her people could adapt the raspberry clafoutis into a take-out item that she could market as the Razz-Ma-Tazz. She couldn't wait to get away, if only for a quick trip to the powder room, to dictate the idea into her little machine.

Leila lived for her work. She was the highest-paid female executive in the gargantuan American fast-food industry, which accounted for 48.5 percent of total food spending nationally—of which her company had 26.31 percent. In the past six years she had built up food sales in retail grocery outlets by inspired spin-offs of her most popular fast-food items into packaged-food retail items, and she was sure the Tofu Pizza would even outsell the company's prepackaged 98 percent fat-free hamburgers.

Sir Freddie had not taken his eyes off the rising white shelf made by the billows of her pigeoned and powdered chest while he talked about horses and tennis rackets during the two hours they had spent together at a table for two he had arranged for that evening (despite the fact that their proper place was at the Commodore's table). He had wanted her to stroll with him among the lifeboats on the Sports Deck after dinner, but she had promised to meet another man.

She danced for an hour or so with Dr. Anson Padgett, the geophysicist authority on the "superplumes" of hot material which, he was explaining to her, were widely believed to have risen eighteen hundred miles to the ocean floor from near the earth's molten core and were having profound consequences for the earth's climate and life-forms. His explanation of his work was thorough even though he seemed to be able to dance without missing a beat all through the abstruse geology. He was an absolutely sensational dancer. They danced tangoes, rumbas, and salsas with his large hand gripping her bottom. Later she slipped away to enjoy a half hour at the craps table in the ship's casino. She had made four consecutive hard eights and had doubled every time. The stickman and the pit boss were mad fans of her because on previous crossings she had put them on the company's potato chip free list, so that each time they reached port, a giant economy-size bag of the chips would be waiting for them. Both men, she thought, probably also entertained secret ideas that, if they made the right moves, they could get into her drawers. It seemed likely and logical to her that the pit boss had okayed the stickman to switch the dice to loads when it was her turn to make a pass. It amused her that she probably had the same effect on heads of state, bellhops, and even on elderly men who couldn't walk without a cane, all of them passing her loaded dice in one form or another, on the wild supposition that, if she won, they would win her, eager and panting.

That night, in the ship's casino, she was either sure that the stickman had switched the dice or that the Venerable Bead was working once again to bring her good luck. She never went anywhere without the ancient star ruby on a thin gold chain around her lovely neck. It was known to the historians of great jewels as the Ahmadabad Ruby, which had been in the possession of the great khans and maharajahs since, as far as was known, the fifth century. In the terrible struggles for power that had punished the Indian subcontinent in the following centuries, it had changed hands four times until, in the seventeenth century, it had come into the possession of a Ukrainian spice trader who had brought it back to Russia, costing him his life under the knout but winning the ruby for a Grand Duchess. It was so old and so priceless that its name had been changed to the Venerable Bead. It had been a gift to Leila on her wedding night from her second husband, the most powerful man in the history of Hollywood, who had inherited it from his father, a close comrade of Joseph Stalin. It weighed 97.643 carets and it was not only irreplaceable but had brought Leila all of the great good luck of her life. It was valued at $1,483,700.

She was $800 ahead when she cashed in and left the casino, alone for the first time in three and a half weeks.

She was wearing a $55,000 sable coat, a $1,483,700 ruby, and a platinum diaphragm. Her dress was a copy of a 1927 evening gown by Mme. Vionnet, which she had had a clever little woman in St. Ann's Villas, London, adapt for 1991. It was made of heavy rose and clinquant paillettes and was just-below-knee length.

She went out on the open deck, high above the tossing, winter seas. The deck was deserted. She stood at the ship's rail looking out at the heavy water. The waves were more than sixty feet high. Mountains of sculpted water collapsed under the illusion of being cathedrals and were replaced by spume. Spray flecked at her face. She wondered how it would feel to be pulled on a rope behind the ship, but the thought made her shiver, so she switched to thinking about the effect of the moonlight on the rolling water.

2

Leila had risen from demonstrating prepacked lunch techniques at a trade school in Dearborn, Michigan, to becoming head of the world's largest fast-food conglomerate. She was the owner of five homes designed by Frank Lloyd Wright and a $12-million Bugatti that was preserved in an underground vault in Indiana.

Miss Aluja's parent company, Food Stuffs Inc., had 17,490 franchise stores worldwide at which franchises took in revenue of $5.9 billion, according to *Pizza Today,* the industry trade paper. In the previous fiscal year Food Stuffs Inc. had revenues of $2.6 billion, netting a profit of $97.4 million. The company recently won exclusive rights to sell pizzas and tunaburgers on all NATO and U.S. Army, Navy, and Marine Corps bases.

Just one of her companies, which manufactured multiflavored pizzas, had a 29.7 percent share of the $5.6-billion world pizza market. Her companies owned nineteen national fast-food chains, comprising a total of 114,720 outlets, from Aunt Abigail's Apple Turnovers Inc. to Taco Loco.

Three careers before she went into the fast-food business, as a film star and as a counterspy, using the assumed theatrical name of Meine Edelfrau, she was earning an average of $63 million a year as "the most famous woman in the world." Her second record album on the Cacaphony label, *I Stand Alone*, from her hit film *Nobody Stands Alone*, sold 7,450,000 copies.

Her life had followed one extraordinary career after another. Every dazzling success, she was sure, had come to her because she was wearing the Venerable Bead. Born a Muslim of Iraqi parents in

Dearborn, she became famous as an evangelical Christian. She became a powerful Washington lawyer for the National Gun Carriers' Association, CANCER (Center for American National Cigarette Education and Research), and for the enormous industrial conglomerate Barkers Hill Enterprises.

Sponsored by both Barkers Hill and Wambly Keifetz, "adviser to presidents," and chairman of the globally powerful Bahama Beaver Bonnet Company, Miss Aluja moved on from Washington to vital work in industrial public relations in New York, where her pervasive influence upon President Osgood Noon was frequently alluded to by those inside the loop. Following her triumphs as "the President's public relations counsel," Miss Aluja formed what was to be the largest fast-food conglomerate in the world, Food Stuffs Inc. of Terre Haute, Indiana, now a $28-billion-dollar company.

Leila Aluja had presided over the finances of an empire that had included nineteen fast-food chains operating in thirty-one countries. Her companies owned a ranking pharmaceutical company; a cable television system that included a national evangelical television network; gambling casinos in Nevada, Aruba, Nassau, and Puerto Rico; seven U.S. senators and sixty-one congressmen; and a chain of ballroom dancing schools. While in Europe, sources at Food Stuffs Inc. who asked to remain anonymous said Miss Aluja had closed fast-food deals worth tens of millions of dollars.

She had pledged $10 million to three universities but had not yet written the checks, although she had accepted honorary degrees as Doctor of Education from two of them.

Miss Aluja had been married and divorced four times: to an unnamed Albanian diplomat; to Joseph Reynard, a colossus among the Hollywood talent agents of his time who was later convicted of spying for the Albanian government; to Ellsworth Carswell, a former CEO and director of the National Gun Carriers' Association, and to Maj. Gen. Mungo Neil, linguist and retired military commander. There were no children.

3

Leila had been conditioned by her country's leaders to feel a sense of mortal alertness against the Communist menace, although she was only an infant when President Truman had invoked his policy of containment, the Truman Doctrine, and his Loyalty Oath, refusing the reentry of such an ominous threat as Charlie Chaplin to the United States while he had been in England to receive a knighthood. All of it had been necessary to beat out the steady alarms that had warned of the Red infection poised to destroy the American dream.

Her parents had been immigrants from Iraq. Her mother had died when Leila was seven years old. In the early years in America, her dad did muscle work for the Detroit mob, performing the occasional hit on demand, but within six years his wiliness had been recognized and he became an assistant on the staff of the family's *consigliere*. Deals came his way before they filtered down to the capos or the soldiers. He became interested in national politics and, with the help of his prime sponsor, the Cloacino family, was elected to Congress from the 19th District, Michigan, when Leila was fifteen years old. As an incumbent, it was a job for life.

From the beginning of her formal education, Leila worked her way through schools. By day she studied under a scholarship at the Richenda Todd Institute of Detroit; by night she attended classes at the Dearborn School of Industrial Culture, established by the automotive industry to improve the quality of the box lunches that workers had been carrying to the workplace, often clogging gas lines of engines with hard-boiled egg discards, causing thousands of costly recalls. It was the hope of the industry that DSIC could develop "snacks," a step on the thousand-mile journey to comprehensive, universally consumed fast food, that would satisfy and nourish automotive workers while building their cholesterol counts and obesity levels.

Quite by chance (and because she was sleeping with a supervisor of the transmission unit division of one of the larger car companies), Leila was chosen at DSIC to head the experimental "snack" project. During her first two weeks in the laboratory, she developed the mayonnaise lamb burger with kasha, served in a pita sleeve, which had the virtue of appealing to the Middle Eastern segment of the work force, Dearborn having the largest Muslim population of any city in the United States. Leila discovered that she had a gift for fast food.

In 1972, following in her father's footsteps (he had been a law student in Baghdad before being forced to flee), she graduated from the law school at Ann Arbor at the head of her class, was editor of the *Law Review,* and had rejected employment offers from the three leading Wall Street law firms so that she could protect her country by serving in the FBI and fighting Communism in the front line.

"I know it sounds egotistical, Dad," she told her father, "but, believe me, if I ever want to go into politics, the voters will see me as having been at the forefront of the Red crusade."

"How you gonna get into the FBI?" her father asked. "I maybe could help, but the Director drives a heavy deal."

"How?"

"If you want his help, and you get elected, you gotta snitch on the Speaker."

"I've been thinking about this for a long time, Dad. I did a good job ferreting out Communists at school and, part-time, at the Dearborn plant and I've had a letter from a big-league association of former FBI agents in Minneapolis called Freedom Now."

"Yeah? So what are they?"

"They have seventy-one hundred clients—American business firms all earning more than five million a year who have reason to believe that their employee rolls were laced with Communists. Freedom Now proves that these executive hunches were right. They expose Communists on American payrolls."

"Yeah?"

"Naturally, they can't all be fresh Communists each time, so when one is turned up, they follow him from new job to new job to insure that he is unemployable until Freedom Now sees to it that he gets work elsewhere so he can be uncovered afresh because that's what the clients are paying for."

"The FBI would hire you for that?"

"That's where I'll need your help."

"Me? Listen, you want it, I'll do it. So I'll be in hock to the director. So what, right?"

"No. I mean your help with the Mob."

"How can the Mob help with the FBI?"

"They keep on the good side of the Director by seeing that he gets the right information at racetracks, which are his hobby. And he doesn't see anything wrong with them because he has said, over and over again, that there is no such thing as the Mafia. So you get the boys to give him a couple of hot horses, then they tell him about me at Freedom Now and get him to hire me."

"Very patriotic. I'm prouda you."

Leila didn't work the gimmick right away because she was offered two times more money to go to work for the Awareness Foundation, a nonprofit, public-service institution founded two months before and whose opposition to Communism had set a new standard for the country. The foundation functioned entirely through grants from the Central Intelligence Agency. Its purpose was to train labor attachés for U.S. embassies and consulates abroad for the overthrow of governments suspected of having Communist leanings.

She became the ultimate interviewer at the foundation. If an applicant got past Leila, he or she was admitted. If not, he was thrown back into the pool of routine espionage. She exposed two "liberal" plants (both muckrakers from intellectual magazines) and seven probable enemy agents.

The Director/CIA, accepted the recommendations of the CIA Committee for Operations and signed an order directing that Leila Aluja be absorbed as an agent of the Central Intelligence Agency at three times the "arrangement" at the Awareness Foundation. The committee citation to the D/CIA read: ". . . that Leila Aluja (file attached) be persuaded to enter this service. On the record of her casework accomplishments, going back to her successes as class monitor in Michigan elementary schools, it is the opinion of this committee that Aluja would rate (in the baseball batting average terms as observed by President Nixon) as follows: Richard Sorge: .425; Colonel Rudolf Abel: .495; James Bond: .657; Leila Aluja: .727. No more gifted anti-Communist hunter exists in our records or in the records of the Soviet Union (confirmed in the Soviet-SMERSH dossier on Aluja which, through an expert deception planned by Miss Aluja, holds her false photographs, finger and voice prints, and genetic IDs). There is no field of espionage, counterespionage, or infiltration at which Aluja does not excel."

Before the CIA could act on her recruitment, the FBI had preempted her services. The intervention of the President and the Senate Intelligence Oversight Committee became necessary when the Director/CIA threatened to take the case directly to the *Reader's Digest*. But a woman in the FBI! To neutralize the shock the Director/FBI permitted a rumor to be spread that Leila was a transvestite. Because the Director was so dead set against women, her service record and paycheck identified her as Lee Aluja and her service photographs were doctored to show her in what were rather a butch rig and haircut. It was a necessary move. The Director had gone on record many times as saying he would never use a woman (professionally or personally), and the Director was never wrong.

In her fourth month of FBI service, while she was still being trained in the Director's methods, all American law enforcement agencies were "privatized." The horrified president was faced with increasing taxes on the wealthy to provide health care for the voters, a vital reelection issue, so rather than cutting Defense expenditures, he had auctioned off the government's law enforcement units among qualified private detective agencies; the Haselgrove Organization had won the bidding.

It was the American way, but at first many news media outlets, most Patagonian and all four opposition politicians, had expressed alarm at the idea of the executive having "a private KGB." The President went directly to the people, stating that a line had to be drawn. Fifty-six of the country's largest corporations, including the Mafia, bought 372 three-minute television spots explaining to the people that America was America (God bless it!). It was the land of free enterprise and the Haselgrove Organization had invested a lot of money in the plan; that the "old" FBI and CIA had been un-American, even Socialist, maybe even Communist, because they had not been required to show a profit while operating with "unaccountable" public funds, and that settled the matter.

In addition to his fabled base headquarters deep in the high Rocky Mountains, Haselgrove had leased the fourteen thousand square feet of the National Security Agency at Fort George Meade, Maryland. At NSA alone, Haselgrove kept 11,539 civilians and 8,217 military busy around the clock. The NSA was reorganized to tie in with the government's dream of a domestic, and ultimately international, network of recording pools by which transistors, those tiny friends of man, could pick up as much as 54 percent of general conversations around the country. When one considers that the larger part of this work was entirely selective, it measures the formidable job that the Haselgrove Organization's computer scientists were able to get done. These "listen-ins" were to be used as "flag samples" of U.S. public opinion and, of course, as evidence in courts of law when they were needed to protect the country from Communism. It was the national hope that, within three years, the recording effort could be established throughout Europe and Latin America.

The recording centers transmitted all flag samples to the NSA multiple conveyor belts that ran under Fort George Meade on a path that was 980 feet long and 560 feet wide. The centers were capable of analyzing the listen-ins on all foreign leaders, excepting the Israeli prime minister, a condition that was under continuing negotiation. These flag samples were fed into advance models of the Cray Y-MP C90 supercomputers for translation into officialese gobbledygook upon eight-by-eleven-inch sheets of paper at the rate of seventy-three feet of documents per minute, then transmitting the documents by computer relay for automatic filing in five separate repositories (as separated as are the Central Adirondacks from the Big Bend country of Texas) in case of enemy attack.

The supercomputers were capable of handling one billion operations a second, or one gigaflop. With sixteen central processing units, the system had a peak performance of sixteen gigaflops. One of these gigaflops had found Leila. She was tapped by the leader and lifted to the top of her profession. Leila Aluja was one of four team leaders employed by the Haselgrove system and the only woman of any rank in the organization above cleaning woman.

It was the year Richard Nixon won his second presidential election; the year the Tasadays, a Stone Age tribe, were discovered living in caves in the southern Philippines; the year the chairman of ITT startled the world by accepting a total annual compensation exceeding $1.6 million. It was fifteen years after the death of Senator Joseph McCarthy (R-Wis., 1908–1957), who had given up his life mostly to booze but certainly also with every gray cell of his far-ranging intellect to the total eradication of Communism whether it existed in dentists' offices, on the faculties of universities, in Hollywood, in embassy library books, on television, or in the United States Army.

The extraordinary exception of admitting a woman into the upper reaches of the great security apparatus had to be made because Mark Haselgrove, leader of the Haselgrove Organization, had discovered that "somewhere in Hollywood" the most dangerous Communist *apparat* ever to threaten the American democracy was operating with clandestine arrogance. It had to be uncovered and ruthlessly eliminated. Haselgrove, the most cunning man-hunter since Javert, had evolved a plan to ferret out the conspiracy while simultaneously creating an inordinate amount of publicity. He needed a beautiful woman agent to infiltrate the filming community by carrying the bona fides of film stardom.

Acting with extreme circumspection, the Haselgrove Organization arranged for the the Melvini family, which ran gambling, vice, labor, agricultural, entertainment, narcotics, and extortion interests in Southern California and (partly) in Las Vegas, to intercede with a principal Hollywood studio. The Melvinis were direct descendents of Ignazio (Lupo the Wolf) Saietta, founder of the Unione Siciliane in the United States, and therefore among the aristocrats of organized crime which—next to the flag, celebrities, and the Pledge of Allegiance—was the most hallowed American institution.

The Melvini family controlled motion-picture craft unions, and therefore had no problem with securing a featured player contract for Miss Aluja, but also, because the family was also into recycled postage stamps, they were able to reduce Leila's mailing costs for her fan mail considerably. Nineteen crime families in the United

States were persuaded to undertake dispersed mailings from sixty-seven key cities directly to the studio whenever a motion picture featuring Leila Aluja appeared on American screens. Such a wide range of postmarks on that many fan letters was the clincher for contract renewal.

For seven months before starting her career as a film actress, the leader threw Leila into a crash course to learn to speak, read, and write Albanian. It was a difficult assignment even for Leila, who had a knack for languages. Even the language's official name, Shqiperi, from a term meaning "to pronounce clearly, intelligibly" confused things for her. She learned the Gheg dialect, which had marked subvarieties and a verb system with many archaic traits, such as the change of a stem vowel in the past tense. Altogether, Gheg, with its strangulated nasal sounds, struck the ear with astonishment. To brush up her conversation (and to hold her under iron, not to say sadistic discipline), the leader assigned her to work as a dance-hall hostess in Manila with instructions to take up with a certain Albanian diplomat in the Philippines on a combined trade mission and intelligence-gathering assignment for the Sigurimi, the dreaded Albanian secret police.

Leila had no trouble at all in worming her way into the Albanian's heart. She was a superb dancer. She was available after the dance hall closed each night. She spoke Albanian. She was a beautiful woman. However, it was the Haselgrove psychological profile of the man which achieved the result. The diplomat's mother, aunts, sisters, and childhood sweetheart had been uncontrollable drunks so, after she met him at the dance hall, Leila began to drink heavily. The diplomat, having spent his life trying desperately to reform the women of his family, fell in love with Leila when, after his pleadings, she gave up alcohol. They were married under Eastern Church rites.

Through the Haselgrove Organization, Leila was able to produce papers that proved her to be an Albanian citizen who had been taken to Paris by her parents when she was two, which accounted for her accented Albanian speech. Her father, the documents established, had been the long-since exterminated patriot, murdered by the Bulgarians, Xeri Kambtar, a friend of Mehmet Shemu, the Albanian premier. When the newlyweds returned to the groom's homeland,

Leila was welcomed warmly by Albanian government circles. To be able to speak Albanian with a charming accent which was now and then impeded by a foreign lilt, she had had to push herself through 3000 hours of Berlitz courses in the record time of 587 hours, a stunning feat.

When her husband died under circumstances which the Sigurimi were able to prove easily to be the work of Greek Republicans, but which had actually been carried out by Haselgrove assassins, Leila's grief was a palpable thing. She threw herself upon Mehmet Shemu, the premier, pleading for the chance to avenge herself and her family. For reasons known only to the Haselgrove Organization, she had herself moved from Tirana, capital of Albania, to the North American School at Beijing, going on to graduate from China's International Relations Institute. She learned Chinese, but she was drilled and coached day and night in Beijing in the Albanian language until she spoke it as flawlessly as any native Gheg. She sensed that, whatever the Haselgrove target was, it had something vital to do with Albanians. Upon graduation, she was infiltrated back into the United States by routes long established by the Sino-Albanian espionage systems. She settled into a modest house in Brentwood, California, that is, modest for Brentwood, a suburb of the film capital.

When he knew she was ready, Mark Haselgrove issued the order that she was to be signed as a featured player at a major Hollywood film studio under a two-picture contract with stairways of options. She worked hard at her craft, sweating out long hours with her dramatic coach and spending many arduous late afternoons sprawled on top of the desk of the head of the studio. She had worked her way up to fees of $165,000 a picture because her fan mail was so prodigious. Her pictures didn't gross prodigiously, but she was a featured player and grosses were always blamed on the director, or the star who was carrying the picture, depending on which the system needed less.

She got an enormous amount of fan mail every year: letters, telegrams, homemade cakes and pizzas shipped by parcel post and special delivery, scapulars, mezzuzahs, rabbits' feet, a crocheted crucifix from the occupational ward of a Dublin hospital, a lapis lazuli portrait of Richard Nixon, and a row of Easter eggs hand-painted by Portuguese housewives. A hysterical (rented) mob, screaming for autographs, was always there, frantic to touch her, as she entered or left her hotel whenever the studio sent her to New York. All that adulation had cost Haselgrove $9,043 and some change to maintain. It took organization, which Big Al Melvini provided, and two people on the payroll, but the profit-to-cost margin was large and the effect Mark Haselgrove had desired was achieved.

Leila was ranked (by high-, middle-, and low-brow film critics) as being one of the worst actresses in film history, including Theda Bara and Natasha Rambova. In polls taken by the New York Film Critics Circle, by a vigilante film committee formed to protect American cinematic art, and by the *Consumers Report*, her work was grievously deplored. However, the critics of the supermarket tabloids ranked her with Garbo and Hepburn because they ran with craft unions that the Melvini family could reach.

She burst into American consciousness, as Narcissus had suddenly appeared to Narcissus, as an icon of the American religion, celebrityhood. In her third screen appearance, in an epic having a cast of thousands, surrounded by hundreds of extras, diverted by the clamor of an epic battle, without a single line to speak during the brief nine seconds her image was flashed on the screen, she had appeared to be so lost from any understanding of what she was supposed to be doing that she had been singled out by Bosley Crowther, film critic of *The New York Times* as ". . . a shocking example of how the art of acting, even wedged into such a mob scene requiring thousands of players, can be botched to ruin the promise of a gigantic cinematic effort."

To give some kind of credence to the arrangement that the Melvinis and the Haselgrove Organization had forced upon the studio, Leila had come to motion pictures from the theater. The leader had decided that if she were "discovered" on Broadway, it would make good filler for her thumbnail biographies that would inevitably appear in the fan magazines. He had one of his people speak to Angelo Partanna, *consigliere* to one of the important New York families, about the plan. By some slipup in planning, she was signed to understudy the most durable actress in the American theater.

In a flurry of insider betting, mostly by studio executives and the Melvini family, the Las Vegas book laid odds of 11–1 against any possible chance that Leila would ever go on in the show because the star had once danced a soft-shoe routine onstage with a compound fracture of the ankle just to block the chance of her understudy from going on. However, on the night of Leila's big chance, the star had a sudden street "accident" on her way to the theater. She required emergency surgery. There was no possibility of her appearing in the show again. Nonetheless, rather than inflict Leila on the audience, despite the possibility of reprisals by theatrical unions, and even though it might provoke an uncontrollably violent response from the ticket holders for being denied the chance to see a hit play at shockingly high ticket prices, the management had closed the show, taking a loss of $96 thousand in returned advance ticket sales. It was a prudent decision. Leila was not at home on the stage. She bumped into furniture, forgot whole pages of her lines, twice had gone to the wrong theater in a panic of tardiness and advance stage fright, and fought constantly with the other women in the cast.

It could have been hard to say where Leila did fit into any scheme of things until her true vocation revealed itself. She was a movie star; period. A movie star was a true celebrity, beatified and magnetized by being seen on the screen, in fan magazines, and gossip columns due to her intimacies with the male stars. Acting simply was not a factor in the equation. She brought her dad a lot of attention in national politics, White House dinners, and organized-crime circles. He believed secretly that Leila had provided the reflected glamour that had gotten him the chairmanship of the House Judiciary Committee.

Leila didn't mind the life of a film star because she knew she was working for American freedoms against an evil empire. The food was good. Mostly—well, marginally—the sex was good. She got an IRS discount on all her clothes, shoes, and makeup because she needed them for professional reasons. She waited for the big break that would transform her from a featured player into a genuine, out-of-my-way movie star. She wanted to make it really big in *The National Enquirer*. She wanted "unauthorized" biographies written about her. She wanted a hotter class of men.

Then everything changed. Within two years, under orders from the Haselgrove Organization, Leila married Joseph Reynard, the biggest film, theatrical, and concert agent in the known world, and he made her a star. He was like insane about her. Not only that; she was very fond of him.

On their wedding night, as he undressed her ritually on the four-poster bed with the full mirror imbedded in the ceiling, while she looked up at the reflection of his hands fondling her, he took off his pajama top as if he had made a sudden impulsive decision, to reveal a huge and glistening star ruby hanging from a gold chain around his neck. She gasped at its beauty, quickly appraising its great value. He lifted the chain over his head and dropped it carefully over hers, hanging the fabulous gem around her neck. Staring hypnotically into her eyes, he told her the story of his father taking him up the mountain many years before, on his father's 112th birthday.

"He took me up on the high mountains of northern Albania, where the eagles nested. He said to me in his direct way which I can never forget, 'You may have wondered for all of your life why I am such a great man and why I have had such prodigious success.' 'Yes, Father,' I said to him. 'I owe it all to this,' my father said, opening his shirt, baring his chest, and showing a huge ruby suspended by a gold chain around his neck. 'This has brought me the good fortune of my life.' 'It's beautiful!' I said. 'I have never seen anything like it! It must be worth a king's ransom!' 'It's worth more than that, my son,' he said. 'It was once valued at seven hundred thousand gold rubles when it hung from the neck of a Russian czarina, but—more than that—it has been my magical talisman, my good luck piece beyond imagination.' 'How did it come to you, Father?' I asked him.

'Early in the century, about 1903, after Stalin and I had knocked over a few banks, we overheard, by chance in a tavern, that a Grand Duke of Imperial Russia and his wife, the Grand Duchess, would be passing through the village that evening. We waylaid his coach a few miles outside town. Stalin wanted only their gold, but I noticed this ruby hanging around his wife's royal neck, so I tore it from her. She cried out that I could take anything she owned but that—it had been in their family for more than nine hundred years, from before the Mongols took Russia, that it was the bearer of her family's good fortune. So I cut her throat to show her she was wrong. Later when I showed the bauble to Stalin and told him the story that went with it, he was greatly amused by the claim that it had been in the family for more than nine hundred years.' 'What bullshit,' he said. 'Nine hundred years ago that family was up to their hips in pig shit.' 'It's a pretty thing, though,' my father replied. 'If it's all right with you, I'll keep it.' 'Keep it with my blessing,' Stalin told my father. 'Nine hundred years, indeed! You should call it the Venerable Bead.' "

"Oh, Joe!" Leila sighed rapturously. "What a romantic story. I shall keep it until I die."

"We are one being now, my darling. My good fortune is yours, and yours is mine, so I pass this jewel, this Venerable Bead, on to you."

"But Joe—" she gasped, clutching the ruby with both hands, "this must be worth a half a million dollars!"

"Perhaps more—much more," he said.

As though guided by the power of the ruby, Reynard had come up with the zinger that eventually would earn Leila $63 million (gross) per year. She had always had a pleasant singing voice and had been able to improvise several classy dance steps in front of the stereo in the Reynard living room. She had a great chest and great legs, which her dramatic coach had said were her best feature. She had enormous commercial sexuality as well as possessed the nerve of eleven Apache Indians. Joe wanted her to be happy, so, if only out of desperation he had said, "What the hell, Leila, you're never going anywhere in the film bidniz as Leila Aluja and those four English kids have built an entire rock industry, so why not we get in on the ground floor?"

"How do you mean?"

"I'll hire some arrangers and a voice coach. We'll get some dancers, a sock choreographer, a rock band, some really punishing amplifiers, a solid video producer, a cushy record deal, and eleven press agents. Then I'll book a national tour. You make like you're dancing. You flash your chest. You sing loud. Rock is a gorronteed gold mine, even if it's impossible to hum. After the tour I'll set you with a movie deal where you're starred over the title, and a flock of product endorsements and, after you hit, you'll do as much television and movies as you think you want."

Leila shrugged. "Sounds okay with me. So when do we start?"

"Tumorra. But you gotta have a new name."

"Like what?"

He paced up and down the room, thinking. "I think I got it! The name alone will get you on the cover of *Time*. It has a classical Italian sound.

"Joe—fahcrissake!—what is it?"

"Meine Edelfrau. That's it. It means 'my lady'—like ma donna. It'll sell a million records. Meine Edelfrau."

As Meine Edelfrau, Leila became "the most famous woman in the world." If the name itself was aphrodisiac to the millions of her fans, a number which grew greater and greater as she toured the world, her presence on stage was a force that sent audiences out of their seats to copulate in the aisles or to beg her to take off the two remaining shreds of clothing she would still be wearing by the end of each performance. Fame, money, and overpowering public lust for celebrity made her the most popular, desirable, and saleable singer-dancer-newsmaker of her time, but she had to travel with six bodyguards and was able to gain time with her husband in public very rarely and then only by wearing a blond wig and inserting a set of celluloid false teeth over her real ones.

Joseph Reynard was hardly the first man in her life. The occasionally oversexed producer or director to one side, she had "dated" the great and near-great of filmdom, statecraft, and the worlds of sports. Nonetheless, Louella Parsons had announced her actual engagement to only two men, with each of whom Leila had thought, before she met Joe Reynard, she would spend the rest of her life, or at least a couple of months. Even now, when she would come upon their photographs suddenly in *Film Fun* or some other glossy magazine, she would get a lump in her heart as big as all memory. She had never been sure which of the two it was whom she really loved: Ueli Munger, the Swiss Casanova, the most bankable leading man on the Warner lot, or the radiation-hot, handsome young director, Freddie Goldberg, whose latest movie, *Cold!*, had outgrossed the combined *Rin-Tin-Tin* pictures, the grossing champions.

Both men were two-time Oscar nominees. Munger had been an intimate of President Kennedy, had double-dated with Sinatra and King Farouk. Goldberg had been voted Man of the Year by the

Junior Republican Exhibitors of Omaha and had already written his first autobiography. Both men had beautiful teeth (done by Dr. Pincus of Beverly Hills). Both men had given restrained but heartbroken interviews to the wire services on the day of Leila's wedding to Joseph Reynard.

When the news hit, racing up and down the canyons and out to Malibu and Palm Springs, that Leila Aluja, the barely featured player of *Betsy Flagg, American, The Film* (I through V) was going to marry Joseph Reynard, sole agent for the Dalai Lama, two Japanese electronics companies, and the BBC, the man credited with having discovered Arnold Schwarzenegger when the actor was merely a 138-pound weakling, no one could talk about anything else. Joe Reynard and the leading lady's wise-cracking best friend! Joe Reynard, the only figure in film history who had ever been awarded an Oscar for agenting! It all had the effect of the San Andreas fault swallowing the entire Universal lot.

Two hours after the announcement hit the trade papers, Ueli Munger, King of the Box Office and idol of millions, made such a violent scene at the Reynard-Aluja luncheon table at the Polo Lounge of the Beverly Hilis Hotel (a favored restaurant of the stars, where the radiant couple were receiving the homage of Hollywood) that Beverly Hills police had to be called and Munger had had to be dragged out of the restaurant. There was national television coverage.

The next morning at a quarter to three, Freddie Goldberg's Javanese exercise trainer at his twelve-bedroom home on his four-acre estate in Beverly Hills had had to call an ambulance. The medics put a stomach pump on the director and were able to thwart his suicide attempt. Although it was hotly denied, the Asian had confirmed to *The National Enquirer* that Goldberg had indeed tried to kill himself by overeating because of the Aluja-Reynard wedding announcement.

Joseph Reynard, the man who had won the prize that had been so coveted by both the greatest male star of the past box office fiscal quarter, and by the screen's ninth greatest director, had always been a mystery man who had, seemingly, appeared out of nowhere.

Reynard wasn't entirely a self-made man. The self-made part was an open book, but the secondary plot of his life, as with so many clangingly successful people, was closed. There were perhaps five or six versions of where he had come from and how he had happened, including how he had won the Notorious Shannon and Pusch Agency in a gin game, but if the real story were known, he would have been ruined, Hollywood superpower or no power, because in 1973, the Communist thing was very heavy. A case could have been made against him that would have made the Hollywood Ten look like founder-backers of Joseph McCarthy (R-Wis.).

There was a lot that Leila Aluja claimed she did not know about Reynard, could not possibly have known, she told the *Modern Screen* interviewer. He had come into her life like a tornado, had swept her off her feet by proposing marriage to her in the Executive Dining Room on the Fox lot. Within twenty minutes the Fox publicity head had flashed her acceptance across the world, before she might have had the chance to take Ueli and/or Freddie aside during an intimate weekend at the Springs to hint, at the very least, at her decision to marry Joseph Reynard. She knew they would have understood because they feared Reynard's power.

4

Joseph Reynard, a native Albanian, had been born Josef Shqitonja. *Shqitonja* meant "fox" in Albanian. The fox was the Albanian national emblem. It appeared on the Albanian flag. His father had been a fox in more ways than six. In the old days when the czar had been very big, his father had been on Stalin's bank-robbing team well before the Russian revolution. Stalin had joked (little notes on sentimental birthday cards) that it was a good thing Albania was small and poor because, if it had been four kilometers bigger and twenty leks richer, his father would have stolen it.

Even the word *yogurt* made Joseph Reynard homesick. He missed the sound of homey old names like Xhafer Ypi and Shefqet Verlaci, and every year, on the anniversary of Stalin's death from trying to swallow a pillow while two Politburo members sat on it, Reynard felt delicately guilty about lounging around as idly as a snake in swimming pools filled with celery tonic.

He was a tall man whose limbs fit him loosely. His ankles flopped when he walked as if he were dealing cards with his feet. His arms floated haphazardly. When he shifted his weight in his office chair, it seemed to be about to capsize. He moved as if he were a partly filled water bed; his memorable characteristic was total relaxation, when all around him people were popping Carafate tabs to control ulcers. He was dressed by London tailors, a symbol of his relief to be out of sheepskins and sandals. His thirty charcoal-gray mohair suits gleamed like an oil slick.

In his Permanent Disguise he was six feet three inches tall wearing elevator shoes, an overcompensation by the short Chinese planners. His nose had been modeled on that of the elder Morgan: quite swollen into a rutabaga shape, roseated, and pitted over an ivory-yellow mustache. His eyebrows were of the same color but thicker. He walked behind a large stomach that had been attached ingeniously to his body by sloping, flesh-colored foam-rubber padding—so ingeniously that although he had been sleeping with Leila Aluja since the second night he had met her, she had no idea that this stomach bulge was not his own.

To support his added height and weight, he had developed the splay-footed walk of a ballerina. The cunning eye pouches, the baldness that extended halfway backward on his mottled crown of flesh and then foliated into a garden of taffy-colored hair, his height, his five-button suits, his stomach, and that walk all confirmed the presence of an awesomely important man of fifty-odd years.

He was an awesomely important man within the walled city of world entertainment. He was, for example, perhaps more powerful in paralyzing the minds of the world public and holding those minds in stasis than Genghis Khan had been to the history of Asia, although not as harsh.

Biologically and chronologically, Josef Shqitonja was thirty-six years old. Underneath all those layers of Permanent Disguise, beyond the two gold teeth, he would be a totally unrecognizable but fine-looking young man. He was descended from Ghegs who had lived north of the Shkumbi River, direct descendents of the Thraco-Illyrian tribes and part of the Roman Catholic minority of Moslem Albania, the motherland of the 115-year-old man.

His father had been such a man. In those mountains his father had had the most magnificent mustache among a race who, even as striplings, seemed to be wearing busbys across their faces and, later in life, to be hiding behind reclining polar bears.

His father's mustache had been so densely furred and gigantic that it had to be combed three times a day with bears' claws to keep it free of small birds and other pests. The secret of its enormous health was raw eagle eggs made into a mousse and rubbed into it. His father had been eighty-four years old when, seeking fresh eggs in a high mountain aerie, he had had to bite off the heads of two eagles. Carrying the four eggs down the sheer face of the icy mountain cliff, he lost his footing and fell sixty-five feet, landing in a thick treetop safely and without having broken the eggs.

Little Josef had been born to his father's favorite wife when the elderly statesman had been eighty-eight years old. The image of a fox had been painted on the infant's cradle and on the thick straps of his sandals. Each night his father would rock him to sleep while he crooned, "You are a Shqitonja, a fox of foxes. Never forget that. The foxiest fox in the box."

Little Josef had been raised on three other majestic tenets as well: (1) the greatness of Joseph Stalin, (2) fear of Serbs and Greeks, and (3) regret that the Turkish Empire, the Sublime Porte which had been Albania's protector, had passed into history. Eleven out of forty-nine Turkish grand viziers had been Albanian and his father had been confident that he would have been appointed to the post had the Turks held on.

Stalin had been no Shqitonja, his father had said, but he had been a great one for bracing a bank. Because of the old friendship, his father, through Stalin, had arranged in 1953 for Josef to study at the Oriental Institute in Moscow, which had been declining since the day it had been founded by Vyacheslav Molotov in 1945. At OI he had mastered Chinese dialects, history, culture, and economic patterns. Now, on a Saturday afternoon in Beverly Hills, thousands of miles away from his beloved Albanian mountains, he was Ambassador Plenipotentiary Incognito of the Chinese People's Republic to the United States of America even though, in the formal, stuffy sense, this was not quite the same thing as being Ambassador to the Government of the United States in Washington. The latter would have been impossible, of course, because China did not recognize the United States.

But it was a job that had to be done. There could be no information without representation and the Soviets had refused to share theirs. The Chinese, to put it simply, looked too Chinese for espionage work inside the United States. The West had China watchers outside China. Josef Shqitonja and his vast *apparat* was China's West-watcher from the inside.

He was a spy master, an uncommon, pervasive, and invisible spy master, not any common spy. He was a trained diplomat. There was a distinction. Ordinary spies did their own laundry. He sent his laundry to be done in Paris each week using his working name. He watched around-the-clock with an alert staff of 236 from coast-to-coast, including seventeen KGB-trained traveling representatives. His people spied and handled the necessary staff assassinations and political dirty tricks. He voted in city, state, and national elections because everyone above the rank of junior agent in the embassy was a not-in-depth American citizen, including Shqitonja. Let the clumsy Soviets claim their diplomatic immunity, General Ha Mat Sun, chief of the 1st and 5th Directorates had said in his commencement address in Beijing. Mat Sun's people could prove they were native-born American citizens because forged certificates of their native American birth had been inserted into local records in small and large American cities across the country. This laid them open to charges of treason and subsequent execution if they were ever caught at spying, but it made all of them eligible for Medicare if and when they reached the age of sixty-five.

The talent-agency business which Shqitonja ran (out of Beverly Hills, New York, and London) had enormous influence over the American entertainment and communications industry, to say nothing of the mentalities of the American people. He sustained couch potatoes. He provided substitute lives through the illusory manifestations of his clients. He decided which of the films exported to the world were to be made, starring which actors, and on what terms. He kept an office at each of the major Hollywood film studios and television networks. His talent agency had grossed almost $200 million a year and gave out $5700 worth of Christmas presents in cigars alone.

Only an Albanian was competitive enough to enter show business on a trainee level, then build such a business in just under six years, but the fact that he was an Albanian and had 236 countrymen helping him meant everything. He was a Shqitonja, an Albanian fox. The fact that a woman in the Referentura Section was the actual boss of the whole operation was only a peculiarity of the system.

Joseph Reynard had a house with a quarter-mile indoor jogging track on four acres in the heart of Beverly Hills. It was entirely walled, with seventeen bedrooms, a twelve-car underground garage, a lacrosse field, and a two-level swimming pool. He lived by each word of Chairman Mao's lines, "It is good if it ends good" and

"That we, the poorer born/Whose baser stars do shut us up in wishes/Might with the effects of time/Follow our friends."

But with all his position and power and his thirty charcoal-gray suits, excepting his union with Leila Aluja, he was not a happy man. How he longed for freedom from material things. He had power, he had position, but he had no money. His Sino-Albanian masters paid him a flat $1000 a month plus expenses. He was forced to maintain an exalted life-style the demands of which were beyond extravagance, on an expense account. It was generous enough, but it was impossible to put anything aside under that sort of arrangement. He had no salary, no stock options, no ownership of anything. The solution to money problems had become an obsession with him. His own great-grandfather had been the inventor of yogurt, but had never known how to set up a commercial empire with it. He could have been richer than Exxon if only the 130 square miles of the massive limestone extension of the Dinaric Alps, in a valley 6,300-feet high, had lent itself to the worldwide launching of a product such as yogurt. But the sad fact was, the old man hadn't even known what it was he had invented until his daughter-in-law had named it.

His own father was a man who dominated Stalin to the point of actually becoming the crucial counselor, the brain beyond the Union of Soviet Socialist Republics, the man who had dictated Stalin's every move, and who because of his admiration for Stalin, had been forced to take over the same guidance for the major policies of the People's Republic of China as well—all of which leading to the Cold War situation whereby the Soviets and the Chinese were utterly dependent upon Albania to fix their destinies. All that, and yet there he was, possessor of the name but not the game, a lackey working for $1000 dollars a month and expenses, owning practically nothing but thirty suits and a few shirts and ties.

But he had Leila's love. That was priceless. He gave her love and a career in return and that brought them both joy.

He looked back on his prodigious labor of transforming himself from a sheep farmer to a great talent agent. The climb had been long and hard: the two years of drudgery as a janitor in the apartment house on Granovsky Street where Serov and Rudenko had lived, where Khrushchev lived; the freezing year as a car-wash attendent at Lubiyanka Prison to work his way through college, to pay for the two-thirds that the Albanian state stipend did not cover. His father had urged him to Moscow to get his degree, beyond all his sons, when the Albanian Party leader Enver Hoxha himself had been educated in Paris where the food was so much better.

He never knew anything more thrilling (until the night he had met Leila Aluja) than when he was admitted to the International Relations Institute. His heart still swelled with affectionate nostalgia as he thought of that massive old building on the corner of Krymskaya Square.

IRI had a Western and an Eastern curriculum. Because Shqitonja had transferred from the Oriental Institute and knew Chinese so well, because he was Albanian and Albania was under the protection of China, he was assigned to the Western division to study North American showbiz dialects, American showbiz customs, haircuts, regional costumes, and folk dancing. Later, on his first day on the new job in Palm Springs, California, he had dressed himself so colorfully and had worn such a conforming hairstyle that he had become invisible instantly.

The day after he graduated from IRI in Moscow, he was granted a fortnight's leave in Tirana, the Albanian capital, where he was issued a jeep from the motor pool, which meant that the Minister of Commerce would have to do without a car until Josef returned from his visit home.

He had driven across the narrow coastal shelf toward the mountains where his father lived, riding along the continuations of the ancient Roman Via Appia which, having ended in Italy at Brindisi, continued on the other side of the Adriatic as Egnatia Street to run to Constantinople. It had not been repaired since the time of the Romans but, on the other hand, not many cars had used it.

That beautiful day stayed with Joseph Reynard. He was going home, driving through stands of willows and white beeches. The abundant wildlife of his boyhood was no longer there. It had been pushed to the utmost forests by the national shortage of drinking water. He had never forgotten his father's urgent advice, "Always live near a river," which was why he had bought a duplex at the very edge of eastern Manhattan for his frequent trips into New York after he had reached the pinnacle of power.

To that key advice, his father had added, "And look out for the Sigurimi." The Albanian Secret Police. Russian trained. Chinese inspired. Worse than either. If he were to have his choice among falling into the hands of the torturers of the KGB, or into the merciless complacencies of the 5th Directorate in Beijing with its "gift of a thousand deaths," or the one elderly man and his great-granddaughter who constituted the interrogation team of the Sigurimi, he would skip into the arms of either the Russians or the Chinese. His father always crossed himself reflexively when he heard the name of Maj. Gen. Mihalleq Zicishti, the Sigurimi chief.

Drinking in the smell of the all-Albanian gasoline fumes, so reminiscent of boiled cabbage and entrapped miner's feet, he could see his father's *katun* in the distance. A ram came tearing out of the front door of the main house, scattering chickens ahead of him. As Josef braked the car, his father came charging out, mustache unfurled, to greet him.

His father was bigger than Josef in all the dimensions. His hands were huge and their bulging veins so large that it was as though moles were burrowing under his skin. Only his piercing black eyes, his scimitar nose, and his mottled bald head could be seen above his shirt buttons. The frozen waterfall of his great mustache covered his mouth, his chin, and the sides of his throat, wholly obscuring his shoulders.

He embraced Josef, then led him into the house where aunts, wives, and nieces had been assembled. There was a sense of family awe in the loud greetings and many tears of joy because no one in their collective memory, beyond Josef's father and an aunt, had ever ventured more than twelve miles beyond the village, which was the center of the universe. Josef changed into sheepskins and sandals since foreign clothes tended to make the family suspicious. They all sat at the family table with stone jugs of fig *raki* placed at accessible intervals along the table top.

"Say something in Chinese," his father commanded after they had been reassembled.

Josef went into the great "Shall I or shall I not exist? That is the question" from Chairman Mao's famous pamphlet *Small Village,* which began, "Now is the winter of our discontent."

He declaimed interchangeably in the Mandarin and Cantonese dialects, throwing in some slang of the Keichow, Liaoning, Yunan, and Fukien districts. Josef mimed wherever it was seemly to mime. All were greatly moved when he finished twelve minutes later. His father was very proud.

His father began to speak from behind his mustache in that voice which recalled boulders being ground into rocks, the rocks into gravel, then into sand, that voice which hurled itself or coaxed itself into a sonic spin out of the rifling within his throat. "I have been talking to Chairman Mao, my boy," he said, "and I can tell you that you are going to China."

"I see," Josef said.

"We are a family of travelers. Before you, my sister Nezhmije was a traveler. She went to America and became very, very rich, so we never heard from her again. May it be that the Shqitonjas who are called upon to travel always get rich. May you get as rich as I did when I traveled to Imperial Russia and as rich as my sister."

"Thank you, Papa."

"You may be asking yourself, Why China? What could be as strange as an Albanian in China?"

"I have trained as a diplomat, Papa. We have an embassy in China."

"You will never see the inside of that embassy, son. But by serving China, you will be serving Albania. They are our natural allies."

"Perhaps you could explain that, Papa."

"I was the closest friend to Josif Vissarionovich Dzhugashvili, the theology student who worked for the cause inside Imperial Russia where the fear and death were, while others who walked into history lived in London, or Zurich, or the Bronx in the Yew Ess of Ay. Dhugie, as I called him, had the power of life or death over hundreds of millions of people, and he had the sense to use it. Power is like ice. If you don't use it, it melts away. Because we were buddies, rootin', tootin', shootin' pals, he protected our country from the Serbs, the Montenegrins, the Bulgarians, the Italians, and the Greeks. We are weak. We have to depend on protectors. We are very small and we are surrounded by enemies; therefore, our history has been a constant search for a powerful, foreign protector—the more powerful, the better; the more distant, the best. We had the Turks since 1403. Then as the Turks got weak, the Hungarians and the Italians got stronger. We went up and down. We became independent after the Balkan Wars of 1912." He grimaced. "But independence is a very bad thing for us. The Serbs swallowed a half-million Albanians in the Kosmet, the Greeks took two hundred thousand more, and the Montenegrins carved out all of Shkodër. Thank God for the first World War."

He broke wind in dramatic punctuation. As one chorus, the assembled wives all cried out, "God bless you!"

"We needed a protector desperately," Josef's father said. "We grabbed at the Italians in 1934. Then came World War Two and we were filled again with Greeks, Yugoslavs, and Germans. In 1946 we were almost swallowed whole by Yugoslavia. Who wants a protector who is right on his border? So we took the Russians and they made our secret police work. But now old Dhugie is gone and the Russians have made friends with Tito. We had to find a new protector. This time, the very best, because China is ten thousand miles away. The Russians don't want to upset this protector, so they will sit on the Yugoslavs. We are saved once again, my boy, and it has made a great career for you. *Tungjat jeta!"* he roared. The two banged their stone jars together, grinned broadly, and drank deeply.

5

After two weeks of dreading the *raki* hangovers and the obligatory orgies in the haylofts with the local farm girls, Josef went down the mountain to Tirana to report to the Foreign Office of the Chief of Cadres (Eastern Section), where he was issued an Albanian Foreign Service passport. He filled out documents that needed to be deposited with their corresponding organizations; an internal passport, a *Komonsol* card; transit cards for the industrial, military, and oil regions; a credit card for the Albanian telegraph agency; and an application for credit with the New China News Agency. He arranged to have his subscription to the *Anuari Statistikor i Republikes Popullore te Shqiperise* forwarded to Beijing. He memorized and signed *Rules of Behavior Abroad* and took an oath that he would live by them or suffer punishment by the Sigurimi.

A fishing boat took him across the forty-seven miles of the Adriatic Sea to Italy, where he landed without disturbing the Italian immigration authorities. A car took him inland to Perugia, where he joined a bus tour of Americans en route to picket the Vatican on behalf of birth control. He carried a forged American passport in the name of Henry Emmet, banker. He flew from Rome to Hong Kong, where he disappeared into a Chinese military airport at Kwang-Chou.

He was met at the Beijing Airport by two Chinese who spoke to him only in the arcane showbiz dialect of midtown Manhattan and central Beverly Hills. He was ordered to speak only English until he had attained proficiency in Showbiz American. He was issued reasonable facsimiles of American clothes, and he did not see the inside of the Albanian legation during his entire two-year course of graduate studies.

His superiors assigned him to a girl named Marilyn Fu, who spoke groovy U.S. musician jive talk. She had her ways of relaxing him. The food was excellent.

He began the most intensive period of studies of his life, brutally exhausting work at "Chinese pace"—classes, seminars, and lab work eleven hours a day for seven days a week, all of it requiring six hours of grinding book study in his quarters, which were shared with six other Albanians.

Two of his classmates had been at IRI with him; the other four had come to Beijing from scattered Albanian legations around the world. Their ages ranged from twenty-two to sixty. The only two women in the class were the oldest in the group. One of these wore violet corduroy bloomers under a black burlap kilt.

The size of the class trebled within the first two months until the student body was almost 280 Albanians in all, speaking the Showbiz dialects of Las Vegas, Miami, Southern California, and central Manhattan. They studied karate, the same techniques that Chairman Mao had put to use in order to overthrow governments in Africa and Southeast Asia, for environmental protection as well as to counter the stresses of the constant power struggles within the American film and television industries. They were taught micro-photography, gin rummy card manipulation, and theatrical agency procedures including such skills as reading small print upside-down from fifteen feet across a room, treating men as though they were fragile women, and women as though they were annoying men. The curriculum placed most emphasis on theatrical agency practices and U.S. tax evasion methods.

An essential part of the Total Disappearance course (4 points, 6 semesters) was the system of Permanent Disguise, which had been devised by Lt. Gen. Ha Mat Sun, chief of the 1st and 5th Directorates. The instructor of the Permanent Disguise class, who was a qualified makeup man as well as a plastic surgeon, explained the reasoning behind the necessity for the disguises by Sino-Albanian agents in the United States: "You are going into a country where very little is what it seems to be," he said. "Great leaders, using Permanent Disguises which totally deceive the population, mask their ineptitude and indifference with these disguises which show them to be warm-hearted, amiable, and wholly lovable fellows. One of their great leaders had the boyish cast of a collegian, but few women were safe in his company. Another was a poor country boy who rose to become a country school teacher. Other than that, he had existed by the grace of nothing but politics, yet he left an estate of twenty-two million dollars.

"The use of Permanent Disguises extends downward through their savings and loan executives, also to the people who lead the manufacture of their automobiles, to their legislators who have actually been able to pass laws legalizing bribes for themselves called Political Action Committees, as well as to the extraordinarily effective, apparently benevolent health care systems and insurance and pharmaceutical companies. All of them wear concerned and kindly Permanent Disguises so that they may make more and more money while giving fewer and fewer services, the key objective of the nation. Oh, yes, ladies and gentlemen, if you hope to succeed in your American missions, you must master the art of Permanent Disguise."

The Sino-Albanian policy was that all secret agents in the United States would wear a Permanent Disguise, which would not be removed at any time and which did not require renewal for periods of as long as eight years.

At first Josef wondered, considering the amazing efficiency of the Permanent Disguises, why the Chinese themselves did not enter the United States and do their own espionage work because any chosen features could be duplicated, and the Chinese (mostly) were tiny enough to make wonderfully believable Hollywood agents.

Shqitonja graduated at the head of his class. His father was so elated by the news that he sent a gallon of yogurt flavored with thirty-year-old Hungarian Barat Palinka, 150-proof apricot brandy, by the Chinese diplomatic pouch from Tirana.

On the day before actual commencement exercises, Josef was summoned to the Foreign Office of the Chief of Cadres (Western Section) in the Chinese Foreign Ministry. Although Josef didn't know it at the time, the place in which the meeting was held was a replica of the private office of Leonard Shannon, founder of Notorious Shannon and Pusch in Beverly Hills, California. The floors were paved with lapis lazuli containing facsimile autographs of past and present Notorious Shannon clients, set in brightly sparkling semiprecious stones. The Shannon trademark and good-luck piece, a platinum bagel, rested on the center of the highly polished desk.

The Chief of Cadres was a plump, sardonic Cantonese. He alternated leers and sneers as though conveying his knowledge of the impenetrable. Due to his intensive training, Shqitonja recognized it as the perpetual expression employed by all film company executives who earned more than $1,634,782 a year.

"Siddown, Joe," the tiny chief said. "This is it, sweedhott."

Shqitonja sat. The chief pushed a huge box of cigars toward him with the heel of an alligator shoe that rested on the desk. Josef took a cigar and lit it. It was made of cabbage leaves and argol, but it had been expertly rolled by an agent who had obviously studied the art in Havana.

"You ain't no dummy, bubbie," the chief said. "You got yahself the best score inna whole school."

"I'm Shqitonja and we try harder," Josef shrugged.

"So all right. You cut for the coast tumorra. You go in at Guatamala and you come out heah." He wheeled in his chair and stabbed a tiny finger at Tijuana, Mexico, on a wall map behind himself. "You got five weeks to set yahself with any of the Big Three agencies. After that, the only way to go is up—and we'll be watchin'."

"What do we have on some agency with a big front but maybe a small cash position?"

"That's a good qvestion, boychik. The name of the agency is Notorious Shannon and Pusch. They got a good list, but Shannon plays golf like he was Ike and Pusch plays the horses like he was Pittsburgh Phil. For maybe ninety grand, depending on how you play it, you could like take over the whole schmear, fake oak paneling and all. But you gotta get in first. You gotta get to know all three sets of their books, then, as soon as you can, you gotta start to move classmates in for when after you ease Shannon and Pusch out so the list stays with the office and you are set to grow. Dig?"

"That I can do. Then what?"

"Then you make it the biggest talent agency inna industry. That's your cover. One cover for three hundred illegals in a bidniz packed with interchangables—little guys with little brief cases, crazy haircuts, tweed fedoras—they can get lost in any crowd in the States, baby, and because they're always talking shop and nobody listens. Capeesh?"

Josef nodded solemnly.

"You leave maybe thirty of the dumber ones to run the agency and the other two-seventy or so handle our thing."

"No Referentura? No rezident? Or am I the rezident?"

"How can you be rezident, baby? You are out in front."

"Then what am I?"

"You are ambassador. That's the rank you hold."

Josef was dumbfounded. He flinched at the statement, staring at the Chief of Cadres as a puce flush rose from his throat to fill his face. "You are giving me *ambassador*?"

The chief moved to placate him, swinging his feet off the desk to ease the pain. "Relax, bubbie. The heart's got its reasons. Don't tell us how to rob a train."

"After the way I worked? With my marks at IRI? You got to be kidding, Sam!"

"Keep it sweatless, kid," the tiny Chinese said. "You have the flash spot. You have the expense account. You are a tall guy and tall guys always work in front."

"Who's the rezident?"

"Don't ask arreddy. You'll know when the right time comes." He grinned. "All things come to them which waits for it. You know the s.o.p. Referentura and Intelligence got to be under Political and you are Diplomatic. Go sue City Hall. Are you with us?"

Josef nodded glumly.

"Atsa my boy," the chief said gaily. "So here's the drill. Notorious Shannon needs you to build the television and the lecture departments. They need rock-tour bidniz and concert bookings. So you gotta build a chain of legit branch offices across the country and Chairman Mao wants you to pick up a solid record label and keep your eye out for a movie studio so we can justify the big operation. Okay?"

"I dig."

"Make as much *tsaar* for the Russians as you can. In a quiet way.

You know, like you could strand the Red Army chorus in Terre Haute or something."

"How do I report?"

"The rezident will handle it. You have no contact, in or out. That's full-time stuff, believe me, and you gotta build the agency. Anyway, the rezident would make a lousy agent. She likes actors."

"A woman?"

"Why not?"

"And she's the boss?"

"Right. Hey, you wanna big laugh?"

"I'll take two if you've got a spare."

"The Russians is gung nuts because none of the news media crowd in Rangoon goes to their swimming pool anymore. They all go to ours. How about that?"

"Very funny."

"Chairman Mao is like to bust a gut."

Josef shrugged.

"We move you out tumorra. Happy second act, baby. And hey! You gotta new name. Who can spell Shqitonja?"

"What's my name?"

The diminutive Chinese shuffled through papers on his desk. "Here it is," he said, "Joseph Reynard. How's that for a crazy moniker?"

6

He drove a rental Corvette north into San Diego with the bullfight crowd. The course in Deja-Vu USA (4 points, 2 semesters) was working like a watch. Nothing seemed strange to him except the people, but he realized that, in southern California, the people must seen strange to each other.

He turned the car toward Palm Springs, where he closed the deal for the ownership of Notorious Shannon in a gin rummy game with Phil Pusch. Pusch had learned card mechanics working in carnivals, then, later on, for Meyer Lansky's sporting enterprises, but Joseph had been taught how to work and win at college (Western Division) in Beijing. After two hours of play, Pusch suggested one final game, three across, which would decide whether Joseph would win control of the Notorious Shannon Agency. Leonard Shannon had quietly sold out to Pusch three years before in order to get on with his dream of playing every golf course in the non-Communist world.

Within four months, Joseph had one-third of his classmates at work behind Notorious Shannon desks. They began to bring in important new business, actors being so sensitive to rumor and superstition that it was a straight agitprop operation: slander, forged "proof" of malfeasance with clients' funds, or the distribution of a few Rolls-Royces or houses among the box-office leaders. By the eighth month, Notorious Shannon was the biggest talent agency in the business.

The branch offices were building. The big band department was fattening up. Concerts and lectures had tripled their income while television was growing into a gold mine.

When he decided he had all the major studios and independents eating out of his hand, Joseph felt that he had reached the point where he could ask for a salary in addition to the expense account on which he had been operating. Meanwhile, his secretary murmured through the intercom that Peggy Flinn, one of the file clerks, insisted on seeing him. He consulted his secret file. Flinn was an Albanian named Liri Frasheri, born in Sazan. He told his secretary to send her in.

She was a quite small, fragile-appearing woman in her late fifties with a white Dutch-boy bob. She wore Space Shoes and a shoulder-strap purse. She locked his office door behind her with a key from the purse. While Joseph stared, uncomprehending, she lit a cigarette and threw the spent match on his $4,000 carpet.

"Hey! What's witchew?" Joseph yelled.

She sat down. "I am the rezident," she said in Russian.

Joe sat down with a crash. "Welcome, Comrade," he answered weakly. "How long have you been here?"

"I was in charge of the file room at Notorious Shannon for two years before you got here," she said, switching to American speech. "You are a very classy boy. And don't think I didn't pass that word to Chowmeinsville."

"Am I permitted to ask the general outline of your assignment?"

"*Po,*" she answered, slipping into Albanian with the word for *yes*. He had the grisly thought that the word *no,* which was *jo,* was his own name.

"We will operate on the Russian system," Miss Flinn said in Albanian despite the irrevocable law that all languages except Showbiz American were forbidden, showing the extent of her power and the security of her position.

"I am rezident for State Security, for the Chief Intelligence Directorate, the Ministry of Foreign Affairs, and the Ministry of Foreign Trade." She smiled sweetly. "Russian operation, Chinese budget. I am also in charge of all security matters for all intelligence departments of the Chinese People's Republic, as follows," she said, shifting into Cantonese. "The State Committee for the Coordination of Scientific Research, the Council for the Affairs of Religious Sects, the Committee of Chinese Women's Interests Among American Women, the Committee of Youth Organizations, the

Patrice Lumumba Memorial Fund for Counter-Revolution, and the Central Committee of the Communist Party of the Chinese People's Republic."

"Are you also Sigurimi?" Josef gulped.

"No cheap jokes, please. I report to the First and Fifth Directorates in Beijing." She leaned forward for emphasis. "All communications from Gen. Ha Mat Sun come directly to me." She lapsed into Albanian for absolute clarity. *"A me kuptoni?"*

"I understand."

Miss Flinn stood up. "Okay, doll. So let's let it slink out in the alley and see who shoots it down." She rippled fingers at him and started out of the room.

"Uh—Miss Flinn?"

"Yes, lover?"

"When do we settle on some kind of a salary for me? Also, with the money I'm bringing into this business I think I'm entitled to maybe some stock options."

"Boychik—you arreddy got the biggest expense account in fillum history. What more do you want?"

"Well! Like a little for a rainy day?"

"Do I get a salary? Do I get stock options? Do I get to eat at Chasen's? Do I get to lay gorgeous movie stahs? We're working for a guvvamint, fahcrissake. Straighten up, Joe." She unlocked the door and left the room.

He wheeled in his chair and stared out hopelessly at the monotonously perfect climate thinking that if he could get his hands on some real money, he would defect. He was entitled to some fair share of the profits. He was acquiring film companies for them, getting $10 and $12 million fees for actors with enough points to have them piling up art collections, fahcrissake, but what did he have? Bupkis! A lousy expense account that they were trying to tell him was some kind of big deal. For two cents more, he would strip off the Permanent Disguise and woo Leila all over again. But he had to have a bundle of money. He couldn't swing it on a nontransferrable expense account, no matter how unlimited.

7

Joe had to know more about Peggy Flinn. She was the enormous boulder standing in the narrow mountain path over which he would have to make his way if the time ever came to escape. He dominated the Albanian community, the in-group of Beverly Hills, but Peggy Flinn dominated him and that was more than he could stomach.

Three evenings after his first meeting with the rezident, two hours after the office had closed, he strolled into the Referentura, which was forbidden territory for him even though he was ambassador. The door to the rezident's office was closed, but he went in to make sure she was not there. He saw a few freshly decoded cables in the Signals basket on her desk. He riffled through them reflexively because that was the basic training of any agent, secret or showbiz. He was riveted by the third signal in the stack, written in Russian.

1st Directorate
HUSTLEGRAM

Top Secret/FYEO
March 18th

GREETINGS

The State Committee for Foreign Economic Relations parenthesis Tirana parenthesis has signaled to the Council of Ministers, CPR, that New York attorney, Courtney Wolgast, 29 Broadway, representing estate of Mrs. Timor Coolidge, has mailed inquiry seeking wherabouts of Albanian Josef Dhelper, who is heir to $4,489,232.

Advise confirmation of status of attorney, identity of Mrs. Timor Coolidge, and of your positive apprehension of legatee (Dhelper). If your investigations prove him to be deceased, a reasonable facsimile of him will be forwarded to you from Beijing. Confirm.

The designation HUSTLEGRAM meant that a mandatory informational reply within seventy-two hours was necessary.

Joseph understood the signal instantly. His father had told him — too many times for him to have forgotten it—the story of the great fortune of his sister, Josef's aunt who had become a Mrs. Timor Coolidge. He had had a general idea from his father that Auntie Nezhmije was loaded, but nothing like this. The husband hadn't even been in showbiz, fahcrissake. Aunt Mezhie must have been as wise as his father because she had designated Josef Dhelper as her heir. That got him off the hook with the Sigurimi. Dhelper was the Albanian word for Reynard, the French word for *fox,* the English word for Shqitonja, because she knew $4,489,232, an amount bigger than the Albanian Pentagon's annual budget, could cause a lot of trouble in Albania and she had wanted the Shqitonjas to have the time to think and to scheme a safe way to get their hands on the money and to be able to keep it.

He pocketed the signal and strolled out of the rezident's office unseen. Back in his own office, consulting a Manhattan telephone directory, he confirmed that Courtney Wolgast had offices at 29 Broadway and that he lived at 14 East 90th Street. Joseph began to plot his escape, as complicated as he knew that could become—not a plan, just a widening desire. He would need to take the money and Leila with him wherever he went. But Leila, as Meine Edelfrau, a.k.a. "the Material Girl," had become a worldwide celebrity who was earning more money than the gross national product of Albania plus Macdeonia. It would mean that he would have to run out on his clients, leaving them at the mercy of film companies and television networks. They were artists, they needed him, but he needed that $4,489,232 even more. Ueli Munger's twelve-picture deal at Paramount at $8 million a picture plus points; Freddie Goldberg's two back-to-back blockbusters, nine $5 million scripts ready to be sold; the merger of Sony with the State of California—they were all pending. More than $210 million in commissions was involved. He had to put all of that out of his head. First things first.

He telephoned Leila Aluja's message center, maintained for Leila's identity as Meine Edelfrau; she had no other identity any longer.

"Sweedhott," he said into the automatic tape at the other end of the line, which would transfer the message to Leila no matter where she was in the world, "I gotta rush call to New York. You'll be closing at Soldiers Field in Chicago, then you layover for the weekend, so meet me at the Bottom of the Cage, in New York, at six-thirty on Saturday. Love yah, Joe." The Bottom of the Cage was Leila's favorite restaurant anywhere.

He checked that he had all seventeen of his credit cards, took $12,500 traveling money from his wall safe, and left for the airport. He checked into a hotel penthouse suite on East 64th Street, and had a good night's sleep. He telephoned Courtney Wolgast at his office at 9:25 the following morning.

"This is Josef Dhelper," he said when he got Mr. Wolgast on the phone. "I have been told that you made an inquiry—"

"Made an inquiry? What the devil is the matter with your people? I made that inquiry four months ago and I haven't heard a word from anyone."

Josef almost collapsed with relief that his countrymen would never become famous for the anxious observation of the passage of time or that the Chinese had never bothered to be as efficient, say, as the Swiss. "It's the bureaucracy, counselor," he answered smoothly. "Only the police department really works. But I assure you, I got word of your letter only yesterday evening."

"Ah. Well. Yes. I see. Nonetheless, I must get this thing moving and off the books, as they say." He wheezed. It was an old voice, not old in the calendar sense, as perhaps it could be said about his father's old voice but reminiscent of Santa Claus's voice, very old. "Can you lunch with me at the Harvard Club next week?"

"The *Har*-vard Club???" Joseph's voice broke. Not even the cunning, resourceful Colonel Abel, the James Bond of Soviet espionage, had been crafty enough to penetrate the Harvard Club, citadel of the American nomenclature's secret power. The tremendous opportunity made him speak very rapidly. "No, no, sir. Not next week," he said. "To-day. It must be to-day."

"My dear man, I have been waiting for you for four months and—"

"That is not my fault. It must be today."

"I am sorry. I have a very busy day today."

"Then tomorrow. I know tomorrow is Saturday, but we could meet in the afternoon. I have so little time, you see and—"

"Yes. I quite understand, Mr. Dhelper. Tomorrow at four o'clock then? At the bar in the Harvard Club?"

Joseph disconnected and began to compute. Now that the inquiry had been forwarded by the creaking bureaucracy in Tirana to the ancient Confucian mandarinate in Beijing and, after aeons, had undergone a sort of osmosis into the form of an active signal from the 1st Directorate, it was alive among the Security forces, the part of modern politics which actually worked, which had the best minds, which existed to hunt and bring down.

The Chinese would believe that the sleepy bureaucracy of Tirana had bucked the information through to get it off their desks and to forget it, but when it had moved from Tirana to Beijing, by the very act of its moving, it had come to the attention of the Sigurimi.

The Sigurimi would understand why it had been bucked to the Chinese who had both the budget and the manpower in New York to run this down. But $4,489,232 was involved, an amount far, far bigger to Albania than it was to China. It would take any Sigurimi section chief about twelve hours of checking to discover that Josef Dhelper was really Josef Shqitonja, their own man. Sooner or later the information would have to be shared with the Chinese, then the 5th Directorate as well as the Sigurimi would be after him and his money.

Therefore, it was good-bye, Leila. He knew he had to explain to her except that there was no way to explain. He was already on the run. Good-bye, Leila. Good-bye, my darling.

But he was a Shqitonja! He felt the chilled steel of family pride reinforce his spine. He must find a way to keep the legacy and Leila as well. She needed him. She was just starting to score international success as Meine Edelfrau. Her concerts in Tibet had been tremendous money winners. She had had sensational reviews on the tour and she was doing tremendous business, but she was also a very dopey little broad who could hardly think her way through breakfast. Besides, she was a terrible, terrible actress who couldn't survive if she didn't have him behind her, staring down the studios and daring them to make any move that would end her career. She had a simultaneous four-network contract to be finalized for the most spectacular television special ever broadcast. There was two million eight waiting in line to be picked up for some basketball shoe endorsement. She couldn't handle stuff like that. No one but he could handle stuff like that. He couldn't desert her. He could not throw her to the wolves in the snow behind the careening droshky because, in a wonderful sense, she *was* the droshky that was pulling his life forward.

He would have to do two important things before he met Courtney Wolgast tomorrow afternoon, he thought. He would have to arrange for emergency funds through his New York office, then he would have to strip off his Permanent Disguise.

8

Under instruction from Mark Haselgrove, Leila had fallen in with the dominant Albanian crowd in Beverly Hills. She was passed from cocktail to dinner party as she slowly arrived at the surmisal that Joseph Reynard was the absolute leader of the tightly knit Albanian clique. But he seemed to avoid Albanian social gatherings; in fact, he did not seem to acknowledge its existence. That made Leila suspicious. He spoke Albanian. All the Albanian crowd in movies and show biz patently saw him as their leader. But if Albanian clients needed to talk to him, they came to his office and spoke only in English. It was, therefore, all the more remarkable—but who can account for the accidental catastrophes of love?—that Joe had met Leila at all since it was not possible, considering the quality of her work as an actress, that an agency as powerful and as respected as Notorious Shannon and Pusch would have represented her.

Reynard seemed to be unreachable, yet she knew that the Haselgrove Organization would not accept that. Then, entirely by accident, dressed as either Sonny or Cher, Leila managed to trip and fall into Joseph Reynard's lap at a dinner party at Cecil B. DeMille's house.

They fell helplessly and hopelessly in love. This did not alter her reflexive ferocity about her work as an American patriot. Her central task was to determine who was Joseph Reynard's boss—who was the overall rezident and which one was the Sigurimi representative. By ferreting out who was the rezident controlling the entire Sino-Albanian spy network, she would be able to identify Joseph

Reynard's place in the scheme of things. This revelation almost shattered her, but it was too late to turn back. She knew she loved Joseph Reynard, yet she loved the flag more.

She could not bear to think of what would happen when the case was closed. She was utterly torn. She would find herself asking desperately for advice from a photograph of J. Edgar Hoover, which she kept in a locket hung around her neck. She wrote "Dear Abby" letters to Barry Goldwater. She held long prayer sessions with Louis B. Mayer, both of them kneeling on the vicuña rug that covered the floor of his office. Aghast, she found herself devoting more and more time to planning Joe's escape after his arrest and conviction because then she would be assigned by the Haselgrove Organization to find him again, yet she hated herself for thinking that way. Always, in her daydreams, she vowed that the second time she caught him it would not be for Mark Haselgrove but for herself.

The conflict which this kind of "turncoat" thinking inflicted upon her jarred her soul. She had to keep telling herself that she loved Joseph Reynard, yes, but she loved the free-market system more. Still, she would think wistfully, no flag ever designed could do to her what Joe did to her. Had she even sensed that his prodigious skills in bed were merely the result of his having gotten top grades in Sexual Persuasion II, a popular elective at the institute in Beijing, she might have pulled up stakes, rushed off to China, and formed a friendship with the professor who taught the course.

The terrible thing was, she couldn't blame Joe for having been a Communist. He couldn't help it. It wasn't as though he had been a Texas boy or an Indiana boy who had converted to Communism, betraying his country. He was only doing what, to him, must have seemed to be the right thing—even the patriotic thing where the Albanians were concerned. He wasn't entirely a spy, after all, she rationalized. He was partly a diplomat. It was just like the thousands and thousands of young American lawyers who had wanted to be florists or schoolteachers, as she had wanted to be, but society and the system wouldn't let them; they were forced into being lawyers, as she had been forced to exterminate Communism wherever it lurked.

STOP! her soul cried out in mortal torment, but her heart dragged her onward toward the abyss. Ultimately, she could arrest him, sure, because that was her job, her duty, but after that? Would he ever speak to her again when he found out at his trial who she was? Ah, the hell with it. The only way she could stay steady and helpful would be to live from minute to minute.

9

Joseph Reynard stood totally still and stared at the facade of the Harvard Club from across 44th Street. He was where every Russian, Chinese, and Albanian boy who had ever hoped to make his mark in espionage had vowed, in their hearts, to be standing one day. He crossed the street and entered the building, his bowels frozen with fear. He entered what he had been taught to believe was the inner center of American government.

The security agent guarding the door was a white-haired man with a white mustache who was dressed in the club livery. He stopped Joe short with a piercing glance. Joe knew he would be searched. The agent's hand darted into the top drawer of a tall desk. Joseph waited for the gun to appear. He was sweating.

The man's hand reappeared holding eyeglasses, which he put on with great care, a clever psychological ploy to intimidate the visitor, Joe thought. Joe imagined the security man, undoubtedly a 10th Dan, karate, demanding in a blurred but menacing voice to know who Joe expected to see. I am a Harvard man, Joe shrilled inside his skull, desperate to keep a firm grip on his cover, using General Mat Sun's concept called Method Espionage, wherein the spy becomes the image he has conceived.

"What name, sor?"

"You will please tell Mr. Courtney Wolgast that Mr. Josef Dhelper is here."

It came over Joe all at once that his man was in fact Allan Dulles, the dreaded former head of the Central Intelligence Agency! Nothing had been heard of Dulles since the President had broken him and taken away his Party rank. And this was how they would do it. Americans hated to waste anything except money. This would be their equivalent of Commissar of Hydro-Electric Installations at Kerke-Vilyuski in Yukutshakaya. He snapped a picture of Dulles with his belt-buckle camera just before the man turned away saying, "Dis way, sor," with an assumed Irish intonation.

He followed Dulles. The next few moments would tell if this were all a trap. He was led into a small, darkly paneled bar to a short round-faced man with white, wavy hair who wore an old-fashioned wing collar of the type which had once caused Comrade Lenin to seem to smile. The man wore a boutonniere as big as a cabbage in the lapel of a dark suit. Joe had the feeling that this was what his father might look like behind his mustache were it ever to fall off.

"St. Joseph's helper is here, sor," Dulles said before he left them.

"What did he say?" Joe asked.

"Tom is getting along, Mr. Dhelper," Mr. Wolgast said with an indulgent smile. "He doesn't hear names like he used to. How do you do, sir? I am Courtney Wolgast. What will you have to drink?"

They shook hands.

"Say!" Mr. Wolgast said with delighted surprise. "That was an Odd Fellows grip, wasn't it?" Joe paled. Unthinkingly, he had used the Sigurimi handshake, which was used only for emergency identification.

"I would like a Southern Comfort on the rocks," he said shakily.

"Sorry?"

"One Southern Comfort. On the rocks."

"Is that an Albanian drink?"

"No. Actually, it was developed in St. Louis by the bartender Louis Herron in 1875." Joe had chosen bourbon as his thesis topic in Conversational Standards (1 point, 2 trimesters). "It is a patented drink, but anyone can make it. You add fresh peaches and peach brandy to bonded bourbon and let it stand in an oak barrel for eight months. One hundred and ten proof."

"Say! Make that two, George."

"You will be pleased with it," Joe said. "By the way, do you happen to know the name of the fourth man on the field in the days of Tinkers-to-Evers-to-Chance and their baseball combinations?"

"No, frankly, I don't."

"Harry Steinfeldt. The third baseman."

"Really? Well, I'll be damned." Mr. Wolgast picked up his Southern Comfort, waved it at Joe, and tried to recover command of the conversation. "So they finally, actually gave you my letter?" he said.

"Oh, well," Joe said, remembering at all times that he was an American citizen. "What do a bunch of Commies know about forwarding mail? Right?"

"I suppose the charitable thing to think was that the letter was misplaced."

"The main thing is—I got it."

"Can you prove you are Josef Dhelper?"

"Yes."

"You seem to me—that is at first glance at least—to be considerably older than thirty-six, you know."

Joe shrugged. "I am anxiety prone," he said. "You should talk to my Rorschach technician."

"Do you have any other name?"

His aunt had been a Shqitonja and all Shqitoinjas thought alike. Even when the thinking was convoluted, it was logical. "My name is Josef Shqitonja," he said. "*Dhelper* is the Albanian word for *Reynard,* the French *fox*. It is the custom of my family to use *Dhelper* when it seems necessary."

Mr. Wolgast was smiling. "That's better," he said. "No one could possibly fake a name such as Shqitonja."

Joe gloated. How exquisitely fatal it would have been if the Sigurimi had sent a substitute legatee to claim the estate.

"Can you prove who you are?" Mr. Wolgast asked.

"My passport."

"It could be forged."

"I suppose you expected me to show you a Communist Party membership card? I am a native-born American."

Mr. Wolgast coughed heavily. Joe thought he had swallowed the wrong way until, with consternation, as he looked up, two men were talking in low drawls on the other side of the bar. One of them was William F. Buckley, Jr., he was certain of it. But Buckley was a Yale man! Why was he here? Joe was determined not to panic.

"Your aunt's will suggests the only reliable identification: your most unusual distinguishing physical marks, the little flowers."

Joe blushed.

"You do have a scarlet birthmark mounted on your left buttock in the shape of a pansy?"

"I personally prefer to refer to the flower in the French—*un pensée*—a little thought, as it were," Joe replied.

"An afterthought," Mr. Wolgast reminded him. "Just a little joke."

Joe had forgotten his birthmarks because he was never in a position to see them. Again he reveled in the consternation of the Sigurimi had they sent a substitute legatee. His birthmarks had been the pride of the family, but no one else knew about them.

"And do you have a tiny but perfectly formed jonquil on your right haunch?"

"Yes."

"In that case, I have three experts waiting to examine you in a room upstairs."

"Experts?"

"One is a dermatologist, another is a tattooist, and the third is a botanist. If they pass you unanimously, the estate will accept you as the rightful heir." Mr. Wolgast lifted his glass. "Good luck, sir," he said.

"You brought the money with you? The legacy? In a bank check form, of course."

"It isn't all that simple, Mr. Shqitonja. Your aunt had quite some respect for the wily Albanian Secret Police, so the will holds one quite demanding clause, you see, which needs to be executed before you can collect."

"A clause?"

"Yes."

"Not one cent without the clause?"

"That's right."

Joe felt ill. Not only did the rotten democracies make a man defect from his mother land and her client country in order to get their tainted money, but the money itself was controlled from the grave.

Mr. Wolgast guided him out of the bar toward a dark staircase.

Joe wondered how he could prove that he had actually been in such a place so that the rezident would believe his photographs were legitimate. As they passed a table, he palmed an ash tray with HARVARD CLUB printed on it, slipping it deftly into his pocket. The barman added the item to Attorney Wolgast's bill.

10

The dermatologist and the tattooist were in agreement that the birthmarks were a natural part of Joe's skin and they left immediately. However, the botanist, a Dr. Gordon Manning, became so caught up with the perfection of the jonquil birthmark that he stayed on to try to persuade Joe to pose for a photograph of his right rear buttock because he was certain he could get the cover on the leading botanical trade journal with it. Failing this, for Joseph Reynard was an inherently modest man, Dr. Manning said, "If you won't consent to have your jonquil photographed, perhaps you'll come to our house for dinner next Sunday night. I make a rather famous veal marengo and I can't wait to show your jonquil to my sons—themselves rather well known botanists."

"Dr. Manning—I think if you—" Mr. Wolgast tried to interject.

"You must be out of your mind," Joe said to the botanist, raising his voice due to the nervousness of standing around the Harvard Club without trousers. "Go away or something. Out! I will do nothing of the sort."

Dr. Manning left in a huff and Mr. Wolgast pulled a long face. "I am afraid your tirade will cost the estate exactly double in consultation fees," he said.

Joe snorted as he climbed into his trousers. They walked down the staircase in silence. Joe was tense. It was essential that he get a signal off to Beijing confirming receipt of the information about the estate. Also, he had the sickening feeling that the dermatologist had taken his fingerprints when he had asked him to hold the examining mirror. He sighed like a tin whistle, relieved as he remembered that he was wearing plastic fingerprints which were replicas of J. Edgar Hoover's and which were used by Sino-Albainan bank-robbing teams to throw the FBI off the scene and to tie up the Director in endless cross-questioning.

He became aware, in his preoccupation, that Attorney Wolgast was speaking, ". . . to show your jonquil to the New York Law Society, but I quite understand how you feel. At any rate, I accept you as the rightful heir, my boy. And now, if we can sit down in the library, I will read the will to you."

"I don't have the time for that today, Mr. Wolgast. I am so sorry, but I have a very important meeting."

"Whatever you say, sir."

"Do you think it will take much time to execute the clause?"

"Hard to say. Up to you, actually."

"But, suppose I become ill or incapacitated?"

"Then the estate goes to the Friendly Sons of St. Patrick."

"I must have time to think. I had not anticipated such complications. May we meet tomorrow to read the will?"

"Tomorrow is Sunday."

"It must be tomorrow. It should be right now, but I have an important meeting and must have time to think."

"Very well."

"Will we meet here?"

"At my flat, I think. I'm in the book. Ten o'clock tomorrow morning? Will that be suitable?"

"Thank you, Mr. Wolgast. I am most grateful."

They shook hands at the foot of the stairs. Joe slipped out of the building. He had taken thirty-seven photographs of the interiors, personnel, Allan Dulles, Arthur Schlesinger, and William F. Buckley, Jr. He hurried toward his office on 40th Street, thinking that he had never faced so many problems in his life.

11

When Joe arrived, Notorious Shannon's office building was quite deserted. The watchman, who looked like a second-generation Swede and who had the letters H, E, L, L, O T, H, E, R, E tattoed on the backs of his stubby fingers, greeted him by name and took him aloft in the Notorious Shannon private elevator. When Joe left the elevator, the watchman dropped the car two floors, waited for thirty seconds, then ascended again to Joe's floor. He propped open the elevator, ran eleven paces down the corridor, and entered a door marked CLOSET, after unlocking it.

He sat in front of a compact radio transmitter and slipped earphones over his square blond head and, almost instantly, began to transcribe the signal that Joe was sending in code from the main transmitter in the Referentura section. The coded message said the following: *Garble duck. Yes to Youngstein. Pepperdog will carry the day for his titled godmother and the Dodgers is playing nice ball. Garble Gaston.*

As the signal was transmitted, it was also intercepted by the NSA monitor, under lease to the Haselgrove Organization, on Governor's Island in Upper New York Harbor and was automatically retransmitted for decoding at the Fort George Meade headquarters outside Washington. The decoded message was on Mark Haselgrove's desk within thirty-six minutes after its transmission to Beijing, but the message to Haselgrove, despite efficient deciphering, still read as if it were in code: *Have confirmed Wolgast representations and will stand by to receive substitute legateee. Frasheri.* Frasheri was the rezident's birth name.

Haselgrove issued instructions to a lieutenant, "Run Wolgast and Frasheri through the memory banks. Check surrogate records for all registrations in all cities showing a lawyer named Wolgast or Frasheri. If a will is located, have one copy sent to me and prepare a hold envelope for Leila Aluja. Do you read me?"

"I read you, chief."

Behind the door marked CLOSET, the watchman folded the transmitter-pickup into the wall and returned to the elevator to wait a few floors below Joe's floor. He made a telephone call from the elevator car.

He was the totally invisible rezident for the Chinese People's Republic, Peggy Flinn's direct superior. In the entire *apparat,* only she knew he existed. To the occupants of the building, he was good, old Nat Gannis. To Peggy Flinn-Frasheri, he was Maj. Nako Gega of the Albanian Sigurimi, the most dangerous man she had ever met in a lifetime of espionage.

12

Leila Aluja was the only thing on Joseph Reynard's mind as he waved good night to the watchman to walk uptown to the Bottom of the Cage on East 61st Street. At that moment, she and her motorcycle and unmarked cars escort were leaving behind La Guardia to get to Manhattan. As usual, she had to be protected from the hundreds of fans who had picked up the rumor that she would be arriving from Chicago sometime that day. They demanded her autograph and fought to touch her, screaming "Meine Edelfrau!" over and over again while police fought them off while trying simultaneously to get her into a convoy.

As she rode into New York behind the sirens, she wondered what Joe could be planning. His message had sounded so ominous, as if he needed her. If it had to be that way, she thought, they would cancel the rest of her tour; there were only two dates to go anyway.

After nine years of intense training, Joe knew he should have been thinking about his constant peril. He should have had his mind set on analyzing the mental processes of the Sigurimi or just thinking of those four ominous words, *General Ha Mat Sun,* but he was hopelessly in love and he felt in his bones that the events of that day were going to change everything in their lives. How could he explain when he removed the Permanent Disguise? He would be transformed from a corpulent, cucumber-nosed, balding beyond-middle-age man into a vibrant type whom, instinctively, one knows jogs at 5:15 every morning. How could he tell her? Would she still love him? What could he say to her?

Unable to get a taxi, he was walking north on Madison Avenue coming up to 50th Street. Somehow, he reasoned, he would have to make Leila understand that they would have to be separated for a little while. But he didn't know for how long. He couldn't begin to judge how long the execution of that clause would take and she certainly couldn't be with him while he executed it because heaven only knew what his aunt might have dreamed up to make him earn every cent of her bequest and because, as Meine Edelfrau, Leila would be too conspicuous. He kept shaking his head like a punch-drunk fighter as he walked, saying no to himself as he imagined himself saying to her, "I am quitting my $180,000,000 a year gross business, Leila, so that I can inherit $4,489,232." No American could possibly understand that. Worse, how could he explain to her that she could not come with him while he overtook the money?

As he approached 50th Street, he was followed by the 5th Directorate operative on permanent detail. Joe had let himself forget that he was under total surveillance. The man from the 5th was wearing an American Legion dress uniform and was unaware that he was being followed by a Sigurimi agent whom Major Gega had ordered to watch Joe. He was dressed as a butcher's helper in a stained white apron. The Sigurimi man assumed he was being followed because he was a member of the most illegal of all Sino-Albanian illegals in the country, but he could not spot the tail. Behind him, dressed as a Western Union messenger, came a Haselgrove operative who was driven nearly frantic to find a men's room, but he was forbidden by duty to leave such a chain of suspects that stretched out ahead of him.

A Department of Sanitation worker was hosing down 50th Street and this very nearly made the Haselgrove man double over with the power of suggestion.

As the long, northbound procession passed an emergency sewer excavation which was working under the merry sign DIG WE MUST, the Sigurimi man gave a secret hand signal of greeting to the Albanians who were digging on some random Chinese assignment—underground agents in the truest sense as they cached counterfeit money and fluorine flasks or hid bodies or bombs beneath the surface of the city.

Marching south, from the opposite direction, approaching the corner of 50th Street and Madison Avenue, was a flashy blonde who was wearing a mink coat as big as a housing development because she was the mistress of a wholesale furrier, who was following her without her knowledge. The furrier was badly winded in trying to keep up with her and his corset was cutting into him cruelly. Behind him, although he was not entirely unconscious of it, stalked a private detective who had been hired by the furrier's wife to gather evidence for a long-planned divorce action.

Walking east, crossing Madison Avenue at right angles to the two oppositional files of people came an invisibly linked unit of three: (1) a woman shopper who had just tucked change from $500 into her purse, (2) a professional pickpocket named Wendell Lowrie III, and (3) a New York City detective from the Pickpocket Squad who ambled along comfortably in Lowrie's wake, waiting for him to make his move for the purse.

The fated thing happened at the southeast corner of 50th and Madison. The young, blond woman, who was a visual mnemonic, spotted her most recent lover, an apprentice jockey, as he walked westward, taking tiny strides. She squealed to catch his attention, failed, then leaned across the agent from the 5th Directorate to catch the jockey's sleeve, blocking the eastbound trio and causing a collision with the woman shopper and Wendell Lowrie III, just as the furrier saw the blonde embrace the jockey, causing him to leap forward in rage at the moment Wendell Lowrie made his move for the shopper's purse and the detective lunged at Lowrie. The man from the 5th Directorate and the Sigurimi man became a part of the scrambled mob as if pulled in by a rope, which also drew in the Haselgrove operative, who fell on top.

Joseph Reynard, immersed in his problems, kept moving northward, unaware of the shocking pileup behind him. As two uniformed police from a patrol car moved in to break up what appeared to be a street riot, the false Western Union messenger wet his pants.

13

The Bottom of the Cage was a Swedish-Hawaiian restaurant with a relaxingly unpolitical atmosphere. The waiters wore Swedish student caps and paper-flower leis and they served a full ounce and half of bourbon. As he waited for Leila at the wicker bar, Joe forced ten dollars on the head waiter and arranged to have a corner table for two. Leila arrived ten minutes after he had.

"There was a terrific rumble at Madison and Fiftieth," she said excitedly. "We got caught in the jam it caused. A legionnaire went berserk or something."

"Damn! I missed it. I was just there. What will you have, dear one?"

"A bourbon martini?" She knew bourbon was his hobby and she wanted to flatter him.

"Not a good mix, sweedhott."

They were seated at a corner table, adoring each other, unable to stop touching each other over and over under the table. Leila ordered *akta akoldaddsoppa med ostranger med sas bourbon* and Joe had *jarpe i gryta med gaslever och tryffel is sas bourbon*. They both had the poi and pineapple curry in large cocconuts, which usually goes well with a Swedish-Hawaiian meal. "And food snobs say we Americans don't have our own cuisine," Leila said tartly. "Oh, Joe! I don't suppose I'll ever know why I'm so crazy about you."

"I wish you could have known me when I was younger."

"Come on, Joe. You know you were never younger."

"Well, I was. And I wasn't such a bad-looking fellow at thirty-six."

Leila knew exactly how he had looked when he had attended the International Relations Institute at Beijing because when she had been a student there, she had pored over all the yearbooks and their snapshots and stories of his class. Much later, when she saw him wearing the Permanent Disguise, she had looked right through it to the face of the gorgeous young man in the photographs from his days in China. She remembered having her Haselgrove unit sergeant check through the records of the Evelyn Hunt Children's Haven, which he had told her had been the only home he had ever known, and she had been flabbergasted to find his record there, filled with all the anonymous details.

"These people can be thorough," she wrote in her report to Mark Haselgrove, "because each one is responsible for the placement of his own record in as many files as the cover demands. If his cover is blown, it would be his own fault, therefore each agent does this part of the job very well indeed. I strongly urge you to think about installing just a certain amount of such decentralization. We are much too rigid as we are."

Almost two hours into their ecstatic dinner, the headwaiter glided into place on the discreet side of Joe and whispered that a Miss Peggy Flinn was at the bar and insisted upon speaking to him about an urgent business matter. Joe was so concerned by the news that he almost overturned the table in his speed to get to the bar.

"Honey! What's the matter?"

Joe told the maître d' to say he would be right there, then he explained to Leila, "It's a woman from the office, a late worker. They must have called from the coast about the merger. I won't be a minute." He didn't listen for her response. The furniture of his mind was crashing into the walls of his head. He must have made a fatal slip somewhere that day.

As he approached the bar, Miss Flinn greeted him with pleasant diffidence. Under her Dutch-boy white bob she was wearing a smart Mickey Mouse sweater pin and rhinestone-pimpled harlequin eyeglasses. Joe greeted her cordially, careful to be as patronizing as she had ordered him to be with her in public. They sat side-by-side on high, leather bar stools.

"Well, well, Miss Flinn," he said hollowly. "What brings you here, for out crying loud."

Her eyes were so cold that he had the illusion of staring into the window of a fish store. She spoke in a low voice that did not project any farther than she wished it to project. "You signed my name to a priority signal today," she said.

Joe turned stripes of red and white and the stripes began to revolve about his head and body as on an electric barber pole. He had goofed. They had planted an intercept, a freshman-year gimmick at IRI. It had to be the building watchman, that Swede with the tattoos.

"But you were at the bew-dee parlor," Joe said.

"It was a Hustlegram!" she snarled. "You should have found me! The office had the number."

"Would I have sent such a signal if it had not reflected the greatest credit on you? Have you asked yourself that? Eh? It was a relay about some Albanian who had inherited some money—"

"Some money??? Almost five million dollars! Our entire defense budget!"

"That's what made it so important! They wanted immediate action and I got it for them—but in your name! I verified everything with the lawyer this afternoon at the Harvard Club." He threw the name away. "And he is big. Very big."

"The *Harvard* Club?" Her expression changed totally. Her jaw dropped.

"Whattle yiz have, friends?" the bartender asked, leaning between them.

"A vodka scaffa," Miss Flinn said.

"A bourbon crusta, Herman, thank you," Joe added.

"Some chartreuse in the scaffa, little lady?"

"Absinthe."

As the barman moved away, Joe tried to remember that he was a Shqitonja, a fox, but he was shaken. They had tailed and taped him. Too many years of the soft life and he had forgotten the most important thing he had ever been taught—that for the rest of his life he would be under surveillance wherever he was. How else could Flinn have pinned him down in one of the twenty-seven thousand bars in the city? How could he have forgotten the things which had made the step-motherland great?

He assumed an approximation of an air of smug confidence as he went on about the Harvard Club. "Not even Colonel Abel has ever been in there. I worked every second because I was representing you. I photographed constantly. You will be interested to know," he drawled, "that Allan Dulles is the main security guard on that door. I have photographs of Arthur Schlesinger and William F. Buckley, Jr., as they briefed agents. The photographs will be on your desk in the morning as your own espionage coup."

"Joe!" Miss Flinn was overwhelmed.

"One scaffa, one crusta," the bartender said.

"Thank you, Herman."

"What did the lawyer say?" Miss Flinn asked, her hand on his sleeve.

"I have prepared a full report. It will be on your desk in the morning."

"And?"

"I pretended to be a relative of the legatee who, I told him, was on holiday but would return in about a week."

"Good. That was very good."

"Beijing or Tirana can surely have a substitute here in, say, ten days?"

"No question. I am also very pleased that there is a rational explanation for what you did, but never do it again. You understand?"

"May I join you?" Leila stood at Miss Flinn's elbow, smiling radiantly. She had been listening to the conversation from across the room, using a tiny parabolic device that transmitted to an earpiece which had been fitted surgically within her left ear.

Joe almost choked on his crusta. As soon as he was able to, he said, "Miss Flinn—may I present my wife, Meine Edelfrau?"

Miss Flinn fell apart just as any American would when faced with a towering, overpowering celebrity. "Miss—Mrs.—Meine Edelfrau, what an unexpected honor!" She shook hands maniacally with Leila, climbed down the tiny rope ladder on the bar stool, and left the restaurant. As she emerged into the street, an elderly, "blind" Negro guitar player who was a member of the Haselgrove team, picked up her trail behind the 5th Directorate man who followed Miss Flinn. Behind the three figures a Sigurimi agent shuffled along dressed as a nun.

Inside the Bottom of the Cage Leila was convinced she had cracked the case. It was all over. She knew who the spymaster was, the rezident, and now they could close the net. She gloated, then she remembered Joe. How was she going to save Joe?

"What a delicious drink!" she said as she tasted Joe's crusta. "Who was that woman?"

"The office manager."

"How did she find us here?"

"I always tell the answering service when we have a big deal on the fire."

"She seemed upset. She left so abruptly."

"She was upset. She needed a friend. She turned to me for help."

"What happened?"

"Her mother just had another child."

They walked toward Park Avenue. It was a warm night. Leila held his arm closely and looked up into his face adoringly while thinking that she must get to a telephone to report her discovery of Flinn's identity.

"I have to talk to you, baby," Joe said softly, but, she thought, rather hoarsely. His face looked haggard.

"Joe—what's wrong?"

"I—I may have to go away for a little while," he said. She dragged him to a stop on the Park Avenue traffic island. Steel rivers of gleaming cars moved on either side of them, breathing poison and making noises of power with the relentlessness of Satan seeking the ruin of souls. She was almost certain the he didn't suspect her in any way, just as certain as she was that he loved her.

"It's that Flinn woman. What did she tell you that has you so upset?" Dirt from the sky sifted down on them steadily.

"No, no. Nothing like that. I had this—this thing come up and I have to go away for a little while."

"What thing?"

"An opportunity. Which I am absolutely pledged not to discuss."

"Where are you going?"

"I won't know until tomorrow. Leila, please—just trust me. When I come back, a lot of things will be changed, but I promise you—I won't be gone long."

"But what's the opportunity? If I only know that, I won't worry so much."

"Well—" he made useless movements with his hands. All of his training screamed at him that he had already told her too much, that he must not tell her any more. But he couldn't withstand the blinding glare of the love that was coming from her eyes. He began to tell the truth in a shifty way so that she would be sure he was lying, a lousy cover story no matter how she looked at it.

"I—I may have come into a lot of money, but to get the money there is this clause and—well, I have to go away and do the things the clause says or I can't get the money."

He shrugged. She blinked while she reasoned that, if he wanted her to think he was lying, then it was important for her to look bewildered, then a little hurt, then to be a dead-game sport and show him that, if this was the way he wanted it, then that was how it would have to be.

Biting her lip, she looked up at him and said, "If that's the way you want it, Joe, then that's the way it has to be."

Joe was enormously relieved. The traffic light turned red. She took his arm again. They walked silently across the street toward Lexington Avenue. Leila stopped them in front of a bar, which was three steps down from the sidewalk, and said she had to find a john.

While Joe ordered two bourbon smashes, she went to the ladies' room and found a telephone. She dialed the Haselgrove night service, which was in an undertaking parlor on Lexington.

"Night detail? Three-one-eight here. Do you have anything on a will that might involve Foxy? Ah, that's great. Oh, perfect. Now—he'll drop me off at the apartment, then probably make a phone call. In about twenty minutes. I want a tape on the call. Yeah, yeah. He is not the head man, just as we thought. *Nummer eins* is a woman—about fifty-seven, Dutch-boy white bob, junk glasses, and Space Shoes. Has a Buffalo, New York, accent, but it could be Iowa. Our agent, Coomber, was tending bar there tonight and he got her prints on a glass. They'll probably turn out to be J. Edgar Hoover's, as usual, but that's what we want to know. Yeah. Right. Twenty minutes."

They strolled to the entrance of the tall, white apartment building between Lex and Third in which Leila kept an apartment under her

Aluja name for those times when she was on tour as Meine Edelfrau and had a chance to pop into New York. As the doorman pulled open the entrance door, Joe kissed her on the cheek. "Gotta pick up the morning papers, baby," he said, "but don't roll over in bed too fast, you might crush me." He beamed at her dotingly, deploring his gold teeth. He snapped his mouth shut and left. Leila waited a few moments until she saw a tall, skinny hiker wearing a knapsack and khaki clothes fall in behind the Sigurimi man who was tailing Joe.

When she got to the apartment, she called the Haselgrove night detail again, throwing the cut-off switch which would turn the Sigurimi line tap into a recording of Leila and her alleged mother discussing the most mindless banalities. Joe didn't know about the counterwire but, of course, being a pro, she was sure that he suspected it had been installed.

A block away, Joe went into a drugstore. While he got change from the cashier, the hiker and the Sigurimi nun got into the two telephone booths on either side of the only empty booth Joe could use. Before Joe had begun to dial, they had their stethoscopic bugs working to record on tape whatever he could say.

"Mr. Courtney Wolgast, please," Joe was saying into the telephone.

"This is he," a gentle voice replied.

"This is Josef Shqitonja, sir. I am sorry to have to disturb you."

"Not at all, Mr. Shqitonja, I assure you. I was washing the parrot as a matter of fact."

"I wish to change our meeting place for tomorrow."

"As you wish."

"Please meet me on the upper deck, outside, on the port side of the Staten Island ferryboat which leaves closest to ten o'clock in the morning?"

"Port is the right side of a boat, isn't it?"

"The left. Is it quite legal to read a will on a ferryboat?"

"Oh quite legal. And how very pleasant. Splendid. Ten o'clock then."

Joe disconnected. He left the drugstore and walked slowly up Lexington Avenue. The Sigurimi man relieving the nun stayed about 30 feet behind Joe, walking a honey-colored daschund. He saw Joe into the apartment building, then crossed the street to a maroon Chevrolet. He put the daschund in the rear seat. The Air-Call on his pocket began to buzz, which meant Major Gega wanted him to telephone. He put on the car light to dial the car telephone and was instantly revealed to the French agent in the Service de Documentair et Contra-Espionnage who was seated in a parked car just across the street. It was one of those terrible accidents of history.

From the car, the French agent telephoned his chief, who was dining at La Grenouille on East 52nd Street.

"This is Cloutier," the agent said. "I have just seen the Butcher of Oran."

"Vive de Gaulle," the chief's voice said crisply. Cloutier nodded and replaced the phone. He took a revolver out of a holster and began to screw a silencer to the front of the barrel.

In the undertaking parlor on Lexington, the hiker, whose name was Lou Amjac, was listening to the playback of Joe's phone conversation as he changed into a white shirt, a dark tie, and a dark suit. He had carrot-red hair that was as soft as lanugo. "They had a man in the booth behind him," he said to the night detail man who, to give the establishment a ring of truth, was embalming the body of an elderly male Caucasian.

"So they know what they know," the embalmer said, working steadily. "Here's the dial number count. He called Wolgast, Courtney, fourteen East Ninetieth. Get up there and keep him safe."

14

Out of the sixty-three thousand Albanians living in the United States, only the rezident, Peggy Flinn, knew who Maj. Nako Gega was. From the neighborhood bowling team to the news agent who supplied him with every secret agent paperback that was printed, he was just good-natured Nat Gannis, a happy-go-lucky Bronxite with a Hoe Avenue accent. He was capable of frightening the rezident into numbness as she passed in and out of the building and he smiled at her humbly. She was merely the watchdog for the Chinese. He watched Albanians for Albania.

During World War Two, Major Gega had been stationed in Switzerland for Soviet Intelligence as enforcer for Rudolf Roessler, the master spy whose pipeline to the German High Command had predicted the German invasion of Russia. In Switzerland, Major Gega had discovered *kalbsbratwurst* and *pain croustillant* flavored with caraway. Thirty-two years later, the walls and shelves of the three closets in his small Bronx apartment were lined with boxes of the Swiss products and, with various experimental spreads he had contrived, they were the only foods he would eat outside of Albania.

He sat on a high stool facing his tiny kitchenette and worked with intense concentration on making alternate canapés: peanut butter and herring; cucumber, yogurt, and garlic. He fought off a desire amounting to lust to begin tasting until he had arranged seven of the caparisoned *knackbrots* of each flavor on a large platter. At last he settled down to chew luxuriously, waiting for a response to his Air-Call Page, the marvelous gadget, "a forty-mile extension of your telephone bell," that the telephone company had developed for espionage work.

Off-duty, the major wore Hawaiian sports shirts, mirrored eyeglasses, a scarlet baseball cap, gnome-tight slacks, and a cigar to make himself unobtrusive. He was effective at his work because everything about him was so deceptive. He had the concentric roundness of a model endomorph under a plump, pink, jolly face. His pinkness and sky-blue eyes gave him a look of innocent dependability.

The Sigurimi scorned the concept of Permanent Disguise advocated by the Chinese. The Sigurimi didn't need any hedges against blown cover; they had to keep their cover intact because they had a very limited budget. When they were recalled to Tirana for rotation or instructions, they had to stow away to the European west coast, then hitchhike to Albania. This dramatized that they simply could not afford to make mistakes.

As he chewed the burdened *pain croustillant,* he studied a secret agent novel, making technical notes for his card file. He tried to complete reading one secret agent novel each night. From each he extracted professional tips and techniques to be mailed back to his home office.

Depending on the signal that he was awaiting from Albania, the major might have to visit Wolgast, Courtney, that night. He put aside the book and began a serious analysis of the character of the rezident. Had the woman used Shqitonja as a dupe, ordering him to acknowledge receipt of the signal to contact Wolgast, Courtney, so she could protest innocence if any counter-revolutionary plot were uncovered? That could be. And that would account for Shqitonja's actions.

The major wanted to favor Shqitonja because of the national (and his personal) admiration for his father, a great bank robber and exalted patriot by any definition. Could it possibly be that the rezident wanted to frame Shqitonja for reasons of her own? Or did she actually believe that only she had access to transmitting apparatus and that no cut-in existed? If she were that naive, she shouldn't be rezident.

For maximum pleasure, he was concentrating on the retsina when the shortwave light went on. He set down the glass, crossed the room, opened the high steel door, then slipped on the headphones. He transcribed the coded message on the yellow foolscap in bright green ink. Then he slid out the code book from between the diverting covers of a volume of Richard Nixon's speeches and went to work.

> SIGURIMI TOPSIDE GREETINGS: ELIMINATE REZIDENT STOP SECURE WOLGAST COURTNEY FOR MAXIMUM ADJACENCY TO LEGATEEE BUT KEEP HARMLESS/BLOODLESS ADVISING HIM YOU CLOSE RELATIVE WHO WILL DELIVER LEGATEEE TO HIM IN EIGHT DAYS STOP. SEND THREE (3) ROLLS SCOTCH TAPE AND ONE-HALF CASE LOG CABIN MAPLE SYRUP CONFIRM STOP.

The major tapped out receipt confirmation. He called the number of his number-one's Air-call Page and allowed seven minutes for this man, Shavto, to call back.

The major dressed in a dark suit, a white shirt, and a dark tie. He sat next to the phone and thought about the rezident. No call back from Shavto. He pulled steel shutters down in front of all the windows and locked them in place. Still no call. He put on a dark felt hat and left the building. He walked rapidly toward Lexington Avenue. To the west, on 61st, he saw two police cars parked at eccentric angles to the curb, surrounded by a crowd. He edged and elbowed through the crowd and looked down at the dead face of Shavto, laying half in the gutter, half on the sidewalk, executed at random by the French because he had resembled a tyrant of World War Two.

The rezident! Nat Gannis thought instantly. The rezident had followed Shavto, who was following Shqitonja, and had shot him. Why? What was going on?

He crossed the street to the maroon Chevrolet, where the Sigurimi man had been alive so short a time before, and unlocked its curbside door. Absentmindedly he patted the dachshund, who licked his hand. He shut himself inside the car, all windows closed. He unlocked the glove compartment and turned on the tape recorder, rewinding it until he came to the beginning of Shqitonja's conversation with Wolgast, Courtney. A will. So money was involved. Enough money to have upset Tirana to the point where they had ordered the elimination of the rezident. He must read this will, the major decided. He must have a talk with Wolgast, Courtney, tonight. At least he knew now why the rezident had ordered Shqitonja to take the job of contacting Wolgast, Courtney, and why she had killed poor Shavto who was lying in the gutter across the street. He had to get on with his stewardship over Wolgast, Courtney, and with the elimination of the rezident.

15

As Joe slipped the key into the door of their apartment, Leila murmured into the telephone, "He just came back. I have to hang up." She dropped the receiver into its place, then flew as if a butterfly, her arms wide, her transparent peignoir at full flap, across two rooms to the man she loved. He turned for just an instant to bolt the door. As he did, she reached out and snapped a switch on the underside of a hall table, cutting off the banal bug in order to numb the Sigurimi and setting up a pretaped conversation she and Joe had had months before.

They stood gaping at each other, as still as statues of Cupids at Forest Lawn, admiring each other with whole hearts and seeing themselves canonized in that admiration which reaffirmed their love. Then Joe said, "Whaddayuh know? No papers."

"All the better to know you, my dear," Leila cried and, like the wolf leaping upon Red Riding Hood's grandma, wrapped her legs and arms around him and swallowed a third of his lower face in a yawning kiss. They grunted, struggled, and bleated. Carrying her meaty body, which was like a serpent around him, Joe toppled backward across their large bed, two rooms away. She stopped kissing him and began to rip off his clothes, her eyes glazed as she delved for the treasure, moaning like a musical saw. She set to work on him with a concentration that stopped all the clocks in the apartment, concealing time and turning memory into sensation.

The telephone rang. She carried on with the feast. It rang again and again until she shouted the ritual word for losers at bingo and grabbed the telephone. It was Mark Haselgrove again, speaking with his low whisper without greeting. "If you can't cover a simple telephone call, Aluja," he said, "what are you doing on my team? I am not interested that the subject has returned. I was talking to you and no one terminates a conversation with me until termination has been indicated by me. No matter. Get dressed."

"How did you know I was—"

"Damnit, Aluja! What is television for—entertainment? When you are in that apartment, you are on camera." Leila's orbicularis oculi muscle spun her eyeballs abruptly backward in a nightmare of embarrassment. She realized instantly that not only had he televised what she and Joe had ever done on that bed but that he had recorded it on tape and had sold it to stag reel distributors throughout Latin America. Then she realized that exposure like that would help her prime cover as Meine Edelfrau and she relaxed, her face gradually losing the color of an eggplant.

She looked down quickly at Joe, who seemed to be recovering from the coronary occlusion he always slipped into after they had spooned for a little while. Haselgrove was saying, ". . . be in New York for a very short time and I must meet with you."

She was startled. He was never anywhere but inside the old Strategic Air Command headquarters about ninety-seven miles from Denver where he ran worldwide security from inside a large mountain.

"The City of New York is privatizing the New York Police Department," Haselgrove explained. "It's nothing to bother you, but I had to come in for the signing. All right. There is a car waiting at the door of your building. You have nineteen minutes to make it to the solitary cell of the Arsenal Police Station in Central Park." He disconnected.

Joe was shaking his head groggily. Leila raced to the nearest clothes closet, throwing off her negligee as she ran. Nude, her figure was better, slightly fuller but just as firm as the statuette on the hood of a Rolls-Royce.

Joe tried to struggle up into a half-sitting position, looking exotic in his patented garters, black shoes, and socks below nothing at all. "Whatta you doing?" he asked thickly as she drew on her clothes with the speed of a student fireman.

"My mother is caught in a clothes wringer!" she wailed. "Stay right there, dearest. I'll be back as soon as I can. Oh, Joe, isn't this terrible?" She darted to the bed, dipped down to kiss him on the cheek, then sprinted out of the room.

Joe blinked. He tried again to sit up. "What part did she catch in it?" he yelled after her, but she had gone.

A thin silent young man who was smoking a cigarette, contrary to good health logic, was waiting at the curb as she came out. He was wearing a pressed, starched, laundered secret agent raincoat. He held the car door open for her. She slammed in, banged the door shut, and the car took off behind its siren through crosstown traffic, swinging off lights or going through them. He did not speak. She had too much rank for him.

She was led past the sergeant's desk at the arsenal station as though he was invisible, or she was. They strode through a cluster of detectives, cops, and muggers to descend ancient stone steps. She was aware that the monkey house or the snake house of the zoo was directly overhead. They moved along a sweating corridor and stopped at a steel cell door. The young man rapped on it with the butt of an automatic pistol, but no instructions to enter were heard.

Leila pulled open the cell door. It was empty except for a steel cot, a bucket, a large switchboard, and a white envelope on the pillow of the bed. It was addressed to her.

The message said:

> Aluja: I allowed all the time I could spare but had to be on my way or misshape my work schedule which is tighter tonight because I have agreed to take over all U.S. armed forces military police and shore patrol functions in the Southeast Asian area. You will be taken to the nearest airfield and flown to Denver in my own Stealth fighter-bomber. I have rescheduled our meeting for 4:03 A.M. tomorrow.

Leila tore the note into small pieces, then handed them to the young man, who ate them. He guided her out of the police station and she was seated again in the car.

16

When Peggy Flinn returned to her apartment at 114th Street and Riverside Drive after sitting through two showings of *The Kissing Bandit* at the Thalia, she found a commercial cablegram under her door. She locked the door behind herself, then opened the envelope, peeking at the upper part of the message fearfully. It was from Athens. Who would send her a commercial cablegram from Athens? This was sinister. It was signed Kik. She blushed. It was her pet name for Larushka Skikne, one of her two ex-husbands; he worked in one of the ministries at Tirana.

The message read: "DON'T MEET UNCLE SUGI." Her hand began to tremble. Uncle Sugi was the secret name they had always used for the Sigurimi. Were they after her? They must be after her or else why would Larushka spend so many leks on a cable and travel all the way to Athens to send it?

She made it to a chair and sat down so shakily that she almost missed the seat. My God! The Sigurimi! Even all her boys at the 5th couldn't help her because the Sigurimi frightened them much more than she ever could. Why were they after her? What had she done? The answer came to her like a shell from a cannon's mouth. Shqitonja! Shqitonja had signed her name to that signal. He knew something. He had seen trouble in that will and he was after her job. Absolutely, that was it. That bastard Shqitonja. She would have to nail him even if she had to frame him because it was him or her. She had to have the evidence and have him ready for delivery to the Sigurimi when they came for her, or she was dead. Dead. My God, would they talk first or shoot first?

She called the Referentura and discovered that Shqitonja was spending the night with his wife who, Flinn had thought, was always on the road except for the occasional dinner at Bottom of the Cage. So, she would stake out the apartment building on 61st Street beginning at seven the next morning.

She scrubbed her toes with an ammonia solution to stop the tickling which always happened when she became very frightened, then got into bed. That bastard Shqitonja. She couldn't stand these wise-guy college men with their influential fathers. She would really fix that Shqitonja.

The man with the carrot-red lanugo hair, Lou Amjac, rang Courtney Wolgast's doorbell. He waited a full thirty seconds, then rang again, this time leaning on the bell. The door opened. Mr. Wolgast wore a long nightshirt with a wing collar, a white woolen stocking cap with a long tassel, and mauve woolen bed socks. He was fighting to stop yawning and losing. "At the wrong place, aren't you, young man?" he asked pleasantly, snuffling his teeth and gums in the manner of a leading screen dwarf in a feature-length cartoon that had been released in 1937.

Amjac extended his badge and said, "Mr. Courtney Wolgast?"

While Mr. Wolgast gazed sleepily at the badge, Amjac added, "FBI." To say Haselgrove Security always either called for an explanation or a heated discussion. Mr. Wolgast motioned him inside. "Must be important to make you come this late."

"Yes, sir."

"Sit down, please. Let me see those credentials again." Amjac handed over the leather case and sat on a black-and-white hassock, which Mr. Wolgast had purchased in a souk in Morocco in 1926, a bull-market year. Mr. Wolgast returned the badge. "I am listening, young man," he said gravely.

"Would you like to call our office to verify me, sir?"

"No."

"Because we have to move fast. If you'll get dressed as quickly as you can, I'll explain everything while we move."

Mr. Wolgast left the room without a word and, in a surprisingly short time, while Amjac studied the lyrics on sheet music called

"Ka-Lu-A" on the playing rack of the piano, he reappeared fully dressed carrying a small satchel. "I am ready," he said.

They did not speak in the elevator because it was one of the twenty-three lifts in the city that required a human operator. As they left the building, they were moving so fast that they almost knocked down Major Gega on his way in.

"Awfully sorry," Mr. Wolgast said as he attempted to right the major, staring into his face. Amjac pulled him away, as Major Gega's zygomaticus muscle pulled at his orbicularis oris, producing a jolly grin.

"Not at all," he said, "my fault." He moved up the short flight of entrance steps to the main hall of the building. Amjac pushed Mr. Wolgast into the cab he had kept waiting. It left at once, U-turning on 90th Street to go downtown on Park Avenue.

The doorman blocked Major Gega's way. "I will be visiting Mr. Courtney Wolgast," the major said. "Don't bother to announce me. I am an old friend from Europe and I want to surprise him."

"How old a friend?"

"I don't think that matters, do you?" the major said unpleasantly.

"Yeah. I think it matters a whole lot," the doorman said. "That was Mr. Wolgast you was just starin' at down there. Beat it, buddy."

In the taxi, Amjac was explaining to Mr. Wolgast. "I can't tell you why because no one told me why, but the appointment you were supposed to keep on the Staten Island ferry tomorrow morning has to be changed to a different location and we know how to change it for you if you'll give the okay."

"How and why do you know about that meeting?"

"The man is an important government suspect."

"Of what is he suspected?"

"If it were up to me, I'd tell you."

"Young man, I have been a member of the bar of this state for forty-six years. I have complied with your requests in the best of good faith, but I refuse to cooperate further unless I am given full explanations."

"Then I'll have to make a telephone call."

In a short time, Mr. Wolgast found himself in a most comfortable suite in a towering midtown hotel on the Avenue of the Americas wearing a whiskey in his right hand and a large cigar in his left while worrying about the cover on his parrot's cage while Amjac telephoned from the other room. When day broke over 14 East 90th Street, the bird would be desolated because no one would have removed the cage cover. Still, Mr. Wolgast reasoned, it had had a bath and the cover would prevent drafts. Mr. Amjac returned to the living room.

"Here's the story, Mr. Wolgast. We have good reason to believe that a Communist-terror organization was going to call on you tonight to persuade you to tell them what we wanted to know first."

"But I—what is it that I know that such people would possibly want to know?"

"Josef Shqitonja."

"Who? Oh. The legatee?"

"Yes, sir. Josef Shqitonja is second-in-command of a Red Chinese spy network which of course is run by the Albanians."

"My word!"

"Why were you meeting him tomorrow morning?"

"To read his aunt's will to him."

"What sort of a will is it, Mr. Wolgast? Why would the Chinese—or the Albanians independent of the Chinese, be so interested?"

"I—I don't know." Mr. Wolgast dialed the end of his nose. "It's an unusual enough will in that it requires that a clause be executed by the legatee, but the clause could have no interest to foreigners unless, as Communists, they object to Shqitonja owning that much money."

"How much money?"

"Quite a sum. Four million, four hundred and eighty-nine thousand, two hundred and thirty-two dollars when it was bequeathed over eighteen months ago. Since then it has been appreciating as the markets go up. Mr. Shqitonja's aunt believed in investing in things like pharmaceuticals and communications."

"We will need to be the judges as to whether that clause is of any interest to a foreign power, sir," Mr. Amjac said. "May I have a copy of the will?"

"Not from me, Mr. Amjac," Mr. Wolgast answered, the points of his wing collar quivering. "That is privileged information, sir."

17

A helicopter met Leila at the Lowry Air Force Base at Denver and took her to a wilderness of high mountains, where she was picked up by a Jacometti two-seater made exclusively for the Haselgrove Organization in Kilmoganny, Ireland. It was the personnel transport for Haselgrove Security. Its uniform blackness, its relentless six-wheeled chassis, and the bulletproof comfort of its bubble top had had the effect on the American public which the SS once had had on Europe.

The terrain was pitch-black beyond the headlights of the car, which stopped at a concrete and steel installation in the side of the mountain. Fluorescent lights came on. Armed troops could be seen at attention in the redoubts on either side of the car. An officer conferred with the car's driver in low whispers. Papers were exchanged. The officer signed a receipt for Leila.

The high gates opened electrically. The Jacometti drove into an area approximately forty yards wide, then turned slightly to the right to enter a steel stall that was a hydraulic elevator. The lift car dropped at sickening speed. When it stopped falling, Leila was asked to leave the Jacometti to board a small train that had been painted with the Haselgrove house colors of red, white, and blue.

Each car on the little train could carry one passenger. Leila rode it alone. It moved downward along a spiral passage built on the inside jowl of the mountain. At the foot of the elevator shaft, she guessed she must be seven hundred feet under the mountain. As she looked downward over the cliff which held the railway track, it seemed as though the bottom was yet five hundred feet farther down. Haselgrove certainly believed in personal safety, she thought. Everything was softly illuminated. The ventilation system worked without a hint of fustiness.

At about two-thirds of the way down, the track branched off into a spur line; Leila continued across a widening plateau area, which could be very pleasant, she thought, if one were a gnome or a troll.

The train stopped at a tiny station bearing a blue sign with white letters saying SCHLOSS HASELGROVE. A professionally motherly woman wearing a dirndl came forward, helped Leila down from the little car, and introduced herself as Mrs. Brown. She was all apple cheeks, doughy bosoms, and happy smiles. She led Leila along to a door in the wall of the mountain. "I would say you are a very special little girl," the living symbol of Mother's Day said, "because the only other person to get the two-room apartment under this mountain was Vice President Hazman and then only because our president himself personally asked Mr. Haselgrove for it. Five-star generals get the one-room treatment."

They went into the apartment that was a true replica of every middle-range Ramada Inn motel suite. Leila said, "I am very tired, Mrs. Brown. I have an appointment with Mr. Haselgrove in a little while and I'd like to bathe and nap."

"We have had some of the very biggest people here. I mean your top TV stars and the near-great who had earned the right to see how Mr. Haselgrove was keeping the world safe for all of us and—"

"Do you do karate, Mrs. Brown?"

"Sakes alive, child. The martial arts is at the very heart of our work."

Leila stared at her coldly. "I'm in the same line of work, but I get the two-room suites. Will you leave under your own power, Mrs. Brown?"

Leila ran a tub, but kept her watch on when she got into it. It would be disastrous if she were late again and missed her turn with Haselgrove. She just had to get back to New York before Joe woke up and got hysterical.

She got the bath but not the nap. A hidden loudspeaker asked her to be dressed and ready to leave in seven minutes. A Special Forces master sergeant blindfolded her and put her on one of the cars of the little train. When the blindfold was taken off, she was facing a grizzled Marine Corps brigadier general who had never been taught how to smile. "You are to go through that door in twenty-six seconds, Missy," he snarled. "Take your place, please. Hand on doorknob. You will turn the knob and enter the room on my downbeat."

She stepped forward. The brigadier general stared at his chronometer. She felt the tension she had felt on the two occasions before when she had met with Mark Haselgrove. The first time he had received her behind a screen, as in a confessional. The second he had greeted her with his physical presence: a very tall, bulky man with a face like a used corncob.

The brigadier general's hand swept downward in signal. She turned the knob, opened the door, and entered the room, stepping into a replica of an old-fashioned general store: the smell was marvelous and there were sacks of good red beans and, under worn glass counters, she could see boxes of hunting shells and spools of cotton thread; cans of peaches and baked beans lined the walls. A very short man wearing a visor and bombazine sleeve guards appeared from behind a pile of salt bags. He had curly chestnut hair parted so distinctly down the middle that the part seemed to have been chalked on his head. He had two gold teeth, one directly in front and one in the right canine. A tufted wart grew from his left cheekbone under rimless pince-nez glasses. His eyes were draped with two-tone gray swags. "I was expecting to meet Mr. Mark Haselgrove," Leila said.

"Sit down, little lady," the man said, chuckling. "I am Mark Haselgrove." He led her to one of two rocking chairs in front of a potbellied stove. They sat and rocked. "The Chinese have instituted a policy of Permanent Disguise which is particularly ingenious," Haselgrove said.

"I know."

"You *know*?" His aplomb vanished. He seemed quite annoyed.

"Well, for heaven's sake, Mr. Haselgrove—how do you think *you* know?"

"By enormously expensive and dangerous espionage utilizing a worldwide organization the like of which has never been seen before in history. That's how I know." He glared at her. "The point is—how do you?"

"Mr. Haselgrove! I spent two years at the colleges in Beijing for you. They won't let the American cadres graduate without the Permanent Disguise. You had psyche doctors work me over for four days to pump out everything I knew about this Permanent Disguise policy."

"Aaaaaaahhhh! That was *you*. Well, say, that's very interesting. Hm. Yas."

"I would never have recognized you," Leila said. "That is fabulous makeup."

Haselgrove stood up. "Do I seem taller or shorter to you?"

"You are at least seven inches shorter."

He clapped his hands with glee. "Yes! This is an advance we have made over the Chinese, my dear. I am seven inches shorter because I am wearing Manhole Shoes. Think how useful that can be." He sat down.

"When do we close the ring, Chief?"

"I thought Monday morning. Just before noon. I can't thank you enough, Aluja. You closed a vital case at a most useful time for me. We've just taken over the Royal Canadian Northwest Mounted Police and this is the sort of show which will reassure them tremendously." He smiled at her dreamily.

"And now, my girl. I have this little assassination idea and you are the one to plan the entire operation."

"Mr. H.—about Josef Shqitonja—"

"I was afraid you might have second thoughts there. He is your husband, legally, as we know. That is why I removed you from the scene. Shqitonja will, of course, be arrested with the others at eleven fifty-seven tomorrow morning and whereas that may give you a little sentimental tug, I am sure you understand its necessity."

"He's only one man, Mr. Haselgrove. He can't be any threat."

"Duty first, little lady."

"May I ask one favor?"

"*Ask*—by all means."

"When they take him and they remove his Permanent Disguise—will you photograph him for me? I have to be sure what he really looks like."

"Matte or glossy?" Haselgrove asked.

18

Joe had slept poorly. He kept reaching out for Leila in his sleep only to awaken with a start because she was not there, then to sit up in bed, cursing her mother's clumsiness. What a ridiculous time to do washing, a Saturday night. He ransacked the flat looking for her telephone number but he couldn't find it. Dammit! Why hadn't Leila called him? No matter how entangled her mother had gotten herself in that machine, it certainly couldn't take this long to get her out. At last he fell into a fifth sleep and was battling an unpleasant dream involving his father and the Sigurimi when the telephone on the night table next to his bed began to ring. He clawed at it to get it to his ear. "Hello?"

"Miss Aluja, please." It was a woman's voice.

"Not here."

"Will you tell Miss Aluja, please, that Mr. Shqitonja is not to meet Mr. Wolgast at—"

"Who is this?"

"This is Miss Aluja's answering service."

"What time is it?"

"Eight oh three A.M. Will you tell Miss Aluja, please, that Mr. Shqitonja is not to meet Mr. Wolgast on the Staten Island ferry? He is to go to the top of the Empire State Building at eight-thirty."

"Who left the message?"

"Mr. Courtney Wolgast."

Joe's neuroses curdled. Lou Amjac had made a miscalculation. Leila's telephone number was unlisted, yet Attorney Wolgast had called it. The drill was that only Leila ever answered in that apartment. It was out-of-bounds for Joe.

No one had told Amjac that Leila was not in her apartment at eight in the morning and that Josef Shqitonja would break rules to answer the telephone because he was desperately awaiting a call from Leila.

Joe hung up the phone, staring at it with alarm bells going off inside his head. *How did Attorney Wolgast know to call me at Leila's unlisted number? Meine Edelfrau's supersecret number? How did he know I even knew Leila?*

Somehow he managed to shave without damaging himself dreadfully. He showered. He chose a strong military twill from among the dozen-odd suits he kept at the apartment. The suit would be on the warm side, but it would wear like iron, and he might have to travel far. He checked his money: over $11,000. Wherever he went, he would need to avoid the *rezvedyvatel'ny punkt* where at least one illegal from the murderous 5th Directorate was stationed. The word was out to kill him.

His brain kept demanding impossible information. Was his aunt's last will itself a counterintelligence trap? But what kind of trap? It was all confusing because it had been designed to be confusing. Why? Neither the Chinese nor the Albanians had known about the will, therefore somewhere far behind everything must lurk the dreaded figure of Mark Haselgrove. There could be no other answer to the burning question: How did Attorney Wolgast know to call him at Leila's?

He chose an exquisitely expensive artificial pink rose from his boutonniere collection and pinned it to his left lapel.

That he had to leave some message for Leila fell on him like a collapsing roof of a church. He could not simply desert her. He felt it was as if he were a student again, mixing with the alien Soviet intelligence people and forcing himself to run scared all the time so that every part of him would be sensitive to danger. He could feel the danger now, but, in a strange way, this rankled because Attorney Wolgast could not possibly be a Haselgrove agent. If he were, he would not do anything as clumsy as warning with that telephone call. Still—he reversed his field again—an estate of $4,489,232 would be an effective device to get a man talking about himself, to ask any sort of trick question because all that would seem to be part of the requirements of the will. If that were the case, Attorney

Wolgast would get nothing out of him. Should he keep the appointment? But he knew that, by the mere fact of being a Shqitonja, he was committed to getting the $4,489,232. His father would expect it of him.

There was no going backward. All bridges had been demolished. He had to hear the conditions of the will that morning, then begin to run. If Attorney Wolgast was a Haselgrove man, then Joe would have one more reason to run, but he would be running only from one more ferocious government. And he would be saved by the removal of his Permanent Disguise.

Savor one thing, he told himself. You are a Shqitonja!

He sat at Leila's desk and began to write:

> Dearest, dollink Bubbelchiki:
>
> I must go away and there is no way, at this moment, that I can explain it. Put into your mind that you will wait for me. I will return. I will have undergone a total metamorphosis in every way except in my heart, my dollink. When I return, you will think you will not know me. But before I do I will send you a signal in the form of one of my exquisite little rosebud buttonholes, or a facsimile thereof, of a drawing of a rose or a packet of Burpee Rose Seeds, a telephoned song phrase from (how beautiful!) "Roses Are Blooming in Picardy" or the classical phrase of the leader of the Chinese people, Chairman Mao, "A rose by any other name would smell as sweet."
>
> I have begun to weep. But this is not good-bye. It is, in the truest sense, a beginning for us. I live for your joy and your contentment.
>
> Immer deine, ever thine, oh, boy, your kisses taste like wine.
>
> Joe

19

Peggy Flinn left her apartment building on 114th Street at Riverside Drive at 7:10 A.M., immediately after her wiretapping team assigned to Leila Aluja's telephone learned of the Empire State Building rendezvous. She thought she had made certain that she was not being followed, but was grossly mistaken. She boarded a Broadway bus going south, unaware that Major Gega rode a Vespa a half-block behind. That bastard Shqitonja, she thought all the way downtown. She would win a bonus for overturning this devious, rotten, fair-haired boy, always at the head of his class, that son of an Albanian patriot who was nothing but a dangerous defector. Also, she needed the bonus. On Thursday the pouch had brought a letter from her sister in Vlone. The damned nephew was determined to marry that lazy witch of an Italian girl and to go to work in her father's corset shop in Ravenna. Where would that leave Luba, poor baby, raising a boy who turns out to be a corset salesman, for God's sake?

When Joe emerged from Leila's building, Miss Flinn was ready, inside a 5th Directorate cab, just far enough away form the entrance to his building. Her driver was a good boy and she had plenty on him. Major Gega waited just around the corner, now convinced that the rezident had ordered this rendezvous and that every move she was making emanated waves of guilt.

Lou Amjac and Mr. Wolgast pulled up at the 34th Street side of the Empire State Building in a magenta and green taxi. "You don't think you are coming up with me, do you, Mr. Amjac?" Wolgast asked. "I am sorry, but I couldn't tolerate that."

"Mr. Wolgast, lissenna me! Shqitonja is a spy master. He's just pretending to be your man."

"He's the legatee, Mr. Amjac. The proof of that has been authenticated by experts. My duty is to see that the rightful heir gets the estate. What you and your people do after that is not my concern."

He lifted Amjac's limp hand from his side and shook it. "Good day, sir," he said. "Thank you for your help. If it was help."

Mr. Wolgast entered the skyscraper. Amjac allowed him a three-minute start. Joe's taxi stopped at the building entrance. Amjac saw that Shqitonja was being followed by a short woman with a white Dutch-boy bob. Amjac entered the building behind Miss Flinn. Major Gega followed them. Joe went up in the tower elevator first. Miss Flinn and Amjac took the second car. Major Gega took the third.

The view from the tower showed faintly, miraculously, through the dense air pollution that had risen to a ceiling just below the tower, a tiny section of New Jersey and a piece of Long Island. By squinting downward, it was possible to see buses belching black smoke and the million-odd cars exhaling white smoke with which thousands of tiny people dyed their lungs, creating something gay and frothy as though their chests were packed with saucy black underwear. It was a vantage point from which to view the hell of the future when all the world, urged on by a tilted pope and foaming politicians, spread the Right-to-Life across every mountain and valley, making a single-world city that would be pinned down by a more punishing atmosphere than this one, creating the garbage that was the only food for the lungs.

When Amjac reached the tower, he shambled to the coffee shop where he could pretend to be looking at the view while watching Shqitonja and Mr. Wolgast talk earnestly near a parapet. Miss Flinn had strolled out as if to enjoy the view, her Dutch-boy bob covered with a scarf. Major Gega was nowhere in sight.

Mr. Wolgast was listening to Joe with concern, leaning upon a tightly furled umbrella. "I refuse to continue our discussions," Joe said, "until you explain to my satisfaction how you knew to telephone me at Miss Aluja's apartment and how you got that unlisted telephone number."

Mr. Wolgast looked pained. "Very well. As the legatee, you have a right to know." He took a deep breath. "Last night, after I had retired for the night, the doorbell rang. The caller was an agent of the Federal Bureau of Investigation."

Joe paled to a lizard-belly color.

"This man told me he had been instructed to follow you that evening when you had gone into a drugstore on Second Avenue and he had recorded your conversation with me on some sort of special device those people have. He played the conversation for me. There was no doubt about its authenticity."

"But this is terrible. It is a total invasion of privacy."

"It gets worse, Mr. Shqitonja. He says he was not the only agent following you. An unknown man was in the telephone booth on the other side of you. He undoubtedly, the FBI believes, recorded the conversation as well."

Joe's mind ran on like an ice-covered waterfall, arrested yet dripping anxiety. "Is this leading to how you knew to telephone me at Miss Aluja's?"

"Yes, my boy. It is. Amjac told me he then returned to his office and telephoned his chief for instructions. He was ordered to go to my flat and to remove me for the night in case the opposition, whomever they may be, decided to call on me. We spent the night in a hotel. This morning, in my presence, Mr. Amjac telephoned his chief's answering service with the message to you from me to change the time and place of our meeting today."

"His chief's answering service?"

"I *am* sorry, Mr. Shqitonja."

"But it was Miss Aluja's answering service who called me."

"Yes. So Mr. Amjac told me. I regret to confirm to you that Mr. Amjac's chief is Miss Aluja."

"No!" Joe strangled on the sound. His hands clutched at the older man's sleeves; his face decomposed into small pieces. A bleak dawn rose over the horizon of his dread. That was how, he sang to himself, such a hopelessly lovely girl, such a heartlessly wonderful woman, could pretend to have been in love with an aging, pitted, swollen, bald, and foolish man. He worked it over and over in his mind as a bugler might practice blowing taps before striding out to play it over his own grave. He heard all of it clearly, but his mind was unable to accept it.

He had to run. There was no place to go, but he had to run before multiple sets of hounds. There was the wide world to run in, but no one to run to any longer. Leila would be behind him, not waiting ahead. He had one defense left by which he could elude her: his Permanent Disguise. He would false-trail them, double back, then redouble back to surface with his own original face and form, the shape into which he had been born. Then he would devote the remainder of his days to luring her in, playing her carefully, making her as helpless with love as she had made him, then he would cut her loose into this kind of an icy hurricane in which he now stood.

He became sick and dizzy. "I must sit down, Mr. Wolgast," he said weakly, tottering away, unaware of Miss Flinn, who had moved herself to within ten feet of Mr. Wolgast.

From his hidden position, Major Gega saw his opportunity to carry out his orders and to strike terror into the minds of Attorney Wolgast and Shqitonja. He darted out with the speed of a hunting lion, seized Miss Flinn, and, with enormous strength, lifted her high over his head as he rushed toward the parapet to throw her over into 34th Street, 102 stories below, shouting wildly in Albanian so that Mr. Wolgast should not miss the point of the exercise.

Mr. Wolgast saw the already-dead face of Miss Flinn, listened to her screams, and he acted. He reached out with the handle to his umbrella, hooked it around the major's neck, and pulled violently. The major came backward and so did Miss Flinn.

Gega sprang to his feet and raced toward the elevators. Amjac rushed out of the coffee shop and was knocked unconscious by him. The major entered the elevator as its doors opened, struck down the operator, closed the car door, and disappeared.

Frozen by terror, Joe had stared blankly at all of this, his reflexes beyond his command and his eyes glazed. He had not recognized Major Gega; it was all over so quickly. He stepped over Amjac and strode out to the terrace where Mr. Wolgast was reviving Miss Flinn.

"Miss Flinn!"

"Do you know this woman?" Mr. Wolgast asked him.

"My God, yes."

"It was the damndest thing. The words 'Hello there' were tattooed across his fingers."

"Nat Gannis!"

"Who?"

"Not a name. An Albanian curse." He did not want to acknowledge the Sigurimi to a foreignor. "Nodgahniz. Like *merde* in French." Joe was shaking. The Sigurimi were here already. Somehow they had made a mistake and had gone for the rezident, but they were after him. He had to start running.

"Wha' hoppen?" Miss Flinn said weakly, flat on her back.

"It was Gannis, the watchman," Joe whispered almost into her ear.

She struggled to her feet saying, with awe, "Don't meet Uncle Sugi!" then hurried across the terrace to the elevator bank, stepping over Amjac's unconscious body.

Joe spoke rapidly to Mr. Wolgast. "I have to go away. When we meet again, I will not look like this. Swear it to me. Swear you will not tell that to anyone."

Mr. Wolgast's dignity had the weight of a steamroller. "I am a practicing attorney," he said stiffly. "This is privileged information."

"I will send word—a signal, a symbol. A rose like this one." He touched his lapel. "Or a book by Rose MaCaulay. Or a recording of 'Second Avenue Rose.' Three rose codes in a sequence. And when we meet, because you will not be able to recognize me, I will greet you with the words of Chairman Mao, 'Hath not thy rose a canker, Somerset, hath not thy rose a thorn, Plantagenet?' "

"Chairman Mao?"

"I will say that to you on the telephone, nothing more. Then we will meet in the Rose Room of Heller House in Dover, New Jersey, at noon the following day when—at last—you will read that will to me. Do you understand? Do you agree?"

"Yes. Will you still be a spy then, Mr. Shqitonja?"

"By then I my be dead from being a spy now, Mr. Wolgast. But if I am alive, I will not be a spy then. And bring your experts. You will know me by my birthmarks but in no way else." He turned quickly and half walked, half ran across the terrace, stepping over the fallen Amjac to enter an elevator.

Mr. Wolgast noticed Amjac's body for the first time. He went to it hurriedly, reaching it just as Amjac's eyes were fluttering open. "Oh, Mr. Amjac," he said. "I distinctly told you not to follow me up here."

20

Leila was returned blindfolded to her quarters under the high Rockies at 5:08 A.M. Mountain Time knowing she could not get back to New York before Joe awoke. She was sprawled exhausted in a bathtub when Mrs. Brown entered without knocking. The motherly dearheart was carrying a tray with a large green pill and a glass of water.

"You should have locked your door, shouldn't you have, dear?" Mrs. Brown asked, looking as homely as a cinnamon-covered baked apple. Leila stared at her unpleasantly. She accepted the pill without question and washed it down.

"Could have been cyanide or prussic acid, couldn't it, dear? We should be more on our guard, shouldn't we?"

"Ah, shaddap," Leila said.

"And no matter how much karate one knows, one would be rather helpless seated in a bathtub, don't you think?"

"But you'd need to lean over to get me, wouldn't you, Mrs. Brown? What was the pill for?"

"Mr. Haselgrove wants you to sleep for thirty hours or so, I expect, dear."

"Oh, no!" She could feel the pill working.

"Best to step out of the tub now. If you become a dead weight in there, I'll have to call a Marine or two, and you wouldn't want that, would you?"

Thirty hours later, Leila lay entirely still, her hair spread out on the pillow, with extremely lascivious thoughts of how Joe smelled like baking apricots and how that it was the most wildly arousing smell she had ever known. She felt serene and rested, confident that she would be able to get Joe out after the arrests had been made. Somehow. What the hell. Once he was in the Federal courthouse in Foley Square and they had the security of due process, then Haselgrove would have made his score and have gotten his worldwide publicity; he'd help her get around the details until Joe was sprung—or this would be the last job she would ever do for him. He needed her more then she needed him and he'd better not forget that.

The question gnawing like a ferret at her mind was not whether Joe could be saved after his arrest but whether, after he had been extricated, she should persuade him to work for Haselgrove? He was a highly trained man. But she had doubts. Haselgrove would only make him as a double agent, which meant that he'd either be on the road all the time or that the Sino-Albanians would suspect him and kill him, a pretty lousy way to renew a marriage. The main thing was, if they could work together, he would be safe. She'd still have to keep working for Haselgrove, but Joe thought she was Meine Edelfrau, not the top-secret agent of the Haselgrove Organization. Ah, Joe. You darling, darling man. Then the terrible mistake in her reasoning came to her. If she persuaded Haselgrove to let her recruit Joe, she would have to expose herself to him as a member of the Haselgrove Organization. There would be no question of his believing that she was just little Meine Edelfrau, a world figure, the idol of millions. He would know she had betrayed him.

The loudspeaker concealed somewhere in the bathroom nearby was whispering at her softly. "Get dressed, please, Miss Aluja. Dr. Weiler is on his way to your quarters to take you to Level 31. He will be waiting for you in your sitting room, and he will take you to Mr. Haselgrove."

Leila exploded with pique. "I won't set a foot out of this bed," she yelled, "until you turn that goddamn television camera off me. I am tired of being watched while I'm naked."

There was the slightest pause. "The cameras have been turned off, Miss Aluja. You may proceed with instant dressing. Mr. Haselgrove is waiting."

Leila leaped out of bed, ran to the closet, and shut the door. When she was dressed, she floated out to join Dr. Weiler, a shortish man in a patent medicine doctor's white shift who wore a disreputable mustache and had a nose twitch. He twisted his hands as though they were shaping raw croissants while he spoke, "Please—sit down. We will talk."

"But they said Haselgrove was waiting."

"Don't worry. We allowed. We have six minutes before we go. I must explain everything that we are going to do. You have good bones, I think. The eyes are right, I think. Haselgrove really knows."

"Knows what?"

"What disguise fits who."

"You do the Permanent Disguises?"

"The whole thing. Cosmetic and psychiatric."

"What will I look like?"

"Nice. You'll see."

"Don't you have a sketch? I won't go into this without a sketch."

He smiled slyly. He took a manila envelope from beneath his gown. "This is how you'll look," he said. "Mr. Haselgrove himself gave me this photograph."

She looked at the picture of an extremely attractive young woman who had apparently soft, ash-blond hair. The eyes were violet and charoptic. The nose was snubbed where Leila's was aquiline. The mouth was wider and fuller than Leila's and her perpetual expression seemed to be one of extreme interest, as though shc wouldn't miss a word of any television commercial.

"But—fahcrissake! This was me before they turned me into what I am now."

"I think it's a very nice job they did."

"I always thought I needed a little more forehead."

"No."

"Oh, yes."

"Please, miss. I will give the eyes the slightest epicanthic fold at the corners and that will give the illusion of a higher forehead without damaging the essential effect. Also—do you want a high, small bosom or a big straight-out pair?"

"Big, high, and straight out, I think."

"Maybe I should make the legs just a little knock-kneed? It helps the hemline and keeps the stocking seams straighter. And how about if I make you four inches shorter. We have this new shoe effect."

A Marine gunnery sergeant entered the room. Dr. Weiler became silent. They boarded the little train blindfolded. When the blindfold was removed, Leila was standing in front of Mr. Haselgrove's door with the grizzled Marine general, but Dr. Weiler was not there. She opened the door on cue. Mark Haselgrove (she supposed) was seated in the rocking chair next to the potbellied stove, but his appearance had changed drastically.

"This disguise I am wearing is the painter Haydon's conception of William Wordsworth," he said as he motioned her to a facing chair, "whom I personally believe to have been one of the handsomest men of all time."

"What day is this?" Leila asked, adding as an afterthought, "It's a beautiful makeup."

"I had it done only for you."

"Later. Please. Mr. Haselgrove, Dr. Weiler showed me a photograph of the Permanent Disguise you had chosen for my next assignment, whatever it is. Surely, you realize that that was the face and figure your people had hired to send into China and which was me until the Chinese gave me this Permanent Disguise to send me to Beverly Hills to infiltrate Notorious Shannon?"

"Yes."

"And surely you also realize that by changing me back into what I was, you will be destroying the greatest cover a secret agent ever had—Meine Edelfrau, idol of millions?"

"Yes."

"Then why do it?"

"Because—please sit down, my dear—this may be too sudden a shock for you—but from the moment I saw the photograph of that glorious girl you were before you went into China—I fell head-over-heels in love with you. I adore you, Leila. Or at least I will when Dr. Weiler finishes removing that Permanent Disguise."

She stared at him in traumatic disbelief. She was not acting, which was for the best because she had been characterized by a dozen informed film critics as being a very, *very* bad actress. Her *amour propre* had easily overcome the expression of his inner heart but, for one thing, she had no idea what Haselgrove looked like and, besides, she loved Joe Reynard.

Each time she had met Haselgrove, four times in all, he had been wearing a different Permanent Disguise. No matter what his outer shell looks like, she thought, his soul, his psyche, was like a basketful of cobras. If she had not seen his eyes as he had told her that he loved her, she would have thought it impossible for him to feel any emotion. The tender expression he had beamed out at her had been Adolf Hitler gazing down adoringly at Eva Braun as he had peed on her chest pleading his love.

She stared into the beautiful face which had been William Wordsworth's as he softly spoke the poetry.

Three years she grew in sun and shower,
Then Nature said, "A lovelier flower
On earth was never sown;
This Child I to myself will take;
She shall be mine, and I will make
A Lady of my own."

He mooned up at her, his eyes as pleading as a dachshund's.

"Wordsworth certainly wasn't much of a poet, but he was sure a great-looking guy," Leila said. She had never felt so frightened. This man looked insane, thought insane, and now was living insane. She stammered and choked on the torrent of words that was pouring out of her. "Mr. Haselgrove," she began.

"Call me Mark. Or Markie."

"Markie, don't you think—I mean, Isabel Clifford Fuller is supposed to have been killed in a train wreck. If she shows up again, it will create a lot of confusion. And how will you explain the disappearance of the most visible woman in the world, Meine Edelfrau? I mean, how many times do you think my dad can stand being put through this trauma? When there is a whole world of Permanent Disguises to choose from, why send me out in that Miss Debutante drag, a former Sino-Albanian spy?"

"You weren't listening, Aluja."

"In money alone—income from the Meine Edelfrau industries—

it's going to cost me sixty-four million dollars a year, less cast, crew, and commissions."

He ignored her pleading. "All my life," he said softly, "I have been waiting for someone to love. When I saw your photograph—the way you were before you became the way you are—I knew that all the power I held, all the fear and dread which I commanded"—his voice broke—"meant nothing. All my life, since I was a small boy tearing the wings off houseflies, I have dreamed that the only important thing in the universe was control, control of everything and everyone, but, when I saw that picture of you after you had gone into China, I experienced the most sublime mystery of love any man has ever known, only to have you come out of China as just another drab woman."

"Well, thanks a lot!"

"Another man might slip an engagement ring on your finger or give you a charge account at Neiman-Marcus, but I offer power such as no other woman has ever known. Leona Helmsley will seem like Minnie Mouse when compared to you. You will sit with me, at my right hand, as I give the commands which control the world as we know it."

"But—what about my new assignment?"

"There is no new assignment, Miss Fuller. I was just vamping until I could screw up my courage. With the national news media as witness, we have raided the Notorious Shannon offices all across the country. Nearly three hundred enemy agents have been arrested, and all but three of the ringleaders."

"Who got away?" Leila asked breathlessly.

"Your husband, Shqitonja. The rezident, Peggy Flinn. And a building watchman in New York, Nat Gannis. We need to check him out."

"How did they escape?"

"A good question. I wonder who could have tipped them off?"

"Do you suspect me?"

"Of course I suspect you."

She exploded under the threats and frustrations of seventy-two hours. "What could I tell anyone? That I had been investigating my own husband for three years yet I didn't know anything about any plan to arrest him? I've been in charge of this case but no one ever thought it necessary to tell me that we were going to arrest him until I got all the way out here under this mountain."

She was exalted that Joe was safe and free somewhere, because she was sure that he was working out every detail to return to her wherever she would be. Then, through him, she could recapture the other two and hold them as ransom against Joe's freedom—if only she could hold off this lovesick lunatic in his fucking rocking chair.

"I have absolved you," Haselgrove said, looking wholly inspiring in his William Wordsworth makeup. "As for your Isabel Clifford Fuller disguise, I have decided that is how you will capture these three people."

"How?"

"Where can they go for help? Where can they regroup to await instructions from Tirana and Beijing? As Isabel Clifford Fuller, a Chinese agent in Permanent Disguise, the same woman you were when you graduated from their college in Beijing, you will be making sure that your husband never knows that it was you who betrayed him."

"But how do I know he will even look at me in the Isabel Clifford Fuller disguise? Joe was the biggest agent Hollywood has ever seen. Good-looking women are a dime a dozen to him. In this Leila Aluja/Meine Edelfrau makeup I have something special for him only the way I am now."

"Exactly."

"Exactly what?"

"Do you take me for a fool? Do you think I would send the woman I love back to the man who has the same tragic, joyous chemistry for you as Leila Aluja as I have for you as Isabel Clifford Fuller? No, no, my dearest."

"I feel like my own stand-in!"

"You will seem to have snapped out of amnesia perhaps somewhere on the West Coast in the general region of that railroad wreck I arranged. Shqitonja, in hiding, will send word back to Beijing through channels and wait for instructions. With their budgets they can afford only one hideout point in the United States. Beijing will order you there for regrouping with the others."

"But, Mr. Haselgrove—I mean, Markie—don't you think that—"

"Then you get a voiceprint on Shqitonja and Flinn—and perhaps some genetic traces such as sperm or tears and if they match in our labs—as I am certain they will—we will send in a force to mop up. Then we'll be done with it and you and I can settle down and live happily ever after."

Leila shuddered.

"There is the will, Markie."

"What about it?"

"It isn't some extraneous factor. It had Shqitonja so upset that he kept telling me that he had to go away. It had Peggy Flinn so upset that she broke cover and came to that restaurant—we had never seen her before, so that certainly was unusual—and they discussed a substitute legatee arriving in ten days. There was a lot of tension."

"Are you suggesting that they are not fleeing from our arrest but from something unknown to us?"

"Markie, I *know* Joe Reynard. He didn't have a *clue* that he was about to be arrested. But he was desperate to convey that he had to get away. He's never, never done that before."

"Hm. Uh—what do you propose we do?"

"I say I have to talk to Courtney Wolgast, who we have reason to believe is the last man who talked to Shqitonja. Then, I think I should go back to my apartment, in my Permanent Disguise as Aluja, cancel all the Meine Edelfrau bookings—I had a tour of Japan coming up—and wait for Shqitonja to come back."

"No monkey business!" The violence of the jealousy he projected made every artery and vein in her body feel as though it had been packed with Freon.

"He'll come back, Markie. I know he will. I would stake everything I stand for on that."

"Bring Shqitonja in and I guarantee you a place among ten other people, his intimates, watching a crucial football game with President Nixon in the Oval Office at the White House, perhaps with access to the President's own bookmaker."

"I wouldn't have the brass to intrude on our President while he was recreating," Leila said flatly.

Haselgrove leaned back in the rocker for almost three minutes and closed his eyes. He remained silent as though he were asleep. All that could be heard was the ticking of the cuckoo clocks, which were part of the merchandise of the country-store setting. At last he spoke, clearing his throat carefully first.

"We will do both, I think, Aluja," he said. "You will remain in your Aluja disguise. You will signal Beijing as Isabel Clifford Fuller. If neither of the two hunted Sino-Albanian agents, possibly three, show up at their hideout within two days, you will proceed to your apartment in New York from Beverly Hills, as Leila Aluja—or Meine Edelfrau, as you prefer. If Shqitonja is on the run from them, as a defector, instead of from us, I agree that he very well may return to New York to seek you out as Leila Aluja."

"If he ever left New York."

"Yes. You will have the same quality as invisibility while you pin him down—"

"Pin him down?"

"Figuratively speaking!" Haselgrove snarled, waving his hand with irritability. "Through him you will locate Flinn, then we'll take both of them." Then, as if it had been his own idea all along, he said, "The beauty part is that you'll be in your Aluja Permanent Disguise and he'll be at your mercy."

"Brilliant!"

"However—and this is the part that means the world to me—when you close the case, the time will have come to feed my heart with the tenderness of love; you will return to me here, under this mountain, in the Permanent Disguise of your original form, as Isabel Clifford Fuller."

"How do I that?"

"The complete Fuller Permanent Disguise kit is in that suitcase." He pointed to a handsome piece of airline luggage standing near the door. "Take it with you and—when you have completed a job well done—you will tranform yourself once again into my darling and, together, we shall rule the world."

"Oh, Marky—you make it all sound so—so *thrilling*!"

"I have a meeting with the British Prime Minister tomorrow afternoon about the privatization of Scotland Yard. We must keep up the admiration of the British Parliament because nothing succeeds but success. When I return from London, I must produce the ringleaders for the greatest spy trial in all history. I would prefer that this be Shqitonja because there are still people who get queasy about executing a woman."

"Executing? Josef Shqitonja?

"The Chinese slipped badly by insisting that their people become American citizens. This is treason. The death penalty."

Leila turned as cold as if her blood had been drained from her. Execute Joe? Twenty minutes ago, she told herself, she had been counting the babies she would have with him. But Joe was safe from this maniac because by now he had stripped off his Permanent Disguise and no one would be able to find him. He was safe, but she had lost him. Joe was gone and if he ever came back, how would she ever make him understand why she had betrayed him?

21

Joe had checked into an enormous commercial hotel in midtown under the name of Jonathan Matson. It was a characteristically American hotel where everyone, by hotel-chain policy, was anonymous. Neither the room clerk, the bellman, nor the elevator operator had looked at him because they had been trained to understand that eye contact embarrassed the hotel's guests.

Locked in his room, refusing maid service, rarely ordering room service, and staying behind the bathroom door to sign for sustenance when it arrived, it took Joe three days to remove the Permanent Disguise, a task usually assigned to a skilled plastic surgeon. No anesthetic or cutting was required, or he would have had to use mirror-hypnosis.

The arduous work involved peeling away dozens of layers of false tissue. Mounds of plastic padding that had been shaped to change his facial configuration as well as other visible parts of his body such as his hands, neck, and forehead came away. It was exhausting labor. The teeth gave him the most trouble. They had been modeled on Chairman Mao's and, actually, were entirely wrong for the shape of his face. But the Chinese dentist who had done the job had been a devout patriot so, to him, it had been the only way to go.

As Joe peeled off the last undercoating of five o'clock shadow, the underbeard that had been his trademark as a talent agent, he fell back upon the hotel bed, not even bothering to assay his form of almost eight years ago. He slept through the early evening and the night to awake realizing that he had no clothes that would fit him.

The clothing of Joseph Reynard, talent agent nonpareil, was six to eight sizes too large for his former, now-current frame. His hair was entirely wrong. He would need to get some clothes that fit and have a barber give him a bald-man's crew cut until the hair grew back at the front and top of his head, meanwhile filling in with a good toupee. Good God! He hadn't taken off his ears, huge appendages with lobes that hung down like lavalieres. He went to work, peeling and tugging, until his own normal, pink, exquisitely shaped ears reappeared. All that remained to be done was to unwrap the layer upon layer of gauzelike padding that had been wrapped around his abdominal area in order to give him an authoritative girth, and then he would be back to resembling his old self.

He stood, naked, in front of the full-length mirror, barefoot without the elevator shoes and, for a flash, he felt as if he were back in his father's house, which was just a few dozen leagues away from Guisinje (which was just forty-two miles on foot, mostly downhill, from Memtuna, the Paris of northern Albania). He imagined he could taste the yogurt, the real stuff that had kept this great-grandfather alive well into his 134th year. He imagined he could hear the screams of the eagles in their aeries above his father's house. He could hear Pop's glorious basso voice singing, "Stalin Is a Grand, Old Name." For a second, he was home again.

He went to the house telephone and called one of the dozens of shops that lined the lobby floor. He ordered one blue suit and one gray suit in size 42 (as opposed to 54, which would have been the Joe Reynard size if he had ever bought a suit off the rack, which he had not), two white shirts, six pairs of dark-blue lisle socks, some underwear, and two dark neckties. He longed to order a felt fedora but, as the only man wearing a proper hat in a city of ten million people, he would be immediately conspicuous.

When he was dressed, he stood and sat, full-face and in profile, desperate to find a way to convince Leila that he was Joe Reynard, a bulky, balding man of substance, and not Jonathan Matson, a young blade who might have stepped off the train from Princeton. He deplored the good looks and the proportioned, muscular figure that had been wholly protected by the Permanent Disguise, a bulwark between him and the calendar. Staring at the man he had been and was again, he began to make his plan.

First, he would have to settle his aunt's will. If he was going to be on the run, that roughly five million dollars would come in handy. There wouldn't be any time to have a formal meeting with Mr. Wolgast, so it would have to be done by telephone. He looked up Wolgast's number in the directory and dialed. Mr. Wolgast answered on the second ring.

"Mr. Wolgast," Joe began, "I am going on a somewhat extended trip. I may be gone for some time and there will be no opportunity for us to meet. Therefore, if you would be so kind, perhaps you will tell me by telephone the nature of the clause in my aunt's will which I must perform before I can inherit her estate."

"Certainly, Mr. Shqitonja. Simply really. Your aunt was a very great admirer of her grandfather—your great-grandfather—who had once developed an extraordinary formula for a very, very special yogurt."

"I had been told that, yes."

"Be that as it may, it is your aunt's wish—her stipulation—that you use fifty thousand dollars of the money from her estate to reclaim and redevelop your great-grandfather's formula for the yogurt, and that you market it successfully in the United States."

"Market it or cause it to be marketed?"

"Either will do, Mr. Shqitonja."

"That's all? That's all I have to do to get the five million dollars?"

"Precisely."

"Then I must return to Albania, mustn't I? I must track down whatever it was that my great-grandfather had developed. My father may know the formula."

"Good luck, Mr. Shqitonja."

"Thank you, Mr. Wolgast. Thank you for everything. I will notify you where to send the fifty thousand dollars of seed money."

He had about ten thousand dollars cash. Leila had thirty or forty million stashed away from her work as Meine Edelfrau, so they would have enough to work with until he could inherit his aunt's estate. He had to find Leila. They had to disappear. He removed her file from his attaché case. He flipped through her schedule book and almost collapsed with relief when he saw that she would be working a charity benefit at Madison Square Garden that night singing and demonstrating fifty-one of the positions of the *Kama-sutra* and *The*

Perfumed Garden. It would be no use for him to approach her at the Garden, where she would be surrounded by bodyguards and, being unable to recognize him anyway, she would signal her men to beat him up and toss him aside—standard operating procedure.

The thing to do would be to wait for her inside the apartment on 61st Street. He would, somehow, have to get past the doorman, a main hall security guard, and one of two elevator men, all armed—men who over the past five years he must have given more than a thousand dollars in tips to be sure that they protected Miss Aluja. He called the building superintendent on his room telephone. He spoke in the booming, no-nonsense voice of Joe Reynard.

He did not identify himself. He said, "You know who this is?"

"Yes, Mr. Reynard," the man said.

"Good. I am sending one of my most trusted people to Miss Aluja's apartment. He has a key—and an envelope for you, I might add. Please tell the staff to see that he goes directly to the apartment."

"Yes, Mr. Reynard,"

"His name is Mr. Matson. Jonathan Matson. A youngish man. Rather good-looking."

He was seated in Leila's wing chair with a full view of the front door when she came home somewhat spent from the *Kama-sutra* demonstrations. She shut the door, chain-locked it on the inside, put her suitcase carefully against the wall, then leaned heavily against the door in exhaustion before turning to enter the living room. Then she saw him.

"Joe!"

She saw him as his snapshot from the yearbook for the Class of '59 at the Oriental Institute as it had been imprinted on the forefront of her mind; a dark-eyed, handsome, romantic-looking boy whose face she had never been able to forget.

Joe was stunned, pole-axed, bedazed. What is happening here? he asked himself. Am I here? Am I awake? He looked around himself. All the lights were on. She could see him clearly. *"Joe?"* he said distantly. "How can you say Joe? I'm a different man. How can you know me?"

He could hear his own voice clearly. It was an entirely different voice since he had scooped the little vibrator out of his larynx. Even the accent was different. It was mid-Atlantic, not Showbiz.

She went around the room, throwing little electrical switches.

"What are you doing?" he said with alarm.

"Just throwing the switches to generate the backup system on the sound surveillance," she said. "I always keep their TV surveillance on a backup. All they get is footage of me walking from room to room, or reading in bed."

"Then their cameras didn't get me?"

"No way. Haselgrove's whole strength—and his weakness—is that he's too thorough."

When she finished the work, she pulled up a footstool and sat at his knee.

"You told me you'd be changed when you came back," she said "but you haven't changed—not to me. More hair, yes. Thinner, yes. Less nose, of course. Brighter teeth, certainly. But I'd know you anywhere."

"Baby, I'm three inches shorter, forty pounds lighter."

He walked slowly to the mantle and stared into the large mirror over the fireplace. Only his father would have recognized him, unless this whole thing had been a colossal trick of the mind which the Chinese had played on him. Could it be that the Permanent Disguises the Chinese had claimed to value so highly were just a psychological ploy, that he had always looked the same and that they had brainwashed him to believe he looked different, and therefore he had acted differently and had conducted himself differently? His father had had an old folk saying, "Damned clever, these Chinese," but this was impossible. Yet Leila had known who he was the instant she had seen him. He had never really believed in psychoanalysis, but he felt an urgent need of a very good shrink right now.

"Okay, Leila," he said bluntly, to hang on to his sanity. "What's the story?"

"You want it straight?"

He nodded. He couldn't stop nodding until she came close to him, took his head in both of her hands, and kissed him tenderly. "I was FBI for a while," she said, "then CIA. After that the Haselgrove Organization scooped me up."

He began to shake badly. She led him back to the wing chair and lowered him onto it.

"They got me into the Oriental Institute in Beijing and, by total accident, I came across your picture in your class yearbook. I not only memorized it, I fell in love with it. Then they put me on your trail in California. We met. We got married."

He had become very pale. "Three years. The happiest years of my life. Yet all that time we were spying on each other."

"On each other? You knew about me?"

"You want to hear it from me?"

She nodded.

"Beijing put me onto you after you began to mix with the Albanian crowd in Hollywood. Nobody else, not even the rezident, knew Beijing's suspicions. You were my job and only my job. They knew who all the others were because they worked for us, but there was something fishy about a strange, new Albanian suddenly popping up, so they told me to run you down."

She stared horrified at every word as it came out of his mouth.

"So I traced you back. You were such a terrible actress—no offense, Leila!—that you couldn't even have gotten work in television much less movies unless I got the work for you—no matter how much muscle your father's family had with the unions—but until I could find out who you really were, I had to keep you working, keep you so far out in front that you couldn't possibly disappear—so I thought of the Meine Edelfrau dodge."

"But you were never able to pin anything on me?"

"Nothing. But they wouldn't let me give up and, anyway, I found out that I loved you more than anything in my life."

"Mark Haselgrove is in love with me."

"Why not?"

"He wanted me to take off this Permanent Disguise and go back to looking the way I had looked when I joined the agency, which was the Permanent Disguise the Chinese had put on me, not the real way I am, the way you know, as Leila Aluja, as I am now."

"The American people know about Permanent Disguises?"

"Do you think Ronald Reagan could have looked that good without it? He's a very old man. Ninety-six, in fact. But the Republican Party had to keep him looking like a teenager so, presto, the Permanent Disguise! Goodie Noon, Nixon's hand-picked chairman of the Republican National Committee, actually *is* a teenager, but he brought so much money to the Party in campaign contributions that he had to be made President. He needed to be physically matured—an impossibility mentally—so he was fitted with a Permanent Disguise. It is used throughout the Supreme Court and the Congress. Lunatic right-wing conservatives need to appear to be middle-of-the-roaders. Politicians whose souls had them looking like Central Casting hoodlums had to be made over, to look respectable. I would say we had Permanent Disguises long before the Chinese."

"You mean, the Leila Aluja/Meine Edelfrau look is just a Permanent Disguise? You don't look the way I think you look?"

"Very few Americans do, darling. We see what we want to see."

"I want to see what I'm looking at."

"Mark Haselgrove fell in love with my other face and body, so, maybe you will, too."

"Never!"

"It's just a way of looking at things, dearest."

"What are we going to do?"

"I am the only one outside your family in Albania who knows who you are now or what you look like. Beijing doesn't know. The Sigurimi has forgotten."

"But, you. What are we going to do about you? They know you. And they know you the way you used to be."

"That's easy. I've got my old face in that suitcase in the hall. I'm going to mix the two Permanent Disguises. Isabel Clifford Fuller's eyes and chin. Leila Aluja's nose and cheekbones. Add two and a half inches in height, eleven pounds less weight. Dye the hair red and utilize the English speech of the Sherbourne School and Exeter University."

"You are wonderful! I'm sure you have it all figured out—how we'll get away from Haselgrove and where we'll spend the rest of our lives together."

"I have a few ideas."

"But what do we do? Where do we go? What about my inheritance? I don't want to even think of changing how you look,"

Joe said. "A stranger would be taking over my dreams. Whenever I think of doing anything, it is always with you, only you."

"Nothing changes except our identities and you've already changed yours. I love you, Joe. I love you more than Heloise loved Abelard, more than Ingrid loved Bogie. We are going to fly to Rio by separate routes tonight."

"I haven't told you about the five million dollars?"

"What five million dollars?"

"My aunt's estate. She left me almost five million but, in order to get it, I'm going to have to turn family detective until I find my great-grandfather's formula for what everyone says is the greatest yogurt ever discovered."

"Yogurt?"

"My father will know. But it means I will have to go back to Albania."

"Joe, I can't go to Albania. That's Commie territory. Haselgrove would never let me back into the States again."

"But that's just it! You wait for me here! It's just for a few months. I'll run down the formula, come back to New York with a new name and a new passport, collect the five million, and we'll get married all over again."

"Haselgrove will hunt you down. There's no escaping him unless we can convince him that he has to forget about you."

"How can we do that?"

"I've been thinking. You've said that your father has very terrific connections with the Soviet Union."

"Yes."

"Does that still apply to having real muscle with Brezhnev?"

"Yes."

"Is he influential enough to persuade Brezhnev to privatize the KGB and the military police of the Soviet armed forces and turn them over to Haselgrove on a free market basis?"

"I think so, yes."

"Then we're safe!! We'll hand the whole security thing over to Haselgrove on a platter and he'll turn it into a money-making police force! The Russians will be spared the expense while getting a royalty on the whole operation, and Haselgrove will be so tickled that he will forget he ever heard of you."

"Hey—like wow!"

"Go home. Get your father busy in Moscow. Find the formula for your great-grandfather's yogurt. Baby, we're home free!"

"If we can make the deal with Haselgrove, what are you going to do? You can't stay working for him."

"I'm a lawyer. I'll practice law. My father has friends who can set me up."

PART

2

22

The arrest and incarceration of more than three hundred key Hollywood agents employed by Notorious Shannon was a spectacular feather in Mark Haselgrove's cap though it all but paralyzed the motion picture industry. Only three people were left throughout the entire craft of filmmaking who knew how to make deals, get the right tables in restaurants, actually read a script, or to help an actor write a letter home to mother—in sum, how to make movies. This accounted for such films as *Ishtar, Hudson Hawk,* and *Howard the Duck*. It was to be many years before the vacuum was filled again.

It took Joe Reynard's father four days to make the deal to privatize the KGB and the Soviet military police. After she had talked to Joe from Tirana, Leila made an appointment, which took nine days, through channels with Mark Haselgrove. At last she and Haselgrove met in the boathouse of the old Glenmore Hotel, destroyed by fire some years before, on Big Moose Lake in New York State. With a scraggly gray beard, rubber boots, and the smell of freshwater fish, Haselgrove was disguised as an old woodsman.

Leila laid out the proposition carefully. She told him simply that she loved her husband and that her husband's father had certain connections in the Kremlin that had made it possible for her husband to work out an arrangement whereby Haselgrove would immediately understand that, when he was ready, her husband could return from Albania to live in the United States.

There was a stormy scene. Haselgrove pleaded with Leila, then threatened her for considering leaving him for "a Commie rat." For Haselgrove, the break meant not only a lover's rue but a gnawing chagrin for what he considered to be a loss of power. He ranted that he would isolate her at the Organization's outpost in Tierra del Fuego, overseeing cattle rustlers for the Argentine Territorial Police, which he had taken over. Leila let him talk himself out, then she hit him with the proposition.

"Markie, listen," she said, "my husband's father has some pretty good connections in Moscow and he's been able to arrange for you to take over the operation of the KGB and the Soviet military police. How would you like that?"

"What?"

"You heard me right."

"The KGB? That's tremendous! Is this some kind of a joke?"

She looked at her watch. "In twelve minutes, at the general store, right up there, a call is going to come in from Leonid Brezhnev inviting you to Moscow to discuss the deal."

"Twelve minutes from now? Brezhnev? Jesus, this is tremendous. Let's go."

Haselgrove left for Moscow from Utica, New York, at 5:27 the next morning on his personal prototype of the Stealth bomber, Police Force One.

Before he left, he willingly agreed, in writing with four independent witnesses, to total amnesty for Josef Shqitonja-Reynard and, as a gesture toward helping Leila get started in a law practice, ordered his publicity machine to see that she got the widest acclaim for having risked her life in order to bring dangerous Communist subversion to justice.

In a national media sense, Leila became a heroine to the American people. She had saved them from enslavement by Albania. Their gratitude was expressed not only in admiration and fame but in hard money. She was paid $1,784,600 for the publication rights to the story of her fight, her seeming to be citizen Meine Edelfrau while overcoming a force that could have changed the lives of all Americans by turning them into faceless robots serving a Communist state. She was offered her own television talk show, which she refused. She made public appearances on college campuses and before women's clubs and veterans' organizations. She received $50,000 a lecture (three a week) to tell the story of her long struggle to overcome those who sought to enslave America.

She was received at the White House, feted by the leadership of the two great political parties on Capitol Hill, thus reminding the nation again that it was a citadel of freedom under democracy.

Through it all, Leila remembered Mark Haselgrove's eyes and shuddered under the intuitive flash that if he couldn't have her, he could at least be able to watch her and know what she was doing.

Leila gave herself over to being followed, photographed covertly, to having her most intimate moments televised on tape. She knew her clothing would be tapped with artfully sewn-in microphones smaller than snowflakes, that the money she used would be secretly marked, and that she would never, ever again as long as Mark Haselgrove were alive, be truly alone. Instead of this knowledge bringing her dread, it appealed to her sense of destiny. She would enter history through the portals of the Haselgrove Organization and, perhaps millennia after her civilization had gone, the record would be found deep within the Rocky Mountains, among the flag samples and listen-ins, confounding archaeologists. She gripped the Venerable Bead in her right hand, thought of Joe, and literally lived on her courage.

Before her lecture tour and her appearances with Geraldo, Oprah, Phil, Barbara, Arsenio, Johnny, and Dave, and on the ritual Sunday talk shows, she took a five-day holiday at The Inn at Manitou in northern Ontario and played tennis from morning until night, then she fell exhausted into a vodka and water every evening. Every time she slammed her racquet into a tennis ball, she drove Mark Haselgrove further and further away. When she knew she had him and her life under control again, she went home to her dad to plan her real career in the work she had been educated for and trained to do: the practice of law in protection of the weak and helpless against their predators. She went to Washington to her dad's office in the Capitol.

"Listen, Pop," she said earnestly. "I have an idea. I want you to set me up with the Attorney General so I can do what you always wanted me to do—be a lawyer."

"The Attorney General?" her father said. "Are you kiddin'? Where is the money there?"

"First things first. I want you to set me up as an assistant Federal prosecutor in New York. I gotta get a name for myself as a lawyer."

"A name? What name? Tell me the name of five big lawyers in this country. They don't need names, they need the nerve of nine Apache Indians. Lemme set you with one of the big Washington outfits. There, maybe you won't practice law much, but you'll be more powerful in this town than anybody at the White House."

"Pop! Am I a dummy? I have over fifty million dollars of Meine Edelfrau money in Swiss banks. I could buy my way into any law firm in the country. But first I have to be a star as a lawyer, someone all the lawyers are gonna envy, someone with the kinda glamour they think they could have if they came outta the closet. Set me up with the Federal attorney's office in New York, then in good time every law office in Washington will wish they could get me, and whoever the lucky one is who gets me, they'll have to take me as a senior partner."

Her dad spoke to the Cloacinos in Detroit. The Cloacinos arranged a meeting with Edward S. Price, chairman and CEO of Barkers Hill Enterprises, the investment arm of the American Mafia. Price sent her to Angelo Partanna, *consigliere* to the Prizzi family, which dominated New York (among other places). When there was a confluence of influence— the Congress, the Department of Justice, and the Mafia—a place was made for her as a prosecuting attorney on the staff of the Federal prosecutor for the District of New York. Altogether, it was a living lesson in civics.

Leila threw herself into Federal prosecution with the zeal she had given to her relentless off-scouring of Communists from the face of the American escutcheon. She won case after case, headline after headline. She was famous in *People* magazine as a hostess for the superb little suppers she gave at the brownstone she had leased on East 64th Street.

Through all of it, she never lost sight of where her heart was. There was no way to telephone Joe in his mountain village in northern Albania because there were no telephones; in fact, only a year before, modern science had first brought the village a weekly delivery of mail. She and Joe wrote to each other every week, he outlined his progress (if any) in locating the secret formula for the yogurt and spilled out the pathos of his love for her; her letters never mentioned her newly found fame, just the plodding facts of her hard work to succeed as an assistant Federal prosecutor.

Because she had no way to control her zeal, because she was more ambitious than Attila, despite her basically sinister sponsorship, she became such a publicized threat to organized crime as a Federal prosecutor, in news media fantasies if not in fact, that serious consideration had to be given to moving her upstairs, out of the way. When her father had come up with the solution to have her moved into the lucrative private practice of the law in Washington, everyone was happy and the policy of business-as-usual continued.

23

Within weeks after her father had put in the fix and she was released from duty by the Federal prosecutor, Leila was sitting behind an enormous, elaborately carved Florentine desk that was wired to record any conversations in the room unless she disconnected the system with a knee switch. It was in an office within the Washington law firm of Schwartz, Blacker & Moltonero, of which she was a partner, and which employed 137 lawyers. She faced walls on which were hung paintings by the Neapolitan Francesco Solimeno, two by a pupil of Rembrandt's named Gerard Dou, Franz Kline (two numbing representations of a thick black line on a white background) and by Robert Motherwell (an equally baffling graphic something). The paintings seemed to tell what the mind of the world had been and what it had become.

The room was boastful, almost the equal in its braggadocio to the office of the founding partner Malachi Olgilvie, which displayed four Caravaggios (although he was not a religious man) and a Houdon bust and which had bulletproof windows and eavesdropping equipment woven into the edges of the carpet of the room. Neither law books nor any other paraphernalia of legal practice was visible in any of the partners' rooms.

She spoke to her secretary through the intercom. "I need time to work up the backgrounds for the Supreme Court replacement," she said. "Do I have anything on the pad for after lunch?"

"You have a Dr. Nolan at five-thirty, Miss Aluja," her secretary said.

"Who's he?"

"The vice president asked you to see him."

"Oh, shit! Okay, nothing else, please."

She went back to poring over the backgrounds of candidates for the high court. The retiring justice had had one Lithuanian and one Argentinian grandparent. His parents had come from the Seattle area and his mother had been a state golf champion. Therefore, it was her brief, as outlined by the White House, to find an ethnic Lithuanian-Argentinian golfer who not only would have name-recognition in the northwest but should also have some background in the law, but no association with marijuana, sexual harassment, or pornography. Thank God for computers, she thought.

Leila had acquired big hair in the totemic style of Dallas women: bleached, lacquered, gelled, sprayed, teased, and stiff as a board. It gave her the structured immobility of an ophiolatrist carrying a large basket of live snakes to church on her head. From her corner office, looking out the window, she could see the White House three blocks to the south and the Capitol in the eastern distance.

Schwartz, Blacker & Moltonero occupied its own nine-story building at K Street and Massachusetts Avenue in Washington. It was near the best lobbyist restaurants: the Lion d'Or, Jean-Pierre, and Joe and Moe's.

The entrance door into the law firm carried the legend "Law Office" under the firm's name. Although it employed 137 lawyers, it wasn't a law office in the old-fashioned sense of Abraham Lincoln and Clarence Darrow, but few Washington law firms were. Leila Aluja's practice was the exception. She was the firm's second litigator. Under rare, even historic, circumstances, when the firm was required to go to court, she sat beside her leader, F. X. O'Connell, Jr. Together they took on or represented governments and colossal corporations in the way that the grand legal battles are now fought: millions of documents winnowed through ever-new software systems and thousands of workers: lawyers, paralegals, outside counsel, in-house counsel—the megacase. The cases dragged on for years, clogging the courts and producing legal bills resembling the costs of any other sort of war.

Counselor Aluja earned fees of $950 an hour when under full sail because of the fame she had made as counsel to clients who had been hauled before Congressional investigating committees that were no longer inquiries to obtain information but were gigantic reflecting mirrors for whichever overweening component could attract the most television attention. With the Congress practicing new subversions of the democratic process, Leila Aluja's kind of law practice was helping to validate the decline of the west.

If anyone had dared to say that Leila Aluja wasn't worth the amounts of treasure she extracted from her clients, Schwartz, Blacker & Montonero would have instituted a lawsuit (handled by a junior associate at $65 an hour). The chief executive of the largest automobile company in the world had said, "If I had done something out-of-line and I knew that F. X. O'Connell or Leila Aluja were coming, I'd probably emigrate to a monastery in central Iceland."

However, as for the bulk of the firm's business, if fair-labeling practices had been in force for the legend on the firm's front door, the billing would have read "Power Brokers and Lobbyists-at-Law."

Schwartz, Blacker & Moltonero represented powerful domestic and foreign clients operating outside the government who needed to have things fixed by people operating inside the government. The firm's diligence in the service of the compliant government had led to laws which had made possible Political Action Committees, those miraculous vehicles by which all American legislators could be bribed legally; deregulation, which had plagued airlines, banks, and insurance companies alike; and savings and loans corruptions, which were crushing both the country's credibility and its electorate.

For its clients, Schwartz, Blacker & Moltonero had devised the method by which Japanese industry or the Israeli government could buy the American Congress. The fees spread around from the legislative needy to the healers changed hands through Schwartz, Blacker & Moltonero, without whom none of the other parts of the system of unequal representation within democracy could have operated as profitably or with such punishing force upon the electorate.

Among others, the firm represented Japan's giant confederation of agricultural cooperatives, its electronic and fiber-optic industries, and its automotive and semiconductor interests in the United States. It counseled Big Oil, the National Bankers Association, the American Physicians Association, and the National Insurance Council. In its necessarily secret compartments it advised clients whose major and minor interests could be said to oppose those of the people of the United States, including the special interests of the most anonymous part of the American economy, organized crime.

It was Schwartz, Blacker & Moltonero, with Leila Aluja as attorney-in-fact, who had interceded with the State Department in the mid-1980s to have Iraq removed from the list of sponsors of international terrorism—despite considerable evidence that Iraq was one of the two main factors in world terrorism—in order to permit arms sales to it by the United States. Arrangements for fees and emoluments had been arranged through Ms. Aluja's father, Congressman Marty Aluja (R.-Mich.)

Although Leila Aluja's reputation as a litigator was her base within the profession of law, the true source of her power lay in her access to the insiders who moved and shook the American government from the closed hearing committees of Congress throughout the bureaucracy to the White House. Access was the true currency of power and when combined with the compounded clout of Schwartz, Blacker & Moltonero and Barkers Hill Enterprises, it defined the inexorable effectiveness of her ability as a fixer and a lobbyist.

To the public, Schwartz, Blacker & Moltonero was invisible, just another law firm. In its most invisible manifestation, the firm was closely bound to American politics and government because it had such an influence as a major fund-raiser and strategist upon the national political committees of both parties and their candidates for the executive, legislative, judicial, military, and appointive branches of national government. It had been powerfully instrumental in bringing about the nominations and elections of four of the most recent Presidents of the United States as well as the multiple leaders of the House and Senate and the heads of all key committees.

The firm was also in a position to move a lot of business into tributary law firms in key cities around the country, firms that exercised less puissant but equally effective leverage upon state and municipal governments, and therefore in the nomination, election, and control of United States Senators and Congressmen.

Schwartz, Blacker & Moltonero, a public corporation, was a wholly owned subsidiary of Barkers Hill Enterprises, a multinational conglomerate charged with reinvesting the profits from narcotics, gambling, prostitution, extortion, usury, pornography, and recycled postage stamps which accrued tax-free to the country's largest organized crime family.

The founding partners of the law firm had long been gone: Schwartz (deceased), Blacker (retired), Moltonero (gaga). The primary founding partner, a super-plotter named Malachi Olgilvie, who had such a compulsion to secrecy that his name appeared nowhere on the firm's letterhead which listed eighteen partners, was said to be "inactive."

Leila Aluja's clients, because they included Barkers Hill Enterprises, were the cream of the Schwartz, Blacker list. One of the jewels in her crown was the Center for American National Cigarette Education and Research (CANCER), which contributed endowed advertising programs for elementary schools through its sponsorship of cigarette-oriented sports programs on a mission to advance young America along the yellow brick road to cigarette achievement.

Her father, Little Marty Aluja, was a nine-term Congressman from the 19th District of Michigan. He had been born Hussein al-Uja al-Tikriti in Iraq, the president of which was his first cousin. He had raised Leila in a glow of memories about the good, old days in Iraq: the Sumerians, the discovers of multiplication, division, and the square root; the foundation of Baghdad in 762; Ur of the Chaldees and the seven-day week; the Assyrians, who had established latitude and longitude; and the Kassites, who had introduced the horse. The core of his constituency was the large Islamic population in Dearborn, Michigan. He sat on the Europe and Middle East Sub-Committee of the Foreign Affairs Committee, among others. The Congressman was a great raconteur. Among his favorite after-dinner stories to the stream of Political Action Committee contributors whom he entertained in Washington was the one about his cousin.

"It was in the early fifties," he would say, drawing on a huge cigar, "in Baghdad." Here he would pause to grin ingratiatingly at his audience of close associates and slush-fund sustainer. "I was just a happy-go-lucky law student at the time. My future depended on the goodwill of the Party. To make a long story shorter, the Party put me in a six-man squad assigned to assassinate the Prime

Minister, a bad guy. But the night before the hit, one of our key shooters came down with a bum appendix. Nobody could think of an instant replacement, so I recommended my kid cousin Saddam Hussein al-Tikriti, who always carried a gun for the sake of his image. He wasn't a very bright kid, but he was ambitious. He had killed his first man when he was fifteen and the score, at twenty, which was when I got him the assignment, was three more. Anyway, the idea was that our car would block the Prime Minister's car while four of us jumped out and pumped lead into him. Well! You can't believe how many things went wrong. Our lookout passed the word that the Prime Minister's car had started its run, but our driver couldn't move his car because the alley was blocked by a delivery truck. But when we ran out into the main street, we saw that the Prime Minister's car was caught in traffic. We rushed out to get him, then things got worse. Two of our people couldn't fire—one had forgotten to put a clip in his weapon, another one's gun jammed. Our leader couldn't get the grenade out of his pocket—it got caught in the lining—but Saddam, who was only supposed to cover our getaway, moved in and started shooting, knocking over the driver and the bodyguard. By this time we were all surrounding the car and all the guns where shooting at once. So what happens? We hit each other. The leader gets killed. I get hit in the chest. Saddam gets hit in the leg, all friendly fire. And what happens to the Prime Minister? Nothing. Not a scratch. So our driver takes us to a Party doctor. I got out through Syria to the States, thank God. Saddam got out to Cairo and was there, drinking a lotta coffee, for a coupla years until the Party finally caught up with the Prime Minister and they brought Saddam home. He worked his way up to being the top assassin, the numero uno hit man the Party had."

Leila's dad was as adorable an old character and as bent a legislator as had ever served in Congress, which made him almost as lovable as Jack the Ripper and more bent than the hunchback of Notre Dame. He was very useful to Leila in her work to make the world safe for massively sinister corporations such as the Bahama Beaver Bonnet Company, one of the owners not only of the United States of America but of the world; and as the Iraqi-American Business Confederation, which represented three major oil companies; the leading automobile manufacturing entity; the widely flung United Electric; eighty-three other American businesses; and the United Congress of American Churches.

Leila Aluja sat on two important presidential commissions. She called the Secretary of State "Jimmy." She had been a United States delegate to the United Nations. She was a renowned hostess and one of the capital city's most desirable dinner partners. She had a standing invitation to Clark Clifford's Christmas buffet; Clifford would greet her in the presence of the most powerful people in Washington, in his silky voice, with "How's my lawyer?"

She had been one of the handful of power brokers invited by the newly elected Ronald Reagan to the famous candlelight dinner at the F Street Club; a guest list had been carefully drawn from the power center of Washington's politicians, lawyer-lobbyists, and influence peddlers. She was the lawyer for Skull & Bones, Goodie Noon's secret society at Yale.

She knew the great and the near-great of five continents and for legendary fees had represented many of them: the crooked bankers, the suborners, the ravening hawks, the pornographers, and the drug barons. Most intimately of all she knew the politicians, their ambitions, and their prices.

She was the little brown mouse who ate fat cats for breakfast.

At a White House reception four nights before, Vice President Hazman had asked her to see someone named Dr. Jim Nolan—something to do with Harvard. She had agreed to see the man as a matter of politeness; there would be very little leverage in it. Dr. Nolan had called the following morning to make an appointment.

It was 5:27 in the evening after a long day when her secretary announced that Dr. Nolan was waiting in the outer office. Leila sighed, braced herself, and said "Send him in."

Nolan was a tall man, not bad-looking, she thought, who insisted on staring directly into her eyes. Other people did that all the time, but he had not only the sort of myopia that gave the intensity of the stare an objectionably possessive quality but also one brown eye and one green eye. The effect was to give his head the impression of being two profiles pasted together. His voice rumbled like Kissinger's but with a slight burr and with none of Kissinger's menace. His clothes were strictly off-the-rack.

"Good afternoon, Dr. Nolan," she said more cheerfully than she felt because she had had a tiring day of getting the IRS straightened out on a misunderstanding about $3,712,000 in back taxes, which could have been a miscarriage of justice in that the man was a very close friend of President Reagan's and a loyal contributor to Republican Party campaign funds, as well as bearing up under the responsibility of finding the President a nominee for the Supreme Court.

Dr. Nolan came on genial and, she thought, just a little smarmy.

"The Vice President didn't seem to know what you wanted to talk to me about," she said.

"I'm in town to see if I can open some doors to research. I'm interested in American business conglomerate support of the private welfare systems."

"Ah?"

"President Reagan said he knew that the burden of charitable works would be taken up happily by the private sector and I had hoped—"

"That *is* fascinating."

"If you could introduce me to the right people at the National Gun Carriers' Association—"

"They aren't a conglomerate."

"But they are such a part of America. And, I thought, if we could study the various philanthropies of, say, Barkers Hill Enterprises and the Bahama Beaver Bonnet Company—"

"Who will you be doing the study for?"

"I've been asked to help out at Harvard. The study will be for foundation and government use and would be published by our university press."

"Let me talk to our people about it."

"Well"—he smiled as boyishly as Ronald Reagan—"it's worth a try."

"I'm having a little dinner party for the Secretary of Defense and a few of the justices on Thursday night. Ellsworth Carswell, an important executive with the National Gun Carriers' Association, and Wambly Keifetz, chairman of Bahama Beaver Bonnet, will be there. I'll introduce you to them, then you'll be on your own. If they like your ideas, the others will."

"You're very kind."

"My secretary will give you the address. It was so nice meeting you, Dr. Nolan."

She made a mental note to warn Keifetz in advance, if not Carswell. There was something fishy about this guy, she thought. It was almost as though someone had set up the meeting so that the man could have her physical identity clearly in mind. Contract killings started that way when the shooter was always from out-of-town. She thought of asking Barkers Hill to check him out, but she realized that his introduction had come through the Vice President's office, so he had to be entirely legitimate.

"Recheck this guy with the Veep's office," she said to her secretary through the intercom.

24

"Dearest, dolling Pupchen," Joe's letter said.

Almost three interminable years have gone by and still we are thousands of miles apart. I have talked to hundreds of people who knew my great-grandfather, dozens who have eaten his yogurt, but I have met no one who has any idea of how it was made. My father has suggested that we bring in the Sigurimi, our secret police, to widen the investigation, but I oppose this because if they thought we were that desperate to find the formula, then it would be valuable enough for them to pursue the search independently of me.

My father has remembered an old woman who stirred the milk for my great-grandfather when he made the yogurt that my aunt is so determined that I bring to the world. There is a possibility that the woman may remember the secret ingredient or ingredients which make it so remarkable. It must indeed be remarkable. My father says she is somewhere around 158 years old (people are long-lived in these mountains, I know, but that is preposterous even considering my father's great age). I keep asking myself, Is it possible that her extraordinary age is the result of eating my great-grandfather's yogurt? I grow dizzy when I consider that. I think of the hundreds of millions, even billions of dollars that such a product could earn. I think of the world's cemetery grounds laying barren because of fewer and fewer bodies available, of empty hospitals, of the president of the American Medical Association standing on a windy street corner desperately hoping to sell a few apples. I am beginning to think there are more implications here than meet the eye.

The woman lives about four thousand feet above us, to the northwest. There are no roads. I shall have to make my way on foot with a rough map my father has drawn for me. It is estimated that it will take me four days to reach her village, then my father says I must count on spending at least a week up there before I undertake the four-day return. Needless to say, there will be no letter next week. But don't let this stop you from sending your letter so that it will be here when I return.

I love you eternally. I ache to hold you. I worry night and day that so much time has gone by that you, with the great variety of your life and work, will allow me to grow dimmer and dimmer in your memory. I know I could not bear this were it to happen. I try not to think such morbid thoughts, but this is one of those days when I (almost) think that our separation isn't worth the four million–odd dollars it will bring.

Darling, sweet Schatzie:

I know that this time you are going to meet the person who has the secret of the yogurt. Then you can telegraph Mr. Wolgast from Tirana and come back here to win your inheritance. But if that remarkable old woman—I'm sorry, Joe, but I just can't believe that she can be 158 years old, no matter how old your father says she is—does have the secret of the yogurt it might be a really remarkable dietary discovery and I can't wait to try it myself. But we must keep it out of Mark Haselgrove's reach. I can't bear the idea of that monster chugging on and on until he is 158 and has swallowed all the police departments of the world.

> We are tremendously busy here. There is some sort of silly conflict going on about my Supreme Court nominee, some nonsense about his fondling a ten-year-old boy in the men's room of the 137th Street IRT station—the same old routine. Politics as usual. The President is going to lead a crusading force of American motorcycle manufacturers to Italy to put a stop to Italy's almost immoral export of Vespas—noisy, smelly machines that are too well made, which the president says constitutes unfair practice.
>
> I am making extraordinary amounts of money and I have my own share of influence in this town, I suppose, but I am not really happy about what I am doing. I have always wanted to be a schoolteacher and, some day, a principal of a school or, failing that, Secretary of Education.
>
> I bring this up because—and you've got to forgive me for this, my darling, I got so low and became so lonely that I just lost my head and married a man named Ellsworth Carswell. He was an important executive with the all-powerful National Gun Carriers' Association, a vital client of the firm, and my partners also thought it would be a good move. The marriage didn't last, of course. He was no Joe Shqitonja. There was no bigamy involved, you may be sure. We have so many lawyers in this firm that I was able to divorce you at almost no cost. It was just a formality, dearest. Now that I have divorced Ellsworth Carswell, there will be no problem, not that there ever was, to us marrying again.

Leila didn't only love children, she enjoyed children, but her ex-husband, Ellsworth Carswell, had given her a sort of venereal disease that left her barren. What might have been a boon to some other career women was a tragic loss to Leila. She wept while she was sleeping. She dreamed that she was lactating, then awoke to bitter disappointment.

Although she had divorced her husband and refused ever to see him again, except on a professional basis, she did talk to him on the telephone, charging his principal, the National Gun Carriers' Association, at her going hourly rate, because he was a key player with an important client and there could be no excuse for bringing personal matters into business.

She hated obliterating the Constitution of the United States every day of her life on behalf of the NGA, but that was the principal rationale of her work. She detested politicians (excepting her father) and continued to do what she was doing (she told herself) only because she had been raised in a Muslim family in which the father's word was law. Perhaps for more than any other reason, it was because her father had never had the chance to pass the bar examinations in Baghdad all those long years ago, again because of yet a different set of politicians. He wanted more than anything else for his daughter to be a leading American lawyer, a successful and powerful lawyer in the American way, a mover, not a scholar, an invisible power, even if Leila hadn't often had the opportunity to really practice law since she had arrived in Washington (in the sense that doctrinaire lawyers practiced law) because her work as a fixer so far overshadowed her work as a litigator.

At thirty-four, she married Ellsworth Carswell, an antihumanist and an amateur of cocaine, whom Leila felt couldn't be described without using the letter *S*: short, stocky, swarthy, salty, suspicious, shrewd, sanguinary, shallow, and a shit. Most of all, the word *cynical*, which should have been spelled with and *s*, applied to him like paint to a barn.

Carswell operated entirely within Washington, D.C., as Director of NGA's Alliance for Congressional Cooperation. He was third in line to be chief operating officer—as well as being a member of the Board of Directors of the National Gun Carriers' Association, a servant of the U.S. Constitution. He was also Director of Public Affairs for the Citizens' Committee for the Right to Shoot to Kill, and executive secretary of the Inner-City Sportsmen for Osgood Noon, which had accounted for more citizen deaths than the Korean and Vietnam wars combined.

At thirty-three, she had left public office as assistant Federal prosecutor for New York armed with the NGA sponsorship and the prestigious and profitable Barkers Hill Enterprises account. She had moved to Washington to practice lobbying and influence peddling at the mainstream law firm of Schwartz, Blacker & Moltonero, bringing with her, as well as NGA, Barkers Hill and the National Charismatic and Evangelical Confederation of Television Pulpits as clients.

In one holistic trine she defended the American right to be defrauded by organized crime, protected the right of citizens to arm themselves and thereby to drive the American homicide rate to heights beyond the imagination of the world, and guarded the public's right to worship their God, with a flick of their remote television control, without ever needing to get out of bed on Sunday morning.

By extending the membership of the National Charismatic and Evangelical Confederation of Television Pulpits to the White House and to the Congress, she had been able to guide Dr. Homer Farnsworthy, an ordained cleric and an authority on the American flag, to a crucial place at President Noon's side, insuring the safety of the flag, bringing ever-closer the realization of the hope for prayer in the schools and the repeal of the Satanic capital gains tax.

Nonetheless, all of the power that accrued to her had very little meaning. She had told her third ex-husband, early in their courting days, that she wished she could have been a schoolteacher. He had been so deeply shocked by her confession that she never mentioned it again. "A schoolteacher," he had said with revulsion. "What kind of money do you think people like that bring in?"

"It's not the money," she had protested, fighting the shame which his remark had brought her, "it's the chance to be with kids, to help them, to help to make them better people." She knew it was, along with self-respect, about the most important power anyone could have.

Little *x*'s had appeared over each of Carswell's eyes. She couldn't remember having seen anyone look so baffled. "There are good people and bad people, Leila," he said. "There are no other kind and nothing anyone can do will ever change that except that when bad people get money they become better people. I think you will agree that Ronald Reagan proved that."

Reminding herself that he was entitled to his opinion even though she could not possibly agree with him, she closed the issue within her mind. If he had not infected her reproductive system and had not taken away her meaning and her chance for peace and joyousness, she might have doomed herself by remaining his wife.

Because of the aura he had helped to bring to her, that of being the lawyer for the National Gun Carriers' Association, the most feared lobby in the nation's history, she had deluded herself into believing that he was her kind of guy, until he ripped out of her any hope of ever having a child of her own.

He was a sort of cripple, something she didn't understand until she divorced him. She knew, as long as she stayed where she was and did what she did, she would be a kind of a cripple as well. She had become convinced that the more money people had, the more confused they became because they were confronted with more choices. She plotted that some day—perhaps after her father had retired—something good must come out of her life. She knew which buttons to push. She would have her father and the law firm behind her and could set herself up with a new incoming administration and have herself made Secretary of Education.

Until that day came, she would dedicate herself to the law, a sacred calling. She knew, as every other practicing lawyer did, that as defining as being known as the lawyer for the NGA and CANCER was, her principal client, Barkers Hill Enterprises, was perhaps the most important single account with which any law firm anywhere could have been endowed. Barkers Hill, with whom her dad was closely associated, had provided her father's solution to the unfavorable publicity she had been bringing to organized crime by her too-conscientious prosecution. Barkers Hill Enterprises was the legitimate arm of organized crime in the United States, its holding company, its prodigious money laundry, its investment arm and principal fixer, its briber, and its avenger and adjudicator.

After the divorce, she acquired a big house in McLean, Virginia, where she took refuge in the impersonal presence of the mighty, where she entertained Senators and Congressmen, justices, White House aides, Hollywood political groupies, the joint chiefs and the great armaments makers, oracular Sunday television talk-show stars, and the powerful New York dressmakers. She made money, accepted dazzling presidential appointments, and became a key figure in the burgeoning American establishment, even though her mother had been a Yazidi who considered Satan a fallen angel who would one day be reconciled with God.

25

Leila was in her office at Schwartz, Blacker & Moltonero at 11:07 A.M. on a dismally wet Tuesday when she received a logged and taped telephone call from her third ex-husband. The call could not be tapped because as it was sent to the telephone number he had dialed from a telephone booth in Georgetown, the call had been shifted around at random by computer, through a series of other telephone numbers until, seemingly at random, it came through Leila Aluja's private line. If it had been possible to bug her private line, which it was not, the computer would have broken down the sounds of the telephone conversations into separate vowel and consonant divisions that could be reassembled into coherent words only by Leila's manipulation of her work station.

"Listen, hon," Carswell said, "we're gonna need a lotta help with this proposed flamethrower legislation the NGA dumped on me."

"Flamethrowers? Legislation?"

"Three of NGA's big client companies have been able to pick up a tremendous arms pile of them, so now we have to make them legal for civilian use and make them a constitutional staple in the American home."

"But, Jesus, Ellsworth—"

"What? The Pentagon is gonna unload them for three dollars a rattle, but they're gonna retail for two hundred and nine eighty-five, and are a bargain even at that price. Two million units. And it fits right into our overall strategy."

"But, Jesus, Ellsworth! Flamethrowers!"

"Not to worry. There will be an obligatory seven-day waiting period, personally endorsed by Ronald Reagan."

"I mean—can a kid operate a flamethrower?"

"Whatta you mean?"

"Suppose some child gets in the line-of-fire of one of those things? The flamethrower could incinerate it."

"For crissake, Leila!"

"Ellsworth—fahcrissake! The Federal Center for Disease Control just reported that one out of every five high school students in this country carries a weapon!"

"Ah—kids. You know kids."

"Suppose some maniac kid turned a flamethrower on a schoolyard?"

"Baby, you are talking a lotta meaningless impossibilities."

"A maniac did it with an assault rifle and the President backed him up!"

"Sure, it's possible that some kids loitering in schoolyards could get a little charred—but the greater good is the safety and protection that flamethrowers can give us by allowing each citizen, armed and ready, to defend his rights under the Constitution."

"That's a lot of crap, and you know it. A handful of farmers wrote that stuff over two hundred years ago. It doesn't make any sense today."

"Doesn't make any sense! We're talking about the American Constitution here!"

"It was 1787! They had just fought a war with a citizen army! They had no money, except what they printed! They had no police force! They were surrounded by Indians! So, in a wilderness country, they needed to have every household armed because every family had to protect itself."

"What's gotten into you? Are you denying the Constitution of the United States of America? It says all citizens have the right to keep and bear arms. You know that. It's a sacred right. Besides, the strategy part of the exercise comes out when the sportsmen of the inner cities start buying this lulu. The whole geshrei about assault rifles and handguns is bound to die down because they'll seem harmless in comparison, and the President will be vindicated for being the only one in the country, besides the NGA, who believed in making the sale of personal weapons in supermarkets possible."

"The NGA is on very shaky ground and they know it."

"Shaky? The NGA?"

"The Supreme Court has never ruled on the constitutionality of that Second Amendment crap."

"Ruled? *Ruled?* It's a part of the sacred Constitution of the United States of America!"

"Seventy-seven years after those farmers felt it necessary to put in that amendment, the Fourteenth Amendment was added. It says—and every American should know it by heart—'No State shall make or enforce any law which shall abridge the privileges or immunities of citizens of the United States; nor shall any State deprive any person of life, liberty or property without due process of law; nor deny to any person within its jurisdiction the equal protection of the laws.' "

"What the hell does that mean?"

"It means that someday somebody is going to sue the NGA for conspiracy to murder and when the case is taken to the Supreme Court, the Fourteenth Amendment will force the court to rule against the NGA."

"Holy shit, Leila! Please! Don't mention that to anybody else!"

"Which brings us to these barbaric flamethrowers."

"Why do you think our three biggest gun manufacturers are willing to take the heat on this? They knew that flamethrowers—because of their smell, a very heavy gasoline smell—will be just a passing fad, but shotguns and assault rifles, where the year-in, year-out profit is, are forever."

Because he did so much cocaine, his sentences came out as rapid bursts, through his clotted nasal passages, as if strings of Chinese firecrackers were igniting and exploding throughout his adenoids, alarming the immediate neighborhood, which included his brain.

She sighed. "Okay, Ellsworth, what do you want?" She felt a numbing coldness forming deep in her stomach. She was overcome with an even greater distaste for Ellsworth Carswell than she had ever noticed before. She peered around corners of the future to seek on-rushing justice which, as it must to all men, sooner or later, would overtake this pointless creep and his murderous organization.

"We need a law passed in this session of Congress which will define flamethrowers as recreational weapons and allow their sale in supermarkets and gas stations."

"That's going to cost a lot of money."

"You provide the footwork, we'll provide the clout. Listen, Big Oil is behind this all the way. Flamethrowers use a lotta gasoline."

"Carswell, this is the craziest idea the NGA has ever had."

"Baby! This is an A-one priority! We've lost 527,000 members in the past two years! This will bring them back! Flamethrowers are the novelty weapons which will get people interested in defending the American home again! There are people out there who would shred the Constitution even as we are talking here, if they could get handguns and assault rifles outlawed! Then what? Where would law and order be? What are the American people gonna use to defend themselves? The ACLU? What happens to profits?" She could hear him scratching his Bulgarian radish-grower's mustache on the telephone, as he did whenever he was excited.

26

The midnight gala for the "Kurds for Saddam" movement, held in the reception rooms of the Department of State, had been organized at President Noon's suggestion to allay the suffering of a brutalized people and yet not interfere in the internal affairs of Iraq, which would have been completely forbidden due to intense presidential morality ever since Noon had wiped out the infrastructure of the country but had allowed Saddam to carry on.

The gala was attended by the cream of Washington's power establishment. Beauties of both sexes had been flown in from Hollywood. The great dressmakers had been trucked in from New York. The policy makers of the American meaning were assembled for a cause which was close to the President's heart. All the people who really mattered were there, dressed to the nines, jostling each other to stand on the left side of photographs.

A slate of great regional American chefs had contributed a buffet menu of authentic Kurdish dishes: ravioli filled with goose liver and duck meat and tossed in a melted sage-butter sauce, paper-thin *bresaola* with a cluster of shiitake mushrooms and greens. The dishes were served on brightly burnished brass plates in a room that oozed power and elegance. The state reception rooms were more elegant, in a rich, understated way, than anything at Versailles or, for that matter, in any Cecil B. DeMille production.

Wearing a recreation of one of Mme. Vionnet's 1930 black velvet evening dresses having a twelve-inch white ermine hem that fell as straight as a Doric column when she was not in motion, Leila's big hair fell down to her shoulders, framing her face. She had arrived at

11:45 P.M. and found herself staring across the great, crowded room to see her third ex-husband entering, causing her to gag. She whirled away and blindly joined the line at one of the buffet tables and, within seconds, she was followed in the line by Dr. Jim Nolan.

Her eyes went blank when he greeted her by name, so he reintroduced himself.

"I'm the man Vice President Hazman sent to you for an introduction to the NGA and Barkers Hill Enterprises."

"Oh! Yes!"

"Jim Nolan."

Of course. *Doctor* Nolan."

He was taller than she was, which was always good, she thought. Carswell had been shorter and she had never been comfortable with that, except in bed. Dr. Nolan had good color, good hair, nice teeth, and if she could get used to looking at a man whose clothes expounded a walk-up-a-flight-and-save-ten-dollars philosophy instead of having been cut by one of those awesome English tailors who appeared at Barney's, as advertised, twice a year, she thought she could agree that they set off his very, very masculine frame very, very well. He was tall, but not gangly, she decided. She rather liked his sandy, off-blond hair, which was surprising she thought because usually she detested blond men, not that he was blond, just blondish. He had the admirable body-type usually associated with athletes. The peripheral cross-reference to the words *sexual athlete* flashed across her consciousness, but she wasn't having any of that.

Still, she thought, it had been a long time since she had taken a man to bed, or had been taken there. Joe had become just a vague memory of happy times gone forever unless he really cranked up that yogurt swindle and got paid off by his aunt's estate. It had been easy to abstain as much as she had because every time she had as much as a thought about sex, she would be stricken with the loathsome memory of Ellsworth Carswell, making her retch reflexively. However, contemplating the abstract idea of having sex with this pleasant man did not make her want to vomit. Quite the contrary.

"Do you like walnut cake?" she blurted.

"Yes. Indeed, I do. May I get you some?"

"No, no. I was just asking." Her personal chef, a Mme. de Caunteton, who traveled with Leila whenever she shifted base, whether from McLean or to Monaco or to New York, made the most fault-free walnut cake in the (known) world.

Leila put a spoonful of larks'-tongue pâté on her plate. "How did you get on with Keifetz and Carswell?"

"We had very pleasant chats. They were quite courteous, actually, but they told me, because of the unrest in Iraq, you know, the war, that their people were extremely busy right now. They felt it would be a quick war, however, and asked me to call them in the spring."

"Ah. Too bad," Leila said, inhaling his male odors.

Dr. Nolan helped himself to some creamed cappelletti with a Gruyère sauce in slices of truffle, placing it beside the chrysanthemum salad on his plate. Everything served, the White House press release had said, could have been cooked and served in the tents of Kurdistan . . .

Leila put a small helping of haggis and another tasting of larks'-tongue pâté on her plate. "What is that?" she asked, watching Dr. Nolan continuing to serve himself.

"I think it's a sort of rabbit pie with a little pickled lamb thrown in. Very nice. It must be a national dish. Shall we find a place to sit?"

She decided (for the third time) that he was rather good-looking. She also had the impression that he really couldn't be making any kind of living at all because he had admitted that he had attended these freeloading affairs before and she had never seen such a heaped-up plate.

They found places to sit against a far wall. An out-of-sight orchestra was playing dance music.

"Jim is an unusual name," she said.

"I suppose so. It's sort of a family name. Its meaning is much disputed. The original meaning of the name in Hebrew is 'seized by the heel.' " He shrugged. "Perhaps we're birds of a feather. Leila is an unusual name."

"It's Persian. Originally."

"Byron used it in *The Gilaour*, didn't he? You have sort of a Persian look. I suppose you're of Sicilian descent."

"Guess again."

"You're not Arabic?"

"Entirely. Tell me—with this research you're doing—are you in the political science department at Harvard?"

"Not actually. My basic discipline—it's sort of abstruse—" Dr. Nolan managed to talk and eat at the same time, as daintily as plates-on-the-lap call for, but somehow he had scoffed the whole huge plateful down before her eyes in the short time they had been talking. Leila was a consecrated gourmet (in a controlled, dietetic way), so she loved to see men eat. She knew Mme. Caunteton had baked a *karithopita*, a Greek walnut cake, that very morning. She was beginning to think it might be nice if she invited this fine-looking man home with her beforc it got too late—in more ways than one.

"I'm a mitochondrial geneticist." Dr. Nolan said. "You know, DNA and all that stuff."

"No. Really? What is that?"

"Oh, well," he said helplessly, "the fact is, all human life did arise from one common ancestor—a woman who lived in sub-Saharan Africa about two hundred thousand years ago."

"But that's absolutely fascinating!"

"She was tracked down by mitochondrial DNA. The pattern of one person's DNA is unique, but it can be compared with the DNA of others, dead and alive, making it possible to construct genealogical trees through unbroken chains of mothers back to the mother of us all."

"But—Africa? My father always told us that the Garden of Eden had been in Iraq."

"That's what the paleoanthropologists used to say, based on old bones and flaked flints and shards of pottery, because of folklore like the Bible, and because the Middle East forms a bridge between Africa and Asia. But the one reason that they were never able to prove that particular Garden of Eden siting is that paleontologists have not been able to devise a comprehensive and universally acceptable code for what constitutes a modern human, while the mitochondrial geneticists most certainly have."

"If you really do like walnut cake, I baked one this morning. And I have some rousing Ethiopian coffee to go with it."

"Cake?"

"At my house. Just over the Chain Bridge."

"Well! I *love* walnut cake."

27

At 10:17 P.M., just less than twenty minutes before the start of the Department of State reception, Freeman "Butch" Owlsley, CEO of the National Gun Carriers' Association, watchdog of American Constitutional rights (Second Amendment), was shot to death with his two bodyguards, Alvin M. Myrtle and Jonas Freistein, as thcy were descending from the doorway of a discriminating Washington brothel in the northwestern section of the city. Reflexively, the police, because the brothel had been on the Pad for so long, protected the public from the knowledge of where Mr. Owlsley had spent the evening or that he was an ardent S&M enthusiast.

Butch Owlsley had led the NGA to its greatest expansion in membership. Under his leadership, the organization's influence with elected officials had also soared, to the dismay of gun-control advocates and the families of people who had died from gunshot wounds. Butch Owlsley had held sixty-eight national shooting records with pistol, military rifle, small-bore rifle, shotgun, automatic weapons, derringers, and small cannon. He was one of the seven civilians since the Revolutionary War who had received a special Army award for marksmanship. He had joined the NGA as a junior member at the age of ten. In a quarrel with schoolmates when he was fourteen, he shot three classmates to death and was convicted of murder, but the verdict was overturned by a higher court which ruled that the trial judge's jury instructions had been incomplete. However, when young Owlsley testified on his own behalf, he said something that was in direct opposition to the mantra of the NGA. He was to regret bitterly his comments for the rest of his life. He apologized eloquently later in his autobiography *Guns Don't Kill People*. Shamefaced, in an agony of self-recrimination, he admitted that, in order to avoid execution, he had said, "I didn't kill those boys. Them guns killed 'em."

Butch Owlsley was affectionately known as "Mr. NGA."

Immediately following the tragedy (Owlsley and his two bodyguards had left three wives, five mistresses, and sixteen children among them), the news media, blacked out until they could get their bearings, were forced to observe the tactful oversights by the police for almost two hours.

When the ugly background of the story broke, the public shuddered in revulsion, wishing it could afford to hang out in such an elegant knocking shop even if there were obvious risks, but, nonetheless, they almost buckled under the encroaching anxiety of whether the odd circumstances of the Owlsley murders could threaten their rights under the Second Amendment to the Constitution, and whether the National Gun Carriers' Association's tradition could be sustained to protect them.

The weapon that had destroyed the three men was a sportsman's favorite: the mighty Ithaca Mag-10 Roadblocker. Chambered for disastrously powerful 10-gauge cartridges, the automatic shotgun had a rubber butt and a pad for the shooter's added comfort. It had delivered three rounds of projectiles, which would have had sufficient force to ventilate the body of an armored personnel carrier and create terrible carnage upon the people inside.

Mr. Owlsley's head and his left arm had been blown off. The torsos of the two bodyguards had been separated from their hips by the force of the two hits. The requisite television shots of shrouded bodies being rolled on gurneys into ambulances were shown, making it seem as if the three men had merely dropped off to sleep. The murder weapon, a favorite of enthusiasts everywhere, had been flung on top of the badly ruined bodies that had been scattered as if unpackaged chunks of meat, all across the stone steps leading into the building. The killer had tossed a sealed envelope on top of these scraps. It contained a single message: "People don't kill people. Guns kills people."

A massive outcry seemed to wail across the nation wherever sportsmen and gun lovers gathered, a scream of anguish that made

King Lear's cry of agony seem like a chuckle. The head shooter of the American people had been shot to death with one of the guns that he had insisted were every American's right to shoot. All reason was topsy-turvy. A world of order and tranquility, except for the persistent sound of gunfire in all American cities, had been stood upon its head.

An emergency NGA board meeting was called for 4:15 P.M. the following afternoon to dam up any negative responses to the Owlsley shooting, such as public confusion over whether the biter had been bit. But, before the meeting could be convened, the crazed killer, relentlessly defying all logic, struck again.

28

Dr. Nolan *did* love walnut cake. He ate almost all of it, excepting about two slices. Leila had reached the point where she was considering telling him that she thought she might slip into something more comfortable, because she felt she had to do *some*thing to get him away from the cake. She started wondering just why she had yanked him away from that reception and had brought him all the way out to Virginia when the goddamn telephone rang—her hot line, her altogether private telephone—so she had to excuse herself and leave him with the rest of the walnut cake to find out that it was her loathsome third ex-husband calling.

"For crissake, Fletch!" she screeched into the phone. "It's twelve-fifty in the morning!"

"Leila, listen. I'm sorry. Listen. Somebody shot Butch Owlsley and blew his head off."

"*Whaaaaaaaat?*" She went cool and lawyerly. The sexual ambitions that had been building over the past hour were gone. She was instantly desexed. The NGA paid Schwartz, Blacker & Moltonero a retainer of a million and a half a year plus. Duty came before any conjectural chance at copulation.

"Wait!" Carswell said. "Whoever did it also killed Butch's two bodyguards, then left a note."

"A note?"

"It said: 'People don't kill people. Guns kill people.' "

"Holy *shit*!" she exploded. "That's a deliberate perversion of the NGA's byword, its central canon, its apothegm, its words to live by!"

"It makes you want to throw up. So whatta we gonna do?"

Leila paid out her counsel like so many ice cubes.

"Call an emergency board meeting for tomorrow afternoon," she said. "Demand that Goodie Noon call out every government investigative agency—the FBI, the CIA, the DIA, the SEC, the IRS, the FDIA, DEA, and the U.S. Customs Service—this is obviously the work of a drug-crazed madman—invoke the investigative arm of the postal service, the District of Columbia police department, and make a public plea that the cities of over one million population, from Canada to Mexico City, send in to Washington a token force of their best investigators so that the fiend who gunned down Butch Owlsley and his two goons may be run to earth. Are you writing all this down, Fletch?"

"Yes. Yes, I am."

"The country can't be allowed to look at this as any ordinary murder, some little knockoff with a Saturday night special. What gun did they use, by the way?"

"An Ithaca Mag-10 Roadblocker."

"My God! Even Butch wouldn't have wanted to be hit with a thing like that!"

"It's a real son-of-a-bitch of a weapon," Carswell said admiringly.

"Butch Owlsley stood for the Second Amendment to the Bill of Rights of the American Constitution!" Leila barked, her sense of duty overcoming a feeling of revulsion. "For the sake of everything this country stands for, you've got to have this city crawling with cops wherever civilized people gather because this murder strikes at the core of the American meaning, equal rights for every citizen under existing and unwritten gun laws."

"You're right. My God, this wasn't just a man, a human being, who was shot to death; this was a symbol of law and order throughout the land."

"Yes! Now—tell Goodie Noon that you want what's left of Butch Owlsley's body laid out in a sealed casket in the rotunda of the Capitol. Send telegrams to every branch office of the NGA, all fifty-four of them throughout the United States and Canada, telling them to pour the memberships into Washington by plane, train, car, and bus to form a thirty-six-hour vigil in an endless procession around that casket, while the television cameras turn, paying tribute to the man who gave his life so that they might continue to shoot off guns, reminding America of the meaning of what it could lose."

"That's beautiful, Leila. Utterly, utterly beautiful."

"Now—have the board authorize the transfer of five million into the NGA's lobbying war chest, then, while our people see that word is spread all over the Hill, I want you to reintroduce the betrayal resolution into the minutes of the board meeting, and our people will see to it that all of this gets to every individual Congressman and Senator."

"Five million—betrayal resolution," Carswell muttered into the phone as he scribbled the notes.

"Have the board vote the posting of a reward of one hundred thousand dollars for information leading to the arrest and conviction, et cetera. Demand that the House of Representatives appropriate an equal amount and see that the White House puts Osgood Noon on every news show tomorrow, on or off the golf course, responding to the outrageousness of this revolting, rotten crime. Do you have that?"

"Yes, Leila." He was overwhelmed by her dedication. He knew she *hated* the NGA and everything it stood for and yet, because she had taken the lawyers' equivalent of the Hippocratic oath, although he had certainly never heard of any even remotely equivalent oath for a lawyer, or maybe because she had accepted NGA money or maybe for some tilted reason she felt she was required to earn the money, she was taking this problem on as if it had happened to a member of her family. She was an exemplary woman and he had lost her. He loved her as he had never loved anyone else, not even his dog, Captain, way back before the world had closed in on him.

"All right," Leila said rapidly. "You've got to beef up the NGA's PACs—especially that juicy Congressional Victory Fund—with at least five million dollars so that it can be spread around the House and the Senate so that the lunatic antihandgun lobby can't try to exploit Butch's shooting and that goddamn note to their advantage. Allocate not less than ten thousand dollars per each member of record per year as direct financial support."

"Got it."

"Have Goodie Noon call all five living Republican past-presidents to an emergency conference at the White House tomorrow morning—Nixon, Ford, both Reagans, and Bush—fly them in on Stealth bombers, covered by the networks, Nixon from Central China; the two former co-Presidents, Ron and Nancy, from California; Jerry Ford from the Pebble Beach golf course; and George Bush from his permanent chili cookout somewhere in Texas. Get them to Washington for a massive joint press conference with Goodie Noon from the newsroom of the White House in time for every morning talk show at 8 A.M., making sure that every one of them repeats the proper, official slogan over and over again that 'Guns don't kill people. People kill people.' The entire credibility of the National Gun Carriers' Association is at stake."

By God, Carswell though, he had to find a way to see that she got credit for all of this. He had burst into her mind with a problem out of left field and she had responded as Hank Cinq had on St. Crispin's Day—more than that—the way Herodotus—or was it Cincinnatus—or maybe Winkelreid—whoever had taken all those spears in the gut at some bridge somewhere so that his people might be free. Whoever or whatever, she was his heroine. And he had lost her.

"I feel very humble, Leila," he said. "You have saved the NGA because you can think on your feet. You're a day saver and a life saver."

"Go!" she bugled into the phone. "Preserve the Second Amendment! Save your country!"

She hung up the phone, filled with excitement, pride, and self-loathing, and wondered what she was going to do about Jim Nolan.

She was almost beside herself with elation. This could be the end of the NGA! She could be less one more client on her way out to becoming a schoolteacher.

Dr. Nolan was standing in the doorway as Leila turned away from the telephone. "You were brilliant," he said. "You would have made a great general of the armies."

For whatever reason, and there were many of them, Leila burst into tears. Dr. Nolan moved across the room and, very carefully, put his arms around her, resting her head on his shoulder and stroking her hair gently. "Whatever it is that has happened," he said, "it has been a terrible shock to you. There is no better cure than a good cry."

"Oh, Jim!" she sobbed. She turned her tear-stained face upward to stare into his eyes, with a rough approximation of Nancy Reagan's helplessly adoring gaze whenever she looked at her man. No living male could have resisted the abject defenselessness of that appeal. Dr. Nolan embraced her, grasping her with one hand in the area of her crotch, and kissed her with the consecration of a man who has far, far more dedicated things in mind.

Dr. Nolan was a tiger in the sheets. Leila had never experienced (nor had she expected) stamina like this from an academic. The entire bed was damp with passion when her preset alarm clock began ringing at 6:30 A.M. They had been at it for four hours! As she pulled herself away from him, struggling feebly to get herself disentangled from his arms, his legs, and the sticky sheets, he became aroused again. Chaotic emotions and sensations between down-to-earth exhaustion and up-to-heaven ecstasy manipulated her like a cosmic yo-yo all over again until, for a number of times which had gone beyond her counting, she went off again like a jaguar in heat.

Before their carnal enshrinement had passed as much as a halfway mark, Leila told Nolan everything: of the acrimony that had resulted from her marriage, the tragedy of lost motherhood, and of her bitter anguish over her role in life.

"But," Dr. Nolan remonstrated with her, "why? You are one of the great figures in Washington life, a key lawyer-lobbyist. You are the friend of presidents, you represent the mighty movers of the destiny of this country."

"If you only knew," she moaned. "Did you ever hear anyone in the gun or tobacco business say out loud that's what they did for a living? I have clients in the Mafia who are prouder and more open about selling cocaine."

"But, you have power, money—"

"What does it *mean*? I wanted to be a schoolteacher. I wanted to have children of my own. That's what real power is."

"You will. It's not too late. You will."

Her despair exploded within her. She clung to him, sobbing and trying to talk while he stroked her back and tried to pat the grief gently out of her. "I can never have children," she said. "He infected me with one of those loathsome diseases and before I knew what had happened to me, he had robbed me of everything—everything!"

Leila had followed ambition for most of her life. In one aberrant moment she had succumbed to womanly feelings. She had been fond of Ellsworth Carswell during their courtship and the early days of their marriage before he had given her the clap, but essentially—and she accepted this wholeheartedly—she was marrying a powerful client when she married him. The NGA was the most powerful force in the nation, next to Political Action Committees. Her law partners had been encouraging when she had talked over the possibility with them at the regular Monday meeting.

"He's third man on the NGA pole now," F. X. O'Connell said. "Someday—with the love of a good lawyer—he could be top man."

Jim Nolan was something else. She loved him. She was so completely absorbed in him, his life, and his work that she knew, deep, deep down inside herself, that after she had made just five million dollars more, she would quit the Washington rat race and go off with Jim to qualify for her teaching certificate, then pull a few strings at the White House to get herself placed in a clean little school filled with clean, pretty, adorable kids and, well, let the other guy knock himself out.

"This is your life, Leila Aluja," she told herself on a very private tape recording that she kept in her wall safe at home and that she played back mistily after Jim had brought her home, night after night, following their long talks about the past and the future so that he would know the kind of a woman he was getting. "So make it perfect. Live it with the man you love, doing the things you were meant to do."

29

At 12:07 P.M. on the day following Freeman Owlsley's assassination, an unknown assailant shot and killed the wife and two children of the executive vice president of the National Gun Carriers' Association, Mrs. Jerrold Brownlee and her twin sons, Timothy and Raymond, aged seven. They had been crossing the playground of the Gareth T. Orchard Day School in Alexandria, Virginia, en route to the family automobile, when they were taken out with a Winchester bolt-action hunting rifle using the popular sportsman's "elephant" cartridge, the .458 Magnum that was capable, to every hunter's delight, of achieving a velocity of 2,040 feet per second, generating some 4,620 foot-pounds of energy. The weapon had been thrown on top of the badly fragmentized bodies.

Alexandria police lieutenant Jacob "Jack" Ramen told the news media that he had not realized how much devastating carnage such sporting weapons could deliver. "Jesus," he told the evening news cameras, "if anybody ever shot a deer or a peasant with one of these things, there wouldn't be anything left."

The police and the news media instantly linked the killings of Mrs. Brownlee and her sons to the murders of Freeman Owlsley, late chief executive director of the National Gun Carriers' Association, and his bodyguards, because the same typed message accompanied each of the homicides: "People don't kill people. Guns kill people." Regarding the terrible crimes, officials of the NGA were baffled as to any possible motivation other than the enforced conviction that the killer was "some kind of crazy antigun nut."

Boyishly and enthusiastically, his mouth curling upward toward the right side of his face, President Osgood Noon stated at his daily press conference for the print media, as well as at his daily press conference with the electronic press, then at his biweekly press conference with the secondary school/grammar school press, followed by the daily conference with the shopping news media which came on the heels of his press conference with the religious press, "This may be the work of some kind of a crazy antigun nut. And I'll tell you another thing, this kind of antigun monkey business has got to stop. I don't like it one bit. It is a violation of the Constitution of the United States and I'm here to tell you that it will not stand."

Goodie Noon ordered FBI Director Clement W. Farnsley to take personal charge of the case and to make his reports directly to the President "until you have this heinous killer treed and hog-tied in a corner without a leg to stand on."

In a closed-circuit address organized by White House aides to reassure Riflemen of America, a subsidiary of the NGA and a sportman's organization that had been fighting tooth-and-nail against the dangerous, lunatic activists who were trying to ban handguns, the president said plaintively, "For gosh sakes, where will this nut strike next?" Then he drove off in his $600,000 powerboat for some "President in action" television coverage.

In his confidential orders to the FBI chief, delivered at the foot of the gangway to the Marine Corps helicopter that was about to take the President and Mrs. Noon to Camp David for the traditional five-day weekend, Osgood Noon said shrewdly, "Listen—we could be looking straight at the eternal triangle here. Don't overlook that. Wife of the executive veep and the head honcho of the whole schmear was shot. What? Could the killer be the husband? Don't overlook that. Don't see how there can be any other reason for these killings."

"A great angle, Mr. President."

The instant, official media (and public) linking of the murders to the National Gun Carriers' Association itself (in one way or another) was a curious one because, above all the consciences in America, the NGA had given more support to the Second Amendment to the Constitution of the United States than any other public or private entity in the nation's history.

30

In 1992, the NGA had revenues of $97,933,893. To defend the Second Amendment of the U.S. Constitution, its Alliance for Congressional Cooperation (ACC) had spent $27,732,302, and various educational committees within its body had spent $31,930,442 on its public relations effort to generate a universal understanding of its patriotic aims.

The heart, soul, core, gall, balls, and greed of the NGA was in ACC. Nearly 125 antigun bills had been proposed in Congress in 1992. The ACC had organized the Congressional Victory Fund (CVF), one of the most successful Chinese boxes of PACs within PACs that had ever been crafted. PACs, or Political Action Committees, had been invented by the U.S. Congress so that it could be bribed legally, and no institution or organization had rushed in to bribe the legislators with more efficiency than the NCA's ACC. The PACs formed by the Congressional Victory Fund totaled $16,938,007 in 1992 and were used vigorously on behalf of friends of the NGA or against enemies of the second Amendment of the Constitution.

Each year the Alliance for Congressional Cooperation generated more than two million letters to Capitol Hill, so that the legislature could point to reasons for justification of its bland issuance of license to murder, and raised more than $7 million to pay for that justification. Over 14.3 million pieces of legislative, political, and informational mailings were produced by the ACC, comprising 3,170 different mailings sent to state associations and clubs, Mafia families, newspapers, firearms dealers, and state legislators. The mailings included letters, postcards, mailgrams, computer calls, bumper stickers, and phone banks.

The central meaning of the NGA was that 2,653,861 dues-paying gun carriers had taken total control over whether 249,000,000 people could be shot to death as they strolled through their cities and towns, although the Supreme Court had never ruled that the Constitution protects the unfettered right of citizens to own, aim, and shoot guns at other citizens. The gun carriers' movement was dedicated to the death of living things—birds of the air, beasts of the field, and people—provided that these were accomplished through the use of firearms.

At the emergency meeting of the NGA Board of Directors, held in the long, wide boardroom at NGA national headquarters, which could be converted instantly into a shooting gallery for target practice by members of the executive staff, Ellsworth Carswell was elected as executive director and CEO of the entire gun-carrying national crusade. The man who would normally have been next in line for the job, E. Jerrold Brownlee, had shot himself to death using a Colt .45-caliber revolver through which he had discharged an elongated version of the obsolete .44 Russian cartridge; together they made up for in bulk what they lacked in velocity, delivering 310 foot-pounds of energy. Brownlee had explained the reasons for his choice of weapon and cartridge in his farewell note (so that the details could be included in the association's weekly newsletter), which had stated, otherwise, that he did not wish to live on without his wife and children and that he felt that their violent deaths by gunfire had proved that he had wasted his life.

The letter was destroyed on the spot after it had been read aloud to the assembled Board of Directors with a great deal of distaste.

The emergency board meeting was opened by Carswell (after he had had the chance to snort three lines of Colombian vegetable matter in the john), with an expression of thanks to Leila Aluja of Schwartz, Blacker & Moltonero for her advice and counsel. The board voted its gratitude in the form of passing a resolution to award Ms. Aluja with a Georgie, the silver, pearl-handled service revolver, which was the NGA's highest Award of Merit, named for

General George S. Patton, a man who had gone to bed every night fully armed.

"That these tragedies should have happened on the eve of our annual convention and shoot-out at Valley Forge is almost more than I can bear," Carswell said. "It will be hard times for all of us to sit on that platform and face the membership without the inspiration of Butch Owlsley and Jerry Brownlee leading us. May I ask you to stand for thirty seconds of silent prayer for the rest of the souls of those two great men?"

The directors got to their feet, clasping their hands before themselves and bowing their heads. The more patriotic among them wept. It was one of those unforgettable moments for network television, Ellsworth Carswell thought, mentally kicking himself for not having activated a hidden camera in the room.

When the memory-moment had passed and the men and Leila had taken their seats again around the great table, it was agreed that a petition would be presented to the mayor of the District of Columbia to drape all street lampposts with black crepe in mourning for the fallen NGA leaders. The board immediately carried the motion, but modified it to command its two million–odd members to telegraph President Noon at the White House to issue a proclamation that would provide for the mourning decoration of all street lamps in every city of more than twenty thousand in population.

"It is not just that Butch and Jerry and Jerry's wonderful little spouse and kiddies have been blown away," said Gunther Bamborg, representative of the largest machine gun–producing entity in the nation, and a supplier of arms to 113 dependent nations, "but it's that goddamn letter the killer left behind. If people start taking it seriously that guns kill people, we could have a real crisis on our hands. We got to snow public opinion for eight feet over their heads, so let's start with proper mourning for Butch."

"What did I tell you?" President Noon said to his FBI chief via satellite telephone between Camp David and Washington. "It's *cherchez la femme* every time. Husband killed wife and her lover. Terrible measure to have to take, but so are wars. Case closed."

"A great angle, Mr. President."

"It's a wrap-up. And although it's a terrible, terrible thing, thank

God it takes the onus off gun-loving Americans who shoot to preserve our Constitution." As always, the President had it wrong, or at least, skewed. The NGA, pinned down under the weight of the two notes that had pointed to the possibility of guns having the ability to kill people, as well as the bleak admissions in the suicide note left by its executive vice president, faced the worst crisis of its long, profitable existence.

Dramatically, Ellsworth Carswell reintroduced the "betrayal" resolution and pushed it through to a unanimous vote for the third time in two years, a key statement of intent that warned every American politician (and turned each individual's blood to lumpy turds) then in office and all who would follow them in office as follows: *"The membership of the National Gun Carriers' Association . . . pledges that we shall not soon forgive and shall never forget the betrayals of those politicians who once sought our support and who will need it again."*

"We must triple our threats to politicians," Carswell told the assembled board. "They have to be reminded constantly that we know who our friends are. And, of course, spread some money around."

"Some of them may snap under the strain," Big Slim Fonseca, a director who had once loaded George Bush's shotguns in East Texas said. "They are swaying and dizzy under the threats we lay on them as it is."

"Big deal," Carswell sneered. "Did you ever hear of one of them turning down the cash?"

The amount of five million dollars was transferred to the NGA's lobbying war chest, targeted directly at the goal of dispelling linkages the Congress might have assumed to exist between the heinous murders and the crazed notes that had been left behind, which had indicated, in their insane way, that guns had had something to do with the deaths of NGA leaders of the NGA and their families.

"Someone is trying on some kind of sick irony," Carswell said, "hoping to make a connection between the untimely deaths of these dear people and our nation's legal right to bear arms."

"Still," Angelo Partanna, the Mafia's representative on the

board, who was known as The Grandfather of Practical Pistol Shooting said, "if there is a connection, this nut could try to hit you next."

"I am armed," Ellsworth Carswell said courageously.

"There was nobody who moved around this city who was more armed than Butch Owlsley," Partanna said. "He wore two ankle holsters, two crotch holsters, a small-of-the-back pistol, two sleeve derringers, and a forty-five automatic tucked into his waistband, and so did his two bodyguards. But still somebody blew him away."

Immediately, funds were voted for round-the-clock protection of Carswell and other executive officers. The director who owned *The Mercenary Soldier,* one of the nation's most popular weekly magazines, said he would round up a crew of armed bodyguards before the meeting had concluded; he was as good as his word.

As the protection took effect, Ellsworth Carswell, intimidated by the unwholesome mien of the eight men in his guard, summoned them to his outer office and laid down the law. "First, you men are going to have to agree to bathe and shave not less than twice a week and you are going to have to use a strong masculine deodorant. Remember, you now represent the NGA. Second, you are going to have to clean up your language. Obscenities give guns a bad name. Third, you will all go out right now and buy blue serge suits, white shirts, and black ties. The National Gun Carriers' Association is not a gypsy camp."

31

Somehow Ellsworth Carswell got through the day. He listened to the last anxiety-ridden officer of the NGA wailing into his face, checked his personal weapons before he went out into the street, summoned his cleaned-up bodyguards, then went home to his apartment. After he had taken a shower, he looked inside the refrigerator and the larder and then went out shopping. After one trip with them, he decided he couldn't stand to have bodyguards hulking around him wherever he went. He felt like an idiot walking along the aisles of the supermarket with eight lumpy men standing around while he peered in at the labels on the frozen vegetables. He was sure he had caught one of them smirking when he put three packages of Bird's Eye yellow squash into the shopping cart, the fucking carnivore.

He decided to have them transferred to guard the body of his new second in command, reassigned to Washington from the Houston office, Benito Juarez Bennett, who was said to be able to sign his name on a plaster wall with bullets from two Smith & Wesson Model 659s shot simultaneously with left and right hands, and which packed fourteen 9mm rounds into their staggered-line box magazines. For fancy wall designs, such as Valentine hearts, the American Flag, or Mother's Day symbols, Bennett shot with an Israeli Desert Eagle automatic, chambered in .44 Magnum, truly a gun for serious handgun enthusiasts. It measured 10.25 inches overall, Ellsworth thought with admiration, weighed 3.75 pounds when empty, and fed a 7-round magazine.

It was odd how those things developed, he mused. Benito Bennett was flashy with handguns (he was a graduate of the American Pistol Institute at Paulden, Arizona, and the Northeast Pistol Institute at Union, New Jersey, and earned a doctorate at the Lethal Force Institute of Concord, New Hampshire), but he was really only a so-so shot with assault rifles, the sportsman's friend, such as the Armalite, or even the Czech Vz.58, which doubled the AK-47's rate of fire.

Bennett was going to have to shape up, Ellsworth thought, if he expected to survive as NGA's regional director for the Washington area. Handguns were all right for crack dealers and pimps, but NGA men were expected to pull their weight with shotguns and rifles, laser sights or no laser sights.

It had been a wistful kind of a day. Ellsworth had taken over the leadership of a great American institution after having had such a long, and, in a way, intimate kind of a talk with his ex-wife, then passing on her leadership principles to the board as his own. And now he had a future of doing coke until he died and making the world safe for people who desperately wanted to shoot guns at any living thing as long as he and the NGA could assure them that the means to murder were legal under a Constitutional tradition, as the NGA had interpreted it.

Ellsworth hadn't always done coke. After he had married Leila, well, he felt stupid. He had never been what people might have called keen-minded and, what with the insomnia brought on by worrying all the time about keeping up with his wife intellectually—or maybe *mentally* was the better word—and trying to clear up his general fuzzymindedness, he had tried cocaine. It had helped him. He was much more alert, perhaps even overalert, doubling his insomnia, and he had been driven to feeling he needed to practice sex—the movements and positions, the gargles and the mewings, all the attitudes that he hadn't really ever been able to figure out, compared to the kind of sex that people were delivering all the time in hard-porn movies, which he rented and ran early in the morning when he couldn't sleep but when Leila was ticking off her eight and a half hours. To have the feeling that he was really pleasuring his beautiful wife, whom he loved beyond even his own belief, he got started on learning advanced sex techniques by reading sex manuals, then practicing on hookers and—Jesus!—one of them had given him the clap; he hadn't had any idea that he had such a loathsome thing when he passed it on to his sweet, wonderful wife, who then banished him from her life forever.

He had just stumbled across the calendar since then. He thought about her constantly, obsessively. He did his work mechanically and he knew by the tone of Leila's voice over the telephone in the course of their daily business conversations, as much by what she said to him as how she said it, that she had a loathing for the National Gun Carriers' Association and everything it stood for.

"What can a gun do except maim or kill?" she had told him over and over again. "Its only reason for being is to convey a deadly projectile along a long or shorter tube so that it will rip and tear and destroy whatever the living thing at which it is aimed. How can we justify such things? Going into the twenty-first century, can anybody possibly say with a straight face that we have to shoot the animals we eat? Or the vegetables? How can the President of the United States, over and over and over again, repeat the same ridiculous nonsense that we must defend the archaic Second Amendment to the Constitution when it means that living things are going to be killed or crippled? Why, fahcrissake, do I have to be the lawyer for American guns and cigarettes, the two things internationally that kill more people than do wars?"

He had tried to reason with her, pointing to the amounts of money that guns and cigarettes were contributing to their little family's earnings, but she was disconsolate.

Considering that the NGA was paying him $292,000 a year and expenses, Ellsworth had simply refused to listen to her. But, after she had banished him from her life, he began to see more and more how important the matter was to her. He could understand why she had to continue to defend the NGA professionally while it defended guns because her end of the deal was somewhere around $480,000 a year plus expenses (and from cigarettes $610,000 a year plus expenses).

It was a very, very American dilemma. Her hands had been tied; now that he had lost her, he decided he had to do something about freeing her from her bondage. He wanted more than anything in life to please her, and the only way he could see to make her happy—indirectly and without any hope of allowing her to acknowledge her gratitude to him—would be to destroy the NGA. So he had murdered Butch Owlsley, following with the shooting of Mrs. Brownlee and her two boys in the classical NGA setting of an American schoolyard.

The Owlsley job had been easy. Nobody would miss Butch. The two bodyguards, after all, had to accept risks as part of their jobs. But the work on Mrs. Brownlee and the twins—who needed to be shot for public relations reasons—had been hard because she had been such a nice woman. It had all been proven when President Noon had been persuaded to limit the magazines for automatic rifles to twelve rounds, a repugnant act for him; the only thing that had forced him to such an extreme was the public outcry over the shooting of children in a schoolyard. Noon stood for a kinder and gentler America, providing it carried guns.

Behind the intelligence and power in Leila's voice on the telephone when Ellsworth had called with the news of the NGA shootings—pretending to ask her advice but really listening for her instinctive response—he had heard the exultation, the overtones of jubilant rejoicing that a blow had been struck at the NGA, the triumphant shadings of glee that she had not known she was showing and therefore did not repress.

He had brought her joy! He had pleased her and, now that he had found the lost key to her happiness, he would continue to please her.

He packed carefully before going to bed. The convention at Valley Forge would open at ten the next morning in an outdoor amphitheater. The long-range weather forecast had been good. Perfect weather had been promised. He packed two suits, just in case anyone spilled something on him, and a full uniform of a commandant of the French Foreign Legion. The Legion uniform would be the official costume throughout this year's convention, as the David Crockett buckskin fringes and the raccoon hats had been the theme at the Alamo meeting in '91. His kepi was spotless; his desert boots were shined to a fare-the-well.

The whole, grand old gang would be there, hawking their guns and bullets and sniper sights from 161 booths hustling everything from smokeless gunpowder to recoil pads and laser sights or scopes. The members would have a chance to fondle CCI ammo, Speer bullets, small-arms ammo, Brenneke slugs, and all sorts of automatic reloading equipment. It would be an old-time, good-ole-boy carnival of octagon rifle barrels, Lansky sharpeners, holsters and slings, pistol scopes, speedloaders and, above all, stacks of *The Mercenary Soldier*.

And there would be hours-into-days of gun seminars: forty-two discussion groups over five days. He would miss the Gun Collectors' Committee meeting, the sessions on handgun hunting and gunfighter guns, and the three-hour seminars called Reloading—A Rewarding Hobby. Wistfully, he realized he would have to forgo the meeting on the National Firearms Museum Fund, which this year would surmise upon which weapons Andy Warhol and Pablo Picasso would have used to assert their rights under the Second Amendment to shoot guns. He sighed at the thought of missing the thrilling session called The Celebrity World Stands Up for the Constitution with genuine celebrity speakers from the big soap operas and an hour or two of dignified counsel on the right to bear and keep arms from Charlton Heston.

Guns were a damn sight better company than women (excepting Leila), he thought. A fellow could go off by himself and some good ol' buddies in a primeval forest with forty or fifty six-packs of Coors, or stalk through the inner cities in search of prime targets, which was the way a real man was intended by God and the Constitution to get his jollies.

But he had other work to do.

He packed an empty tooth-powder can with three ounces of reliable Bolivian cocaine. Through trial and error, and because of some very sound advice from knowing NGA members, he had narrowed down his favorite area for coca-leaf production to the Cochabamba highlands of Bolivia. Just 8,448 sweet feet above sea level was the premium condition for producing the best leaves, according to executives of the Medellín cartel, staunch supporters of the NGA.

He went to his gun cabinet that covered one entire thirty-foot wall of the rather large study and that held a sportsman's assortment of rifles, shotguns, machine guns, and a superb collection of handguns. If everything worked out, he could make his shot from a concealing copse on the periphery of the arena. It would only be a matter of slipping away from the dais while the Senator made his life-crushing speech. He was a long-winded, on-going speaker, so there would be plenty of time to get into place to make the kill.

He would be able to rejoin the confusion on the stage almost immediately after the hit, after activating the tape he had prepared for broadcast over the amphitheater's public address system.

He decided to use the semiautomatic rifle PSG1 from Heckler & Koch, a really reliable German firm. It was chambered for 7.62mm, had an emphatic weight of 17.85 pounds plus a 20-round magazine. Its muzzle velocity of 2,821 feet per second would take the top right off the Senator's head tomorrow evening.

If, however, for whatever reason the outdoor shot would not be feasible, he would have to make the kill inside the Senator's hotel suite. He chose the powerful Czech M52 automatic for the job. It had a sensible weight of 2.11 pounds with its loaded eight-round magazine that chambered a devastating 7.62mm bottleneck cartridge with a muzzle velocity of 1,600 feet per second. That would separate the Senator from himself, then probably go through the wall of the building and a few tree trunks on the outside. He would go for a series of explosions in the Senator's central chest area. He sincerely hoped, if he did have to do the work in the hotel suite, that the Senator wouldn't be having one of his usual young men as company, because he hated excessive messes.

But what a loss for the NGA! What deep and lasting happiness it would bring Leila! Senator James Felspar Aukins (R.-N.C.), chairman of the Senate Judiciary Committee, keynoter at the convention, was the greatest friend the NGA had ever had in the Congress of the United States even if he did come expensively. Not only that! He was the spokesman for the enormously profitable cigarette industry in his great state. How thrice pleased Leila would be!

32

When the stream of bullets from the Heckler & Koch blew Senator Aukins backward to crash into the cyclorama with such force that the bulky remnant of his body tore a gaping hole in the backdrop, riotous anarchy took over among 5,314 NGA delegates. From somewhere, crazing the membership, the public address system kept rasping out two sentences at top volume over and over again, saying, *"Guns kill people. People don't kill people."* It seemed like forever before somebody found a way to turn it off.

There was a confusion of action and reaction. More than four thousand armed delegates, including several hundred women who produced pistols from their shoulder holsters and handbags, threatened each other with the guns in the sheer excitement of panic because no one knew who had fired the terrible shots that had destroyed Senator Aukin or if the guns would be turned on them. Overzealously, perhaps nerved up by the pandemonium which had struck, confused by the incessant message from the public address system, but also excited by the chance to shoot somebody, fifty-six NGA members shot and wounded seventy-one fellow NGA members, thirty-one fatally. Because mandatory NGA target practice leading to marksman proficiency had honed the aiming accuracy of each of the shooters, the results were tragic if altogether in keeping with NGA aims.

Police, sheriff's deputies, and FBI were everywhere, but ultimately it would be impossible to sort out who had done the actual killings because of the compounded confusion, the number of wounded who needed medical attention, and the proud fact that every member of the convention had been carrying at least one firearm in defense of the Second Amendment to the Constitution of the United States. Although vehicles as small as station wagons were commandeered and ambulances were driven to the scene from nearby army bases as well as hospitals, temporary surgical facilities, some without benefit of any anesthesia on hand, had to be set up in the convention booths which, a short time before, had been selling holsters, ammunition, and Israeli "Desert Eagle" semiautomatic pistols.

The dead included two members of the NGA board of directors and four regional supervisors. Police conjecture established by the news media claimed, much later, that "at least" two of those killings had been opportunistic, resulting from past grudges, but that the remainder were hotly defended as having been protecting the rights of all Americans under the Second Amendment.

The Valley Forge shootings established a new American record for the greatest number of mass (civilian) slayings in U.S. history. NGA historians recorded proudly that, at their own convention, more people had been shot to death (and wounded) than the previous tallies of the twenty-one dead at McDonald's in San Ysidro, California, in 1984, or the sixteen shot to death in Austin, Texas, in August 1966, or the fourteen shot and killed at the post office in Edmond, Oklahoma, in August 1986, or the thirteen blasted out of their lives in Camden, New Jersey, by a man who said, "I'd have killed a thousand if I'd had enough bullets," or the thirteen people who were fatally shot in their heads in a robbery at a gambling club in Seattle in February 1983, or the twenty-three murdered by a semiautomatic pistol in a cafeteria at Kileen, Texas. Previous scorekeepers had credited the NGA only indirectly for all those other hundred-odd corpses, but the thirty-two dead at Valley Forge were proudly all NGA dead, shot down by NGA guns in the hands of NGA insider-shooters.

Instantly, by a vote of 247 to 177, the House of Representatives rejected a hastily proposed ban on the sale and ownership of semiautomatic weapons and multiple-bullet gun clips. Representative Todd D. Thanatos (D.-Miss.), long a beneficiary of NGA largesse, spoke out for the House membership when he said, "It was not guns that caused those deaths. It could just as well have been a barrel of gasoline or a land mine filled with dynamite. Or AIDS."

Without hesitation, even while the carnage was being counted, President Noon came out for a ban of gun clips that held more than fifteen bullets. "We gotta draw a line," he said.

Ellsworth Carswell, acting CEO of the National Gun Carriers' Association, praised the House vote, saying that he now hoped that Congress would move to build larger prisons and appoint tougher judges. "I don't honestly think that Congressmen vote differently than their constituents want them to vote, " he said.

An NGA survey, taken following the various shootings of the membership by the membership and reported to the membership in the NGA's glossy monthly *The American Shooter*, showed that the most popular weapon of choice by overcharged members at the convention was the Beretta 93R, a 9mm weapon weighing 2.47 pounds with a 15-round magazine in place, featuring selective fire capability for three-shot full-auto bursts with a folding grip to steady the shooter's aim when his left thumb was hooked through the oversized trigger guards. NGA members throughout the country took note of this and Beretta sales soared.

Reflexively, 1,271,382 telegrams, telephone calls, faxes, and teletypes signed by members of the NGA and sent by the sixty-three NGA regional offices in the fifty states, Puerto Rico, Guam, Grenada, Panama, Nicaragua, and Tel Aviv, flooded the White House and the offices of the United States Senate and House of Representatives, demanding that the murderer of Senator Aukins be brought to justice, but not mentioning the fifty-six overwrought NGA members who had fired their guns indiscriminately at fellow NGA members at the Valley Forge convention. Coincidentally, a miracle of shared syntax really, every message of the hundreds of thousands photographed by the network television cameras in great piles at the White House, closed with the same refrain: "Guns don't kill people. People kill people," which was the correct and proper way to recite the NGA mantra.

President Noon led the nation in mourning. After banning the import of all foreign semiautomatic weapons (although not going so far as to ban the manufacture and sale of domestic semiautomatic weapons on the grounds that they had been "made by Americans for

Americans") and suggesting that ammunition clips be limited to fifteen rounds, he authorized the burial of all thirty-one victims in Arlington Cemetery. He wore a black armband on his golfing, fishing, hunting and speedboating sportswear. He pleaded with the nation for a token eight-hour cease-fire on all target practice on people of the inner cities. "Someone has gone too far with this shooting," he said. "We gotta draw a line."

International network and cable television coverage was intense, the continuous around-the-clock programming costing the television networks an estimated $3.4 million in lost advertising time. Two hundred and ten thousand NGA members from forty-six states of the Union attended the funeral, either marching or watching from the curbside as the cortege passed by along Pennsylvania Avenue from the Capitol to the White House, where Osgood Noon joined the saddened procession, slow-marching to the heartbreaking tempos of the dirges being played by the U.S. Marine Corps band, at the head of twelve hundred civilian sportsmen who carried their assault rifles reversed, barrels pointing backward into the ground, following the fifty-six caskets, three to a caisson, with Senator Aukins's little dog trotting mournfully between the wheels of the gun carriage holding the Senator's mortal remains. The cortege turned left at 23rd Street, then crossed the Arlington Memorial Bridge to the national cemetery, where ministers of eleven Protestant denominations, a priest, a rabbi, a mullah, and a Scoutmaster delivered benedictions and the thirty-one loyal Gun Carriers were laid to rest. At graveside, the thirty riflemen fired a simultaneous volley into the sky, which fell to earth some forty-six yards away, wounding a flap of nuns praying at a bishop's tomb.

33

Dr. Jim Nolan, who was neither a statistical appraiser of private enterprise philanthropies nor a mitochondrial geneticist, as he had represented himself to Leila Aluja, sat across the desk in a windowless room in the Treasury Department of the United States. It was a secret office at the end of a labyrinth twelve stories below street level in Washington, D.C., at the brain center of the Deep Cover Section. There, he answered questions put to him by his superiors, Richard Gallagher, DDCS, and John Kullers, Deputy Director (Inquisitions).

"You are convinced that the woman can deliver solid evidence?" Gallagher said.

"Yes, sir. That is, in terms of our game plan."

"Lay it out for me."

"She is psychologically repelled by the NGA, not only for the usual reasons but because one of her ex-husbands is now its executive director."

"Nonetheless, she's a lawyer," Gallagher said. "Those people are beyond feelings in the normal sense. Have you examined her tax returns?"

"Yes, sir. Squeaky clean, every one of them. Going back beyond the statute of limitations on an average annual income of two million, three a year."

"God—and she's such a fine-looking woman."

"Yes, sir. Absolutely a superb-looking woman."

"And so rich."

"I wouldn't say exactly rich, sir. A few million, yes, but not rich in any way the Reagans would call rich. Say well-to-do."

"What's the general plan?" Kullers said.

"I thought we should encourage her to let us gain access to the NGA secret accounting—the real set of books—which, from what she tells me, are kept in Baghdad and in Libya. Then, through that decoy, although all of it will be just a ploy really because we know the NGA is untouchable because of the extent of their Congressional protection, we can blackmail her with the threat of NGA reprisals for giving us that information, and gradually move her into the other area of the investigation, toward our real target, Barkers Hill Enterprises."

"Barkers Hill is the hardest nut of all to crack, Jim," Gallagher said grimly. "Eliot Ness succeeded in his assault on a relatively parochial branch of that activity when he crushed the Capone mob, but that was sixty years ago and Barkers Hill makes the Capone people seem like a gang of thrifty spinsters who are plotting a midnight raid on the refrigerator."

"Leila Aluja is the key, sir," Dr. Nolan said. "If we can turn her, Barkers Hill can have no secrets. Edward S. Price included."

"Is she as ambivalent about Barkers Hill as she is about the NGA and CANCER?"

"No, sir. I think she rather admires the Mafia as a matter of fact. She is an American, and they have been the greatest service organization this country has ever known. Also, they've done a great deal to advance her father's fortune as a Congressman and they were the force behind moving her out of the Federal prosecutor's office into such a comfortable income—into Washington and the bracket she is in today."

"How long do you think the job will take?"

Dr. Nolan sighed. "I have no idea. I'm going to have to wriggle my way further into her confidence, then—when the time seems to be right—I am going to have to confront her, threaten her, bribe her with her own ambitions—"

"Ambitions?" Kullers said, startled. "How can a lawyer go any higher than manipulating the government of the the United States?"

"She wants to be a schoolteacher. Her dream of glory is to make school principal. When the time comes, Treasury may have to ask Education to intervene."

It had been the most difficult meeting of his life. He had been trained at betrayal by the great teachers of undercover action, but he had never sat in a chair, facing his chief, breaking his own heart. He loved Leila. Vaguely, he had deluded himself into believing that, sure, she would be sent away to some women's correctional facility for five or ten years or so, but that when the gates to that facility had reopened, releasing her, he would be there with a bouquet of flowers and a large automobile to sweep her away from the bitter memories.

She was a lawyer, he had told himself again and again. She loves and respects the law as much as I do; therefore, she knows as well as I do that she must pay the price for her sins against the law.

But now, as he left the heavily guarded underground bank vault that was DDCS's office, all of that confidence in how everything would work out had left him. He loved her. She loved him. He was going to send her away, stripping her of everything. He would have gladly offered her his right arm, if that could have been of any possible use to her. If he could only turn back the clock to the first hours of their love together, before she had begun to spill all of the information that was going to lead to her conviction.

He would wait for her, no matter how long her sentence. He would bribe the beauty operator at the women's prison to give her those few extra attentions that could make all the difference to a woman's self-respect.

He loved her. He had betrayed her, but he loved her. But if it contributed to the downfall of the National Gun Carriers' Association, the cigarette industry, and to handicapping grievously the continuance of the Mafia in the United States, he would have to do the job and leave sentimentality to the greeting card companies.

34

The burden of stress had been placed squarely upon Leila. The NGA turned to her to make all the arrangements for the mass burials at Arlington Cemetery, the Air Force flyovers, and the President leading the march in slow cadence behind the caissons carrying the caskets along the route of the cortege for massed television coverage. All this had to be coordinated with the membership drive opportunity that the mass murders had made possible for the NGA and which, when tallied at the end of the ensuing quarter, would result in 13,482 new members nationwide. The Lord taketh away, but the Lord giveth as well.

She worked directly with Ellsworth Carswell on the arrangements and she felt it was oddly touching the way he tried to anticipate her needs and to ease her tasks in every possible way. The feeling made her uncomfortable in an exhilarated way. She felt as if she were doing the County Kilkenny marching step in a St. Patrick's Day parade: two steps forward and one step backward. She didn't want to step backward if it meant going directly toward another punishing emotional encounter with Ellsworth. He was a callous, masochistic spoiler and she intended to keep telling herself that until this icky feeling went away. She wasn't sure about going forward toward Jim Nolan. There were areas in his courtship that screamed warnings at her like sirens in the night. She wasn't sure what they were, but even though she felt herself caring for him more and more as time went on, something within her shrank from trusting him.

On the second night, working late at her office on a draft of a presidential proclamation with which Goodie Noon would declare

Second Amendment Day and urge the cities, towns, villages, farms, inner cities, and mine shafts of the nation to enter 24 hours of mourning, she began to get that old feeling again. Ellsworth was so sweet when he wasn't doing cocaine, she thought. He was genuinely helpful and, well, even loving. Then, a vision of herself entangled in an extraordinary position, wholly unclothed under and around Jim Nolan, flashed across her mind, but she told herself instantly that that was all right, that she was a grown, divorced woman with certain corporeal needs having nothing to do with this freakish return of affection for her ex-husband.

"How about instead of a military squad," she said hurriedly, trying to blank out the compelling memory of the hours upon a bed, on the floor, and on Dr. Nolan's pool table, "we have the NGA board of directors fire the funeral knell volley over the massed graves at Arlington?"

"That's brilliant!" Carswell said.

"Rifles or handguns—or both?"

"I think handguns. It would focus the attention of the inner cities and there is something romantic about twenty-four portly, extremely successful men pulling their weapons out of their shoulder holsters and firing them over the coffins. It would inspire the American people and encourage them to wear shoulder holsters."

"For Christ's sake, Ellsworth! This is a funeral, not a sales promotion. We'll use a company of Marines."

"Whatever you say."

"But, on the other hand, it would be nice and I'm sure he'd want to do it because it's such a grand photo opportunity—we could ask the President to fire just one lone shotgun salute into the air over the caskets. It would make the twelve o'clock news, the five o'clock news, the evening news, and all the morning shows right across the country. It's a knell for a dead Senator, don't forget."

"And a Senator who was shot to death."

"But with a rifle. The President should fire a rifle."

"Leila?"

"Yes?"

"When this is all behind us, when our lives return to normal, I was wondering if—sometime soon—you'd let me invite you to a candlelit dinner at my place—just the two of us—just like the old days."

"First kick the coke then we'll talk about it."

"You will? All I have to do is stop snorting vegetables and you'll actually—"

"Three months of no cocaine and I'll have dinner with you wherever you say." She *hated* compassion. She *detested* poignancy, but she had fallen right into a finer-feelings trap. No matter. She was a woman with woman's feelings. Besides, he could never give up cocaine. There was no candlelit dinner to worry about.

When the funerals were over and President Noon had flown off with an entourage of forty bodyguards, secretaries, aides, and close staff members, his wife, and his literary dog to judge an *eisteddfod* in Wales before flying on to officiate at a Finno-Ugric ceremony in Lapland, at which he would receive a large, beautifully carved wooden hammer, and be appointed that year's Thundergod—with extensive television coverage—Leila, exhausted, told her law partners she needed a week off. She flew with the Venerable Bead in the firm's Gulfstream III to the Bahamas, where she planned to have six days of complete silence and some bone fishing on Andros Island. With only a staff of servants at the law firm's getaway villa, she was almost alone.

It was a rambling, comfortable house on about four acres facing the ocean. It had an orange-tile roof, a large swimming pool, and a tennis court. The large, airy room assigned to her had two ceiling fans and a private patio with an Arabian fountain and a caged mynah bird, who chirped an endless store of sentences in Cockney and in the Bahamian dialect.

On the first day she rested. On the second she fished, but all the fish were stronger than she was, which exhausted her again, so, on the third day, she sat limply on a deserted beach, wearing a pale green bikini, a white balibuntal straw hat, and the glowing red Bead. She was reading when Jim Nolan came jogging up from the horizon.

"My God! Leila! Leila Aluja! What are you doing here?"

She stared at him blankly.

"What a wonderful surprise!" He played the scene as Olivier

might have, betraying a wholly earnest sort of pleasure at finding her on a deserted beach so unexpectedly.

"What are you doing here?" Leila asked dazedly, feeling vague stirrings.

"Jogging. I'm staying with some friends up the beach."

He sat on the sand beside her. They chatted until it was lunchtime. In the next few days they fished, swam, and drank some good wine, but also spent approximately fourteen hours on a bed in the Schwartz, Blacker & Moltonero villa after Leila had turned off the audio and video surveillance systems. However, as designed by the founding partner of the law firm, Malachi Olgilvie, disconnecting the primary systems immediately cut in identical backup systems, so every orthodox and experimental position they underwent in their pursuit of love, every grunt and squeal of ecstasy, all the reflective sweat which the violent exercises produced, the overlapping dialogue, bleats, yelps, and groans, some wildly self-indulgent, some conventional, was on the record for the managing partner of Schwartz, Blacker & Moltonero to review.

Leila was an operatically vocal and outrageously expressive kind of sex partner; she heralded each orgasm as if it were the first ever experienced by woman since the dawn of time and the evolution of the species. She came like a lunch whistle, finding a vocabulary with such desperate intensity as to threaten the glass in the windows and to send mice, roaches, and all other animal life scurrying out of the house to safety.

Through it all, Jim Nolan worked assiduously, putting to the task every technique he had been taught at "The Farm," the Deep Cover School where agents in his cadre were trained under conditions simulating everything they would encounter in the field. Suspicious of the probability of a backup surveillance system, he did his best to shield his face from the camera, but Leila's enormous engagement with the inspiration of copulation gave her unexpected strengths. Again and again, her hips would send him spinning into the air, and when he came down, he would be flat on his back and Leila would be on top of him, his face bared to the cameras.

In one of the intense clinches, as they writhed and sang out incoherently to sink back into utterly unguarded looseness, Jim Nolan said, "I have thought many times of your dream."

"My dream?"

"To be a schoolteacher, then maybe later the principal of a small-town school."

"It was just a dream."

"Why should it be?"

"There is no possible way it could happen."

"Ah—there must be lots of ways. Just at random, take the Witness Protection Program."

"How do you mean?"

"If you went into that, they could set you up in whatever small town you chose, settle the right credentials on you, and place you with just the right small school."

"They could? But what would I be doing in the Witness Protection Program?"

"It was just an example. There are more ways to skin a cat than you have dreamed of, Horatia."

The abandoned couple were circumspect, they felt, because they always confined their lovemaking to nighttime, when they imagined the native staff wouldn't be aware of what they were doing. What they were doing they did perfervidly and with a sense of dedication. When the time came to go home, Leila had convinced herself that she was, at last, in love again.

35

Dearest Leila:

Almost four years later and I think I have found the secret of my great-grandfather's yogurt. I slipped badly in a high mountain pass leading up to the old woman's village. My burro fell on top of me, breaking my leg, but it could be that the warmth of his body kept me alive for the seventeen hours before, by a divine stroke of luck, a man from the village found me. He had been out for a walk to see a friend in Yugoslavia; within nine hours he was able to return from the village with bearers and an improvised stretcher. The exposure from the cold brought on pneumonia, so, after the midwife had set the compound fracture of my leg, I was immobile. It is thanks to my father's name that I survived. They were grateful to him for some forgotten favor he had done for them, they said (this favor turned out to be the gift of my great-grandfather's yogurt). As time went on, I came to realize that it was the name, Shqitonja, that had electrified these people to undertake the prodigies of emergency transportation and folk medicine which, without any question, saved my life.

The grim promises of the yogurt are something we must think about. Eating it has extended the average age of the people of this village above the Crna Gora border to 142 years. The *average* age. The yogurt can more than double the life span. In this village, seventy-nine years old is so far considered middle-age.

Now read this!

The present heavyweight boxing champion of the world is from this village. He is ninety-eight years old!

It gets worse: Only two people settled in this tiny place 163 years ago and today there are more than 1,200 scattered across the mountainside up here. They have lost 30 percent to accidents such as falling off the mountain or to disagreements over goats or women, but the original founders of the village are still alive and well and the founding woman just had twins, the sixth generation of her offspring.

All my life I have been deluded into thinking that my great-grandfather, having discovered his yogurt, had never found a way to market it to the world because he was too unsophisticated. I have learned directly from the old woman who stirs the yogurt that he had forbidden those who knew the secret to allow it to be passed on. One family is the custodian of the formula. They are like priests of a religion. I can't really understand why because the stuff isn't sold; it is community property.

I was shocked to read in your letters that your husband had infected you with such a disease, but hardly as shocked as I was by the news that you had divorced me and taken another husband. Now you have divorced him and I wonder if I shall ever see you again. But I am too tired to go on now. You must keep sending your wonderful letters to me at my father's house. I am sure I will be well enough to make the return journey by next summer and, in the meantime, they keep me fattened up here with their astounding yogurt.

With all my love into eternity,
Joe

36

Ellsworth Carswell quit coke cold turkey. He was so enthralled with the promise of starting over with Leila again that he seemed to have forgotten that he had ever snorted away his nasal membrane. His nose took on a normal color. The backs of his hands stopped itching. He no longer spoke sounding as if he had thirty Kleenexes caught in his throat. At he end of each week of total abstinence, he called Leila so she could be up-to-date on the score. "Five weeks down, seven to go," he said.

"What?"

"I've been off the vegetable powders for five weeks. So we will have a candlelit dinner date seven weeks from now."

"Ellsworth! That's tremendous!"

"Just the love of a good woman. Nothing to it."

She was thrilled—for Ellsworth's sake—but after a week in the Bahamas and four days back in Washington, she had become so absorbed in Jim Nolan that she had had trouble following what Carswell was trying to say while he told her of his triumph.

Dr. Nolan was handling her carefully. Never before any of their sexual events would he ask any questions about her work. But almost always afterward, when they lay as spent and gasping as bass on the floor of a rowboat, he would try on various approaches that might get her talking about her work so that he could find the handle which would open some of the doors he wanted to enter.

On the third strenuous night on Andros Island he murmured, as they lay with her head resting like a sack of wheat on his chest, with his hairy arm holding her shoulders, "What kind of a man is Edward S. Price?"

"Price?" she answered, muffled, after about six beats.

"Of Barkers Hill Enterprises."

"Oh, that Price. He's a smooth, very dull man who is probably the sole support of the world's greatest tailor."

"I saw him once. By accident, in Brooklyn."

"Edward Price? In *Brook*lyn?

"Not only that, he was with Angelo Partanna, the *consigliere* of the Prizzi crime family."

"Little Mr. Partanna? A crime family?"

"It sure was a funny combination. You know Partanna?"

"I met him—twice, I think—in Mr. Price's office in New York."

By the time Ellsworth Carswell was into his fourth week of abstinence, Jim Nolan had also skirted, gingerly, areas of the National Gun Carriers' Association and CANCER, the Center for American National Cigarette Education and Research. He was just warming her up to an awareness of his interest in her law practice to the point where, in the last night of Leila's Bahamas stay, as careful and as skillful as Nolan's questions had been, her wonder about the quality of his interest was compounded.

On the fifth day of Leila's return to the law offices in Washington, the managing partner, Franklin M. Heller, asked her via the intercom system if she would meet him in his office. "Something has come up," he rumbled, "rather important."

His office was a replica of a Vermont country lawyer's room at the turn of the last century. Heller sat beside a vast rolltop desk, securely locked, with a brass spittoon at his feet. A 1901 calendar displaying the Crackerjack sailorboy and his dog was the single wall decoration, except for the faked rows of bookshelves holding only the spines of volumes of Blackstone. The floor was made of bare wooden planks. Franklin Marx Heller was a stout man with heavy dark bags that hung like sporrans under his eyes. He wore a navy-blue beret at all times, in or out of the law offices.

Mr. Heller conducted the meeting with the same authority with which he superintended breakfast at home: stern, overpowering, fair.

There were no preliminaries. "The man with whom you were sleeping on Andros Island," Heller said when Leila had been seated as comfortably as was possible upon an upright, pine-hewn chair, "is a Federal investigator."

"*Whaaaaaaaaat?*" She stared at him glassily. Her eyes focused into realization. "You son-of-a-bitch, you had a backup in that house!"

"Audio and video."

"My God!"

"No harm done, dear. You obviously didn't know about him. Although you should have made it your entire business to find out."

"Know about him? *Know?* How could the man be a Federal agent? He's a mitochondrial geneticist."

"Jim Nolan is his nom de guerre. His real name is Harvey Zendt. He's been a professional civil servant since he finished two years as a retail shoe salesman in Pittsburgh. He spent eighteen months enrolled at the Treasury's Deep Cover School—they call it 'The Farm'—learning the various techniques with which he won your—ah—admiration."

"Frank! You're wrong! He was sent to me by the Vice President of the United States."

"Precisely," Mr. Heller said.

"Precisely what?"

"How better could a secret investigator for the United States government gain access"—he cleared his throat—"access, that is, to the leading Washington law firm, the innermost core of American government, unless he was introduced to you by the Vice President of the United States."

"Hazman is going to pay for this."

"You were *supposed* to check the reference out with the White House Chief of Staff, under the protocols which were set up in the Reagan administration, and not just accept any White House introduction willy-nilly on its face value."

"But this is preposterous! The man was so disingenuous. Never—by word or deed—did he even slightly compromise himself."

"I seem to remember one or two leading questions he put to you about Edward S. Price and the cigarette education program, to name two. He was rather probing, I thought, about the NGA. I was greatly surprised that alarm bells didn't go off inside your head when he mentioned the Witness Protection Program."

"But what did he want? What is he after? What branch does he come from?" Her world was crashing down upon her head. She was up to her hips in bitter ashes.

"He's from the Deep Cover Section at Treasury."

"My God!"

"They are out to break Barkers Hill Enterprises, the NGA, and the entire cigarette education program directed at American youth. And all just to collect a few billion dollars in evaded taxes!"

"They must have gone mad to think they could go after the NGA. But I am going to crucify that son-of-a-bitch myself." She wanted to shriek, weep, and tear out her hair. She loved him, truly, completely, with a woman's honesty, and he had mocked her. He had humiliated her in front of her partners. He had come to her like a Judas raised on Spanish fly, and she had to get back to her office with the doors closed so she could begin to plot his destruction. What kind of a schoolgirl had she become that she could be so bemooned over the first thing that had appealed to her in a pair of trousers since her divorce? Heller's rumbling voice broke into her grief.

"More vitally, Leila. We want you to review every moment you spent with him. We want you to be certain, beyond the shadow of a doubt, that you did not betray a single professional confidence."

"I did not. I could say that it could have been that I almost did, but I did not. And I thank you for bringing this to my attention." The last sentence was the most difficult she had ever had to say.

"Let me state, in summation," Franklin Heller told her in his native didactic way, "that once more we have a profound reason to thank our founder, Malachi Olgilvie, now in far-off Syria, for his foresight in installing that automatic backup system. Remember where you heard it first."

37

Her heart breaking, she methodically set to work to destroy Jim Nolan. After thinking, which involved scribbled notes in her own kind of shorthand on a yellow legal pad—seven pages of it—after inviting the chairman of the Republican National Committee to her office, after telephoning and receiving calls back from the White House, after refusing to take two calls from Jim Nolan, she was driven by Arpad Steiner, her bodyguard-chauffeur, to her house in Virginia. At home, she dined on a large *kalbsbratwurst* with three rashers of bacon, some fried onions, and a seeded Kaiser roll with a glass of Montrachet '61. She refused to take two more calls from Dr. Nolan and instead prepared for bed: a warm bath and a sleeping pill—an extraordinary decision for Leila. She slept for nine hours, then, refreshed and objective, she telephoned the Secretary of the Treasury from her bed and made an appointment to lunch with him in his private dining room that day.

They had carrot juice cocktails before lunch. The food was plain but excellent: grilled mushrooms, rutabaga omelets, Melba toast, salad, and coffee. The Secretary suggested that they get to the business at hand while at lunch rather than waiting until the decaffeinated coffee had been served.

"A really sweet opportunity has come up, Win," she said. "They tell me that the senior senator from North Carolina—the one who was shot at the NGA convention— North Carolina *is* your state, isn't it, Win?" she asked gently.

He nodded.

"The Party would like you to run for his seat."

Winikus's eyes grew wider. His pupils dilated. Otherwise he didn't change expression.

"I hadn't heard anything about Lester resigning."

"The President is going to name him as Ambassador to the USSR. Something about cigarette exports."

"Well, that's a very big deal. The market for real cigarettes over there is tremendous."

"The question is, Will you make the run?"

"Well, I'd like to talk it over with the President."

"He's all for it. Absolutely gung ho about the idea."

"How come that you—of all people—are the one to tell me about this?"

"It all may seem involved, but it isn't when you analyze it. We—my law firm—represent CANCER and most of the other American cigarette interests."

Winikus nodded.

"We also represent the NGA and a really large conglomerate called Barkers Hill Enterprises. Every one of those is a large campaign contributor—as they would be to your campaign, of course."

Winikus's expression loosened. "But what's my connection?" he asked.

"As a son of North Carolina, you support and sustain the cigarette industry, right? As a native of a wonderful outdoors state, you support guns and hunting, right? As a member of Osgood Noon's administration, you support the Second Amendment to the Constitution, right? And as an American leader, you support the business community."

"So?"

"So your own Treasury Department is sponsoring a Deep Cover investigation sworn to destroy CANCER, the NGA, and Barkers Hill Enterprises."

"No!"

"It has to be stopped, Win. Your man on the case—he calls himself Dr. Jim Nolan, but his passport name is Harvey Zendt—has to be transferred to American Samoa."

Winikus made notes on a pad on the table beside him, stared at her grimly, then, all at once, as if the entire message had at last struck home, said, “Consider it done, Leila. I’ll talk to Modred at the RNC and get back to you.”

38

Leila had Arpad Steiner drive her to Washington's National Airport on the morning that Dr. Nolan's flight left for American Samoa, via Los Angeles. She wore her dazzling black-and-white houndstooth check suit, which made her stand out in the airport crowd like a mushroom cloud. She saw him as he left the American Airlines departure desk, but he didn't see her. She had to make two separate passes up and down in his general area until he noticed her and called out. She turned, looking as if she were puzzled by a greeting at such a place, then recognized him, and smiled sweetly.

"Jim! What a surprise!"

He rushed to her, crashing into two little old ladies on the way. It took a few minutes to get them on their feet again and to brush them while he apologized. Leila stood serenely in place, not making a move toward him, not entering the chaos he had caused. At last he got away.

"Leila! My God! I've been trying to reach you for ten days."

"You have? What a pity. I've been in Paris. Helping out the trade delegation with the Common Market. Didn't my office tell you that?"

"They told me nothing. I called you at home. I called you at the Senate and—"

"Is anything the matter?"

"I've been transferred to American Samoa."

"S*amoa*?"

"They hit me with it like a bolt of lightning."

"Harvard? Harvard transferred you to—*where*?"

"Well—yes. They have some new attack on the project in mind, I think."

"But your research! With Wambly Keifetz and the NGA."

"It was all very, very sudden and I wanted to say—well, I wanted to say good-bye."

"Jim! I'm beginning to feel like the woman in *Casablanca,* that wonderful movie. Samoa! How romantic! How long will you be gone?"

"It's an indefinite assignment."

"You mean—it might be for *years*?"

"Leila, I was thinking—well, you're a wonderfully well-connected woman and I have been wondering if you could—well—do anything to have this transfer canceled. Considering what we have come to mean to each other."

"Me? How, Jim? What could I do? If I am connected, as you say, it is entirely inside the Beltway. I don't know a soul at Harvard. But I could ask around."

The announcement of the departure of Dr. Nolan's flight came over the PA system.

"Los Angeles and Samoa," Leila said. "They're calling your flight, darling. How very sad that it should end like this." Like a death ray, she beamed a sweet, sweet smile directly into his face. "But it isn't the end, is it? I'm sure you'll be back here in no time at all." As she stared into his eyes, her expression hardened like quick-freeze BB shot scattering contempt all over him.

He caught his lower lip between his teeth, turned abruptly, and walked toward the long finger leading to the plane, fumbling with his ticket and his boarding pass.

"Don't forget to write," Leila called after him, holding back a rush of tears.

Dr. Nolan's departure for Samoa happened on the day before the end of the twelve weeks in which Ellsworth Carswell was to have proven his independence from cocaine. He sent Leila an enormous bouquet of flowers with a note that said, "What with twelve weeks of absolute freedom from Colombian vegetables, I hereby claim my prize of one candlelit dinner at my apartment on Friday, the 10th."

The news of Ellsworth's achievement and the idea of dining alone with him the way they had been, long ago, both thrilled and depressed Leila. She was thrilled with his victory over his affliction, if it were true, and remotely excited by the memory of his fervor in the sack. The sensual elation was offset by the concomitant memory of the infection he had left inside her, which made her remember what she would never be able to forget, that she could never have children because of him. Such a tidal wave of disgust overcame her that she had to walk unsteadily to a couch and lay down. She stared at the ceiling and went over everything he had said and done to expiate his sins against himself and her, remembering the inevitability of her own death and knowing that, what with the work load she carried and the fact that her last chance at loving someone had shot itself in the head, she decided that maybe Ellsworth, if she could get him away from the NGA now that he was off coke, could be her last best hope for loving anyone or being loved. She got off the couch and went back to her desk. She dictated into the machine a fax that accepted, with pleasure, Mr. Carswell's gracious invitation to a candlelit supper at his home.

3 9

Ellsworth Carswell had not kicked the cocaine habit. Because it had clogged his nasal passages as well as the sounds of his voice and had made certain cosmetic changes in the complexion of his nose, taking it from dead, fish-belly white to cherry-red, then back again, which was utterly out of synchrony with the other colors of the skin on his face—both annoyances that would make it simple for Leila to detect that he might not be free of the cocaine habit—he now mixed it with heroin and smoked it. The problems with his complexion and his vocal delivery vanished. More than that, the system, called "crack" he believed, delivered a new, perhaps briefer, but a far more consuming kind of high.

By the morning of the scheduled candlelit dinner, Ellsworth had had an in-depth conference with the maître d' of Leila's favorite French restaurant—at which she had conducted so many millions of dollars' worth of influence peddling—and arranged for a menu of Leila's absolutely favorite nutriments: Consommé Royale, Sole de la Manche au Vermouth, Poularde Demi-Deuil, Coeur de Laitue, Bombe Osgood Noon, and Café.

The strong beef broth made with ground lean beef, chopped celery, carrots, onions, and leeks would be simmered for four hours, strained through a cheesecloth, topped with a custard garnish made of whole eggs and light cream, firmed in the oven, then cut into small pieces. The sole to be served on that wonderful evening had not yet arrived from France and would not for nine hours. It would be poached with butter, chopped shallots, and sweet Italian vermouth and then served in a sauce made with the liquid of the sole, cream, egg yolks, and butter. A superb bottle of Montrachet '61, Leila's favorite, would be there with the fish. The Poularde Demi-Deuil would be carved, in Ellsworth's apartment, by the restaurant's *écuyer tranchant*. It was Leila's favorite dish: the chicken baked to a golden brown, the sauce made with dry white wine and brown sauce, butter and brandy, and the lot garnished with diced carrots, turnips, mushrooms, truffles, and celery. With this triumph would come the magnificent Bonnes Mare '37, as ruby-red, he thought, as the Venerable Bead, which lay, wherever she was, upon Leila's billowing bosom.

"There is no substitute for beauty," Ellsworth told the maître d' gravely at the trial supper, "and no compromise with perfection."

The Bombe Osgood Noon seemed to have been made entirely of air and ice cream. The problems of the actual dinner settled, Ellsworth sat down to ponder what else he could do to fill Leila's heart with joy. The answer came to him almost immediately.

40

Very nearly in a daze, Leila listened at the telephone in her office while an official-sounding voice told her that Ellsworth Carswell was being held on charges of multiple homicides and that he requested that she be notified as his attorney and would she come at once to the city jail.

"I don't understand," she said.

"Are you Leila Aluja, attorney in the law firm of Schwartz, Blacker and Moltonero?"

"Yes."

"This is Sergeant John Lahr? At the D.C. jail detention facility?"

"Yes?"

"We are holding Mr. Carswell, your client, prior to his transfer to the Lorton Reformatory off Interstate Ninety-five?"

"On what charges?"

"Attempted multiple homicides?"

"Multiple *homi*cides? Ellsworth *Cars*well? That's impossible. Let me talk to my client."

There was a long pause while Carswell's chained right hand was freed from his leg irons so he could take the telephone.

"Hi, hon," he said, attempting blitheness but projecting bleak despair.

"What is this, Ellsworth?"

"Well—"

"Your voice sounds all clogged up. Are you all right?"

"Well—"

"Are you on—never mind. What is this nonsense about multiple homicides?"

"Well, maybe you'd better get down here."

She hung up the telephone, staring at it as though it had betrayed her. She gargled something into the intercom, crossed the room, put on her hat and coat, picked up her attaché case, and left the office.

Ellsworth Carswell had been arrested in the Capitol building as he was entering a Senate hearing room, coked to the hairline, where the Senate Judiciary Committee was about to open the fourth day of hearings on proposed antihandgun legislation containing amendments that had been framed by the National Gun Carriers' Association. This committee was perhaps the most august, measured, and fair as the grateful financial contributions from an intense but widely ranging system of Political Action Committees would permit it to be. It was one of the most susceptible of all of the relentlessly probing arms of any legislature in the world, as it reached out for justice (as its special-interest contributors saw it).

Carswell had been summoned to testify before the committee as an official witness. He had arrived in the company limousine, had waddled into the Capitol building looking curiously overpacked and top-heavy. He had been apprehended at the entrance to the committee hearing room by a security guard who had become suspicious because of the extraordinary bulkiness of the jacket Carswell was wearing. Without being asked to show identification, and protesting loudly, he was taken off to an anteroom and searched. He was found to be carrying three .357 Magnum Israeli Desert Eagle machine pistols, each measuring 10.25 inches and weighing 3.75 pounds (when empty, which they were not). Each pistol was loaded with nine rounds for automatic fire. Also, in his jacket and trouser pockets, Carswell was carrying three grenades.

After three security men had been able to get control over the hysteria that these weapons had caused them, considering the neighborhood and the tenants who were threatened—the incident occurred almost immediately after rather contentious conduct by the committee in its solemn procedures concerning a Supreme Court confirmation—after they had (reflexively) beaten Carswell rather thoroughly while they pressed their demands for information concerning his intentions, one of them, having ripped Carswell's wallet from the right rear pocket of his trousers, suddenly began frantically to attempt to pull his colleagues off the suspect.

"Hey! Jesus! Wait! No! No!" he shouted.

The security men stopped hitting Carswell, although they kept a tight hold on him. "What, Eddie?" the calmest man asked.

"This is Ellsworth Carswell, the president of the National Gun Carriers'. He's got top clearance."

"So?"

"So he's probably on the list as an official witness. Those guns he had were probably just exhibits for the committee."

"Three guns this size? Grenades?"

"Eddie! He's the head of the NGA! The entire House and the Senate and the White House will be all over us if we get on the wrong side of this guy. We'll all be transferred to Guam."

"Holy shit!"

The large men all began to brush Carswell's clothing, to get him straightened out again. "A natural mistake, sir," said the spokesman, who had found Carswell's wallet.

There was wildness in Carswell's eyes. "Gimme my guns," he said.

"Rules is rules, sir," a shortish, plump officer said. "No firearms allowed in the committee rooms. But when you are called to testify, we can bring the guns to you. Unloaded."

"Un*loaded*?" Carswell said frantically. "How can I mow down the committee if the guns are unloaded?"

"Whatta you mean?"

"I'm going to blow those rats out through the wall of the building," Carswell said earnestly.

That was when they decided to arrest him. He made a violent fuss, needing to be subdued. He was turned over to the City Police at a discreet side entrance to the great building. En route to the police car, still in the hallowed halls of Congress, Carswell somehow obtained possession of the holstered pistol strapped at the side of one of the squad of cops who were escorting him. He took a snapshot with the gun at a passing senator, quite elderly and nimble, but although Carswell was a sure shot with any kind of handgun, the guards had been all over him in an instant, so the shot had gone wild, missing the legislator and damaging a valuable chandelier.

They needed to subdue him again, so he was somewhat badly beaten when they had him confined and handcuffed on the floor of the rear area of the police car. His face was swollen and beginning to discolor. He regained consciousness en route to the jail and demanded to talk to his lawyer. It was not until he had been assured that they would call his lawyer that he began to confess. He began to babble the confession because one of the cops asked him if he had really intended to shoot down the committee. He told them he intended to shoot anyone and everyone who advocated the use of guns under the archaic protection of a constitutional amendment that had been written to meet the needs of citizens who had been dead for more than two hundred years.

On the way to the station house, he ranted about who he had already shot and why he had shot them. The cops, listening with glazed eyes, wondered how they had gotten mixed up with stuff like this, stuff which could mean the end of their careers. This guy *was* the NGA! The meaning of the words rang like a knell inside their heads.

Immediately upon arrival at the detention facility of E Street, SE, Carswell was asked to repeat his confession to a stenographer who typed it, and Carswell signed it before Leila was summoned.

Leila brought a photographer with an electronic camera that could record sequenced shots on television tape, then project the results in instant replay on a television screen. She brought an electronic box that could make color prints directly from the television screen. She brought a legal stenographer with her. She told the police captain in charge that she wanted absolute privacy with her client and the assurance that nothing which would be exchanged between her and her client would be recorded and that if it were later produced as recorded evidence after she had his signed assurance that there would be no eavesdropping, that she would press felony charges against him, have him stripped of his badge and his pension and slammed into a Federal prison. She demanded a copy of the alleged confession that her client was said to have made.

Leila read the confession before she saw Carswell. Every small detail of the murders—of Butch Owlsley and his bodyguards, of Mrs. Brownlee and her two children, which had led to the suicide of an NGA key executive, of Senator Aukins and the thirty-one attendant, inadvertent slayings at Valley Forge as well as his plan to murder the entire House Judiciary Committee—had been dictated deliberately to a police stenographer, then signed clearly by Carswell with what was undoubtedly his signature.

She had seen and done many terrible things since she had come to Washington, but this was so unattainably beyond belief that she imagined that somewhere along the way since she had awakened safely in her bed that morning, she had been drugged with some strange, new, hypnotic, and psychotropic narcotic now producing this cruel illusion.

At that moment, Ellsworth Carswell was brought into the room.

She looked at his battered face, at his twitching, warped posture, at the hideous discoloration and enforced malformation of his features and his carriage and, turning to her photographer, said, "I want every angle, frame by frame. We're going to project these shots on a giant screen in successions of courtrooms right up to the highest court in the land. They beat this phony confession out of him."

When the photographer finished his work, Leila told the photographer and the stenographer to leave the room. "First we'll talk," she said to Carswell, "then you'll dictate a statement."

When they were alone, she stared at him, long and hard, and said, "How did all this happen to you this morning?"

"I wanted to make you happy."

"Ellsworth—please. How did they get you to say all those wild things about killing Butch Owlsley and the others?"

"But I did kill them," he said piteously. "I did it for you." His voice broke into a sob. He sat across the table from her, weeping. It was as if the scene had reverted uncountable aeons to the time when Cain had tried to explain to his mom why he had had to kill his bubba, Abel.

"I killed them for you. I mean, Butch was Butch and he stood for the NGA. Mrs. Brownlee and the kids were symbols of children being shot down in schoolyards and in the streets all over America only to have our President tell everyone that the way to curb murders by guns in the streets was to reduce the ammunition clips from fifteen bullets to ten. Brownlee shot himself because he suddenly saw the light and Senator Aukins stood not only for the use of guns in the streets, on the farm, and in the home, but for cigarettes as well, and it isn't possible to say which is more deadly. You were against all these things. They made you unhappy. I had made you unhappy by passing along that grievous disease and I wanted to make everything right again for you. I wanted you to be happy. So I shot those people."

She couldn't speak. She was able to reach across to grasp his hands with both of hers. They sat fused into each other for many seconds while she counted eternities and wondered what to do next.

What are we going to do? she asked herself. Who is more guilty, me, the Founding Fathers who wrote the Second Amendment so that the NGA people could hustle it for a buck, or this insane little man?

"It's a challenging ethical question all right," Carswell agreed stoutly, as though he were reading her mind, dabbing at his cheeks with a disreputable handkerchief and hiccupping uncontrollably.

"The photographs will prove beyond a doubt that the police tortured you to get a confession, that the whole thing is a scheme by the antihandgun lobby to discredit the NGA. Then we'll plead insanity and you'll be cleared."

He looks so forlorn, Leila thought. How had he gotten so confused? Certainly she had yelled at him and wept at him and had rejected him with excuses about his commitment to the NGA, about cigarettes and politicians, all of it a blind to cover her real loss, the right to be a mother and the God-given chance to have children, which he had taken away from her. Because of the illusory power and the money that had flowed from representing the NGA, Barkers Hill, CANCER, and the President's obsessive war mania, and by helping to build the great PACs, she had cheated herself out of her final chance, the chance to be a schoolteacher, to immerse herself in a sea of children. Now, somehow, it had taken this terrible turning, which had led to thirty-nine cold-blooded murders.

"You are insane, Ellsworth. That is, not in any way sane. You are mentally diseased and immediately certifiable," she said.

"I admit it all does sound sort of wiggy," he said, "but I assure you, everything I did was rational. All of it, every one of those killings, had a clear reason for being. I am afraid I would have to resist any defense based upon insanity."

41

With every newspaper and every radio and television station trumpeting the confession of the serial gun murders by the head of the NGA, Leila was summoned directly out of the meeting with Carswell to a hastily summoned meeting of the Board of Directors of the NGA. The decision to call an emergency meeting of the board had been made so quickly that there had been little time to rearrange the shooting gallery into a proper meeting room, but a table and chairs were in place even if the gun racks and targets were still showing.

The board itself was usually an impressive gathering of American leaders: well tailored, portly, rubicund, and, in that special way undertakers are, jolly. That collective surface mood had changed for this emergency meeting however. Their very incomes had been threatened. Moreover, they had been betrayed by an underling whom they had sponsored well and paid well, and this foulness of the human spirit had made them savage and remorselessly vindictive.

Basil Schute, formerly Honorary Chief Arsenal Officer, had been asked, temporarily, to preside over the meeting. Every one of the sixteen directors wore a black suit with a mourning armband, a black tie, and a white shirt. Schute, a hogshead of a man emanating a powerful man smell, was dressed entirely by L. L. Bean, from his mocassins to his khaki-colored duck knickerbockers and his John Wayne–style hat worn indoors and out, which had trout flies hooked into the sweatband. Schute was the outright owner and sole manufacturer of ammunition for handguns and rifles that exploded upon impact, causing irreversible damage and having 4.6 times the fatality probability of ordinary missiles. Therefore, due to the popularity of the item in the great housing projects of the inner cities, he had become an NGA leader overnight. He was envied and sought after. If he wanted it, the vacant leadership of the NGA would be his for the asking.

"I stand here as a symbolic voice for our fallen," he said. He had a high, almost falsetto register to which he seemed to be listening intently and appearing unable to control his impatience with when it was silent. His voice, like that of so many great men, was his mirror. "If it is my fate to follow them, so be it."

There were cries of "Hear! Hear!"

"I have asked NGA legal counsel Leila Aluja of Schwartz, Blacker, and Moltonero to meet with that martyr to our cause, Ellsworth Carswell, whom the police are now attempting to railroad for a crime which he could not possibly have committed. I can only conclude that all this is a plot by that Brady woman and her antihandgun cabal to discredit this organization through their allies the police."

Except for the occasional member, preoccupied with the peril which his livelihood faced, who would absentmindedly and morosely make a snapshot with a handgun at one of the moving targets at the far end of the chamber, the room was morbidly silent as Leila entered. Before Leila had a chance to take the empty seat at Schute's right hand far up at the head of the table, Schute said, "Is it true? Are the police out to frame Ellsworth?"

She stared at him, unable to conceal her pity, not only for his ignorance, but over the fact that a man of his enormous bulk and outright smelly shagginess could have such a squeaky child's voice. "They have a full confession," she told the entire meeting. "Not only did he intend to shoot down all members of the Senate Judiciary Committee, but he told the police that he had killed Owlsley and the bodyguards, Mrs. Brownlee and the children, and Senator Aukins. He signed the statement to that precise effect."

"Impossible!"

"Ridiculous!"

"Horseshit," Basil Schute said, "if you'll pardon the brusqueness of an old soldier."

"However," Leila continued, "he had been badly beaten, probably because he had resisted arrest. He had every right to be where he was when they took him. He had been subpoenaed to appear as an expert witness before the committee."

She nodded across the room to the technicians who had accompanied her. "I have photographs of his brutalized condition," she said to the meeting, "and will establish at his trial that he was beaten by the police into signing that confession. The police, as we know, are enemies of the NGA." She nodded at her staff. "Run it," she said.

The board of directors of the NGA sat rapt and horrified as shot after shot of Ellsworth Carswell's mutilated and swollen face appeared on the forty-by-fifty-foot television screen at the end of the room. When the showing was over, Leila nodded to her crew, who left the room.

"That is absolutely barbarous!" Schute shrilled.

The meeting was in an uproar.

"You've got to do something about this," Schute said to Leila over the cacophony of shocked protest from the members.

"What do you mean?"

"How will you prove his innocence?"

"He refuses to try to establish his innocence, so I am going to plead insanity."

"*Insan*ity?"

"He was completely around the bend when he did those shootings."

There were outcries of "Now, just a little minute here, Counselor" and "Ellsworth Carswell wouldn't harm a fly"—a rhubarb.

"I'm sorry, madam," Basil Schute said with the sternness of a fusillade of his own patented bullets, "but the CEO of the NGA cannot possibly allow him to plead insanity. It would be making a shatterproof case that guns, not people, kill people. It would say before the television cameras of the world that anyone who owned a gun, carried a gun, or fired a gun—who kept or bore arms—was to one degree or another insane. A fifty-billion-dollar industry would be destroyed. The entire political structure of this country would be altered irretrievably."

"I don't understand. Do you want him to be executed or, after an eternity of trials and appeals, condemned to life imprisonment?"

"It is not only the case of Ellsworth Carswell who would be on trial," Schute answered her curtly. "It would be the Second Amendment to the Constitution of the United States of America and the right of all Americans to keep and bear arms."

"But, how then are we to—"

"Our sponsors," Schute thundered, "the people who pay your not inconsiderable fees, sold more than four million nonmilitary firearms last year. That's 1,376,000 pistols, 622,000 revolvers, 1,382,000 rifles, and 688,000 shotguns. Almost alone, we have built the homicide rate in a relatively small city such as Dallas to be the highest in the country, perhaps the world, and sixty or seventy American cities are pushing for that distinction right behind. What do you think would happen to that sales curve if the National Gun Carriers' Association announced that people who shot at other people with those weapons were insane? Where would the vital civilian ammunition industry be? Yes, sure, there are still two hundred million guns in circulation throughout the land of the free, and they will still be circulating for fifty years, maybe longer, but the NGA represents a growth industry."

"Carswell has said to me that he will testify under oath that he murdered or caused the murders of thirty-nine people," Leila said angrily. "Any court would take that automatically as grounds for insanity."

"Carswell was the key officer of the NGA when he shot those people—if he did, which all here sincerely doubt," Schute said flatly. "So if you plead that he is insane, where would that leave the rest of us in this room who advocate—indeed insist upon—the right of the American people to shoot guns at whomsoever they choose?"

"Get that through your head, counselor," a voice from halfway down the table shouted. "If you plead the executive director of the NGA insane, you'll not only be giving the Judas kiss to this powerful and vindictive organization but you'll be bringing down the wrath of the entire Congress and the President of the United States, the entire defense establishment including NATO, and the pillars of the Mafia upon yourself. No one can survive that. We—and they because of us—would exact a terrible revenge."

"Then what in heaven's name are we supposed to do?"

A silence fell upon the room. Men stared at the table or at their shoes. At last, Basil Schute spoke. "That is for you to determine. That is what we pay you for."

She shrugged as if at last the whole thing were out of her hands. "Then there is only one thing to do. The NGA must arrange for a presidential pardon for Ellsworth."

There was a thickening silence while the directors weighed Leila's solution in balance then the room resounded with hearty, deeply appreciative applause.

"What a superb solution!" Schute said, grinning broadly and rubbing his hands. "Solomonic. Goodie Noon is not only a sportsman who wants to bring the privilege of guns to the inner cities but he is inclined to cooperate with us all the way, what with an election year being almost upon him."

"It will keep him on television two hours a day—his dream!" shouted a director at the far end of the table.

"And it is all so politically correct!" another voice exclaimed.

"There is a possibility of a news media outcry," Leila murmured.

"Negative propaganda can be spin-dried of course," Schute said amiably, "and pinned on a lot of radical hotheads. But if there is any appreciable outcry, we will arrange to have both the Senate and the House endorse the pardon; we'll put Ellsworth on every deep-thinking Sunday-morning talk show, plus 'Geraldo Rivera,' and the shooting in the streets can go on as before."

Rightly, Osgood Noon quietly refused to consider the possibility of a pardon for Ellsworth Carswell on the entirely just grounds that he had not been tried or found guilty of any offense. "Due process," the President said to the NGA committee who presented him with the informal petition. "Due process. *Then* the pardon."

The Justice Department conducted a sub-rosa investigation of the charges against Carswell. The case was dismissed before trial due to a lack of evidence, but Carswell was held at a medical facility in Pecos County, Texas, where he remained, under sedation, for the next eleven years.

PART

3

42

The National Gun Carriers' Association had more clout by many many times than did Leila's dad, who rallied behind her: the Congress; the Mafia, whose solid front was organized by Barkers Hill Enterprises; and all the reserve forces of power, including the White House, which Schwartz, Blacker & Moltonero could bring to bear to keep Leila in Washington. However, in the view of the National Gun Carriers', Ellsworth Carswell had tried (and failed) to disgrace the NGA in the eyes of the nation just as if the Constitution were a meaningless scrap of paper. Its officers and membership could not forgive Leila for having married Carswell in the first place, even if she had divorced him almost immediately, and even if she had refused to talk to him except on business. She had not been able to shuck off Carswell's insanity charge, so the subsequent presidential pardon had had no purpose. To have allowed the CEO of the NGA to be committed to an insane asylum for allegedly having popped a few people was unforgiveable. She was the NGA lawyer. It was her job to protect the NGA and the American Constitution. The whole ugly business had been aired and had given the news media a chance to infer that it was guns that killed people, not people who killed people, as was the total truth. Furthermore, her foot-dragging had forced the officers of the NGA to remind President Noon from whence they were coming in their effort to force him to pardon Carswell's alleged insanity, making him legally sane again and thereby showing respect for guns and the Constitution. But by that time, all the harm had been done.

The NGA flatly refused not only to have Leila continue to set foot in Washington but even refused to allow her to practice law anywhere in the United States. "She's antigun and she knows it," Basil Schute said, "and no antigun has any place in this country." It was a humiliating time. Leila was run out of town just as if she had been tarred and feathered and slung on a pole.

Given her background, her politics, and the amount of money she had accumulated both as a Washington lawyer and as Meine Edelfrau, there was no place she could go but into public relations. She had dazzling connections. She was a public figure, a supercelebrity whose counsels would be observed by the news media and by the Sunday talk shows, which did the serious thinking for the nation. Having fought Communism for so long, she knew everything there was to know about deceit, treachery, and the straight road to the American way. She had money to invest and entrée to the highest plateaus, so she found a haven as executive vice president of the country's largest and most influential mass-persuasion entity: International Communications Industries.

Leila bought her way into the firm out of the extraordinary fortune she had built as Meine Edelfrau, but she had left that personality far behind when she began the practice of law in New York. Meine Edelfrau had disappeared almost as Elvis and Marilyn had—just gone, not dead, not missing, just gone. It was widely rumored that the famous singer-dancer had entered a convent "somewhere in southern Czechoslovakia." She became part of folklore, like Ronald Reagan, someone people would swear they had seen alive.

As the rumors spread across the world, Czech tourism reported sharp increases in visitors demanding to see old convents. Special tours were arranged. Every year more and more American visitors returned to their hometowns after peering around corners in countless nunneries, saying that they had seen Meine Edelfrau, that she was alive and well and praying for all of us.

For a brief moment Leila toyed with the idea of becoming a schoolteacher, but almost instantly she saw how impractical that would be. She felt she didn't have enough experience with children who, she had been told, could be very difficult at times and who could hardly be called fastidious about their personal habits. Looked at squarely, she saw that needing to spend that much time with children could violate her sense of order. "You're just stuck with being a realist," she told herself, although silently she wished children well.

Leila's offices were in a building that loomed over Manhattan Island in New York. Slyly, even invisibly, she dictated news, opinion, and national policy from a high-ceilinged office decorated in what could only have been called state-of-the-art because its character was so far beyond what had preceded it in interior design that the culture had not yet had the time to put words to it.

The floor of the room seemed to have been covered by a large, colorful rug. But the design within the rug moved and never stopped moving. It was a forty-by-thirty-two-foot glass tank below the level of the floor surface; throughout the illuminated interior of the tank were invisible glass-walled courses channeled by walls that had been plotted in a hypnotic, labyrinthian design. Its animated colors were spectacular. In the areas between the channeling walls, exotic green and gold water plants grew and swayed in the soft, electrically induced currents of water through which swam gold, blue, emerald, and aquamarine tropical fish: cichlids, butterfly fish, angelfish, kissing gourami, and shining, darting, or suspended varieties, all forming a living rug with ultramontane patterns that changed with the movements of the life within itself.

The patterns on the walls of the room also moved. By back-projection on three walls of the room, moving-picture montages were continually replaced by other brightly colored images, each wall telling a different visual story. An endless reenactment of the Big Bang theory of creation appeared on the west wall, which faced the occupant's enormous, deeply-carved Florentine desk of the high Renaissance. On the north wall, to Leila's right, the montageur showed television footage of the primary election activity by the people of New Hampshire surrounding the choice of Osgood Noon as the Republican presidential candidate: great cheering crowds in town halls, the patient candidate slogging through the snow. Because his campaign television commercials had struck such a low denominator, the designer had his cliff-top audience staring far, far downward at a tiny figure, Osgood Noon exhorting them while mired in deep pig slurry while the hoarsely cawing Palestinian sununu birds circled overhead ready to swoop upon the awful kill at the polls. On the south wall were evolving film clips from the cinematic work of Andy Warhol including *My Hustler, Eat, Blue Movie, Nude Restaurant* and, from his motionless epic, *Empire*.

All three wall montages moiled ceaselessly and silently in endless peristaltic action, like bowels clenching and unclenching, trying to purge themselves of the fecal overstuffing of a moribund civilization.

Behind Leila, forming the east wall of the vast room, through a large plate-glass window, was a panoramic view of midtown Manhattan, the East River and, beyond, beautiful Queens, its vehicles, people, and lack of colors punctuated by repetitive shootings at, and evasive actions by, the threatened population. It provided a *tableau vivant* that balanced the punishment offered on the other three walls.

Leila felt comfortable within her own style of the cosmos. The spiral nebulae of the great galaxies across fifty million light-years of outer space, nested within universes that fit so neatly into each other, each one with dwarf stars, red giants, suns, quasars, black holes, and planets that fit into other great and smaller universes, like wood atoms in a pipe bowl, reassured her complex mind while startling and often dismaying the people who came to consult her. Chaos was function. Confusion was one of the primary working tools of her business. Continually divert the eye and you divert the mind. The spirit will follow and the national culture will reconstruct itself, a principal proven by television and politicians. It was an article of faith in the practice of her profession.

The entrance to the room was through double doors centered within the animated areas of the creation of the universe.

The furniture in the room had been imported from the study of Friedrich Nietzsche at Naumburg, then reupholstered with cured lion pelts—giving the room a distinct hint of the Ubermensch. The re-covered horsehair upholstery to one side, it was entirely Biedermeier: curved supports and chair backs, veneers in mahogany, light birch, grained ash, pear, and cherry. The carved, rolled sides of the facing nine-place sofas were ornamented with curved-neck swans, cornucopiae, griffins, and foliage, all gilded.

A copy of *Also Sprach Zarathustra*—containing a stunningly convincing forgery of Nietzsche's handwriting, which said, "Fur Evelyn von Jagen, meine unbetungswurdig Uberfrau, Immer,

Nietzsche"—lay on the large, low table where all the pieces of a Japanese war game had been assembled.

Inevitably, left alone in the room for a moment, the new client would pick up the book and, just as Leila returned, be found reading the inscription. Leila would explain that Evelyn von Jagen had been her maternal grandmother, then she would use her translation of the inscription to explain her own theory of supermen as the definition related to her clients, whose destiny it was, she told them, to dominate their worlds.

At 6:12 P.M. Leila Aluja, one of the three partners of International Communications Industries, which was the leading PR company of the world, was still at her desk/easel working at the desktop publishing unit, composing headlines to be assigned to the nation's newspapers for the next day's editions. She was a striking woman: eyes like black kumquats, rose-over-olive skin, big hair, animal-white teeth. She was wearing (in the office only and for that afternoon only) one of Geoffrey Beene's front-slashed casuals which revealed her operatically beautiful legs, thigh to ankle. Her honey-colored hair was arranged in the Grecian style of the Second Empire. Its styling and color would be changed the following week to a blue-black stylized bob with bangs. She would wear tailored slacks. The changes gave her mystery and a need-to-know inevitability while confusing her clients, who were never quite sure of who she was or if she were meant to be taken seriously, as well as reconfirming her priesthood in the religion of constant change, that phenomenon which kept people from thinking—the American way.

ICI had 8,700 employees in 56 offices in 11 countries. The company billed $341,000,000 in gross fees annually. Leila's division was charged (primarily) with molding international public opinion to conform with the lofty aims of the United States Department of Defense. Leila Aluja (indirectly) was the personal public relations consultant to President Noon, maintaining a conduit of counsel to the White House through Wambly Keifetz (because the NGA had forbidden the President from talking to her directly) and to the CEO of the Bahama Beaver Bonnet Company; she was "adviser of Presidents." Aluja stayed far from the White House, indeed well away from Washington, because although she did Goodie Noon's thinking on Department of Defense matters, and on the elimination of the capital gains tax, which was the President's sole domestic economic "program," it was required that she remain "invisible," lest the NGA strike the President from office.

Due to Leila's continuing (invisible) advice, on behalf of her clients the Joint Chiefs of Staff, Goodie Noon believed in secure government. His national security adviser was a four-star general. A Marine Corps commandant ran the FBI, an Air Force general headed the CIA, and a fleet admiral sat at the helm of the National Security Agency—all of these firmly held Haselgrove Organization operations. The law required the Secretary of Defense to be a civilian, shaking Goodie Noon badly when he was forced to face this grisly fact. He had been told that White House lobbyists could persuade the Congress to rescind that law, but a telephone conversation with his predecessor had convinced him that the astrology wasn't right for such a move. Nonetheless, all other cabinet secretaries were former or present high-ranking military executives, including Agriculture, which was run by a former commandant of the Coast Guard. "No one is going to try throwing a sneak punch at an outfit like this one," the President had told his wife.

If there was a drawback to the rationale, and every system has its so-called negatives, it was that the Noon government was almost continually engaged in gigantic weapons-manufacturing programs totaling hundreds of billions of dollars as well as in "small" wars and enormously expensive homecoming parades. As his advisers assured Goodie, expensive weapons needed to be tested in combat even if it did result in a few hundred thousand dead people, and the flag and bunting manufacturers were entitled to support.

Her fees for shaping the President's image came out of the U.S. Overseas Construction and Rehabilitation Service, paid to Bahama Beaver as a contractor, then transmitted to an ICI number account in Aruba or Hong Kong. ICI reimbursed Bahama Beaver for its tax indebtedness through overlapping fees for counseling services which ICI performed directly for Bahama Beaver Bonnet. The taxpayers never felt the bite and, even if they did, they could go back to sleep knowing that their leader was getting the most expensive, and therefore the highest quality advice.

The ICI counsel and manipulations had won Goodie Noon historically high ratings in the public opinion polls despite his thirst for wars and his assaults upon civil rights, women's views on abortion, the Supreme Court, the national economy, the environment from the North Slope to the wetlands of Florida, health care, and its staggeringly increasing costs, education, and freedom of speech. Making all that failure possible was the rigid rule that all polls were restricted to sampling the opinion of 1,247 people, chosen at random by the Republican National Committee out of 247,000,000 and through which Goodie Noon was proclaimed weekly as the most popular American President in history. It was an airtight, tamperproof system, which had been proven during all the Reagan years.

When he was not savaging domestic institutions, Goodie Noon was preternaturally taken up with meeting and greeting foreign heads of state, always standing on the left of the photographs (pointing at some invisible object to demonstrate his hegemony) for readers who only read the opening name of a caption. He had visited all the (known) countries of the world, some as many as thirteen times, at heavily unnecessary expense. He had one domestic policy: that the reduction of the capital gains tax, which no one but he seemed capable of understanding, would bring instant prosperity to the country.

A hunger for popularity was Goodie Noon's most shining characteristic. This psychological bulimia went far beyond any implication that universal popularity might assure his reelection in the first elective office he had ever held. To Goodie, life was an ongoing, endless, and all-absorbing popularity contest. More than anything else, from boyhood, he had lusted not only to be universally admired but to be "one of the boys" excelling in the manly sports.

He had won his *D* for deviousness in the great game of life because he had had to be devious. "Of course you a pathological liar, sugah," his wife, Oona, had explained. "Who wouldn't be in your position of bein' an appointee all your life, dependent on the kindness of elected people who treated you like a grovelin' dog? You had to kiss ass to get where you got. Now that you been elected to somethin', that cain't be espected to change you habits of a lifetime. You a trained, conditioned, and forceful, if transparent liar, and the polls show that at least 1,247 people love you fo' it."

He would lean over and kiss her cheek every time she said that, taking time out of a busy schedule.

Leila Aluja and ICI had been in charge of projecting Goodie Noon's destiny (just as Ronald Reagan's formidable essence had been crafted by astrologers) since the time when the owners of the country had chosen Goodie to be the nation's President after an interminable career of never being elected to anything, but always being appointed to tasks because he was such a generous Party contributor.

When clients complained to her that the constant activity on the walls and the floor of her office made it impossible for them to think (which was the reason why the hallucinatory montages were there at all), she would tell them, "The world hears the language of symbols over the noise of self. Here, in this room, we are surrounded by that language. The source of all life—water, vegetation, and fish—are at our feet. There—on the west wall—is the origin of the universe, a cacophony of chaos out of which time wrested order. There—the north wall—the triumph of hypocrisy and cant over reason in democracy, of the upward mobility of devious mediocrity. Here—on the south wall—the ever-downward spiral of art and American aspiration lifted in triumph to a mountaintop of reverberating acclaim. Combined, the floor of this room and its three walls are the meaning of public relations, the modern metaphysical science, while behind me lives its market, the minds and purses of the great American people."

All that was delivered with quiet burning sincerity, bowling over her defenseless prospects. Aluja was a master of the horseshit incantations of the great PR fakirs. She had told Donald Trump, ". . . for you are the American Beethoven and your theme must recur, and recur, and recur."

For exceedingly large sums of money, International Communications Industries had formed the images of Barkers Hill Enterprises, the conglomerates' conglomerate, the holding company for the untaxed billions of the great Mafia families of the country, as well as the tobacco conspiracy to kill more people than the National Gun Carriers' Association or the entire cocaine output of Bolivia and Colombia; the real estate lobby, whose ceaseless campaign promised investors riches beyond the wildest greed-dreams of banks and insurance companies; savings and loan institutions, which had dropped the paralyzing weight of an $11,234 debt upon the heads of every man, woman, and child in America.

Leila, and ICI, had shown more than one foreign government that they could go right over the head of the President of the United States by instructing their paid and unpaid lobbies to bribe the Congress through its Political Action Committees. At first there was resistance by clients because it was reasoned that, if foreign governments interfered with the functions of American government to the detriment of the American people, that their agents could be charged with treason. Leila had easily convinced them of the foolishness of that notion. "If you want to milk the American government," she taught them, "you have to do it through the Congress. Only the Congress can bring charges of treason. Your people will have bought the Congress; you will own it. So who is going to charge treason?"

There was little hope for succor, or even for the slightest wisp of pity from the black hole that was Washington. The government of the United States represented a peddler's marketplace funded by an elite business class and foreign governments, not the people who had elected it. The Congress was on the take. Over the short five-year period from 1985 to 1990, totally nongovernmental Political Action Committees paid members of the Congress $26.8 million, making the United States the only western democracy in which legislative elections were entirely funded by private interests. You got what you paid for and, if you didn't pay, you didn't get. After five thousand years of trial and error, prostitution had been refined to this.

Just as invisibly, ICI now represented Goodie Noon, forty-third President of the United States, as a personal account with fees and charges ostensibly paid for (should there ever be a formal investigation) by dear friends of the President's, such as the Bahama Beaver Bonnet Company, the Teamsters Union, the heavy armaments manufacturers, the Mafia, Big Oil, and the financial community, but actually routed through devious paths from covert Department of Defense funds. This was made possible because the country had gradually, since the endless "small" wars following

Korea and Vietnam, become a corporate military state, a clone of the ghastly stasis which had destroyed the USSR.

It was a marvel of waste through scientific pillaging after the disappearance of its forever menacing enemy, the Soviet Union and all its vassals. The Pentagon was still seeking more than $500 billion from taxpayers already maimed by the failing economy, for "about one hundred major weapons acquisition programs" to "protect" a nation whose single seventy-year-old threat—Soviet Communism—had passed into history. The $500 billion worth of "protection" was for a country that was at the mercy of its politicians, therefore unable to afford health care for millions of its citizens or to fight to stave off their strangling by the contaminated environment.

Professional military imaginations soared to the fantasy of $95 billion for new fighter planes that had no conceivable military opponent. Gadget bombers, at $16 billion each, were rushed through over the protests of both the news media and the people (a strange alliance). To the $24 billion already wasted on research for Star Wars, the DOD was looking for $20 billion more. A C-17 troop transport was ticketed at $17 billion until, at last, DOD spending exceeded the combined net profits of all American corporations all in the sacred name of Goodie Noon's Nifty World Order, for want of a better excuse.

The national economy was held at ransom by the whims of threatened defense spending cuts. Entire regions of the country lived in fear that their share of the tens of thousands of jobs that depended upon the ultimate deaths or misery of hundreds of thousands of unknown people somewhere out in the world would be canceled by a horror known as "the peace dividend."

Leila Aluja and her truth machines sold all this to the people through every leak in the national dike of overcommunications. From celluloid buttons to Sunday-morning talk shows, her stooges hammered away at the almost nonexistent attention span of the public paying for all of it with the message that the generals hated war and that their beloved President hated war but that half a trillion smackers had to be spent on the most heinous weapons of destruction if the flag was to be protected.

The military had more employees than the rest of the government combined, all of it making possible continuing international violence, which assured the total control of American capital. The military prospered. The national infrastructure rotted. Education was no longer affordable, the environment reeked of death, an unbridgeable chasm ruptured the live-and-let-live tradition between rich and poor, medical costs and health care spiraled far out of reach of the enormous population under sixty-five, expanding racism was becoming a greater infection than AIDS, and a progressively greater proportion of the people were forced into homelessness, hunger, and disease. It was the thrust of the enforced downward spiral of the West, the irreversible slide into oblivion, while the nations of the Pacific Rim rose like suns in the east.

While the American armies marched and its Air Force bombed the minds and hearts of American couch potatoes with "uncanny accuracy" (88,500 tons of bombs were dropped on Iraq, with 70 percent of these missing their targets) dropping the message of an eternal state of war down the chimneys of their souls.

Goodie Noon followed the parade as the proclaimed commander-in-chief and scored more on-camera time on world television than even he had ever dreamed of. They were *watching* him! They were *hearing* him! They *loved* him! He was the leader of the Free World, greedily oblivious to the unbearable fact that building and operating the armed forces and their industrial base was the primary activity of government despite a lot of crap that got printed about education, civil rights, abortion, bank disasters, sexual harassment, inflation, and nonsense like that.

After the little wars, which had cost more than $70 billion, it was Leila Aluja's brief from the Pentagon that cleared the path allowing Goodie Noon to re-arm the Middle East, for there was nothing he enjoyed more than exciting wars against underarmed, primitive enemies, believing—as the Pentagon had taught him—that the little wars were not only good for business but even better for his central helplessness, popularity. Through a third party, "the friend of Presidents," Wambly Keifetz, Leila had subtly but surely planted deep within his psyche the most wistful hope of Goodie Noon's life. It was his secret dream that perhaps, during his term of office, an American civil war might be arranged, transforming him into a modern Abraham Lincoln, with all the attendant spiritual greatness and popularity marching on with his truth beyond the grave, yet giving the military a chance to test their weapons right on home grounds.

Heaven knows she was a busy woman, but she certainly wasn't getting much sex. If it were only a matter of sex, that could have been arranged, but she needed a man. Joe had become a legend in her life, almost reduced to being no more than a rumor. He had been a darling man when he was there, of course, but the fact was, he wasn't. She couldn't very well enjoy breakfast or go to the theater with a bunch of letters, which had been arriving less and less frequently anyway. Maybe someday he would bring the yogurt down from the mountain. In the meantime she was getting antsy.

43

Leila's wedding to Professor Mungo Neil was attended by the military, social, economic, political, and show biz leadership of the Western hemisphere. People who had not been invited just faded away; health and influence were ruined; connections and the respect that the community had previously given to them were gone. The wedding presents showered on the bride and groom were displayed, row upon row, in locked, tamperproof glass cases guarded by uniformed, armed men throughout the main exhibit hall of the Javits Center in New York. The bride announced that the "extra" Houdon busts that had been received as wedding gifts would be donated to American museums, in itself a tax deduction for the bride of well over $620,000. The groom had no need of tax deductions. He was the sole professor of Gaelic studies at Columbia University.

To accommodate *die Prominenten,* the awesomely distinguished wedding guests (Donald Trump, Geraldo, and Oprah Winfrey were in a front pew), the wedding was held in the Episcopal cathedral of St. John the Divine, with its capacity for twelve thousand celebrants. General Norman Schwarzkopf (USA, ret.), stern but jolly in his battle fatigues, gave away the bride. Mrs. Imelda Marcos was matron of honor. Although the two men had never met, the President of the Irish Republic had been persuaded by the State Department to be the groom's best man.

In a giddy romantic way, the wedding was a love match. In every sense, Leila had literally swept her husband off his seat while she felt such stirrings of awe for his learning, attraction by his bearing, and headiness due to his man smell, that she was, helplessly, a woman in love. It was some kind of glittering miracle that the couple ever met because—on the surface—their worlds were so far apart. Their encounter could have happened in an RKO-Radio picture starring Fred Astaire and Ginger Rogers, produced by Pandro S. Berman and directed by Hermes Pan with a plot which would have had Miss Rogers as a millionaire heiress who secretly, in her heart of hearts, wished more than anything in the world that she could be a schoolteacher when, through a series of fortuitous, not to say happy-go-lucky, circumstances she meets a genuine college professor who is a terrific dancer.

The Pentagon had arranged with Columbia University, as a birthday surprise for Leila, an honorary degree as Doctor of Education to be conferred on her at its June commencement exercises. More than anything, Leila had told anyone who would listen, she wanted to help to mold America's children and their future, no matter what the sacrifice to herself. One day, when her work was done and her Presidential Medal of Freedom had been locked away in a safe-deposit box with, say, another $10 million, she was going to find her way to a little schoolhouse somewhere in this great country of ours and breathe new meaning into McGuffy's reader for eager children.

On the same day Leila was to receive her Doctor of Education degree, the man she had not yet met but whom she was destined to marry was to be awarded the Daithi Hanly Medal for Gaelgoiri, funded by the Kilmoganny Foundation.

Leila had anointed herself heavily with tuberose perfume, a scent which, unknown to her, repelled men, but which, because she liked the scent, she was sure attracted men. It was one of nature's sweeter jokes. Dr. Neil, Leila's benchmate, was more negatively susceptible to the perfume than most other men.

Capped and gowned, the side-by-side professor and the aspiring schoolteacher sat rather high up at the extreme end of the seventh row of the bleachers that had been erected so the honorees could be more easily identified in an outdoor, artificially landscaped glade on the campus; they faced the entire graduating class and their families. The couple had not been introduced to each other. Leila's staff had told her that the man who would be seated on her other side would be, by far, the more profitable to converse with, if it came to that.

Through an unforeseen calculation, before they had had the chance to introduce themselves, if that had been in the cards, Professor Neil fell off the stands, just disappearing and leaving an even greater blank space beside Leila. He had been edging farther and farther away from the awful smell when he dropped off the end of the row.

She had just decided that it would be friendly, or at least tension settling, to acknowledge that Dr. Neil was beside her, just as the man on the other side, the geologist John Jackson, had graciously acknowledged her. It was then that Leila noticed that Dr. Neil was gone, but she could not fathom how he could have disappeared because, sitting at the end of the line, he would have had to cross her to get out.

From a height of fourteen feet, it had been rather a bad fall. When the ceremonies had begun, Leila was sure she heard small moans from an area almost directly below her. While trying to maintain an attitude of respectful attention to the rites evolving in front of her, she sidled to the end of the row, looked down, and saw the semi-unconscious Dr. Neil trying to pull himself up into a sitting position on the ground, but falling back pitiably with each attempt.

Leila was not a $41,000-a-week executive because she was indecisive. She stood up, sidled across the row to the down aisle, and, as unobtrusively as possible, which wasn't entirely unobtrusive, made her way, wearing the voluminous robes of a scholar-to-be, to the dais itself, then faded around toward the back of the underside of the stand, catching the eye of a uniformed campus policeman. She pulled him out of sight under the stands. "The man next to me up there just fell off. He's lying unconscious under the stands on the other side," she said.

They scrabbled with some difficulty under the stands to Dr. Neil's side. The cop took one look and said, "I'll get a stretcher." He darted off.

Dr. Neil had six cracked ribs, fractures of the cuneiform bone on the outer side of the foot and sesamoid bones of the right wrist, and a line fracture of the right ulna and an enormous black eye.

Both Leila and Dr. Neil were at St. Luke's Hospital on West 114th Street when Leila's honorary degree was announced on campus at Columbia. A whispered explanation was made to the provost and, when he told the story to the assembly, a warm public tribute of sustained applause was paid to Leila for her gallantry and unselfishness.

Leila filled Dr. Neil's hospital room with flowers. She had him moved from a ward to a private room. She visited him every day. As he lay there, semiconscious from hospital dope, she would study the settled integuement of his face, Lincolnesque with just a touch of Meyer Lansky, she thought. She stared down at him, at first with curiosity then, more and more, tenderly. She admired the statement his eyebrows made and the nose that might well in the past have been fitted on the face of George Washington or any malefactor of great wealth in the Roman Julian house. He had nobility of nose and a dark, scowling set of eyebrows, she thought. Before she had ever spoken to him, she fell in love with him.

Had she known that he had been a poor orphan boy, raised in an institution for waifs in Hoboken, New Jersey, had she been made aware of the circumstances of his early life, she might have wept at the hospital bedside not out of any such scorned emotion as pity, but from total, overwhelming admiration.

When he had been released into the world from the orphanage, at sixteen, he had made his way as an itinerant bootblack who, whenever he had earned the necessary three dollars to sustain himself for the day and to pay for his lodging, clothing, and food, and to put a bit aside for his education, would spend the rest of his time studying: morning, noon, and night—day-extension courses and night-extension courses until he had mastered ancient Gaelic and primeval Irish history. Living as he did among hundreds of Italian-Americans, he had reasoned that a scholar's knowledge of the Irish language and history would make him stand out like a flame upon the sea.

It hadn't been all that easy. For twenty-three years he had studied languages and earned linguisitic academic degrees until at last he had felt qualified to compete for the newly made chair of Gaelic Studies at Columbia. He had been one of the scholastic finds of the year. The chair had been endowed by a sentimental Irish-American savings and loan tycoon who had named it for his mother, calling it the Mary Slavin Chair of Gaelic Studies. Soon after so endowing the chair, he had been sentenced for grand fraud and misappropriation, but the Slavin Trust continued, earning heavy interest on the funding provided.

Mungo was so absorbed by the scholarly demands of his professorship that it had never bothered him, if he had noticed at all, that the enrollment to his classes had never exceeded two students.

When he was well out of anesthetic, she introduced herself. "I am Leila Aluja. We were seated together at the commencement when you fell off."

He tried to smile, nodded, and tried not to inhale. "You smell differently today," Dr. Neil said.

"Smell?"

"You were wearing some extraordinary perfume. I was edging away from it when I fell off."

"I don't understand," Leila persisted. "What smell?"

"No matter, really. It was just an illusion. You smell really quite nice today."

He could not remember ever seeing a more exotically beautiful woman than this angel of mercy who was always beside his bed whenever he awoke. She was some sort of Latina, he thought. He tried out Castilian Spanish on her, then a few of the South American Indio-Hispanic dialects, but he could see that she wasn't receiving him. It became a problem to be solved. As a linguist and as a scholar, he would not ask her directly, but would keep trying various language forms. He always drew a blank. When she happened to mention that her father had been born in the Iraqi village of Uja, Dr. Neil twigged. He poured out a greeting in the form of a twelfth-century Arabic love poem that was rather erotic, but he had never had reason to interpret it that way.

"I don't speak any of that native gook talk," Leila said. "My father figured we never could use it."

The sweetness, the naivete of her approach to language, the great base of every culture of world history, had wrung sympathy from his heart. He had to see more of her. He had to know her better.

After his release from the hospital, he asked her to a dance at Youth House, off-campus at Columbia, which her schedule wouldn't allow her to accept. He telephoned her formally suggesting boat rides on the Staten Island ferry, visits to the Central Park Zoo, and hikes across Van Cortlandt Park. At the beginning, she thought he must be teasing with such invitations, but when she did accept a luncheon date and discovered that lunch was served from an ambulant frankfurter wagon in the garment district, she began to understand that he was very, very poor and this was so quaint that it reached her heart.

Dr. Neil was in no way a ladies' man. He was shy to the point of being withdrawn. He had neither knowledge nor interest in the world in which Leila moved, or in any other sphere beyond fifth-century Ireland. He was a scholar and, for all his dignity, a naive man who seemed unaccustomed to twentieth-century ways.

Within four months they were engaged. There was no ring because he said the ancient Gaels had preferred to paint a ring of blue around the third toe on the left foot, a sensible identity tag if one did not wear shoes. He never expanded on this lore, but gave her one exquisite artificial white lilac which, he said, because it was made of wax (and if it were properly cared for) should last forever. Leila wept at the beauty of the thought.

The wedding reception at Leila's apartment overlooking the East River and beautiful Queens followed their engagement by eleven months. The newly made and deliriously contented Doctor of Education had had her chef, Mme. de Caunteton, who had been trained at Examen de Fin D'Apprentissage de Patissier, make several walnut cakes from a priceless recipe that seemed to go with anything, tea, cocaine, or alcohol. It was soon established that, if there was anything Professor Neil really doted on, it was walnut cake.

At the reception, as she circulated, she kept returning to his side again and again, at first delighted that he was enjoying the cake and saying so, then slightly alarmed when she realized that he must be eating his fourth slice of it.

They had decided to live on at Leila's triplex apartment with its indoor boccie court, because Dr. Neil resided at the YMCA, which would have objected on sexist policy grounds had Leila wished to live there with him. Her limousine drove him to the Columbia campus each morning after it had dropped her off at her office. They had long talks about the teaching life, Leila's dream of Utopia, and the responsibilities it entailed. Dr. Neil was brave about becoming a part of Leila's circle of friends, never criticizing their little cocaine tics, always trying to keep up with their conversations, mainly about money or the current war; a preponderance of the guests were high-ranking uniformed military.

Dr. Neil was a shortish, dark-complected man with blondish hair who collected old railway memorabilia. Out of what had to be the meager savings of an obscure academic (the Neils kept separate financial accounts), he had just acquired a vast Dublin-to-Limerick collection, intact, for $400, which included 122 public and employee timetables, 317 marked lantern black-and-white negatives, 2,774 adult and school weekly passes, system passes, tickets, forms, a rule book, transfers, and company publications. In a larky moment, he had confided in Leila that he could double his investment in the collection if he could be persuaded to sell it in ten or twelve years' time. When Leila's friends got into talks about money and investments, he would always be ready to join in with accounts of his collection.

44

She had been married three months and four days when the terrible letter arrived. "Flame of my heart," the letter said,

> This is not to blame you for what has happened. We both know that almost eight years have compelled us to be apart. I could not stand it any longer. I left Albania and came to New York, having followed in my doomed, distant way, every step of your brilliant career. The day I arrived was the day after your wedding. My heart imploded! I went to the little church of St. Kerghiz the Armenian and stayed there for two days, on my knees, praying for pity.
>
> It is all right. I understand. You are young and healthy and beautiful and it would have been unnatural to expect you to wait forever for me. But eight years? What is eight years? My father has been married to one of his wives for seventy-nine years. But, no! I do not reproach you. I will mourn you for the rest of my life, which may be a very, very long time because I have eaten so much of my great-grandfather's yogurt. I will sit in dim rooms staring out at our past together at what I can see now were not only the golden years of Hollywood but the shining, golden years of our lives.
>
> I have seen Mr. Wolgast. Tomorrow I shall return to Albania. I told him that I must renounce my four million–odd dollars of inheritance because nothing

would ever let me release the secret of my great-grandfather's yogurt. He was deeply sympathetic. He told me that my aunt would have been proud of me, that what I had gone through to find and weigh the perils of my great-grandfather's yogurt had been a test of my character which I had passed. I did not reveal to him that the rightness of my decision had been entirely due to my having worn the Venerable Bead upon my person for so many years, just as that wonderful object has brought so much luck to you.

He told me that, to show my aunt's appreciation of my decision, that I was to get the *total* amount of her entire estate, $52 million and some change. After the estate is settled, I intend to lease a small island in the Society group in the South Pacific and spend a few years planning the best way to give this money away.

The secret ingredient of the yogurt is the fighting bulls of Spain, or rather the cows of that ferocious breed—because the bulls get their physical conformations from the father but their aggressiveness and courage from the mother. The milk from which my village makes the yogurt comes from the mothers of the most celebrated, courageous, and strong fighting bulls in Spain. You may be certain that this secret formula will never become a scourge upon the world.

There are approximately five billion people on our planet today. In many places the food supply is threatened, rivers and lakes and even oceans are polluted, millions upon millions of cars clog our highways, poisoning the air. Every month there are more millions of homeless. There is vast unemployment. Great nations shirk from helping the weakest among their people because there isn't enough of everything to go around. If my great-grandfather's yogurt were released upon the world, there would be starvation, pestilence, and terrible wars to try to solve the problems of the heinous population explosion which the yogurt would bring with it as billions upon millions of more and more people would crowd upon the planet slurping the yogurt while the conservative Republicans in the United States would clamor to have the Congress pass laws forbidding abortions. The world population would soar to ten billion, twenty billion!—as generation upon generation doubled and tripled their unnatural lifetimes of the five billion people who fight for survival today.

I shall love you forever,
Joe

4 5

Perhaps it was an attempt by Dr. Neil to even the status balance which existed between them, when as time went on and the marriage matured, he began to throw into his conversation phrases from the early Irish language from the pre-Christian period of Ireland (A.D. 431) through the beginning of the Norse occupation (A.D. 828).

By the second year of their marriage, Dr. Neil had become a cornucopia of incomprehensible puns in the early Gaelic language. He would tell dirty jokes in pre-Christian Gaelic at dinner parties for some of the most distinguished (military) guests ever assembled. When Leila returned utterly ex*haus*ted after a hard day at the office, he would transfix her with conversation entirely in early Gaelic. He gargled gutterally at her in Gaelic, during apogees of copulation, crying out incomprehensible petitions in a Dark Ages articulation of ecstasy. It turned Leila off. It spoiled whatever plans for orgasm she might have had.

Then, when he would have recovered, while she would have lain under him like a stretched length of unbearably taut piano wire, he would begin again with the persistence of a professional storyteller, the *seanbchaidhthe,* telling tales of hauntings, pixies, giants, and banshees, laughing maniacally at the ancient Gaelic jokes, singing ballads, gasping his pleasure. He would sweep on through the tragic story of Balor and his unprophesied death at the hands of his grandson Lug (which he would explain, in English, as being essentially the same as that of Acrisius and Perseus).

Leila would try to break in at this first sign of language

comprehension saying, "But who are Acrisius and Perseus?" But he would be onto some other yarn: of Deirdre and the sons of Usnach, or narratives of the Mythological and Ulster cycles. Early on she had explained patiently that she could not comprehend what he was saying to her and had insisted that, at least, he translate the jokes. When he did, they were all stale traveling-salesmen stories (or their fifth-century equivalent).

Leila began by being confused by all this, moved into feeling flummoxed, then experienced despair. She suggested gently, then more firmly, then stridently, that he allow her to make an "exploratory" appointment for him with a conservatively based psychiatrist. "What would I say to him, Leila? That I, a professor of Gaelic studies, occasionally slip into Gaelic speech modes? It is a pure, ancient, and honorable language unlike the jargon spoken by our guests, the generals and the admirals."

As time went on, Mungo became more and more tiresome. When he did speak to her in English (beyond "please pass the salt"), it was usually to mock her profession. "Paying people like you to apologize and boast for some confederation of blackguards is one of the great flimflams of humanity," he would say. He found great glee in analyzing the morals of her clients. "Jay-zus!" he would chortle. "To think that brigands like the Mafia and the American Medical Association could believe that they had to hire press agents to survive totally violates the mind."

They had been married for three years, but after the first two years of the Gaelic patter and his attacks on the policies of American military leaders, Leila had convinced herself, even though it hurt her deeply, that she had had enough of him. She talked to a marriage counselor whom Mungo refused to see. She worked out her emotional problems with a psychiatrist, but Mungo mocked her. She couldn't just walk away from him without trying to make him tell her where they had gone wrong, but he would only laugh at her gratingly and gargle at her in Gaelic.

Both Dr. Carlos McCarry, her conservative psychiatrist, and Mrs. Hunt-Wilmot, the marriage counselor, told Leila that it was an open-and-shut case of envy, that Mungo felt inferior because of his wife's success and distinction in the face of the community's (at best) toleration of his scholarship. Their concurrence of judgment about Mungo bought Leila no relief.

In self-defense she began an affair with a famous sports dentist, a really attractive, tall, toothy, blond fellow named Mario Van Slyke. Leila had seen his picture in *Sports Illustrated* and instantly felt sexually bonded to him. She had never done it on a dental chair, but she knew they were all fully reclinable, with a firmness which should really produce results.

The coupling happened, taking both of them (almost) by surprise, on a Saturday afternoon when no other patients were expected and there were no dental assistants in the office. She had suggested (with a roguish smile) that he administer nitrous oxide, called "laughing gas," as if anyone had ever laughed while doing what Leila and Dr. Van Slyke were so intent on doing, because she knew that dentists believed that many women became sexually imaginative under its influence. He had smirked but had readily agreed.

While he prepared her for the nitrous oxide, he told her about St. Appollonia.

"She was a native Egyptian," Dr. Van Slyke explained, "this won't hurt, you'll feel nothing." He adjusted the anesthetic mask over her nose and mouth. "She had switched to Christianity in the third century A.D., offending her neighbors to the point where they had pried out all her teeth with a hammer and chisel."

"How cruel," Leila said, muffled.

"What was that?" He removed the mask so she could speak.

"I said—how cruel." He replaced the mask and began the inflow of nitrous oxide and oxygen, bending close to her and saying softly, "This evolved into a subsequent community view that she should be beatified as the patron saint of dentistry. Isn't that a charming story?"

She nodded vigorously, wondering when he would make his move.

Leila was a new patient of Dr. Van Slyke's. Usually, he treated boxers, football players, hockey and lacrosse players, jockeys, and baseball batters who had had their teeth knocked out in the normal course of their work. It was a rich field for a modern healer because sports had become the third largest American industry, after oil and entertainment. The Americans were so far ahead in sports dentistry that even the Japanese had despaired of ever catching up to them. To buttress his prestige, Van Slyke was the inventor of the Van Slyke cantilevered mouthguard, which was guaranteed to protect teeth in any contact sport but which was not yet universally worn because it was so difficult to get into the mouth.

His picture in *Sports Illustrated* had shown a tall, extremely handsome man flashing magnificent (implanted) teeth, which had been encased in structural porcelain jackets by Dr. Pincus of Beverly Hills at professional rates. These had been reinforced with bonding to an internal metal structure, making them not only beautiful but virtually indestructible. They were the teeth of tomorrow.

For Leila, what with the acclaim that had been paid to Van Slyke as a sports dentist, his exciting good looks, and those awesome teeth, it was lust at first sight. He seemed to Leila to be everything that her husband was not.

It hadn't been easy to get an appointment. There was no question of getting through to the doctor himself, and the nurse or receptionist or whoever kept asking Leila what her sports affiliation was, insisting on a description of her injuries. At first Leila had said that she wanted a dental checkup, but the secretary, or whatever, wasn't having any of that, so Leila, inflamed by the photographs in *Sports Illustrated,* had been forced to ask Edward S. Price at Barkers Hill Enterprises to line up some sporting references for her. Within twenty-four hours she had Mutts Franconi, who controlled the boxing industry, Vince Mortadella, who ran the two football leagues, and Little Morris Kaplan, who handled the all-sports book in Vegas. Each one of them was happy to call Dr. Van Slyke and secure an appointment for her for the first Saturday of the month.

"Ka-Lu-A" was being played on the Muzak system, amplified by large earphones provided by Dr. Van Slyke and accompanied by the hiss of the nitrous oxide gas. She allowed her hand to leave her side. It lifted itself to Dr. Van Slyke's crotch and squeezed gently. She looked up directly into his startled eyes.

Once she had gotten used to the unusual siting, it was an exciting happening. Needless to say, Dr. Van Slyke didn't gargle on in Dark Ages Gaelic while he pleasured her. Nonetheless, he seemed to be entirely experienced, even if that did seem irrational, considering the relatively slight number of women who might have lost teeth in contact sports.

She got a firm grip with her legs around his chest, arched her back against the firmness of the narrow upholstery, and endeavored in every way, including pants and bleatings, to make it a memorable moment. When Dr. Van Slyke reached the climax, he was so excited that he almost fell off her; only the strength in her legs held him in place, preventing what might have been a serious accident for, having not withdrawn from her, he would have taken her with him in the fall.

They became good friends after that first dental appointment.

Each Saturday, while her husband played the excessively vigorous Irish national game of hurling at Van Cortlandt Park on the Parade Field near 252nd Street and Broadway, Leila and Dr. Van Slyke met atop his narrow dental chair on 57th Street. Hurling, a running game of bash, crash, and smash, combined the more violent assaults of lacrosse and hockey, and required at least three generations of Irish blood on both sides to participate in the game even as a spectator. The club with which it was played was called a hurley; it was used to smite the small, hard leather ball and all teammates and opponents within range.

Mungo had been drawn to the game because hurleys had decorated the monuments of twelfth-century Irish chieftains.

As it happened, on the fifth Saturday afternoon of the Leila–Van Slyke trysts, Mungo Neil was struck so violently with several hurleys wielded by opposing players, that fourteen of his upper and lower front teeth had been knocked out. Professor Neil was bleeding profusely but he was fully conscious. The team doctor took one look and said, "We've got to get this man to a sports dentist." He telephoned the offices of the Gaelic Athletic Association, which immediately ordered that they take Professor Neil to Dr. Van Slyke for surgery, the professor being the 206th hurling player they had referred to him. While the emergency party sped to Dr. Van Slyke's office in an expensive Japanese automobile behind a police motorcycle escort, the GAA representative got on the phone, but, after sixteen consecutive rings, failed to get an answer at Dr. Van Slyke's office.

Absentmindedly, his concentration entirely upon the afternoon's program on the dental chair, Dr. Van Slyke had neglected to lock the outer door of his office. The two burly GAA men, still dressed in the green T-shirts and khaki shorts of their play, supporting Mungo Neil, lurched into the outer reception room and kept going into the dental offices. Almost instantly, they crossed the threshold of the passion pit.

Leila, hearing the sounds, looked up over Dr. Van Slyke's shoulder directly into her husband's face.

"Mungo!" she cried out.

Professor Neil, seeing in an instant the meaning of the horizontal tableau, began to curse steadily in Gaelic, using terrible fifth-century Gaelic oaths, his enunciation badly impeded by his lack of teeth. His two teammates were able to comprehend snatches of what he was shouting. They averted their faces in modesty.

Dr. Van Slyke became aware that someone else was in the room as soon as the strange gargled shouts had begun to escape from Professor Neil's throat. He twisted his head, still in full missionary position, and saw the three men. Outraged by this invasion of his privacy, he attempted to extricate himself from Leila while simultaneously trying to leap off and away from her to confront the intruders. He took a bad fall in a defenseless position from the high, fully reclined dental chair.

Professor Neil raced out of the offices, his two teammates in hot pursuit. Leila was able to get an ambulance by calling 911 and within twenty-three minutes Dr. Van Slyke was taken to Roosevelt Hospital, where the fractures were splinted or cast in plaster and where he was placed in traction. The sports world mourned.

46

Leila was frantic. She did her best to observe what she saw as her responsibility to Dr. Van Slyke by seeing that he had everything: doctors, flowers, and privacy. At every possible opportunity all during that awful first evening and night, she telephoned Mungo at home and at the university, but there was no reply. She had him paged at the Innisfail Ballroom and at Costello's bar and grill. She arranged with the Commandant at Bedloe's Island to send out a squad of soldiers-in-mufti to tour up and down Third Avenue and throughout Queens looking for Mungo. He had disappeared.

Through it all, she was torn by puzzlement and guilt. There had been more than fifteen million people in the metropolitan area on the day he had burst into the Van Slyke surgery to find them so flagrantly *delicto*. How could *her* husband, who had been playing an archaic Celtic game nine miles north of the office of a dentist whose name she had learned entirely at random and which she had never shared with Mungo, have burst in upon her just as she was about to achieve an illicit orgasm?

On the one hand, he had seemed to be in trauma and even had seemed to be talking with yards of flannel in his mouth. She had looked into his eyes, screamed his name, and Dr. Van Slyke had then somehow fallen off her in some angular, freakish manner and had fractured his pelvis and the femur of his right leg while snapping a collarbone. How had it all happened? Had it actually happened? But it must have happened because Dr. Van Slyke was unconscious on arrival at the hospital and she had been required to fill out as much of his vital information as she had, which was little enough.

Between waits for the doctors to emerge with bulletins, she kept telephoning Mungo. Either he hadn't gone home or he would not answer the phone.

It was after eight o'clock that evening when she left the hospital and returned to the triplex apartment to be alone with the Rothkos, Chagalls, Motherwells, and Klines, with the fabulous Regency tables and breakfronts on which she had tied up substantial capital for photo-opportunity reasons in case *Architectural Digest* wanted to do a feature.

Throughout their marriage Mungo had insisted on paying, on a pro rata basis, for the amount of space taken up by his cot and his clothes closet, his bathroom, the area of the dining room occupied by his chair, his end of the dining table, and a small corner of a study which he had insisted on sharing with Leila, although she had never used it. He had estimated as his share of the cost of the twenty-four-room apartment on two floors overlooking the East River, which had cost his wife $3,409,000, to be $1,114 annually, paid off in monthly payments of $92.85, which still represented a strain on his income from teaching what was not an intensely popular course at the university. He was such a stubborn man, Leila thought.

Mungo did not appear at the apartment until the following day, a Sunday, at 11:20 A.M. He said he had come back to get his clothes and his books. He went directly to their bedroom, intending to pack, he said. He spoke only in English—no jokes, banter, or puns in Gaelic.

He had been able to find another dentist and was wearing temporary upper and lower bridges in the front of his mouth. His manner was sullen; he appeared wholly uninterested in any explanation his wife might have had for the extraordinary position in which he had found her less than twenty-four hours before.

Leila forced the issue. "Where the hell have you been?" she demanded. "How dare you stay out all night, then stroll back in here as if absolutely nothing had happened?"

"Something happened, all right," he said. "And you know what it was."

"That's the point! The whole thing is a misunderstanding!"

"You had better get used to it," Mungo said in English. "I'm clearing out of here and I'm never coming back."

"Mungo!"

"I am moving to the Thirty-fourth Street YMCA, where I'll be more appreciated."

"But why? What has come over you? Have you lost your mind?"

"I saw what I saw. I couldn't believe what I saw, but I saw it and there were two witnesses who told me I saw it."

"Saw *what*?"

"Saw that corrupt dentist pleasuring you with your eyes all glazed as if you were some pervert who could only make it in a dental chair."

"That is utterly ridiculous! He was studying my mouth. He had misplaced his eyeglasses so he had to get up close to make his diagnosis. That is how he works and may be why he is such a great dentist!"

"Please, Leila. Don't insult me any more than you have done."

He continued to pack the single suitcase he owned, throwing things in at random, hardly aware of what he was doing. Leila closed the suitcase and sat on it.

"You don't love me," she sobbed. "You never could have loved me, or you couldn't act like this over a total misunderstanding. I don't know what you *think* you saw. I only know that what was happening when you came into that office was a totally orthodox dental procedure."

"My dear Leila. The man fell to the floor. He landed on his back. How could I not have noticed that he was nude from the waist down? Or have you been able to avoid staring at that erectile fleshy thing?"

"*What* fleshy thing? I have never heard such nonsense and if you say he was nude from the waist downward, then I shall report him to the American Dental Association."

"I had two witnesses, Leila. They saw what I saw."

"Impossible! What you are saying is simply impossible! Anyway, what were you doing in that office in midtown Manhattan—wearing those outlandish shirts and shorts? What were you *doing* there?" The question was fired out of her like a pistol shot. It had all of the stark accusation of the cry from Emile Zola in a French court of law.

"Well—I—"

"Whatever you thought you saw last Saturday afternoon, did it ever occur to your diseased mind—which chose a totally rotten and false interpretation of the true facts—that what you thought you saw was the result of your own cruelty and egomania?"

"What are you talking about?"

"What kind of a marriage had you deliberately manufactured for us? You spoke in Gaelic at breakfast, at dinner—even in bed! You told what you thought were jokes—in Gaelic! We had no marriage. We were an extension of Berlitz."

"I thought it amused you!" Mungo bleated with astonishment.

"How could it amuse me? I couldn't understand one word. And you knew that! But you continued with the torture until I shrank from the need to come back to this beautiful apartment every night. I shuddered whenever I thought of you."

"Get off the suitcase, Leila."

"Mungo, please!" She was surprising herself in the grossest way. She had been under the impression that she had lost all interest in him and she had been actively planning to divorce him. She had been waiting only for the hurling season to be over in Van Cortlandt Park so that the blow could be all the sharper and she had intended, with what she had thought was iron resolve, to tell him that their marriage was over and try to work out some settlement, which would have been fair to him, not that he would have accepted a penny. But she now saw that she loved him! How did that happen? Why had she been born a woman to be forced to suffer such agonies?

"Mungo, forgive me," she said, dropping her chin to her chest, producing several real tears, and making the tactical error of all errors, by throwing herself entirely upon his mercy.

He suddenly seemed to tower over her, an impossibility. He burst into a torrent of impassioned recriminations (in Gaelic) actually saying some pretty terrible things. Then he swept her off the suitcase, slammed it shut, snapped the locks, and carried it out of the room.

The sound of the front door slamming would reverberate forever in her memory.

47

Leila had no time to think of the loss of the only man she now realized she had ever truly loved, and certainly had no time, in any event, to follow up on Mario Van Slyke's medical progress other than seeing that her office had him sent $250 worth of flowers and a charmingly humorous get-well card. On the day that Van Slyke, in traction, had finally persuaded a floor nurse to dial Leila's telephone, then to hold the phone to his ear while he listened for her voice in vain, Wambly Keifetz had summoned her to a meeting in the Department of Defense "safe house," which had been created inside the colossal torch held by the Statue of Liberty on Bedloe's Island in the New York harbor.

Access to the statue was more difficult to obtain than permission to visit the presidential living quarters at the White House. The twelve-acre island had been "hollowed out" to provide living quarters for the 1,378 officers and enlisted personnel who had been based there, secretly.

The Air Force personnel who served aboard Bedloe's, cleared after exhaustive psychological profiling, had signed on for a twelve-year hitch, never to leave their base until their tour had finished. No one had completed more than three years on Bedloe's Island, so it was not yet known how the Defense Department would continue to preserve the secrecy when their twelve years of service expired. Conjecture by personnel above the rank of lieutenant general, the lowest clearance to share the information, was that advanced brainwashing techniques would erase all memory of having served deep inside the greatest symbol, next to the the flag, of American freedom. There was another more persistent rumor at top level, that they would all be awarded the Medal of Honor, then shot.

The interior of the statue was honeycombed with electronic communications equipment and arcane weapons systems that could manage and control attack and counterattack by any enemy force if such backups as NORAD and the flying White House were to be destroyed. Installed in total secrecy, the entire installation had cost $37 billion, paid for out of secret Department of Defense funds.

As "an adviser to Presidents," Wambly Keifetz was one of the five nonmilitary people who had instant access to the complex. The President (if he could be called nonmilitary), the Secretary of Defense, the President's dog, and Leila Aluja were the others.

Showing her radioactive pass at the Manhattan ferry pier to the Green Beret sergeant who was wearing the uniform of a National Parks Service employee, after being voiceprinted and gene-classified to confirm her identity, Leila was permitted to board the ferry to ride to the statue. Even so, she was stripped and body-searched by a burly Air Force enlisted woman who called her "baby."

She was the only passenger aboard the ferry excepting a capacity complement of enlisted men and women of the U.S. Navy dressed in civilian clothes, who were pretending to be tourists while taking up all available spaces aboard the small ship to prevent normal tourists from attempting to make the voyage.

On the island, Leila was escorted by an armed guard of four Marine gunnery sergeants under the command of a Marine Corps major to the pneumatic air chute, which propelled her upward into the torch area of the statue containing the safe house. Her host, Wambly Keifetz, was alone in the room with the director of the Defense Intelligence Agency. A four-star general, he was there as a witness, but remained silent throughout the meeting. By protocol, only Keifetz rose to greet Leila as she entered the room.

Wambly Keifetz, chairman and CEO of the Bahama Beaver Bonnet Company, was a balding, tall, portly man who had been the "best friend" of eight Presidents of the United States and who had founded one of the great American fortunes by so serving. During rare moments when crises had had Presidents pleading with him to accept public office, he had served twice as Secretary of Defense, believing, as Willie Sutton had, that he should go where the money was.

There was no small talk at the meeting. Leila had known the DDIA well for years, had entertained him at her New York apartment many times, but she understood protocol and did not acknowledge that he was present in the room.

Leila and Keifetz were seated side-by-side along a long polished oak table, separated by an electronic console that contained nineteen separate studs.

The Keifetz brief to Leila was simple, direct, and in two parts. "My dear Aluja," he said without any preamble. "The Pentagon R and D and the combined scientific research facilities of forty-six of our leading universities have been working on the development of the equivalent of a brigade of electronic marksmen—not in any way different from any human infantry sharpshooters, but wholly electronic robotic figures, each in the uncanny likeness of the American fighting man, planted deep inside the Ozark Mountains and controlled by two Cray III supercomputers. These marksmen—if the bugs can be worked out—would shoot down any missiles, or hostile planes, approaching from Europe, Asia, Latin America, or South Africa, indeed from any known launching position on the globe, using fusillades of regulation-size bullets which would be armed with miniature atomic war heads, fired from mockups of infantry assault rifles."

"Ronald Reagan would be very, very proud," Leila murmured.

"Precisely. The system has cost $182 billion in secret White House funds so far; its finished cost, in 1999, has been projected at a budgetary $2.5 trillion, which is certain to be ratified by the Congress because they have yet to reject glamorous technology or expensive hardware and since the project has already, unofficially, absorbed multiple billions of taxpayers' money. Now, what the DOD wants me to ask you is this: Do you think this defense concept, at those costs, can be sold to the American people?"

"Is that all?" Leila asked.

"Not quite. There is one more question." Keifetz pressed the ON button on the console and the entire tabletop was illuminated showing a multicolored map of the world. He pressed a second stud.

The map changed instantly. The tabletop showed a map of the southern part of the USSR and most of Asia, as far west as Pakistan and as far east as Japan.

"At the moment," he said, "the Pentagon command is in the advanced stages of strategic planning for a war in Asia which would insure American domination of that continent from the Alaskan Arctic to Australian Antarctica. We have had our little practice wars in Korea, Vietnam, Grenada, Afghanistan, and Iraq and now the Joint Chiefs feel they are ready to make a major strike."

He pressed another button. The map illuminating the table changed to Outer Mongolia, showing how and where it impinged on China and indicating near-adjacency to Korea, Japan, Southeast Asia, and India.

"The battle plan would link attack areas to be established in Antarctica and the Arctic," he continued, "with the central attack command to be established in Inner Mongolia." He pressed a stud and small lights went on along the Sino-Mongolian border.

"We would establish bases in the Gobi Desert, there"—he extended a wooden pointer having a rubber tip—"a terrain in which our troops have been trained in combat during the Iraqi campaign, and in Tausagbulag, there in the east, for air strikes against Korea and Japan; and, there, in the west at Bulgan where, there is reason to believe, great deposits of oil will be found, to dominate and control India, Singapore, Indonesia, China, Korea, and Japan."

"An expensive venture, though," Leila said.

"Only on the surface. Say eight to ten billion."

"But the DOD budget for the next fiscal year is only $591 million."

Keifetz smiled at her indulgently. "In addition to the secret funds, which is the money left over from the previous six fiscal years, there will be plenty of leeway."

"Anyway, it will be a war so Congress will have to put up or get out."

"The Chiefs feel it's a bargain because it will provide a chance to try out new weapons, eliminate principal competitors for world markets, and it would pay out enormous assets of oil. The entire campaign will pay for itself within fifty-three years. It's the sort of enterprise which will get the President all tingly when we tell him about it."

"Interesting," Leila said.

"Now—I have been asked by the Joint Chiefs to put it to you: Can you sell those two brave concepts to the American people?"

"I'd like to think about it, actually."

"If the generals had wanted you to think about it, I would have covered the matter with a fax to your office," Keifetz snarled. "Time is of the essence here. We want an educated guess from the nation's top expert—you. You can do your thinking after you make your decision, just as your President does."

Leila felt an overpowering sense of responsibility. At the same time, she was edified to have been chosen to bring the message from the Joint Chiefs to the American people which would, ultimately, have so much meaning to the lives/deaths of the people of the far Pacific Rim. She moved in on the absolute essentials.

"But is it really necessary to start yet another war?"

"Sweetheart—we can't have billions and billions of dollars tied up in all these wonderful weapons without using them, can we? Did you think the Joint Chiefs were just out to waste the taxpayers' money?"

"Nuclear?"

"It will not be remotely necessary to use even tactical nuclear weapons. The new munitions—fuel-air explosives, penetration bombs, and wide-area clusters—precisely duplicate the same effects. The Multiple-Launch Rocket System can hurl hundreds of individual bombs up to twenty miles—twelve rockets in less than a minute—detonating on an area the size of six football fields for only one point two million dollars per twelve-shot salvo. The Tomahawk has a range of seven hundred miles. We shot two hundred forty of these one-thousand-pounders at Iraq in the first two weeks of the war at a cost of only one point four million dollars per Tomahawk. SLAM, a 'smart' missile, is only one point one million a missile and it throws a five-hundred-pound warhead sixty nautical miles."

"Modern science is wonderful," Leila said.

"The Chiefs' favorite has to be the fuel-air explosive because Asia has really thickly congested populations. This one really is the beauty, packed with volatile fuels so that when the fuels are released in a cloud over the target, the charge is ignited, the vapor cloud explodes into a massive fireball that incinerates everyone and everything—or asphyxiates them—within four hundred square yards. I mean, really, what with Cluster Bomb Units that literally slice hundreds of people at a time into bite-sized pieces, and the Paveway-IIIs which can penetrate the deepest, thickest air raid shelter, we're going to bring Asia to heel in, well, the strategic estimate is eleven days."

"But, Wamb—all those dead people—"

Keifetz shrugged. "Not more than three million one. Why? Does that spook you?"

"It just seems like so many."

"Very, very foreign people, Leila. And it may seem like a lot, but they *have* a lot of people. Over a billion. We'll take out about three million one, give a few, take a few—but in the long run we'll be doing them a favor because the overcrowding is really terrible in some of those areas."

"How many troops will we need to ship out?" she asked crisply, getting a firmer hold on herself, telling herself she was not going to be killing anyone, that she would only be firing up the people and their politicians to give permission to the Joint Chiefs to kill enemies of liberty, while in the long run improving future living conditions in very congested areas.

"Because of the occasional surgical accuracy of our air cover," Keifetz said, "the Chiefs estimate that they can swing the whole thing with a start-up of 725,000 men and a call-up of about 230,000 reservists. You can state with confidence that there will be no ground attack until the principal cities have been leveled."

"This is our chance to put a heavy lock on big television."

"How do you mean?"

"If we play tight with them on the scheduling of all bombings and battles, we'll be handing heavy production values without a cent of outlay by them for one long golden handshake with sponsors from the minute the war starts until th boys come marching home—and after."

"Sounds great. How do you want to do it?"

"I'll tell them we'll provide one hundred percent, dawn-to-dusk production values, giving them a pre-edited flow of visuals, exact, on-the-quarter-hour scheduling with a pre-edited flow of tremendous production values plus quarter-hour scheduling of highlights from the show—massive bombings, civilian chaos, plague results, the works—all of them with guaranteed start and finish times to accommodate their sponsors. Real slaughter, on prime time or for the morning talk shows—right in their laps at absolutely minimum cost to them."

"Terrific, Leila. Absolutely terrific."

"How much time do I have?"

"The timetable calls for the Chiefs to have the President demand the liberation of Outer Mongolia on January tenth, before the mosquito season sets in and before the celebration of their high sports holidays."

"About five months, then."

"Depending on the success of your efforts."

"Will Ronald and Nancy Reagan support this?"

"I am sure the budget provides leeway for that, yes."

"Does President Noon endorse the plan?"

"All things in good time. He'll be told, you may be sure. We're still in the planning stages. But you know Goodie. If he isn't making war, he keeps choking on his foot."

"Then the Congress hasn't been told yet?"

"Each in his turn, after we tell the President, the nation to be served," Keifetz said.

"Will Israel be with us all the way?"

"That is subject to negotiations."

"Will I have the public support of General Schwartzkopf wearing his Desert Storm uniform, his fatigue cap, and all his chest decorations?"

"He is retired, of course, and working on his novel."

"I meant for network television appearances and high-density lecture tours."

"Through sleet, through rain, through dark of night."

"Then our people can do the rest. Give us eighty million dollars and complete access to television networks, from weathermen to soaps, and I think I can say that American public opinion will be rallied behind both crusades even if it means gasoline rationing."

"Bless you, Leila."

"But this time let's have the parades and the massed flags from coast to coast *before* the wars start. It's like a kickoff for a new miniseries on television. They'll enjoy it more because it's real-life drama and they depend on us to follow each big news, shake-'em-up entertainment with an even better and more unexpected entertainment. The dull, grinding old-time reality is gone. Perpetual show biz, wonderfully balanced, tidy daily dramas have taken its place. Judge Thomas in mortal struggle against the law professor. The Keating Five—incredible but titillating. The Kennedys at Palm Beach. Middle East crises upon crises, all of it beautifully scripted, showing defiant little Israel against the world. Well! My people will develop a screenplay for this war that the Chiefs must follow precisely. It will tell the story of American conquest with all of the excitement of a good action movie. This one is bigger than the Gulf War, so it will have to be produced and directed and cast with even more suspense and drama. This time, just as we did in the politics of 'seventy-nine with Ronald Reagan, we really must cast an actor to play the commanding general in the field. That's the patriotic way. Gregory Peck would be good, but Oliver North would be better. I don't think Donald Trump is quite ready for a part like that."

"It's going to be hard to beat jolly, bluff, four-square and fair General Schwartzkopf."

"But it can be done, Wamb. The war, like everything in American life, must play out like a movie with a clear beginning, middle, and end—with heros and villains, with mood music behind the television—which will bring it all to us with some well-staged, breathtakingly brave, if controversial, war correspondents. In short, a thrilling dramatic production will be better than any movie because we will be giving them real life."

"The President will be thrilled by your concept. Even the troops will be lifted up as they watch their field television screens in the foxholes."

"A really good show, well cast, will let our boys know that we are behind them. Starting the parades now, five months before the war, will send them off knowing that the whole country is rooting for them while tipping off the nation that another great entertainment is coming their way."

Suddenly the DDI broke protocol. "There is nothing like a parade to reach the hearts of the television viewer," he said. It was such an old-fashioned, oversimplified, amateur concept that Keifetz and Leila pretended he had not spoken.

"I'd also need not less than four months leeway to get the yellow-ribbon factories into full production," Leila said, "and to have every arms plant back into swing—whether we need them or not—for fullest local employment, and we'll ride the crest of the wave to victory."

"Good. I'll see that the contracts are drawn so that you can get the effort underway."

"I think this time the contracts should be directly with the Security Council of the United Nations, guaranteed by Goodie Noon," Leila said. "Sort of direct from maker to wearer, as it were, keeping the Joint Chiefs as clean as hounds' teeth."

48

Leila lined up the great Sunday morning talk shows which did the heavy thinking for the country; organized the prewar parades; held national contests for Betsy Ross look-alikes; massed the great Hollywood stars, led by Arnold Schwarzenegger, via satellite media tours that beamed dozens of star video interviews to hundreds of television stations to draw enormous support for prewar bond auctions; orchestrated the production of video news releases simulating national news clips; prepared electronic press boxes for local TV coverage of parades and yellow-ribbon factories; and handpicked experts to act as spokesmen who could explain on videotape, radio, print media, live and on satellite television, and on the backs of breakfast food packages and ketchup bottles that America had no choice but to go to the aid of the Mongolian Peoples Republic, a family-owned country rich in oil deposits but whose pricing structures for its potential oil output was threatened by the mullahs of Iran who dominated OPEC.

She outlined speeches written for President Noon, who would appear at the rostrum in the White House pressroom to interrupt the "Phil Donahue Show," professional wrestling programs, and the prime-time soaps to cry out to preserve the liberty of the brave Mongol people. These exhortations were repeated throughout the day via satellite media tours. Goodie, exalted, was on the air for more than twenty-five minutes a day for the first twelve days of the vital public relations push. "We're gonna show them the meaning of freedom, as in free-market economy," he abjured the cameras. "A line in the sand of the Gobi has gotta be drawn around the level playing field."

Leila had the knack of believing in whatever she was paid to do. She sold war with the same high purpose and zeal she brought to her crusades for cigarettes. If the crack industry had been better organized or had any goals beyond making money by killing people, she would have sold the meaning of its effect, slightly modulated from a chemical which produced insanity, to the stuff that dreams are made of. In such professional attitudes she was no different from lawyers, economists, churches, and politicians; each of those callings needed to sell things as being other than what they were if they were to retain the respect of the community and the nation.

Leila coordinated the efforts of the owners of the great communications networks with the industrial opportunities that would be created throughout Asia following the war. She organized write-ins by the schoolchildren of America to Congress, the White House, and General Schwartzkopf, letters from the littlest Americans pleading with their leaders to protect the Khalkha tribesmen and their birthright. She arranged alliances of sister cities between Essex, Massachusetts, and Dzhibkhalantu; Dzhirgalantu and Beverly Hills, California. She worked with the great lobbying organizations in Washington to make sure that the Congress understood that there would be covert Department of Defense funds to keep every one of them entirely solvent via their Political Action Committees if they voted freedom for Outer Mongolia. She worked a fifteen-hour day, but she was never able to get Mungo Neil out of her mind.

He had disappeared. There was no trace of him at Columbia University or at the 34th Street YMCA. She never understood him, she told herself. She had never understood how much she had meant to him to make him try to obliterate his past and everything that had meaning to attempt, in his desperation, to vanish from place and from memory. That realization fell upon her with brutal force. She had gone on believing that he was indifferent to what she thought, contemptuous of what she stood for while, all the time, he had been eating his heart out. Where had she taken the wrong turning? She had tried to give him everything and he had refused it. She had introduced him to some of the great military leaders and Mafia dons of their time but that had meant less than nothing to him.

Mungo had used his scholarship to prove how callous of her

feelings he had become; even his running outbursts in the ancient Gaelic had become clear to her. And yet, because he had imagined that she had been doing something on a dentist's chair which she certainly could not have been doing, he had fled in grief from their lives.

He had seen her as dominating their marriage simply because she earned a million or two a year more than he did, and because she advised the Mafia and the Department of Defense on strategy and tactics while he earned $700 a month and was humiliated by facing classes of never more than two students each semester. Of *course* he had felt an urgent need to display his unique skills, to remind her that not more than nine people in the world, if that many, beyond the Gaeltacht, could converse, even joke, in fifth-century Gaelic. She had been blind and now she had lost him.

She asked Wambly Keifetz to have the FBI and the CIA send their teams out to scour the country to find her husband. After six weeks of intensive searching, Mungo was still missing. She begged Edward S. Price of Barkers Hill Enterprises to ask the Families to make an even more thorough search. She had the State Department seek the cooperation of the Guardai of the Republic of Ireland. Mungo, like most professional Irishmen, had never been to Ireland, but Leila felt that she could not leave any stone unturned. There was no sign of him there.

When the letter arrived five weeks after his disappearance, she was utterly unprepared for it.

> Leila:
>
> This is to ask you to be executor of my will. Moved by the threat to Outer Mongolia's freedom, I have applied for a commission in Army Intelligence. I speak, read and write Mongolian, a few of the Chinese dialects, Hindi, Malay, the ten languages of the Andamese Islands in the Bay of Bengal: Ba, Chari, Kora, Yeru, Juwoi, Kede, Kol, Puchikvar, Unge and Yarava.
>
> I have been made a captain. At the moment I am at the Officers Training School at Fort Ketcham in California and expect to be moved out to Asia tomorrow afternoon

where, at least, I can feel that I can do my part for freedom. I have an account in the amount of $1,317.89 in the Rockefeller Center branch of the East River Savings Bank. If I am killed, please see that this amount (plus interest) goes into a fund for the maintenance of the Innisfail Ballroom on Third Avenue. Innisfail, in case you don't remember our past conversations, is the old poetical name for Ireland, meaning the Island of Fal, from *inis* (island) and *Fail,* the genitive of Fal, named from the wonderful stone brought by the Tuatha De Danann—the ancient divine race of Ireland—which has now been placed under the coronation throne in Westminster Abbey, where it is inaccurately known as the Stone of Scone. I have spent many a happy hour at the ballroom, which (actually) is where I polished my (colloquial) Gaelic accent. In closing, I want to say that I regret ever having met you.

Yours sincerely,
Mungo Neil

She stared at the letter as if Mungo had indeed written it in Gaelic or Mongol or Chinese or Malay. It was incomprehensible. Then the terrible realization was driven home to her. She had sent the man she loved to his possible doom or, at best, to some of the worst meals he had ever eaten, a forty-three-year-old man banished by her own hand to one of the most uncomfortable climates of the world. The Gobi Desert???? Was this a nightmare? Mungo didn't even know when to change his pajamas. He was a helpless boob! He had swallowed all the gunk she had been pumping out into the minds of the American people and had actually gone into the Army!

She and she alone, undertaking a routine professional job of work, doing what she was paid to do, merely stirring up the nation's blood, pride, and patriotism, had swept the only man she had ever really cared for along to doom and horror on her own unrelenting tide of suffocating horseshit. The shooter had been shot; the biter bitten. Fate had tap-danced all over her face. She wanted to lower her head into her hands and weep, but, instead, she paid what she considered to be mocking, if pragmatic, homage to her husband's fractured credibility. She asked the chairman of the Joint Chiefs to have him made a chicken colonel.

For all her worry and self-recrimination, the war was over in eleven days, four days beyond the time estimated by Dr. Kissinger. Nine American combat personnel were the sum total of military casualties; two shot in a quarrel during a crap game, three to AIDS, four MIA. As Dr. Kissinger had predicted sanguinely, exactly four Jeeps were totaled.

The estimated cost of the conflict was $737 billion dollars. Goodie Noon demanded that the have-got nations of the world share in the costs of the war on the grounds that America's thirst for universal liberty had opened a market numerically 2.9 times bigger than the Common Market and the North American Free Market combined and, as if to prove his point, the triumphant armies brought thirty-seven McDonald's outlets to Outer Mongolia.

The uncanny accuracy of the Air Force, while always striving to avoid civilian targets, had razed seventeen of the principal cities of Asia, had (somehow) hit electrical plants, water and sewage systems, schools, food depots, and hospitals so the civilian deaths during and following the war were tremendous, estimated at 3,680,000 fatalities, requiring American aid which had, even at the outset, looked as though it could reach $79 billion, but, as time went on and more relief was needed, the total numbers soared.

The United States was so hard-pressed financially that there was little money for parades to welcome the victorious troops home. Goodie Noon was faced with the impossibility of raising taxes, a bane which was to cost him reelection, but ICI earned $6,250,000 in fees out of the deal and was able to skim another $2 million off the top of the expenses. The war, having proven that the nation needed to be ever-alert to guard and sustain its defenses, made necessary an increased DOD budget for the upcoming year, which was 4.7 percent higher than the calendar year preceding it.

49

Dr. Van Slyke had been released from the hospital by the time Leila was well into the campaign to sell the Asian war to the public, almost five months after Mungo had marched off to war. Although she could hardly spare the time, she had spoken with Dr. Van Slyke twice on the telephone but had put off his ardent invitations for little suppers at his apartment. She had made a bad mistake by going to that sports dentist. One of these days, Mungo would come marching home and she didn't intend to have his heart broken all over again.

The war was over. The many, many parades (fortunately, now charged to the local governments in every city of over one hundred thousand) were so well organized that her staff had them well in hand. War was well out of the way for awhile. The President was "recreating" on his estate on Bland Island, setting up powerboat shots for national television so Leila could concentrate on ruining a major insurance company for Barkers Hill Enterprises, who hoped to buy it on the cheap after it had hit bottom.

It was an interesting exercise in public relations. The insurance company had had a triple-A financial rating for half a century but the scientific placement of rumor, both nationally and in thousands of local communities, had panicked the policyholders and had forced them into a "run" on the company's treasury, thus bringing the company to its knees. Barkers Hill was able to pick it up for five cents on the dollar and to win the gratitude of tens of thousands of terrorized policyholders at the same time.

Just as she was basking in the warm glow of both the fees earned by ICI for this coup and for the bonus that had been voted to her by the board, just when she had never had more reason to be happy, the letter from Mungo arrived.

She was having breakfast on her glass-enclosed terrace on top of the thirty-sixth floor of the apartment building when Trusdale, her Scottish-Jamaican butler, brought her the letter on a silver tray. Leila barked with joy when she saw the postmark, which she couldn't quite identify, but the envelope was from some central Asian country and she was almost certain that she recognized Mungo's handwriting, which affected a Gaelic style of calligraphy so obscure that she wondered how the letter had ever gotten through to her.

She was shaken by the effect of staring at the exotically stamped, mysteriously postmarked envelope. Through all the five long months, the only way she had to learn whether Mungo was safe and unhurt had been through the satellite faxes, so graciously provided her by the Joint Chiefs of Staff. She had heard nothing directly from Mungo. She knew he had been decorated for gallantry, that he had been such a success as an intelligence officer that he had been promoted to brigadier, then to major general as his superior officers had been shot by unspeakable enemy snipers; that he had translated-interpreted for Dr. Kissinger at his crucial meeting with the headman of the Urumchi tribes. This had been a turning point of the war, but he had never so much as acknowledged that she was alive.

Now this letter! Her fingers trembled as she tore open the envelope. Her eyes went at once to the signature. There it was, just over the capital letters DICTATED BUT NOT READ; Mungo Neil, Major General, Fifth Army Corps, 22nd Intelligence Brigade, Somewhere in the Bayan Ulegei, Mongolia (APO 318). She went to the top of the letter and began, avidly, to read. "Leila, please institute divorce proceedings."

Leila felt as if she had been bitten by a yak. The shock was worse than anything she had ever known. How could he just dump his cruelties on her as if he were asking her to pass the salt?

> I have fallen in love with a Kobdo girl (from Khara Usu, actually). She has a sensational sense of humor and her dad is mayor of their village. If there was ever any

> conceivable chance that you would meet her (which there is not), I am sure you would like her enormously (once the language barrier had been overcome). I have been teaching her—her name is Pujan—six words of English each night as we cuddle under goat skins. Have your lawyers achieve the divorce with the shortest delay. It is my devout wish that I never see you again.

Her face was sticky from drenching tears. He had never given her a moment to explain. He had just run out of Dr. Van Slyke's office with some sickeningly false picture in his mind. Then, when he had come home to pack his pathetic little suitcase, he had wanted only to mock her and all of the wonderful years they had had together. A vision of the Christmas cards signed "Mungo and Pujan," packets of safety matches monogrammed *M&P* in scrolled letters, filled her mind. Did he ever intend to come home or was he going to go native, pulling wires to arrange to stay behind until the last of the occupying troops left in thirty or forty years?

Well, she would fix that little son-of-a-bitch and his Pujan. She snatched up the phone beside her bed and called the Secretary of Defense at Thok Daurapka in the Tibetan Autonomous region, where he would eat Thanksgiving turkey with the troops. The DOD operators patched her through to the satellite, then beamed down her call to the working table directly beside the Secretary's bed in no time at all.

"Mr. Secretary," she said when she had him on the line. "It's Leila Aluja, in New York. . . . Oh, fine. Beautiful day here. I can almost see Queens. How're things where you are? . . . Ah, good. . . . That's nice. Mr. Secretary, would you do me the really great favor—I mean now that the hostilities are over—of transferring Maj. Gen. Mungo Neil, my husband, back to New York? . . . Yes. Yes, he's had a wonderful war, but I miss him so. That's the Fifth Army Corps, 22nd Intelligence Brigade. In Outer Mongolia. Oh, thank you, Mr. Secretary, and my warmest and best to Betty Lou when you're talking to her."

50

Eleven days later, while she was pondering the puzzle of how to create everlasting public sympathy for a man who had defrauded a Texas S & L out of $1,650,000,000, her secretary, Miss Chapman, did an unusual thing. Miss Chapman did not call her on the intercom or speak to her on the telephone. She slipped into the room—*slipped* was the only way to describe it, Leila thought—as if she were escaping from some menacing force. She was very pale.

"It's an army general—two stars—out there, Miss Aluja. That is, he is costumed like a general and he says he is a general, but—"

"General Neil?"

"You were expecting him?"

"He's my husband, Marjorie."

"My God!"

"Send him in." Miss Chapman half-backed out of the room. In seconds, Mungo Neil stood in the doorway looking as though he were capable of eating the furniture. He was about to bellow something when the extraordinary decor of the huge room stopped him at first bark. He had never been in Leila's office before, never seen the perpetual-motion rug or the ever-changing Technicolor movies on the walls. The effect, intended to cower men far more sophisticated than mere major generals, worked its miracles on Mungo. He was deflated from a raging bull to something more in line with Elsie the Cow.

Whatever he had come to say was preempted by the confusion of his mind. "How can you work in a visual zoo like this?" he asked dazedly.

She decided not to give him the little talk about the meaning of symbols. "Mungo—you're back. How nice," she said.

"Listen to me, Leila—" he said hoarsely.

"I hope you're not just passing through? Or if you are passing through, you aren't staying in some cramped hotel when your own apartment is right where it always has been."

He was beginning to hyperventilate. "I have been transferred out of the war zone," he said stridently, "and have had my marriage plans shattered."

"Your marriage plans?" Leila said blankly. "What marriage plans? You certainly remember that you are already married?"

"Are you telling me that you didn't get my letter?"

"What letter?"

"The letter in which I asked you to file for a divorce."

"Mungo!"

"And immediately after you got that letter my transfer to New York and separation from the armed services came through by direct orders from the Secretary of Defense and that only could have happened as a result of your interference."

"*My* interference? That's preposterous!"

"What do you think this has done and is doing to my fianceé and the feelings and standing of her family in their village? She's heartbroken, the poor little thing—"

"Is she very little?" Leila asked. "We are told that Asian women are all rather tiny."

"She's a Mongolian! From a ruling family! She stands almost five feet eleven without her mukluks!"

"Ruling family? Five eleven? But you just said she was poor and little."

"Don't jerk me around, Leila," he said threateningly.

She sighed wearily. "I have been trying to carry on, Mungo. Abandoned by my husband—but that is the fate of women whose men go off to war—and now you come storming back, mewling about some fancied wrong I've somehow managed to do to you, howling about a divorce so that you can marry this, this native girl, and I am entirely confused. What is it you want me to do?"

"I want a divorce, goddamnit! Then I want you to have me reinstated in the army and transferred back to Kara Usu to try, for the rest of my life, to right this terrible wrong which has been done to an innocent little girl."

"Little?"

He uttered a string of Gaelic oaths. He flung his cap on the floor and jumped up and down on it.

"Mungo, what do you want from me?"

"A divorce!"

"How can I file for a divorce? Do you expect me to name some native Mongolian girl in a dusty little village twelve thousand miles away, behind some uncharted mountains, as co-respondent?"

"What are you talking about?"

"Did you bring pictures of the two of you in *flagrante delicto*? Are there Mongolian witnesses willing to come forward to testify that you were constantly in each others' company, in and out of the fleshpots of her central Asian metropolis?"

"You goddamn well know the grounds for this divorce. You and that depraved dentist."

"Then you will have the bring the divorce action, won't you, Mungo?" Leila said sweetly. "And in self-defense, I am going to have to charge you and that Mongolian giantess with adultery in a countersuit, am I not? The news media will have a field day: U.S. ARMY GENERAL IN ARMS OF MONGOLIAN WHILE WAR RAGED, WIFE CHARGES. That will look just dandy on your service record, won't it, Mungo? Nothing you could ever do would get you back your rank after that. The DOD will not tolerate such scandal. You will be forced to retire, then what will you do?"

"Damn you, Leila!" he shouted as he began to stride toward the door of the room.

"Go ahead, Mungo," she said. "Run away. It's what you do best. When there seems to be trouble, you run away."

"What else should I do? You have successfully stripped me of my virginity, my tenure as a professor, my Army rank, and of the woman I love. Did you think I would want to remain here to have tea with you?"

"You can't have much money, dear. You have to live somewhere and hotels are too expensive. Your room is still waiting at the apartment, which is so large you will never know I am there. You need time to plan. You need rest after the ordeal of that war. It's yours if you want it, Mungo."

He sighed. He shrugged helplessly. He nodded his agreement.

51

That evening they dined together at the Bottom of the Cage. Leila wasn't all that fond of Swedish-Hawaiian food anymore but she was treading carefully. She had sent him along to the apartment where all the servants knew him; Mme. de Caunteton had been so moved to see him again, moved actually by the two stars on each shoulder of his uniform, that she had embraced him with Gaelic ardor. They had babbled on to each other in rapid French while the rest of the staff beamed on them. Then Madame had rushed off to the kitchen to bake a walnut cake especially for him.

He took up again in his old room, with its etching of King Brian Boru, whose victory at Clontarf in 1014 had ended for all time the possibility of Scandinavian domination of Ireland. The nine hundred–odd books were lining the walls just where he had left them. His Linguaphone apparatus, with Lesson No. 63 in Liturgical Coptic still in the machine, rested where he had left it. Everything had been dusted. His Spartan cot was neatly made. His other pair of shoes, brushed and shined, stood in trees in his closet with his extra suit. He felt a warm sense of homecoming despite the fact that his heart was in the highlands of the Mongol Altai.

Before they left the apartment for the restaurant, he and Leila each had a gin sling, which the butler, Trusdale, made so well. They did not discuss his separation from the army other than Mungo saying he thought he would wear his uniform and decorations just one more time before returning to civilian clothes.

"Ought you not to get off a cable to—uh—the young lady?"

"I had thought of that, actually," Mungo said, staring at the floor, "but dialectical Mongolian doesn't go down very well with Western Union and, even if it did, the people of her village—which is some distance from the capital where, if it were possible, the message would come in—they are an *oral* people, you see. Reading just isn't part of their culture."

"If you could arrange it, Mungo, I would be really happy to pay for a singing telegram."

"No. But the DOD could send a man in. They could get a message through."

"That's a marvelous idea. I'll talk to Wambly Keifetz in the morning. Is there a base camp in the village?"

"No. But there is one quite nearby. I used to bike the sixty-odd miles over the mountains to visit."

"That's what we'll do then."

"Awfully good of you to help me out like this, Leila. Considering the circumstances."

They were having a splendid outing: caring service, rewarding wine, and eye-filling, mouth-watering Swedish-Hawaiian specialties. They were getting along together as if the breach in their marriage had never happened, frequently touching each other across the table, smiling at each other's sallies, and behaving the way things had been between them during the early days of their courtship. Leila did not once mention business or the great politicians and military leaders she dealt with daily. She dropped no names whatever; she was a deeply engaged wife. Mungo did not utter one word of Gaelic, nor did he attempt to rehash any of the agonies of the past.

As they enjoyed dessert—a *chokladglaseradeananasskiivor* with fresh Hawaiian pineapple for Leila and *jordgubbswisp* for Mungo, an apparition loomed before them, advancing from across the room, grinning broadly as he came, holding on to an aluminum hospital walker. It was Mario Van Slyke.

"Oh, my God!" Leila murmured.

"What?"

She thought in gigaflops, like a giant supercomputer capable of handling millions of calculations simultaneously. It would be impossible for Van Slyke to remember Mungo, she reasoned, whom he had seen only in a flash before he fell out of her. Mungo had had no front teeth then. He had been wearing sweaty, wrinkled running shorts and right now he was dressed in a full general officer's uniform, and had all his teeth. Mungo wouldn't remember Van Slyke because, after the dentist had crashed to the floor, Mungo had stared at the incriminating evidence of his erection, not at his face.

"I just remembered I'm not supposed to eat pineapple," she said. "It gives me hives."

"Well, well, well!" Van Slyke said as he hobbled to their table. "What an absolutely marvelous surprise to find you here, Leila." He hovered over them, a man scarcely able to walk, but Leila was damned if she was going to ask him to sit down.

Mungo said, "Please sit down, sir."

"Ah—General Neil—may I present—uh, Dr. Mario Van Slyke?"

The men shook hands, exchanging greetings. Leila almost fainted from the tension the anxiety had caused her, but it was beginning to look as if neither one of them had a clue. A waiter slid a chair under Van Slyke as Leila was saying, "General Neil, my husband, has just returned from the Asian war zone."

"Well, good heavens. How exciting. I saw a great deal of that war on television from my hospital bed right here in New York."

"In an accident, Mr. Van Slyke?" Mungo asked.

"Yes. I took a freak fall and—"

"Amazing, isn't it? I go through a war in which over three million people die and come out without a scratch and you—probably under the most peaceful conditions—"

Oh, no! Leila thought. It's coming. I know it's coming.

"You can't have more peaceful conditions than in a dental office," Van Slyke said.

"*Dent*al office?"

"Yes. I am a sports dentist."

Mungo's face slowly drained of color. It had been field tan, then it went to gray, then green, and while Van Slyke looked at him it had changed to calcimined white.

Mungo tried to speak, but couldn't. He picked up the glass of water in front of him and drained it. He found his voice—hoarse, broken, weak but persisting.

"A sports dentist?" he said dully. "On 57th Street?"

"Well—yes. Gratifying that you should know that."

Leila put a restraining hand on Mungo's forearm, but it was useless.

"You depraved son-of-a-bitch!" Mungo shouted directly into Van Slyke's face. "I am going to break every bone in your body."

Van Slyke's jaw fell toward the floor. He stared at Leila, haunted. "Is he the same—"

Mungo's left hand had him by the clothing on the front of his body and was lifting him upwards so he could get in a more solid punch with his right hand when Leila keened into his ear, "Mungo! Think of the headlines! ARMY GENERAL BEATS CRIPPLE UNCONSCIOUS IN SWEDISH-HAWAIIAN RESTAURANT. Your service record. The facts are overwhelming!"

Blind rage wasn't all that had exploded within General Neil when he had realized who this swine Van Slyke was. Any soppy thoughts about Pujan Kobdo had fled from his mind. It wasn't as if he had momentarily forgotten her. But here he was, in the jungle called New York, where this depraved pervert had seduced the woman he loved while she was under some hideous anesthetic these fellows use. His woman! This indefinably rotten . . . on a grotesque dental chair! How could he have been so blind all these months not to have known how these degenerates worked? Arcane gases! Bland injections. The woman is powerless, then creatures like this have their will upon them. Professional rape! What the hell did he care about a goddamn Army service record? He wasn't in the goddamn Army anymore. He would mop the floor with this debaucher and he didn't give a goddamn what the newspapers would have to say.

"*Mungo!*" Leila had sensed what he was going to do. "Let him mend, bone by bone. Then take him apart," she croaked, desperation in every syllable. Mungo let go of the clothing in his hand and shoved Van Slyke back into his chair.

"All right, you dirty philanderer," he said. "Get out of here. Get your strength back. I'll have people watching you. And when you have every measure of your strength back, I am going to come to get you. I will rebreak every single bone which you broke by God's will on the day you seduced my unconscious wife and I'll leave you in the middle of the Catskill Mountains to walk home. Out!"

Van Slyke, pushing his walker ahead of him with shaking hands, tottered out of the restaurant.

Mungo turned to Leila, his decorations gleaming, his shoulder stars ashine. "My God, Leila, what have I put you through in all these months. I tried you and I convicted you in one swift flash and, just now, looking into that womanizer's face, I saw what I should have known from the beginning—that he had drugged you on that terrible afternoon."

"All's well that ends well, darling," she said softly.

"W. B. Yeats," he said, staring deeply into her eyes, a man in love again.

She leaned across the banquette to kiss him. His lips were soft and warm. The whole world was soft and warm.

52

Although Mungo went back to the apartment with Leila that night and stayed through a late breakfast of Mme. de Caunteton's walnut cake the next morning, he told Leila over coffee that the old feeling just wasn't there anymore.

"I thought the old magic had come back after that degenerate dentist revealed himself last night," he said. "But now, in the cold light of day, it's all different. It just won't work, Leila. I'll always have a soft spot in my head for you but—and there's nothing I can do to change it—my heart belongs back there in the Mongolian hills, with a little girl who means the world to me."

"It's okay, Mungo," Leila said. "I understand. Bygones are just naturally bygones. But let's keep in touch."

"Sure."

Oddly, Leila was relieved. All of the spellbinding romance had gone out of the life she had fooled herself into thinking that they shared. He was a pretty dull piece of work really. She felt she was entitled to one more dig when he asked her to intercede at the Pentagon to have his rank restored and to have him returned to permanent duty in Outer Mongolia.

"You're going back to pig it out with the native girl?" Leila asked wistfully.

"Well, it's the right kind of environment for me," he said lamely. "I'll have my books. I can study languages. I'll have my philological hobbies. I'll think of you, of course, but I just wasn't meant for life in the twentieth century as much as you are."

She called Washington. Everything was straightened out. General

Neil was told to report for reassignment at Fort Axelrod in California for transfer to Outer Mongolia following briefing.

A deep economic depression followed in the next few months. It was caused by Goodie Noon's draining wars, which had utterly bankrupted the country, to the total alarm of the economy, and, in the case of his most recent war no other nation would contribute any share of the war's horrendous cost. The vaunted markets and rich oil deposits in Asia failed to materialize.

Goodie Noon was beaten badly in the ensuing presidential elections by a 69 percent margin. Although there were other reasons for his defeat, perhaps thirty, both the Republican National Committee and the Joint Chiefs demanded a scapegoat. Therefore, Leila, who bore the onus of having advised the President on carrying out an invasion of Asia, and who had sold the entire idea of the war to the American people, was so pilloried by the news media that she was hounded out of the public relations industry.

Wambly Keifetz, principal stockholder of International Communications Industries, broke the news to her. "You will have no credibility left when we leak the background of this whole thing to the news media, Leila. They can never go along with you again because the voters will believe you bamboozled Osgood Noon into taking this country into an insane war that has almost destroyed it. Too bad for you, of course, but I'm afraid we'll have to ask you to resign and leave these offices within the hour because the company has already made an announcement to that effect."

It wasn't fair, but everyone understood each other. The military would regroup, above and beyond any charges of guilt or complicity, and would strengthen its hold on the Congress to insure that there would be no decrease in the defense budget. Wambly Keifetz and other well-placed Noon backers, having made substantial, not to say wildly inordinate, profits out of the war, would now prosper by foreclosing on the country. All that was needed was a fresh personality to take the fall; now that Goodie Noon had served his purpose by being defeated for reelection, who could be better suited than the woman who had once tried to violate the Constitution of the United States of America by trying to bar Americans from their unalienable right to bear arms. She was made-to-order for the role.

Wambly Keifetz allowed her a 22 percent profit on the sale of her stock in ICI. She had, also, in the fullness of time, shared in a comfortable way in the Keifetz group's profits from the war. She wasn't hurting, but she was only thirty-eight years old and she needed to find another career.

She went game fishing off Cabo Blanca on the Chilean coast, remote from television cameras. Her dad's phone calls caught up with her in Buenos Aires.

"Leila? Jesus, I been tryna get you for three days fahcrissake."

"Whatsamatter?"

Her dad had come up with the answer to all her problems. "Lissen," he said, "something terrific has come up that is gonna put you right back up on top."

"Yeah? What?"

"The families have decided they need a new way to wash this tremendous money from shit."

"Shit?"

"Heroin! Cocaine! Whatever!"

"I don't get it."

"They wanna set up a coupla chains of fast-food outlets. Fast food! That's right up your alley and it's a better laundry for them than parking lots and funeral parlors."

"Hey, I might know something about that. From the days at the Dearborn School of Industrial Culture."

"You're takin' the words right outta my mouth. Lissena me. They wanna set up a meet with Edward S. Price, your old client at Barkers Hill, who else? They're ready to make a deal. Whatta you say?"

Suddenly, she felt totally alive again. After years of faking it as a movie star and breaking her back on the road as a singer-dancer, after stealing money for *schtarkers* like the NGA and CANCER in Washington, after pumping thousands of tons of horseshit into the minds of the people, she suddenly felt as if she was her own woman at last. She understood fast food. She knew what the people wanted and she could give it to them and she would be in a spot where she couldn't be anybody's patsy again.

"Pop," she said, "I'll be on the next plane. As soon as I know what it is, I'll have somebody call you in Washington so you can meet my flight when it gets into New York."

Her dad arranged a meeting with Edward S. Price, an old friend and client, and the financial representative of twenty-two families of the United States. Leila was set up as chairman and CEO of the newly formed Food Stuffs Inc. with headquarters in Terre Haute, Indiana.

For the first time in her crowded career, Leila felt as if she were following the path her genes, her training, and her aspirations had destined her to. Everything she had ever learned at the Detroit school came crowding back into her memory plus conceptions that she had never imagined she could have produced. Fast-food concepts tumbled out of her mind in quick succession. She hardly had her franchising operation in place, her research completed, and her staff assembled, when she created, all in one seamless piece, a fast-food chain idea called Pastrami Inc. Within seven months, she had established 119 outlets in 23 cities. It was the money-laundering idea whose time had come with the force of Genghis Khan's hordes sweeping out of Asia. A great dam in perpetual indigestion had been opened. Pastrami Inc. was followed by the Taco Loco and the Hamish MacDougal's Highland Haggis fast-food chains. The formulas for bolted food eaten on the run were developed in Food Stuffs' spotless kitchens in Indiana, the nation's most politically conservative state, where, Mafia analysts directed, Communists would be least likely to attempt to infiltrate the company.

There were gourmets who refused to eat anywhere but at outlets of her Tuna Burger chain, which extended from the Aleutians to Teheran. Her Ole Mole chain with its seven kinds of chiles, its oat-bran tortillas, and its red guacamole was marked by lines of people who would stand patiently even in rain or snow, waiting to be allowed inside to savor its tasty goodness.

Throughout the hurricane of her success, something kept gnawing at her memory, something utterly tremendous that had hidden itself there, something that would dwarf everything else she had ever done, but it would not come to her. Day and night she struggled to remember what it was; she tried hypnosis to bring what she knew to be an absolute El Dorado to the surface of her mind. But nothing worked, not sodium pentathol, the so-called "truth-drug," not sessions with some very expensive psychoanalysts. She exhorted herself to wait, to be patient, that the idea for a golden bonanza would come to her.

Leila Aluja became the factor to be reckoned with in the international food community. Her outlets dominated demographics, food-supply sources, employment pools, and portion costs throughout eastern Europe, Asia, Latin America, the United Kingdom, and North America, in fact very nearly everywhere except Antarctica and France. Food Stuffs led the world in fast-food sales and outlets. It had a $3.4 billion share of the snack-food market, which extended into packaged food such as Deep Fry Tater Slivers, Balsam Chips, and Squirrel Juice, the world's third most popular soft drink. She personified snap, crackle, and pop as well as lip-smackin', finger-lickin' goodness. It was the proud boast of her outlets that a customer could order, be served, and eat any item served in any outlet within six minutes of entering. She became a multimillionaire all over again, courted by paparazzi and Political Action Committee fund raisers alike. She kept her triplex in New York, as well as houses in Rimini, Bimini, and Switzerland. She flew Concorde. She was an intimate of Jackie, the Donald, Elizabeth, Henry, Nancy, Arnie, Madonna, and Oprah. She was distinguished for her adaptations of Mme. Vionnet's clothes of the 1920s.

Most of all she was famous for the Venerable Bead, an ancient jewel of great price and estimated by *The National Enquirer* to be worth over one and a half million dollars.

53

After four and a half action-packed years of ten-hour days and fifty-five-hour weeks, Leila undertook a tour of Europe to check operations, streamline outlet logistics, fire a few people, and to dominate the competition for the hottest fast-food item of six seasons, the Tofu Pizza, an exciting new food opportunity which had just surfaced in Oslo and which, according to industry trade papers, was outselling all other pizzas in history by a 4-to-1 ratio. She had sewn up world rights on a leased forty-year basis. It was the biggest coup in the history of fast food, the biggest mass-market food innovation since the hot dog. She had cabled her home office in code within twenty minutes after she had closed the deal with an advance down payment of $2.5 million. Coded faxes of congratulation had poured in on her from Terre Haute, which, since the establishment of the gigantic chicken ranches by the mayor of the city in the late 1940s, had come to be known as Fast Food City.

In Europe, after she had clinched the deal, Leila studied cash flow, customer traffic, advertising, and employee morale in the principal markets of eleven of her European-based fast-food chains, from Finland to Spanish Morocco. She had pored over demographics and food-supply sources, employment pools, and portion costs for the establishment of two new franchised chains to be called Slot Machine Pasta and Swiftie's, which offered instant licorice-flavored hamburgers. She had had three and a half weeks of hard work and had realized a projected increased profit potential of $9,023,477 for her parent company.

When her work was done, she began her holiday by sailing from

Southampton, England, aboard the maiden voyage of the M. S. *Eros,* an all-new, one-class, no-tipping cruise ship. From her destination, Miami, Leila planned a well-deserved diversion in Barbados, Colombia, and Mexico before returning to work in Terre Haute.

The day she was to leave London, she got the jolt of her life. The memory of the elusive, shining, golden vision for which she had been racking her memory to recall from the day it had come to her three years before, the greatest single opportunity of her dazzling career, for that matter of anyone's career going back to the Sumerian civilization, returned to her whole and dimensional, touched her the way Midas's golden finger had touched dross. It forced her to change her plans, to decide to confine her holiday merely to the ship's crossing so that she could fly directly to Terre Haute from Miami.

Joe Reynard, a man she had not seen in eleven years, someone she hadn't even thought of for almost as long, give a year, take a year, had called her from Albania while she was holding a press conference in her suite at the Berkeley Hotel in London. The conference had been called to observe the United Kingdom publication of the food-oriented sequel to her religious autobiography, a bestseller for sixty-seven weeks in the United States, called *I Cook for the World,* which also had a few previously unrevealed sexy bits about her life.

Her secretary handed her a note which said, "Your ex-husband is on the phone from Albania." Leila excused herself from the meeting and dashed out of the room.

"Joe! My God! What a wonderful surprise!" She gripped the Venerable Bead as it hung around her neck.

"Leila, my sweet, adorable, insatiable woman!"

"Where are you? What's happening?"

"I thought I'd pop over to London to see you."

"Joe, that would be marvelous, but we're leaving London this evening en route to Southampton to board the *Eros* for Florida. I'm going to take a ten-day holiday."

"Well, maybe another time."

"Oh, Joe! What an awful disappointment that I won't see you!"

"Ah, well. Perhaps we can meet in New York after your holiday.

Dinner at Bottom of the Cage would be very nice. Until then, my darling." He disconnected.

At the instant Leila hung up, she remembered what she had been laboring to remember over the past three years. It struck her like a bolt of lightning. She was transformed by greed. Hardly thinking about any consequences, she burst into the room of journalists and said, in an awed, electrifying voice, "I have just closed the deal of the century. I am going to manufacture and distribute a food product that will extend human life to an average of one hundred and fifty years!"

Bedlam ensued. The newsmen hit the phones. The story was out across the world on television and the wire services as fast as it got to the primary London news outlets. Within three hours, calls from every branch of the media began to pour into the hotel to pump Leila for more information, but by that time she was on her way to Dorset.

Leila had earned all the holiday she could get. Food Stuffs Inc. led the world in fast-food sales and in number of fast-food outlets. It extended the distribution of its potato crispies, oat chips, and Squirrel Juice, the world's third most popular soft drink, and it dominated international fast-food sales for short-order foodstuffs in eight international (simulated) ethnic flavors: Mexican, Eastern European, Scottish, Arabic, Italian, Inuit, Pacific Rim, and American.

She rounded out the hard three and a half days in London with a four-day weekend at the company's house in Dorset, St Bart's, with its tailored gardens high on a rose-covered hill overlooking a perfect valley.

Working in the garden alongside the four staff gardeners, and toying with random food ideas on the giant Aga stove, Leila always found peace at St. Bart's. On this leg of an arduous journey, Leila traveled with a small entourage, having sent the bulk of her traveling staff (accountants, lawyers, expediters, and bankers) home. With her were an assistant, Captain Urian, USMC (ret.), and her personal secretary/scullery worker, Miss Chapman, a superb personal adjutant who was also cheerful about the cleaning, peeling, paring, and washing-up chores in the kitchen. Leila did the cooking. It was snack food, she said, but great food.

Major Urian did the coding and handling of all secret recipe communications as well as acted as Leila's physical-fitness trainer. He took Leila through forty-seven minutes of intensive exercises every morning, pushing her to the limit of aerobics and keeping her body weight where it should be. He was a small, muscular man who had a considerable reputation as an amateur contrabassoonist. He explained this aberration wistfully, having learned the art when he had been young. In the evenings, Leila had the major sing to her while Miss Chapman accompanied him on the piano. A dainty man, Major Urian sang with a small voice of the most fragile sensitivity, finish, and charm, although with a fixed range of expression. It was a voice so delicate, so gentle, delivered with a manner so self-effacing that Leila felt, to an outsider, it could sound disturbingly precious.

From St. Bart's, the helicopter service picked her up for an eighteen-minute flight to Chewton Glen, the luxurious country hotel on the south coast. There she hoped to pack into eighteen hours what should have taken ten days: pleasurable dining, golf, and sailing.

The fast-food trade papers of the United States and Europe had given Leila's Tofu Pizza coup wide coverage. And the world coverage of her startling announcement in London had the telephone ringing from the instant she arrived at St. Bart's. Calls came in from Terre Haute and from Edward S. Price at Barkers Hill Enterprises. The Terre Haute directors said that the telephone had also been ringing off the hook; hundreds of people were demanding to know about the new product. What was it? What the hell was going on? Leila said she wasn't going to discuss the matter on any goddamn telephone but that the acquisition was of such enormous importance and it promised such gargantuan profits that she was going to cut her holiday short and fly home directly from Miami. Edward S. Price had only one thing on his mind: If the claims Leila had made to the press were true, and they had damned well better be true because the entire spectrum of the national news media was going crazy over it, he had to be the first to have the product so that it could be passed along to Corrado Prizzi, the grand old man of the Mafia who was then ninety-three years old.

The helicopter flew Leila and her staff directly to Southampton to board the *Eros,* bypassing Chewton Glen with regret because, until the last minute, Leila was on the telephone with everyone from Wambly Keifetz, her principal stockholder, to "dear friends" of Ronald Reagan who, in the hope of extending their savior's life to 150 years, were almost beside themselves with greed. Lobbying for an abolition of the no-third-term amendment went into almost supernaturally high gear.

Leila had taken over the Admiral's Suite aboard the cruise ship with a sense of her sovereignty. Miss Chapman and Major Urian occupied separate single cabins on the same deck and were always on call. Leila was in sustained satellite contact with her people in Terre Haute and with Wambly Keifetz in Washington. She forgave herself for feeling so smug, but she had just turned the world upside-down, so the prospect of a six-and-a-half-day crossing of the North Atlantic was deeply satisfying.

Even if it had been possible, she would not have traded places with anyone. The only thing she lacked to make the whole thing perfect was a man. Leila was very, very fond of men, but in the entire three and a half weeks since she had left Indiana, she had not had a moment to spare for sex or even a little mild flirting.

And so when the two most celebrated men aboard, Sir Alfred Harrison and Dr. Anson Padgett, had begun their pursuit of her, she had accepted that not only as her rightful due but as very much of a physical necessity. She was a fully grown, adult woman with an enormous bed in the very expensive Admiral's Suite. She deserved an outlet for all her juices. Nothing had had a chance to happen yet, but the prospects looked good to her.

When the pit boss and the stickman in the ship's casino seemed to be willing to bend all rules to please her, that came to her as an entirely natural act of homage. She knew, of course, that it was possible that their cooperation had had nothing to do with her winning because around her neck she was wearing, day and night, the most powerful lucky piece in the world.

She had put out of her mind the threats she had received by mail, fax, and telephone since she had walked off with the pizza deal, but she was unable to stop thinking about the miracle yogurt, unable to stop counting the almost uncountable profits. With the vast sums of money that the yogurt would earn, she would gradually buy up the Congress through their Political Action Committees, buy up the White House through irreproachable but vast campaign contributions, and, because she would have at least 110 years ahead of her, gradually take over the rulership of the United States, then of the world. She had never had such delusions of grandeur before, but never had she been within reach of limitless treasure and 110 years of productive life (at the least) to make all of it work for her. Other than deploring that the ethics of her competitors had fallen so low, she gave morals little thought. Joe Reynard had to be some kind of a nut to have refused to exploit such a godsend as his great-grandfather's yogurt. Joe, at heart, had never risen above being just an Albanian peasant boy. When a prize such as eternal youth for everyone was at stake, one had the need and the right to bend a few rules and to squash a few people who got in the way.

Aboard the M. S. *Eros,* she had, of course, been asked to dine at the commodore's table. At dinner the first night at sea, she had been introduced by Commodore Bantry-Fanchon to the other passengers at the table as "a genuine international celebrity"—a designation that made Angela Scolari, across the table, stare into Leila's eyes and smile with derision.

It was turning out to be one of those magical crossings with a really interesting crowd turning up for dinner the first night out. They were eight at the circular table: Sir Alfred Harrison, a former Wimbledon tennis great, someone had told her, and a formidably wealthy man; as well as Dr. Anson Padgett, some kind of world-famous scientist. They had been seated on either side of Leila. Sir Freddie was utterly charming, a virile, exciting sort of man who had all sorts of information on tennis rackets: things like restringing, weights, and balance. Dr. Padgett, who had immediately insisted that Leila call him Anson, knew about things she had never dreamed of happening under the ocean floor. They were both good-looking in a manly way, which made a woman glad to be a woman.

Angela Scolari, an Italian film star who was en route to visit her considerable properties in Florida, was seated at Sir Freddie's left and seemed determined to hog his attention. She was banally beautiful in a statuesque sort of way, Leila thought. One thing was certain. Miss Scolari did not much care for Leila and she made no effort to conceal her distaste.

A huge man with an unspellable and unpronounceable name was seated at Scolari's left. He special-ordered everything: cabbage soup, a seafood pie he called *rakov*, as if the English steward understood what *that* was, and something Leila thought he said was *zrazy*—she couldn't be expected to hear everything at the table—which looked like some kind of stuffed seafood.

Beyond the oddity sat Katherine Norton, an attractive fiftyish Iowa woman with many diamonds. Then was a darling, elderly man named Madox Winkleman, who said he was a Justice of the Peace in Winsted, Connecticut, and who actually wore a corded smoking jacket as if he were dressed for dining at home in some drafty castle.

The ship's captain, Sir Aldwin, Commodore Bantry-Fanchon, presided at the table "when the weather permitted." He was a man of heavy authority who spoke very little. Although it was a relatively smooth crossing, he appeared at dinner only every third night.

The women at the table wanted to talk about the Venerable Bead. This was perfectly normal. Even women who detested Leila would go gushy when they decided they had to know more about the Bead, as if it had not been described and speculated on endlessly in every magazine from *Popular Mechanics* to *Pravda*. What did she have a seventeen-person public relations department for? Leila allowed no one to touch the Bead. That would have diminished its powers.

The problem at the dining table was the special-order freak, Danzig Cortjgurdiew, a tall, portly man who wore a four-button dining suit and two gold teeth under a half-bald, half shaggy head. He seemed to interrupt whenever Leila had the total attention of either Sir Freddie or Dr. Padgett. He would ask the stupidest questions, cutting off the flow of Leila's wit and wisdom and almost driving her up the wall. Just as she'd be about to send either man into helpless laughter with a quip or a sally, the boor would lean across the table and say something dumb like, "I have been reading about you, dear lady. I see you have made the coup of coups." Then Sir Freddie (or Dr. Padgett) would be forced to ask what that could be and they would be dragged into an absolutely mindless discussion. What with the buttinsky and the two *very* attractive men on either side of her, Leila was kept so busy conversationally that she didn't have much chance to chat with the others at the table—other than ocassionally pretending she could not understand Scolari's quite comically accented English.

It all seemed so jolly, so typical of a promising crossing on a great liner, so utterly free of the world and all its demands. But, certainly unknown to Leila, a tragedy was being manufactured in every direction around her. Every passenger dining at the commodore's table was a paid or amateur assassin sent aboard the *Eros* by mortal enemies whom Leila had accumulated during the barbaric swath of time she had cut through life in the years, months, and days before she had boarded the great ship.

54

Not one of them, excepting Angela Scolari, was what he or she seemed. Sir Freddie Harrison wasn't the Scottish knight he represented himself to be. He had no idea of how to play tennis. He was a contract killer, groomed, trained, and employed by the Haselgrove Organization to eliminate Leila while the *Eros* was on the high seas. It was a policy matter. Mark Haselgrove was totally against his team leaders leaving his outfit, particularly those to whom he had professed his love. Harrison was a knife worker who was extremely adept at his work.

Anson Padgett was aboard to do the same job, but for the National Gun Carriers' Association, which had never forgiven Leila for the humiliation she had poured upon them by proving that Ellsworth Carswell had not been insane when he had murdered those thirty-nine people, for not refuting forever in a court of law the blackguard lie that it was guns that killed people, not people who killed people. The result had been a prodigious loss of membership nationally, as if the incidents seemed to remind the American public that guns and insanity went hand-in-hand. The NGA also reasoned that Leila had made them lose face at the White House by allowing the rigmarole of alienation proceedings to drag on and on, forestalling the President's immediate pardon of Carswell.

The NGA tradition, of course, demanded that Padgett employ a gun when he blew Leila away. He planned to use the weapon James Bond had made so popular: a .25-caliber Beretta automatic pistol with a "skeleton grip," which reduced the extra bulk in his shoulder holster. At hand, for an emergency, Padgett also carried a .38-

caliber Centennial Airweight, and a larger Walther PPK. He had been ordered to "finish the job" with a VP70 from Heckler & Koch, which was chambered in 9mm and weighed 2.5 pounds with its 18-round magazine in place. The NGA wanted the credit for the hit spread among several contributing members for internal political reasons.

Angela Scolari was, on the other hand, an amateur at murder, as the saying goes, but she was a Sicilian woman whose family's honor and money had been grossly offended. If Leila did not relent in the course she had chosen vis-à-vis the Tofu Pizza, a certain dosage of cyanide of potassium was going to find its way into Leila's afternoon tea. Scolari had pleaded with her family to allow her to use strychnine because it provided such a horrible, contorted death, but the family tradition of hundreds of years had been cyanide, so Scolari, against her will, was stuck with it.

The dear, little, old gentleman at the commodore's table, Madox Winkleman, was a retired major general of the Special Forces, known as the Green Berets, who was still available for military duty despite his exterior gentleness and his age. He now did "special work" for the Pentagon. The military had been grossly offended by Leila's withdrawal from what they considered to be essential domestic psychological warfare, i.e., the preparation of the spirit of the good people of the Republic into a perpetual frame of mind whereby they would welcome war as a festival, a grand circus, a riotous and endlessly diverting experience during which Leila's messages would have not only entertained them but convinced them that continual wars were good for business. Mr. Winkleman had a move whereby his encroaching forearm would encircle the throat of an offender and, with a deft and agile twist, would break the neck, causing instant (and frequently painless) death. He always murmured "The Soldier's Prayer" over his people after he had done the work on them.

Katherine Norton was the personal representative of Wambly Keifetz, known monarch of all he surveyed, a man who was one of "the owners of the world" due to his simple concept of believing with all his heart that his share was by natural, even Divine, ruling, 2197.63 times greater than anyone else's share. Leila had upset Mr. Keifetz because she had flatly refused to mix pinches of cocaine into the bins of Oat Chips, a strong seller for the Terre Haute food conglomerate, which Leila headed and of which Keifetz was a prime stockholder. Keifetz felt, rightly, that a careful mixture of cocaine with the cereal would tend to increase the demand for it, gradually forcing all other breakfast cereals off the market. Keifetz had vast holdings in the coca leaf in Bolivia, Peru, and Columbia. There was always a certain amount of "overage" (broken stems, diseased leaves, twigs, etc.) after the prime market had been serviced throughout North America and Europe; this could well have been used profitably in breakfast foods. Leila had, for whatever reason, flatly refused to cooperate on the project. She would have to be eliminated so that a more compliant executive could take her place, thus utilizing the "high-in-fiber" plant matter. Mrs. Norton specialized in simulated suicides. She arranged tall building plunges, hangings, shotguns-in-the-mouth, bathtub drownings, and was really quite good at what she did.

Danzig Cortjgurdiew, as utterly opposed to the others, had no economically based grudge against Leila. He intended to kill her to avenge the actor's art. He had formed, and was the sole support of, an organization called Why? (Ltd.). It had devoted the forty-odd years of its existence to fighting the growing invasion of television performers into fields which had been meant by a manifest destiny to have been solely and entirely the preserve of real actors, not the talking mannequins who bumped into each other in soap operas (prime time and daytime), television dramas, situation comedies, and male-bonding adventure series. Cortjgurdiew was the sole officer and, excepting his wife (who was now resting in a state institution), the sole member of the organization.

Cortjgurdiew had succeeded in eliminating forever more than thirty-six television performers, but had, for almost fifteen years, been trying to overtake the woman he regarded as the worst actress in modern American history—albeit in this instance a film actress—and whom his organization had ever deplored as having stained forever the acting art.

He had almost had her while she was appearing in films in Hollywood. She broke his heart when she married the most powerful talent agent in the entertainment business; it meant that more and more screen work would be available to her. Then she had disappeared. The terrible, terrible actress Leila Aluja had vanished just before Cortjgurdiew had been about to strike using a sniper's rifle from an elevated position on a high pass between Hollywood and the valley while Leila would be driving her Bentley convertible to join the great and near-great at lunch in Beverly Hills, but severe arthritis had stricken his trigger finger, a visitation that spread into the carpal tunnel of his right hand, and he had lost his great chance.

By the time he was ready again to bring her down, she had vanished from the film business. Nonetheless, even though she might never act again, the plain fact was that she *might* act again and Cortjgurdiew felt, even so, for the artistic crimes she had committed in the past, she had to be made to pay.

Then Providence had sent her to him. He was in London, reading *The Independent*. He turned the page and there she was, over a story telling of her amazing announcement at a London press conference. He had had an investigative agency follow her to Southampton. He had booked passage aboard the *Eros*. He would kill her before the ship reached Miami.

55

By noon on the second day of the cruise, Leila was certain that she had the total attention of Sir Freddie Harrison. He was *such* an attractive man. She longed to see him in full kilt with his sporran flapping. And such manners! His flowers had arrived at the Admiral's Suite with his crested card and a jeroboam of Charles Heidseck '61 with a beautifully calligraphed note inviting her to an informal luncheon, tête-à-tête, in the area immediately forward of the swimming pool. It was an exclusive area, fitting for a luncheon with a Scottish nobleman. She made a note to have the ship's photographer come by the table in a casual way so that she could have a few eight-by-ten glossies to spread around among *W* and *Quiksnaks* magazine editors.

When Leila arrived at the rendezvous, about twelve minutes late, Sir Freddie was dressed in a smart navy blazer with his family crest embroidered on the patch pocket over his heart, and a stunning off-white ascot. The stewards fawned on him, people went out of their way to greet him—"Good morning, Sir Freddie," etcetera, etcetera. He explained his family motto, "Linger Longer. Win," which he was able to recite in Latin.

Leila was wearing a light chinchilla leotard and the Venerable Bead hanging around her neck. Her hair, styled by a witty Swiss team of coiffeurs who had been flown in from St. Moritz, had been cut into a provoking helmet of curls. Her makeup had been designed by Albert of Warsaw and, watching Sir Freddie, she could see that she was having the desired effect. If she had been a betting woman, she would have wagered the farm that within twenty-four hours, she would have him thrashing in the sack.

"I simply cannot believe how beautiful you are," the baronet said, looking as if he were about to kneel to receive her benison. She was oddly touched by the sincerity of his candor.

"It must be the sea air," Leila replied modestly, gloating that she had him hooked. She adored men who adored her. She wanted to take him by the hand, lead him back to her stateroom, strip off all his lovely clothes, and give him really ample reason to be ecstatic over her. They were thousands of miles away from yogurt and pizzas and haggis and tacos and all the cares which went with them. She was going to devour this man.

"In Hindi, you know," he said, "Leila means 'cosmic sport of kings' or 'cosmic play.'"

"Really? I thought it was a Persian name."

"My mother would have told you it came from a Bulwer-Lytton heroine. Whatever, I simply adore your name—as I adore you."

They had a light lunch. After changing costumes (of course), they shot skeet from the rear deck. As they finished, Dr. Padgett came strolling up and, quite boldly Leila thought, as though he were establishing that Sir Freddie had no exclusive claim to her, asked her to dine with him that evening in the very expensive ship's grill, then to compete as his partner in the tango exhibition that had been planned for the cabaret that evening. As much to challenge Sir Freddie as to pleasure Anson Padgett, she accepted.

She and Sir Freddie had a bracing walk around the Promenade Deck after the skeet. Freddie Harrison wasn't as ardent as Anson but just looking at the expression in his eyes, she could tell that he was falling in love with her.

5 6

Anson Padgett was, simply, a *mar*velous dancer. They each won a Westclox alarm clock as first prizes in the tango contest and were addressed excitedly in rapid Spanish by a small Cuban gentleman as they swayed past his table doing a rumba so authentic that as they left the floor when the music stopped, the entire party of eight at the Cuban table gave them a rising ovation. Leila knew that she had never danced so well, but she (silently) gave all the credit to Padgett. Sir Freddie claimed two of the evening's dances, taking her away from the table for two that she and Anson were sharing, but he was a stiff, indifferent sort of dancer. Nonetheless, his powerful male smell made up for the loss of Anson Padgett as a dance partner. Sir Freddie seemed to see dancing as just an opportunity to hold her in his arms. He was a heavy breather and his conversation was a jumble of half-muttered erotic asides, which Leila pretended she hadn't heard, interspersed with some intense references to tennis racquets.

He would whisper huskily how sweetly their pelvises fit together, something no one had ever said to her before and certainly not something she had expected to hear from a Caledonian aristocrat. As his hand descended just a bit too far down the small of her back, he mumbled something she couldn't quite catch but which seemed to be concluding that she had a perfect ass. He knew how to court a girl. You'll get yours, Freddie baby, she thought.

Toward the end of the evening Anson Padgett didn't dance her back to the table but instead cha-cha-cha-ed them right to an exit from the salon where he had bribed her cabin tabby to be standing by with her wrap. They wandered toward the stern of the ship.

"You are the most deliriously gifted partner I have ever danced with," Anson said. "Your kind of vitality cries out to be released in a naked, primordial way. I adore you, Leila."

He did the ritual thing and took her in his arms as they stood concealed between two lifeboats. Leila felt her self-control slipping away. She was sure that, within moments, they would be doing it standing up, something she didn't appreciate one bit and which was hardly worth the effort, when Freddie Harrison came running up, out of breath, to say that Leila must come back to the salon at once because she had won two entirely free days at Disneyland in the ship's tombola.

The evening ended with all three of them sexually distraught, tense and edgy from a lack of fruition. Leila had been made so irritable by all of it that she refused the offers of both men, individually and collectively, to see her to her cabin.

The next morning, the third day out on the voyage, she worked out strenuously with Major Urian in the ship's gymnasium, showered, was massaged, then took off for her early-morning laps around the ship on the Promenade Deck at six-thirty. She had not strode more than fifty steps when Angela Scolari fell in beside her.

"Good morning, Miss Aluja," she said. "I see we share the same splendid habits."

"Ah, Miss Scolari."

"I have been looking forward to a meeting with you."

"Really?" She couldn't stand the woman who (a) was a vulgar actress and (b) had absolutely fawned all over Sir Freddie Harrison to the embarrassment of nearly everyone at the dinner table.

"I would like to go over some tract charts of Florida property with you."

"With me? Why me?"

"Your company is going to need a plant entirely devoted to the Tofu Pizza and Florida is a labor-intensive state."

"We are Indiana people, Miss Scolari."

"I am prepared to make you such an attractive offer that you will find it impossible to refuse."

"Nonetheless it is out of the question, Miss Scolari."

"Then I put it to you this way. You owe it to me."

"I owe something to *you*?"

"You ruined my father. You stole the Tofu Pizza from him. You had Cosa Nostra people threaten him until he was afraid to leave the house. You had them bomb three of his factories. He never recovered from it. He died of a broken heart."

"Then it was you who has been sending me those terrible letters."

"Maybe yes and maybe no. But if I were you, I would keep a watchful eye on Mrs. Katherine Norton, who dines with us each night."

"Mrs. Norton?"

"She is the agent of the octopus, which is the Japanese tofu industry. You cost them a million tons of fermented soybeans and they are going to take their pound of flesh from you."

"Nonsense. You are a charged-up, out-of-work actress who lives off making sordid little scenes like this."

"I am a Sicilian woman, Miss Aluja. You have stolen from us. You brought death to my father. You have dishonored my family. You must pay—or suffer the consequences."

"Pooh!"

"Pooh? You say pooh to me? That is your answer? Pooh?" Scolari was pale green with outrage and frustration.

"Please, Miss Scolari. No fiery Latin scenes before breakfast."

"I will feed you to the fishes!" Scolari shrilled at her. "You are finished!"

57

There were accidents. That night, Freddie Harrison lingered on the deck, wearing surgical rubber gloves to prevent his fingerprints from lingering as well, within eyeshot of Leila's stateroom, thinking perhaps that some odd chance might bring her out on deck for a last long look at the sea. He could get the job done and get back to his own bed. For whatever reason, a bonus payment was riding on this one, so Harrison assumed that she had been such a naughty girl that the Haselgrove organization was more than routinely interested in blowing her away. Freddie had no idea of Leila's former rank in the outfit. He was strictly a European operator.

He had the good manners to be grateful to Leila for getting him this marvelous cruise with all its good food and wine. Usually the jobs were in one dreadful city or another.

He heard a companionway door open. A woman who was exactly Leila's height and build, a woman whose hairstyle was identical to the way Leila had worn her hair that evening, came out on the deserted deck through the doorway to the passage leading to Leila's suite. She came into the dim light about twelve yards away from him and walked toward the bow of the ship. He grinned with delight as he bent over, pulled his knife out of the sheath strapped around his leg, and threw it in one long, overhand pitch. It struck the woman between the shoulder blades, knocking her forward and down, where she remained, inert, flush on her face.

Freddie took off in the opposite direction and entered the ship at the first doorway. He had earned the bonus.

The murder caused a serious crisis of command aboard the ship.

The body, later identified as being that of Mrs. Katherine Norton, was found by a deck crew assigned to holystone the teak. The ship's command from the commodore through the staff captains to the purser sat in shocked discussion of what to do about such a monstrous happening aboard the maiden voyage of the most expensive ship ever launched.

Except for rejecting the idea of communicating the news of the crime to the owners in Liverpool by radio or telephone for fear of interception, no clear decision was reached.

Then, as if the maiden voyage had been cursed by the gods, two hours after dawn the following day, on the Sports Deck, the passenger Mr. Madox Winkleman had been shot to death by a sniper's rifle fired from an elevated position just as Mr. Winkleman had been approaching, from behind, a deck chair which held the sole presence on the deck, the preeminent food tycoon Miss Leila Aluja. Deck stewards had apprehended the passenger who had fired the rifle which had killed Mr. Winkleman. He was identified as Danzig Cortjgurdiew, who, although he did not seem aware that he had killed Madox Winkleman, was exultant over the delusion that he had shot Miss Aluja. "For over fifteen years," he crowed incoherently to the ship's officers, "I have dreamed of destroying that embodiment of anti-art who had stained and sullied acting beyond the conception of mortal man. At long last, she is gone. Justice dwelt within my hand which pulled the trigger."

Miss Aluja was told by the ship's chaplain that Mr. Winkleman had been struck by lightning during a preprandial stroll upon the Sports Deck.

The ship's officers had hardly had the time to decide to hide the two corpses in safe refrigerators when word came tumbling in upon them that Dr. Anson Padgett had been murdered by poison, which could have been administered only while he had been having breakfast in the ship's Presidential Suite occupied by the same Miss Leila Aluja.

A busy cabin steward had left the breakfast tray in the companionway immediately outside the room while he had entered the suite to set up the breakfast table. Someone having murderous intentions toward either Miss Aluja or Dr. Padgett had sprinkled cyanide of potassium all over a serving of breakfast sausage and bacon. The unfortunate Dr. Padgett had eaten one entire sausage.

Miss Aluja was told, in a visit to her suite by the commodore, the two staff captains, and the purser, who were accompanied by the ship's doctor, that Anson Padgett had died of a massive heart attack. His body had been whisked off to yet a third refrigerator.

On his return to his quarters, Sir Aldwin, Commodore Bantry-Fanchon, locked all doors, sat at his desk, lowered his large, seamed, ruddy face into his hands, and wept. Then he telephoned his owners in Liverpool with the terrible news so that arrangements could be made with the Miami police to meet the *Eros* on arrival and proceed with the arrest of the maniac Danzig Cortjgurdiew, who was undoubtedly responsible for the murders of Mrs. Norton, Mr. Winkleman, and Dr. Padgett.

58

Leila lay in bed with Sir Freddie Harrison. She was shocked out of her skull by the violent deaths of that sweet, sweet Anson Padgett and the dear, little old Mr. Winkleman—to say nothing of the total disappearance of Mrs. Norton. With Scolari absent and the commodore locked in his quarters, the dinner table that evening, displaying five empty places, had depressed her so much that she had had two Ojen cocktails before ordering food, then an entire bottle of Bonnes Mares '61 with her dinner. She ate heartily because, well, she needed strength, and the cuisine aboard was so very good. Later, she and Freddie had danced, then had gambled a little, then, suddenly and even to Freddie entirely unexpectedly, almost as a ritual of mourning for those who, so recently, had been so much with them, they found themselves copulating like cobras in heat upon Leila's bed.

She had never done it with a baronet before. He was a tiger in the sheets. She was spent in a wonderful, profligate, endless way and already his hand, under the sheets, was busying itself again while he made those sounds deep in his throat, which gave her such a sense of power.

She shifted her hips languorously and he stopped what he was doing. That wasn't what she had meant at all. He began to play idly with the Venerable Bead hanging from her neck.

"What a beautiful object," he murmured. After considerable time, as if he were gathering wisps of strength so that he could get on with the caressing, he asked if she always wore the Bead.

"I haven't taken it off since the day I got it," she told him. "It's my good-luck piece. I was just a little girl from Dearborn, Michigan, then I put the Bead around my neck and I became one of the movers and shakers."

"It must be worth half a million dollars."

"If not half a million pounds."

"Leila darling, as you know, I had planned a few chukkers with Prince Charles in Palm Beach, but I can't let you go. I want to go on with you to Barbados and South America. Bone fishing, bullfights, and that restaurant—what do you call it—in Mexico City."

"La Fonda del Refugio," she said dreamily. "Women cooks wearing hairnets and the best Mexican food since Montezuma had Hernando Cortés to lunch."

"Is this an invitation?"

"Not really, Freddie. All bets are off. Something huge is happening and I have to get back to my desk in Terre Haute. Perhaps, if you're still in the States, we'll have a weekend in New York."

On the following night, Freddie said good night to Leila in the ship's casino. She was hardly aware that he had left as she doubled her bets at the craps table. She was $800 ahead when she cashed in and left, alone for the first time in three and a half weeks. She was wearing a $55,000 sable coat, a $1,483,700 ruby, and a platinum diaphragm.

She decided to stroll for a while in the open sea air, plotting her moves, making a mental note to call a few friends in Beverly Hills to make sure that Scolari never worked in Hollywood again. The boat deck was deserted. She stood at the ship's rail looking out at the heavy night sea.

A man dressed in the uniform of a ship's deck steward came up behind her, moving silently. He put one arm around her lower legs and lifted her. Then, with his free hand, he grasped the gold chain which held the Venerable Bead hanging around her neck and jerked it free. She turned and stared into his face.

"*Joe!* Joe, darling!" she screamed as he lifted her until her knees were above the ship's railing. Then he tossed her over into the sea.

She was screaming just before she started downward from a height that equaled fourteen city-building stories, and she screamed even more loudly as she descended into the North Atlantic, as the ship moved away from her at a steady twenty-two knots.

59

The seawater closed over her air-supply ducts. She lost consciousness and, as the tidal air was denied her, she sank slowly toward the ocean floor. Her heart beat feebly for a relatively brief interval, but, soon enough, it stopped. Her body died, but, in the deep cortex of her brain where her incarnate memory lived, she remained alive because memory is an exotic biological phenomenon feeding on calcium, potassium, and sodium currents; on serotonin, acetylcholine, and norepinephrine, the stimulating spices in the stew that had been her life.

Traces of memories of sounds, of encounters, of vistas, of faces and smells, the entire colossal library of the mind as lurid as the American dream filed past, floating on the tiny traces of engrams, stored and transmitted at will by patterns of electromagnetism. Ghosts of forever flickered across an incomprehensible number of neurons, axons, synapses, and dendrites in a malleable circuit, ever-changing as old circuits broke apart and formed new connections, holding fast to the brain's subjective representation of experience.

Her memory bobbled like a cork upon a chaotic sea of deals, money, power, celebrity, sex, television, greed, and politics, the tarnished threads of the true flag. She relived what she had been trained to dream but had never seen, lifetimes flashing past in nanoseconds. But where was she now? What was happening to her?

Within Leila's cerebral cortex and the cutaneous sensory areas, she remembered her father. If he hadn't moved to America, she would have married other people. She might never have found Joe or have gotten the Venerable Bead. A galaxy of false memories rushed into her mind, things which had never happened to her; things she had seen on television or read as headlines in *The National Enquirer* or in one of those commercials with soap opera plots. She had stared at too many videocassettes and, from the ten thousand things she had heard or imagined about other people while her past was dying, she had built a memory.

Her body temperature dropped to 65 degrees Fahrenheit. Her body was dead, but the neurons that exchanged information among one another, across the synapses of her brain, were still ticking over, transmitted by strands of ribonucleic acid, the arrangement of which in hundreds of thousands of subunits were astronomically immense.

Where was she?

Every fragment of information that had ever entered the nerve cells of her brain had changed these RNA molecules. From birth, as information had entered her memory, it had been matched to RNA combinations already present there. As match had succeeded match, thousands every day, Leila remembered. The Delta rhythms were moving at less than four cycles a second, but she remembered. Axons continued to send their signals by hosing neurotransmitters into dendrites. Neurons fired, generating memories, their electrical signals traveling the length of axons, then bursting into microscopic bubbles filled with neurotransmitters that catapulted memory across the synapse, where it was bound to the dendrite on the other side of the gap. Meanwhile, brain cells constantly manufactured and replaced proteins and broke sugar into energy to power those reactions. She was remembering the extraordinary details of her fabulous life at a speed which was far more rapid than time.

She remembered her life . . . which was the price she had paid for her constant betrayal of love and trust. Suddenly, she knew where she was. She was in hell.